Praise for *Tell Me Lies*

"[A] wonderfully fresh, funny, tender, and outrageous story that will delight fans of the comic mystery. There's a hint of Susan Isaacs in her writing, but Crusie is definitely one of a kind."

—*Booklist*

"For lovers of chocolate brownies, fairly explicit sex, and heroines who let it all hang out, an entertaining hardcover debut."

—*Kirkus Reviews*

"*Tell Me Lies* is a mad, passionate, and loudly funny first novel. It is filled with the wit and humor that are Ms. Crusie's trademarks."

—*RT Book Reviews*

"[Jennifer Crusie] has a fine narrative voice and a talent for quotable lines. Mostly, she's a lot of fun."

—*San Jose Mercury News*

"*Tell Me Lies*, by Jennifer Crusie, is a masterstroke of wry examination of truth and lies. . . . Crusie writes with a voice that is brutally funny, alternately in-your-face raucous and so poignant you'll laugh with tears streaming down your cheeks. She transcends comparison, and this tale is a pure gem."

—*BookPage*

Tell Me Lies

Tell Me Lies

Jennifer Crusie

St. Martin's Griffin
New York

TELL ME LIES. Copyright © 1998 by Jennifer Crusie Smith. All rights reserved. Printed in the United States of America. For information, address St. Martin's Press, 175 Fifth Avenue, New York, N.Y. 10010.

www.stmartins.com

The Library of Congress has cataloged the mass market paperback edition as follows:

Crusie, Jennifer
  Tell me lies / Jennifer Crusie.—1st ed.
      p. cm.
    ISBN 978-0-312-96680-5
  1. Man-woman relationship—Fiction.   2. Gossip—Fiction.   I. Title.
  PS3553.R7858 T45 1998
  813'.6—dc21

                                                                97036523

ISBN 978-1-250-02447-3 (trade paperback)

Second St. Martin's Griffin Edition: May 2012

10   9   8   7   6   5   4   3   2   1

For
Mollie Amanda Joanna Smith,
still the most amazing woman I know

Acknowledgments

My thanks to the faculty and students of the Ohio State University Creative Writing Program for reading chunks of this *ad nauseum;* my critique partner, Valerie Taylor, who read all of it *ad nauseum;* and my agent, Meg Ruley, and my editor, Jennifer Enderlin, who loyally swear it's not *nauseum.*

All fiction is gossip.
—*Truman Capote*

Tell Me Lies

Chapter One

One hot August Thursday afternoon, Maddie Faraday reached under the front seat of her husband's Cadillac and pulled out a pair of black lace underpants. They weren't hers.

Up until then it had been a fairly decent day. The microwave had snapped and died when she'd tried to heat a muffin for Em's breakfast, but the sun had been shining on their blue frame house, and the temperature hadn't hit ninety before noon, and Em had been absorbed in planning her school shopping, and contentment had reigned. Even Brent, muttering about what a mess his car was, had cheered up when Maddie volunteered to clean it, something she'd done more from a sense of guilt than a sense of obligation. It seemed fair that she should clean the car since she had summers off from work and he didn't, and she'd been bending over backward to be fair lately because it was so tempting not to be fair. "I don't even like you," she wanted to say. "Why would I clean your car?" But Brent was a good husband by default: he didn't yell, drink his paycheck, hit her, or do most of the other things the country music she loved complained about. He was doing his part, the least she could do was play hers. "Em and I will clean your car this afternoon," she'd said when he'd hugged Em good-bye and was on his way to the door. "Call Howie and have him pick you up on his way out to the company." And Brent had been so surprised, he'd kissed her on the cheek.

Em had done her usual eight-year-old eye roll behind her glasses when she'd heard the good news. But then she'd gotten a calculating look in her eye and become the Angel Daughter, trooping out to Brent's gleaming Caddy after lunch with no protest. Something was up, and Maddie waited for the other shoe to drop while she cleaned the trash out of her husband's front seat and sang along with Roseanne Cash on the tape deck.

Em hauled enough junk from the backseat to fill a cardboard box. "I'm taking this stuff inside and putting it away right now," she announced, her thin arms wrapped around the box, and then she escaped into the bright yellow air-conditioned kitchen while Maddie waved her on from the floor of the front seat.

Maddie reached under the seat and grabbed an Egg McMuffin wrapper as Roseanne sang "Blue Moon with Heartache." Good song, nice day. A screen door wheezed to her right, and she craned her neck to see their next-door neighbor, Mrs. Crosby, shuffle out onto her immaculate little white porch and lean into her immaculate little marigold-edged yard to squint in the direction of Brent's Caddy, which should not have been in the driveway because it was a workday.

Mrs. Crosby was festive today, topping the red leggings that hung on her skinny little thighs with a hot orange T-shirt that said "World's Greatest Grandma," cotton proof that hypocrisy began young in Frog Point, Ohio. Maddie waved and called, "Hello, Mrs. Crosby, we're just cleaning out the car." Mrs. Crosby didn't have the hearing or the eyesight she'd had twenty years ago, but she still had the mouth, and there'd never be an end to the hell she could start if she was ignored. "There was that car," Mrs. Crosby would say, "big as life, just like he didn't have a job to go to." It was easier to wave and yell now than explain later.

Mrs. Crosby flapped her hand at Maddie and shuffled back inside, now sure that nothing interesting was happening in the driveway next door. Maddie stuffed the Egg McMuffin wrapper in her garbage bag, and then she went under the seat after the last of the trash and found the underpants.

Mrs. Crosby had been wrong.

Maddie sat with her bare legs stretched out the car door, and stared stupidly at the lace and elastic dangling from her hand. It took her a minute to figure out what it was because the middle was missing, there were just four black lace triangles held together by loops of black elastic, and then she realized they were panties, crotchless panties. She thought, *Not again*, and *Beth*, and *Thank God Em went inside*, and *Now I can leave him*, and then a car door slammed next door to the left, and she jerked and crumpled the lace into a hard ball that scratched her palm.

Gloria was home. It would be bad if Gloria peered over the big picket fence as she always did and caught Maddie on the floor of Brent's car with another woman's underwear. Roseanne started singing "My Baby Thinks He's a Train," and Maddie snapped the tape player off and groped for sanity.

It was probably paranoid to think that Gloria Meyer could

identify another woman's underwear at forty paces, but this was Frog Point, so there was no room to take chances. If Gloria saw, her nose would twitch, and she'd wave and scuttle inside, and an hour later Maddie's mother would be calling to find out if it was true because she'd heard it from Esther by the toaster ovens at Kmart and now everybody in Frog Point was talking about what a fool Maddie was and what a shame it was for Emily and how it was all Maddie's mother's fault because she hadn't raised Maddie right.

The sunbaked suburban landscape dipped and swerved, and her stomach rose up to meet the curves. She realized she wasn't breathing and filled her lungs with the hot dusty air as the blood pounded in her ears.

Next door, Gloria's screen door slapped shut as she went inside.

Think, Maddie told herself. *Forget the dizzy part.* The talk before had been awful. And Em was old enough to understand now. Em would know.

And then there was her mother. Oh, God, her mother.

Think. Stop panicking. Well, one thing she could do. She could make sure she wasn't a fool again. She could get a divorce. She nodded to herself and then felt like a fool anyway for nodding alone on the floor of a car.

She put her hand on the hot beige leather and pushed herself out of the car to stare at her backyard. Funny how normal everything looked. The pine picket fence was still where it was supposed to be, and the splintered picnic table, and Em's beat-up blue bike, and yet she'd found somebody else's underwear, here on this spot, on Linden Street, between Gloria Meyer and Leona Crosby, right in the middle of her life.

Maddie took a deep breath and walked up the back porch steps and into the cool of her kitchen, making sure to slam the back door, which had started to stick in the heat. It was the details that mattered, like not air-conditioning the outdoors because she was distracted and had let the door pop open. She stood next to the sink and held the pants in her hand, trying for a moment to make them fit into her everyday reality the way Em used to sing along with "Sesame Street": one of these things did not belong here, one of these things was not the same. Yellow Formica counter. Dead microwave. Blue-checked hand towel. Flintstone glass with milk in bottom. Mac-and-cheese pan soaking in sink. Brown calico pot holder with "i love you mom" embroidery.

Black lace crotchless underwear.

"Mom?"

Maddie dropped the underwear into the mac-and-cheese mess with nerveless fingers and shoved it to the bottom of the pan, splashing scummy dishwater on her T-shirt. She turned and saw Em in the doorway, lost in her black oversize Marvin the Martian T-shirt, her baby-fine brown hair curling around her face, vulnerable as only an eight-year-old can be vulnerable.

Maddie leaned on the sink for support. "What, honey?"

"What was that?" Em stared at her, her brown eyes huge behind her glasses.

Maddie stared back stupidly for a moment. "What?"

"That thing." Em came closer, sliding her hip along the yellow counter as she moved, bouncing over the cabinet handles. "That black thing."

"Oh." Maddie blinked at the pants floating in the pan and shoved them under the water again. "It's a scrub thing." She began to scour the mac-and-cheese pan with the wadded-up pants, taking great satisfaction in the way the pale cheese clogged the lace.

"A scrub thing?" Em peered over her arm.

"It's not a very good scrub thing." Maddie let the sodden

lace sink to the bottom of the pan. "I'm getting rid of it. What's up with you? Got everything put away?"

"Yes," Em said, full of virtue. "And I put the box in the basement so nobody would trip over it."

Fear caught at the back of Maddie's throat. Em's virtue was all part of some plan for whatever it was she was up to this time, some plan she could make because her world was secure and ordinary, and it was all about to blow up in her face. Maddie's knees went and she pulled out a kitchen chair and sat down before she fell on the floor and made a fool of herself in front of her daughter.

"Mom?" Em said, and Maddie held out her arms and pulled Em close to her.

"I love you, baby," Maddie said into her hair as she rocked Em back and forth. "I love you so much."

"I love you, too, Mommy." Em pulled away a little. "Are you all right?"

"Yes." Maddie forced herself to let her daughter go. "I'm fine."

"Okay." Em backed up a little and began to sidle out of the kitchen. "Well, if you need me for anything, yell. I'm going to go work on my school list some more. It's pretty long this year. Third grade is harder."

"Right," Maddie said. Whatever it was that Em was going to ask, she'd postponed it until her mother was normal again. But normal was going to be never unless Maddie could handle this mess somehow. The key was in not overreacting. That was the key. Think everyday life. If she hadn't found the underwear, what would she be doing? Finishing the mac-and-cheese pan. Taking out the trash. Today was trash day. She'd definitely be taking out the trash.

She got up and pulled on the blue plastic trash basket under the sink. It stuck, and she pulled on it again and again, gritting her teeth, finally yanking at it savagely until it gave up and popped out. *Damn right*, she thought, and caught her breath. She dumped the water out of the mac-and-cheese pan and threw it and the gross, cheese-encrusted panties in the trash. Overcome with revulsion, she grabbed the can of Lysol out from under the sink and sprayed the trash and her hands until they dripped and her nose stung from the chemical-rich air. Then she dragged the trash outside and upended the basket into the Dumpster at the side of the yard, carefully not looking at Brent's car. She was supposed to bag everything she put into the Dumpster, but today was not a bagging kind of day. She slammed the Dumpster closed and straightened as the screen door of the next house wheezed and bounced. Gloria again.

"Uh, Maddie?" Gloria peered over the fence and pushed a wisp of pale hair behind her ear. Maddie squinted at her in the sunlight. Gloria was pretty in a faint, pale, overbred way. Maybe Brent was cheating with Gloria. She was right next door, so he wouldn't have to make much effort. That was like Brent.

"Maddie, I wanted to ask you, what do you think about the grass?"

Maddie gritted her teeth. "I don't think about the grass much, Gloria." She turned back to the house, knowing she was being rude and not caring. Well, caring a little bit; there was no point in making Gloria feel rejected. Or in giving her a reason to talk, for that matter. She turned to smile at Gloria as she walked past her, but it was feeble. *You can do better than that, damn it*, she told herself, but Gloria wasn't noticing anyway.

"I don't know." Gloria's forehead creased as she frowned. "Don't you think yours is getting a little long? Could you ask Brent to come over tonight to talk about it?"

7

Maddie restrained herself from ripping her neighbor's face off. Gloria Meyer was a pain in the rear, but there was no way she could be sleeping with Brent. For one thing, Gloria would never wear crotchless panties. For another, sex would mean she'd have to stop talking about her damn lawn. "The grass will be okay, Gloria."

"Do you think so? I really think I should talk to Brent." Gloria pursued Maddie obliquely, sliding down her side of the fence much the way Em had slid down the side of the counter.

Maddie reached the steps and didn't stop. "I have to go," she said, and escaped into her kitchen.

She was probably overreacting. Absolutely, she was over-reacting. She was ready to murder Brent, and over what? A pair of underpants that there might very well be a good explanation for. She was behaving as if she were in a bad TV show, the kind that began with a misunderstanding that any idiot could see through, and then continued while the two stars plotted and fought all through the half hour without ever discussing the problem like reasonable people until the last five minutes of the show when they talked and everything was all right in time for the Infiniti commercial. How ridiculous. She'd just wait and mention the pants to Brent when he got home. Like a rational adult.

"Hi, honey. What the *hell* were black lace underpants doing under the front seat of your car?"

Calm down. Be rational.

Eat chocolate.

There was a good idea. Chocolate spurred the production of endorphins, which would calm her down, and was full of caffeine, which would give her the energy to kill her husband. The best of both worlds.

The cupboards were full of canned vegetables and cereal,

but in the freezer, in back of the frozen peas and last week's chicken soup, she found one permafrosted brownie. Thank God. She peeled the plastic wrap from it in strips and then dropped it on the counter where it skated and spun like an ice cube.

Great. And the microwave was broken. A deeper woman might see this as symbolic of the breakdown of her life. Fortunately, she wasn't deep. She'd just eat the damn brownie frozen.

She tried to bite off a piece, but it was like chocolate rock. She yanked open a drawer and pulled out her big carving knife. The brownie sat on the counter, sullen, cold, unresponsive. She poised the knife over it and then slammed it into the heart of the cake, but the knife skidded off the top and gouged the yellow Formica. Brent would be mad about that. Well, too bad. Lately he'd been mad about everything; for the past week, she hadn't done anything right. That was one of the reasons she'd been out there in the heat, cleaning his damn car. She thought of the car and felt her blood pound in her temples. He was doing it again. With Beth? Visions of the perky little redhead loomed before her. Maddie hated perky. The hell with both of them.

Maddie held the knifepoint to the center of the brownie. Precision work. Gritting her teeth, she shoved the knife into the center where it jammed, the brownie still refusing to split into edible chunks. Maddie exhaled through her teeth. She'd never met a more irritating piece of fat and sugar. Just her luck: one damn brownie in the house and it had to be male.

She picked up the knife, and the brownie stuck to the end, impaled. It was a nice image, full of vengeful satisfaction. She carried the knife to the stove, turned up the gas burner, and began to toast the brownie like a marshmallow over the flame. The smell of burning chocolate filled the room.

Who was it this time? Beth? Or somebody new? Her mind ticked over the usual adultery suspects.

Gloria next door?

His secretary, Kristie?

Somebody at the bowling alley?

Somebody he and Howie had built a house for?

Did it matter, really?

Maddie turned the flame up higher. After it happened once, did it matter who it was the next time? This was Brent's fault, he was the one doing it to her. And to Em. Oh, God, Em. She hoped he—

The phone rang, and Maddie snarled in frustration before she turned off the gas and went to answer it, the knifed brownie still in hand. "Hello?"

"Maddie, honey, it's Mama."

Maddie closed her eyes and waited for her mother to say, "Maddie, you'll never guess what I heard about Brent today."

"Maddie? Are you all right, honey? I tried to call about fifteen minutes ago, but there was no answer."

Maddie swallowed. "We were outside cleaning Brent's car." *And guess what we found.* She went into the living room and sank down on her blue-flowered overstuffed couch, stretching the phone cord tight across the room as she dropped. Maybe if she propped the knife up in the living room, Brent would come home and trip over the phone cord and fall onto it. She pictured his body toppling, massive and solid, and the scrunch the knife would make going in.

"Well, it's too hot to clean cars," her mother was saying. "You stay inside."

"We are," Maddie said. "Now." She gripped the knife until her knuckles turned white and gnawed a small chunk off the corner of the brownie. It was hard and icy, but it was chocolate. She sucked on it, making it melt with the heat of her angry mouth, and then swallowed it, choking a little as it went down. *Slow down*, she told herself, and drew in air through her nose.

"Are your allergies acting up?" her mother demanded.

"No."

"Well, take a Benadryl just in case. You sound wheezy. I won't keep you, I just wanted to let you know that you're getting company any minute now."

"You're kidding." Maddie gnawed off another corner of brownie.

"It's Sheriff Henley's nephew, the one you went to high school with."

"Nephew?" The news took a moment to sink in, and then Maddie dropped her knife, brownie and all. C. L. Sturgis. He'd been her first mistake. If she'd stayed a virgin, none of this would be happening. She tried to sound uninterested as she groped around on the navy carpet for the knife. "I don't remember."

Her mother did, but that wasn't unusual. Her mother's memory was a natural database of all the times everybody in town had screwed up, so she'd definitely have a file on C.L. And now her file on Maddie, never small to begin with, was about to get bigger.

"I ran into him outside the police station," her mother was saying. "He was looking for Brent, but I told him you were home this afternoon, so he said he'd try you next."

Thank you, Mother. Where was that damn brownie?

"And oh, Maddie, I was so embarrassed." She lowered her voice. "I couldn't remember his name. I knew he wasn't a Henley because he was Anna's sister's son, but I couldn't for the life of me think of who he was. He was a year behind you in school. He was always in trouble for fighting and such a reckless driver, remember?"

"Sort of." Maddie put her head between her knees so she

could think and found the knife and her brownie on the floor under her legs, only slightly hairy from the carpet. So C.L. was back, was he?

Maddie picked up her knife and shoved herself up off the floor so she could pace. Gee, and just yesterday she'd been thinking her life was boring and empty. Well, bring back yesterday. Her skin prickled and her breath came funny again. She tried to focus on brushing the debris off the brownie, but it was difficult one-handed while she was pacing.

Her mother was still talking. "He married Sheila Bankhead and moved away, but then she left him and took him for everything he had. Don't you remember? Maybe he's come home because she's getting married again. What was his name? Something strange."

Maddie cradled the phone on her shoulder as she dusted the last of the lint off the brownie and her mother ran down a list of wrong names. When her mother ran out of steam, Maddie gave her the right one: "C. L. Sturgis."

"That's him! That Sturgis boy. He should be there any time now." Then her mother's voice changed. "Now, how'd you come to remember his name?"

"Lucky guess." Like she could forget. Well, the hell with C. L. Sturgis. The hell with all men. Especially the hell with Brent. She started to pace again, chewing off chunks of the thawing brownie as she walked.

"Well, anyway, Sheila's marrying Stan Sawyer." Her mother sighed. "He's dumber than squat, but she's probably after his money, not his brains. He just inherited all that Becknell money from his aunt. Cancer. Terrible. At least Sheila's better than that Beth he was dating."

Maddie stopped as her stomach started up her esophagus again, full of brownie this time. Beth. She tested herself, looking for the rage she'd felt for Beth five years before, but it wasn't there. She should be mad at Beth. She definitely didn't like her. But hating Beth didn't solve anything. At least, it hadn't solved anything five years ago. Beth wasn't her problem, even if it turned out that she was the one missing the under-wear. Brent was her problem. She should leave the son of a bitch. Then he could marry Beth. That would be one way to get even with Beth.

Her mother was still talking. Her mother would talk through the Second Coming, doing the play-by-play. "And now the sinners are in the lake of fire. I can see Beth the slut from here. I believe, yes, she's doing the backstroke." Maddie could sympathize; she felt as if she were in the lake of fire, too. Going down for the third time with Brent tied around her neck. She leaned her forehead against the wall as her mother moved on to another topic.

"I talked to Candace Lowery at the bank. She was wearing a beautiful beige jacket. To look at her, you'd never think she was a Lowery."

"Mom." Maddie could hear Frog Point talking now. *She stayed with him after the first time, what did she expect? The way she acts, you'd never think she was a Martindale.* She rolled her shoulders back against the wall and clenched the knife in front of her and ate another chunk of brownie.

"I ran into Treva at Revco. She said Three's home from col-lege for a month. Doesn't that sound like a long time?"

"It sounds nice." Maybe she'd go see Treva. Maybe she'd say all these thoughts out loud, and Treva would make sarcastic remarks about her being paranoid, and they would have a good laugh. They were long overdue. She hadn't talked to Treva since last week.

"Didn't you know? She's your best friend, and you didn't know her son was home?" Her mother's voice was starting to rise.

"We've been busy." Maddie didn't know why she hadn't seen Treva, and at the moment she didn't care. One trauma at a time. She shut down all thought and ate the last of the brownie. It was a very good brownie, considering its circumstances.

"Busy doing what?" her mother said, and then the doorbell rang, and Maddie let her head fall back against the wall.

C.L.

"It's summer," her mother was saying. "Teachers don't do anything in the summer—"

The doorbell rang again, and Maddie straightened away from the wall. "Mom, there's somebody at the door, I have to go."

"That Sturgis boy. Maybe you better talk to him on the porch. You know how people are. I'll hang on until you find out."

"No, Mom, I'm going to go now. I love you." Her mother was still talking as Maddie hung up. Just her luck, she'd answer the door and there would be a serial killer, and he'd murder her on her doorstep, and then at her funeral her mother would tell everybody, "I told her not to hang up, but she never would listen." Some screwups lasted beyond death, and answering the door right now was probably one of them.

She did not need C. L. Sturgis. She especially did not need C. L. Sturgis right now because every time things went wrong with Brent, C. L. Sturgis was the memory that popped into her head. *Things could be worse*, she'd tell herself. *You could have married C. L. Sturgis.* Except that things couldn't get much worse, and C.L. was not that bad a memory, and for all she knew, in the twenty years since he'd lured her into his backseat, he could have improved. Brent hadn't, but that didn't mean C.L. couldn't have.

The doorbell rang again, and Maddie walked into her white-on-white hall and yanked the door open.

Sure enough, there on her porch, lit by the sun, was C. L. Sturgis, choreographed back into her life by her mother and a malignant Fate, looking better than he had any right to after twenty years. He said, "Hey, Maddie," and she adjusted her memory of C.L. at seventeen to the real C.L. at thirty-seven. His face was more lined, and he was taller and broader through the shoulders under his blue-striped shirt, but his dark hair was still thick and rumpled, and his eyebrows still did that V thing that made him look like Satan's delivery boy, and he still had those hot, dark eyes and that wide, brainless, sheepish grin. Yep, it was C.L., all right. Rebel without a clue.

"Maddie? Your mom said it was all right to stop by." C.L.'s voice was light and his grin was still in place, but his dark eyes had cooled to wary. What had she ever done to make him look at her like that? Well, besides dumping him after one night in his backseat. He couldn't still be holding that grudge after twenty years. C.L. took a step back on her porch, and Maddie's frown hardened. Sure he could. The way things were going today, somebody she'd pushed on the playground in second grade was probably heading her way with a grenade.

He ducked his head and peered at her, and for a minute he looked seventeen again, unsure of himself and doubly dangerous because of it. There was nothing worse than C.L. looking vulnerable, she remembered, because he so rarely was. "Uh, bad day?" he asked.

Oh, great. He knew about Brent, too. Maddie scowled harder at him. "What makes you think so?"

He pointed at her left hand. "The knife. Big sucker, too."

She glanced down. She still had the blade clenched in her hand, poised to jab. "I was eating a brownie."

C.L. nodded, looking not relieved at all. "Sure. That would explain it. Listen, I don't want to keep you." His eyes went back to the knife. "Is Brent here?"

It was so surreal. An hour ago, her life had been fine, and now she was talking to C. L. Sturgis, who wanted to talk to her cheating jerk of a husband. "You know, my mother told me you were coming over, but somehow I just didn't believe it."

He kept his eyes on the knife. "Believe it. About Brent—"

The hell with Brent. She waved the knife to get his attention. "Look, C.L., I'm kind of busy right now—"

He reached out and took the knife from her so swiftly that she was left staring at her empty hand. "No offense, Mad, but it's been awhile, and for all I know, you've gone homicidal on me." He stepped back off the porch and shoved the knife up to the hilt into the flower bed by the steps. He still had the same great butt he'd had in high school, Maddie noticed, and from the condition of his jeans, they could have been from high school, too. Then he came back to her and smiled again, and she could have sworn his smile was the same it had been in high school, part happiness, part invitation to trouble. It was impossible to be cold when he hit her with that smile. There was something about C.L. that insisted you smile back even though you knew it was a mistake.

She relaxed, exhaling in relief as some of the tension left her neck. "I'm sorry. I'm having a bad day."

He nodded, warm and sympathetic, and she remembered why she'd climbed into his backseat twenty years before. "That's because you're still living in Frog Point," he said. "Every day here is a bad one. You look great, by the way."

Maddie looked down at her soap-stained pink T-shirt, still blotchy with the water from the sink. "You know, C.L., there's such a thing as carrying politeness too far."

"No," he said. "You really do look great. Just like in high school."

He wanted something. He had to; nobody could look at her and say, "Just like in high school," not after twenty years of wear and tear and Brent. She felt the chill return. "Thanks," she told him. "So what do you want?"

C.L. looked taken aback, but not for long. "Well, now that the chit-chat's out of the way, and we're all unarmed, is Brent home?"

Brent. The son of a bitch. Everywhere she went, there he was. She glared at C.L. "No. I'm busy. Try the office." She swung the door closed, but he put his foot in the way and stopped her.

"Wait a minute. I tried there."

He was closer now, and she realized he'd grown more than shoulders and height since seventeen. There was weight to C.L. now; he was solid, and his dark eyes under the thick fringe of his lashes were sure. He'd grown up.

Too bad Brent hadn't.

Maddie took a deep breath. "Look, this is not my day to watch him, okay? I don't know where he is. It's been nice seeing you, but I have to go."

"I can't believe this." C.L. frowned. For a moment, all his warmth went away, and Maddie took a step back. "There is no way anybody can disappear in this town. You're his wife. You must know where he is."

This Maddie didn't need, her first romantic disaster commenting on her current one. "Look, *I don't know where he is.* Now, go away."

"All right, all right." C.L. held his hands up to ward her off. "All I want to do is talk to him. Mind if I come in?"

"Yes," Maddie said. "I mind a lot." She shoved his foot out of the way with hers and slammed the door, surprising herself with how fast and how mad she was. Two men in her entire life, and they'd both taken her for a ride. Well, the hell with them.

"Maddie?" C.L. said from the other side of the door.

"Not now, C.L. Not now, not ever. Go away." Maddie listened for a moment to see if he was gone, and then jumped when Em said, "Mom?" behind her.

Em stood there with her school list. "I heard you talking. Who was that? You look funny."

Em. Every time she got to a place where she could make jokes and pretend it wasn't happening, there was Em with disaster bearing down on her. She couldn't do this alone anymore. "That was nobody," she told Em. "Let's walk over to Aunt Treva and Mel's."

"All right," Em said, but her eyes were cautious.

Ten minutes later, Maddie stood in her best friend's back doorway, trying to look mentally healthy while Treva blinked up at her, startled.

"Mel's in the family room," Treva said to Em, not taking her eyes off Maddie's face. "Go find her." Once Em was down the hall, Treva grabbed Maddie's arm. "What's wrong with you? You look awful. Is this my fault? I know I haven't called. What's wrong?"

"Brent's cheating on me." Maddie swallowed. "I have to leave him. Divorce him." It was a lot more awful than she'd thought, saying it out loud, and she staggered back a step and threw up her brownie into Treva's bushes.

"Oh, hell," Treva said.

As a semi-mature, rational adult, C. L. Sturgis knew that a crush that had blindsided him in the fifth grade and then come back to wipe him out again in high school could not possibly have any impact on his life now. Then he realized he'd driven four blocks down Linden Street with no idea of where he was going and no idea of where he'd been since he'd seen Maddie in her wet T-shirt. So much for semi-maturity.

Figuring his reputation in town was bad enough, he pulled over and parked his convertible before he ran down a Frog Point citizen while having carnal thoughts about a married woman and got another couple of sins added to the list of Things C.L. Done to Shame Henry and Break Poor Anna's Heart.

He tapped his fingers on the wheel, trying to get his thoughts back where they belonged. No matter how desirable she'd been standing in her doorway, all dark curls and warm curves and cool eyes that made him stupid, Maddie Martindale was history. And all he'd done was talk to her on her porch step, so there was nothing for him to feel guilty about, especially now that he wasn't driving in a lust-fogged stupor. He was an adult in a car he'd paid for, and he had every right to be where he was and to talk to anybody he wanted.

C.L. looked around at the tall old houses, every one of them staring into the well of the street with dark windows, and slid a little farther down in the seat, wincing under guilty memories of toilet-papered trees and soaped windows and potatoes in tailpipes and cherry bombs in mailboxes. Then he caught himself. He hadn't done anything wrong around here for almost twenty years. He was innocent. He could even get out of the car. The hell with Frog Point. He jerked on the emergency brake and got out and slammed the door.

The noise seemed to echo up and down the street. He lit a cigarette and leaned against the car door, wondering why he still had the feeling he was going to get busted for smoking. He was thirty-seven. He was *allowed* to smoke in public.

Across the street, a woman opened her front door and came out on the porch, jerking her head at him suspiciously, no doubt drawn out of her musty living room to see who he was and why he was parked on her street in the middle of the day when a decent man would be at work. She looked familiar, and then he recognized her and realized that he'd parked where he had from force of habit. Mrs. Banister. He'd spent most of his senior year parked right here in front of her house trying to seduce her daughter, Linda, and succeeding an amazing number of times. And now here he was, back one last time, betrayed by his instincts again.

C.L. straightened and waved at her to let her know he wasn't some pervert or, worse, some stranger casing the joint to rip off her Hummels. She squinted at him and then stomped back inside, slamming the door. He couldn't tell whether it was from recognition or heightened suspicion, and he didn't care.

What he cared about was Maddie.

She'd looked unhappy and angry and lost when she'd opened the door, and she'd been brittle and smart-mouthed, not the smiling girl he'd remembered from high school. Whenever he'd thought of Maddie in the past years, he'd remembered her warmth, but she wasn't warm anymore. Somebody had hurt her, and he had an idea who'd been doing the hurting and that made him mad. Somebody should have to pay for all this misery, and he was pretty damn sure that somebody was Brent Faraday.

And C.L. was also pretty damn sure he knew how to do it. His ex-wife, of all people, had handed him the weapon.

"I need you for this, C.L.," Sheila had said on the phone when she'd called him the week before. "I need an accountant I can trust. You can take a long weekend, they love you at that firm you work for, they'll let you take off as long as you want. You were a lousy husband, but you're a damn good accountant." After that come-on, he'd had no problem saying no when she said she was afraid her fiancé might be getting swindled, no problem saying no when she cried, no problem saying no when she offered to sign away her right to alimony since she'd have to give it up when she married Stan anyway. But then she'd said, "*Please*, C.L. All you have to do is come down here and look at the books and tell me if Brent Faraday is ripping Stan off by asking for two hundred and eighty thousand for a quarter of the company. Just yes, he is, or no, he isn't, that's all."

And he'd said, "I'll do it."

He took another long drag on the cigarette, sucking in nicotine to blunt the memory. Sheila had said, "There's probably nothing wrong. After all, it is Brent Faraday," and he'd known there had to be a lot wrong. More than he hated Frog Point, he hated Brent Faraday, who got away with murder while Frog Point loved him, and Maddie married him, and C.L. got caught over and over again.

Thank God all that was behind him now. He was a solid citizen with a solid job and a solid future. He might finally be able to catch Brent at something, he was sincerely hoping he would, but his own days of worrying about getting busted were over.

C.L. was finishing his cigarette, getting ready to leave, when a squad car pulled up behind his Mustang, and a cop got out and came toward him.

Chapter Two

C.L. slumped back against his car. "You have *got* to be kidding me."

"Nope." The cop pushed his hat back on his head, showing off a lot of red hair and freckles, and grinned. "Mrs. Banister called in a suspicious man staring at her house, and Henry sent me over to find out if it was you. This is just like old times, buddy."

"Vince, the old times sucked," C.L. told him. "It may have slipped your mind, but back then you were running *from* the cops, not with them. I told Henry he'd lost his mind when he hired you."

"Hey," Vince protested. "That was a smart move. Henry knew I knew everything about juvenile crimes since I'd committed most of them with you. He was getting an expert.

Now, face the car and spread 'em, C.L. I gotta pat you down."

"Up yours," C.L. said. "Jesus, give a delinquent a little power and he gets delusions of grandeur. Did Henry really know it was me?"

Vince leaned against the car next to C.L. "Henry's got X-ray eyes and ears, you know that. Plus, you're the only stranger we got right now. Narrows down the field considerably. Give me a butt, old buddy."

"And then you'll run me in for bribing a police officer," C.L. said. "Smoke your own."

"I can't." Vince showed the first evidence of gloom since he'd pulled up. "Donna's making me quit."

"You're whipped, boy."

"I got two kids I don't want getting secondhand lung cancer," Vince said, his natural cheerfulness returning. "But since they're both over at the park cheating at softball right now, I guess one of yours won't hurt 'em."

C.L. gave up and passed over his pack. "Cheating, huh? Good to know you're bringing 'em up right."

"I'm just showing 'em everything you taught me, C.L." Vince lit up and took a long drag. "Damn, that's good. Why does everything that's bad for you have to be so damn good?"

C.L. thought of Maddie. "Because God has a lousy sense of humor."

"It's good to have you back, C.L." Vince passed the pack back. "Not a lot of people around here'll make jokes about God. Course, when you get hit by lightning, it'll be what you deserve."

"If it ever happens to me, it'll happen to me here," C.L. said. "I cross the city limits and God paints a target on my forehead."

"And you so innocent and all." Vince stood away from the car. "Well, I got to get back to work since I'm the only thing standing between Frog Point and crime. If you're still around tonight about eight, stop by the Bowl-A-Rama and I'll buy you a beer."

C.L. opened his mouth to tell Vince what he thought of the Bowl-A-Rama and then stopped. Regardless of what he thought of orange plastic and bowling shoes, he liked Vince. It might be good to kick back with old Vince one more time.

And Vince knew almost as much about Frog Point as Henry did.

"You're on," C.L. said.

"Good. Bring the cigarettes." Vince turned to go back to his car. "Try not to get into trouble while you're here. I'd hate to have to arrest you."

"Try," C.L. said, and Vince laughed and drove away.

Well, gee, it was great to be back home. Everybody else got to grow up and get married and have kids and become steady citizens, but he was marked for life. The oldest living juvie in Ohio. Quite an honor. He felt like tp'ing Mrs. Banister's house for spite.

And then he'd go see Maddie for old times' sake.

"Forget Brent," he'd say, "remember the backseat?" Except that wasn't a great memory for her. Or him. The next day he'd gone to her locker to talk to her and she'd turned away.

C.L. winced at the remembered humiliation, still sharp after twenty years. Dumb, dumb, dumb. What was it about high school pain that lasted a lifetime? And how was it that he could ring a doorbell and see Maddie Martindale glaring at him, twenty years older and several pounds heavier, and instantly feel that pain again and feel so damn dumb again and still want her again? *It's pride*, he told himself. It was pride saying, *Hey, I was inept because I was a kid; give me another shot, I'm better now, much better. Really.* Except he was pretty sure that if a miracle happened and he got her again, he'd still blow it just because it was Maddie. And a miracle wasn't going to happen, and he didn't want it to. The past was the past, and it didn't matter anywhere except in Frog Point where what had happened twenty years ago was still news today, and Brent Faraday was still Most Likely to Succeed, and Maddie Martindale was still That Nice Girl, and he was still That Sturgis Boy who was Such a Burden to his Aunt and Uncle. The hell with it.

C.L. straightened and took a final drag on his cigarette. He started to lean into the car to stub the butt out and then stopped himself. What were they going to bust him for if he threw it into the street? Littering?

He flipped the butt into the street and then froze as it landed on a leaf, seeing in his mind the leaf burst into flame, catching other leaves, the fire licking across the road, attacking cars and houses, blackened matchstick frames cracking and falling into the street as gas tanks exploded and raged, and then, at the end of the street, as the smoke cleared, Henry in his sheriff's suit, looking disgusted again.

The butt went out, and C.L. got back in his car, determined to get out of Frog Point before it made him certifiable instead of just temporarily crazed.

"I'm never going to feel the same way about your bushes again," Maddie said when she was drinking microwaved hot tea and lemon in Treva's kitchen. It was a lovely, messy kitchen, full of copper pans and kids' drawings on the refrigerator and bright boxes that said "New!" and "Extra Crisp!" Howie had redone everything so it was now brick and gleaming wood and brass, but it was Treva's kitchen, too, so everything was all jumbled together, and Treva stood in the middle of it, bent over a bowl full of white cheese on her butcher-block island, her frizzy blonde hair making her look like part of the chaos, a dandelion blown there by accident.

"I'm sure my bushes have new feelings for you, too." Treva's voice was tight as she picked up a spoonful of the white gunk from the bowl in front of her and a piece of manicotti from the plate beside her and tried to integrate them. Her hands were shaking, and she pushed too hard, and the pasta split and the cheese fell in a glop back into the bowl, spattering her skinny-ribbed red-striped tank top. "Hell." She dabbed at the stain on her shirt with a dish towel. "Just *hell*."

"What are you doing with that manicotti?" Maddie said, stalling to avoid talking about the thing she'd come to talk about. "Cooking? This isn't like you."

"I needed to." Treva gave up on the towel and picked up another piece of pasta. "You know how sometimes you just have to cook?"

"No," Maddie said. "And neither do you. What's wrong?"

"What's wrong?" Treva waved the pasta at her. "You're getting divorced and you ask *me* what's wrong?"

"I think I'm getting divorced," Maddie said. "I have to think this through."

"Don't think it through," Treva picked up the spoon and went back to work, her hands growing steadier as she talked. "Just divorce the son of a bitch. I've always hated him anyway."

Maddie jerked her chin up in surprise. "Hello? You were matron of honor at the wedding. You waited sixteen years to tell me this?"

"You were in love. It didn't seem like a good time." Treva abandoned her pasta for a moment to take a chunk of pale cheese from the refrigerator and hand it to Maddie. "If you're finished barfing, you can help. Grater's in the second drawer behind you."

Maddie scowled at her. "There's something wrong here."

Treva dropped the spoon in the bowl again and braced herself on the butcher block. "I'm just crazy right now. I have a lot on my mind. And I hate him." She focused on Maddie. "All right, enough stalling. What did he do this time?"

Maddie stood and got the grater and a bowl out of Treva's cupboard. Then she began to grate the cheese into the bowl so she wouldn't have to meet Treva's eyes. "I found black lace crotchless underwear under the front seat of his car. It rattled me a little."

"Oh." Treva blinked. "Well, yeah. That would rattle me, too. Crotchless underwear, huh?" She bit her lip. "Beth?"

"I don't know." Maddie grated harder. "They didn't have a name tag. I don't think I care. I mean, Beth didn't make me any promises, Brent did. If I was a good person, I'd feel sorry for Beth."

"Oh, cut me a break." Treva went back to her manicotti. "I know you're the original good girl, but that's pushing it."

"Okay, look, I don't like her," Maddie said. "She slept with my husband, and I still want to spit when I see her. But it was awful for her. She thought she was doing the right thing by coming and telling me, and it just blew up in her face." She stopped grating to remember Beth's face, blank with incomprehension as Brent told her it was over. "I think she loved him."

Treva snorted and Maddie went back to grating. Grating was a pretty good anesthetic. You had to be careful of your knuckles and remember to turn the cheese, but when you were done, you had grated cheese. Not every form of distraction came with a by-product. From now on, she was grating her own cheese. "You need one of those plastic boxes with the grater in the lid," she told Treva. "I think Rubbermaid makes it. Or Tupperware."

"I have so much Rubbermaid and Tupperware now that I

have to buy more Rubbermaid to organize it," Treva told her. "I'll probably die from fluorocarbon poisoning. Forget plastic and tell me you really are going to divorce the son of a bitch this time."

Maddie flinched. "Maybe I'll just kill him. Except that I'd screw that up, too. Maybe I could hire somebody to kill him. The paperboy hates him, too. Maybe we could do a deal."

Treva pounced. "Do you hate him?"

Did she? She was furious with him for getting them all into this mess, but that didn't mean she hated him. She wasn't sure she cared enough about him to hate him. Dislike was in the picture, of course. "Only if he's having an affair," she told Treva. "If he isn't having an affair, I only don't like him. It's the cheating part that's going to make me want him dead in twisted wreckage on the interstate."

"That would be good, too," Treva said. "If we knew a brake line from a garden hose, we could cut his."

"We could cut them both just to make sure," Maddie said, grateful for any change of subject. "Except that would ruin Gloria's life because she lives for the neighborhood grass."

"I heard Gloria's getting a divorce," Treva said. "Call your mother and find out why. If I've heard about it, your mother has photocopies of the complaint."

Maddie winced. "That's the way it's going to be for me, too, isn't it? The wires will be humming, and people will be very sympathetic, and they'll pat Em on the head, and her teachers will call and say they understand why her work has fallen off, and the kids will ask her about it on the playground."

"Em will survive." Treva stuffed another manicotti.

"I want more for her than survival," Maddie said. "I want warmth and love and security. She loves Brent so much."

Treva looked at her with visible contempt. "So you're going

to stay with a cheating scum for the sake of your child? Cut me a break."

Maddie glared at her. "Hey, would you take Mel away from Howie?"

Treva stopped in midscoop, and her knuckles turned white as she gripped the spoon. "I would do anything to protect my children. But I wouldn't stay with a man like Brent."

"Then there's my mother," Maddie said. "A small point, I know."

"Are you kidding?" Treva shook her head. "I wouldn't want to explain *anything* to your mother. But if you think you're going to keep this from her, you can forget it. That woman is Velcro for gossip."

"And my mother-in-law. Helena's never liked me much anyway. She's going to blacken my name six ways to Sunday."

"You're younger than she is," Treva said. "She resents it. Your mistake."

"And then there's the rest of the town." Maddie went back to grating since anything was better than contemplating her future. "Frog Point is going to have a field day."

"Over you? Not a chance." Disdain sat strangely on Treva's cartoon face. "Nobody would say anything bad about Maddie Martindale, the Perpetual Virgin of Frog Point. Not even a demon like Helena Faraday."

Maddie jerked her head up at the venom in Treva's voice. "What?"

Treva frowned her apology. "I'm sorry. But if you weren't my best friend, you'd be pretty hard to take. To tell you the truth, this is kind of a relief."

Maddie sat with her mouth open, trying to think of something to say. This was not like Treva. Treva laughed and made jokes and offered unconditional support; she did not lash out without warning. "Well," Maddie said, stalling for time. "I'm glad it's working out for somebody."

Treva dropped her spoon and came around the butcher block to sink into the chair across from Maddie. "I'm sorry. I'm sorry. Forget I said that. You'll be fine." Maddie stared back bleakly, and Treva picked up speed. "You haven't done anything wrong. Hell, you're the perfect wife and mother. Besides, who cares? Jesus, Maddie, you can't live your life to make this damn town happy." Treva leaned back. "Although come to think of it, you always have, haven't you? Clean in thought, word, and deed?"

"I don't know about thought," Maddie said, trying to recover from Treva's onslaught. "Sometimes I have fantasies of standing downtown in front of the bank and screaming, 'Fuck, fuck, fuck!' just to see what people would do. Or running naked down Main Street. I really think about it, even though I know I'll never do it."

"I'd pay money to see it," Treva said. "Actually, I wouldn't pay money to see you, but I'd pay double to see people's faces."

"But I can't do it." Maddie put the grater down and leaned closer to make her point. "It would be stupid and pointless and embarrassing, and it would be awful for my family. It's *easier* to do the right thing, you know?"

"Not for all of us." Treva scooted her chair back so roughly the legs squeaked. "Some of us found it was easier to do the wrong thing, and we're still paying."

Maddie blinked at her, fighting her way through present trauma to past pain. "Is this about Three? Because nobody gives a damn that you had to get married twenty years ago."

"Before graduation?" Treva went back to her butcher block. "Nobody will ever forget. I could find the cure for cancer, and they'd say, 'Treva Hanes—you know, the one who had to get married before she graduated—discovered the cure for cancer.' Nobody forgets in this town." She shoved the manicotti pan to one side and began to wipe down the counter. "But they won't touch you. You do everything right. You married your high school sweetheart and never looked at anyone else. Hell, they'll put up a shrine."

"Treva, have we got a problem here?" Maddie said. "Because this is not like you, and while I would love to be sympathetic, my life is in meltdown already. I need you on this."

"Right." Treva bit her lip. "Right. I'm sorry. I've just had such a lousy week. And now this. It's just awful. I feel awful about everything."

"Well, at least you got dinner out of it." Maddie stretched to hand her the bowl of grated cheese and the rest of the block of Parmesan.

"No, grate the whole thing," Treva said.

"For one pan of manicotti?"

Treva opened the refrigerator and gestured, and Maddie craned her neck to see past her. Five more pans of manicotti sat already stuffed on the shelves.

Maddie slumped back, appalled. "Treva, we have to talk. This isn't good. What's wrong with you?"

"You should talk. All I have is a lot of pasta. You have crotchless underwear." Treva slammed the refrigerator door. "What are you going to do? Whatever it is, I want to help."

Maddie opened her mouth to ask what was wrong again and stopped, blocked by Treva's bland stonewall stare, the stare that had gotten Treva out of any number of confrontations in her life. Whatever it was that was bothering Treva was not going to be discussed. Period. Maddie gave up and went back to her own problems. "I'll confront him when he gets home, I guess. I don't know what to do. I don't have any proof. I threw the pants away."

Treva rolled her eyes. "You don't need proof. This is divorce; not murder."

Murder. It had such a nice clean sound compared to *divorce.* "Wait," Maddie said. "The day is not over yet."

"Did you ask about the puppy yet?" Mel asked Em.

"No," Em said. "It's not a good time."

"Well, then, I have *excellent* news about Jason Norris."

They'd climbed into Mel's tree house, the one she'd inherited from her older brother, and now Em leaned back on the old blue couch pillows they'd liberated from the family room and tried to decide whether or not to dump all her worries on her best friend. Mel looked like her mother—skinny, blonde, and freckle-cute—but she had a mind trained on Nintendo and every R-rated video in town. She'd be the best person in the world to talk to about the trouble at home. Em just wasn't sure she wanted to talk about it. Talking might make it real.

"Dierdre White told me Richelle Tandy is *crazy* about him," Mel went on, "but Jason is *definitely* not interested."

Neither was Em at the moment. "He told me all girls have cooties."

Mel sat up. "Well, see, that's *great*. He's *talking* to you. According to my mom, boys aren't verbal, so if they do anything more than *grunt*, it's a good sign."

Em shook her head. "He also tried to chase me around the pool with a frog. Like I'd be afraid of a frog. He's a mess."

"Well, I think he's *cute*." Mel frowned at her. "Are you okay? Last week you thought he was cute, too."

Em gave up. "There's something really wrong at my house."

"Your parents fighting?" Mel shrugged. "No big deal. Mine fight *all* the time."

"They do?" Em was distracted for a moment, trying to imagine her uncle Howie yelling. It was hard to imagine Uncle Howie even talking back to Aunt Treva, but then it was hard to imagine anybody talking back to Aunt Treva.

Mel rummaged around in the old suitcase they'd swiped as a treasure chest and pulled out a crumpled pack of Oreos. "Sure. Last week it was about the grass." She took a cookie and passed the package to Em. "Of course, they didn't know I was listening."

"The grass?" Em pushed her glasses back up the bridge of her nose to see the package better. No bugs. She took a cookie and bit into it. It was stale and soft, but it was a bugless Oreo in a tree house, so it was still pretty good. A breeze came up and blew through the window and even more through the cracks between the boards Three had nailed up in his early carpentry days. The cracks made it better. Anybody could nail boards close together; only Three would build in air conditioning.

Mel swallowed her Oreo. "Yeah, the grass." She unscrewed the next crumbling cookie and licked at the icing. "Dad came home and said"—she made her voice deep and rocked her head from side to side—"'Jesus, Treva, you don't even teach during the summer and you expect me to cut the damn grass after all day at work,' and Mom said"—Mel put a squeaky edge on her own contralto—"'Jesus yourself, I'm not going to have a heart attack to cut the goddamn grass. You want it cut, you cut it.'"

"Were they mad?" Em asked, fascinated.

"Nah." Mel slumped down beside her on the cushions and crammed half of the Oreo in her mouth, talking around the black crumbs. "They get tired, and they bitch at each other, and then they say something dumb, and then they do it."

Em blinked. "Oh."

Mel nodded. "Like Mom says, 'Okay, fine, I'll cut the grass, but if I get all hot and sweaty, that's it, 'cause I'm only getting hot and sweaty once tonight,' and Dad says, 'Well, maybe I can cut the grass later; why don't we talk about it?' and Mom says, 'Well, I don't know, that grass is getting pretty long,' and my dad grabs her hand and says, 'Step into my office and we'll discuss it,' and my mom laughs and they go back to their room and do it." She bit into the second half of her Oreo. "I tried to listen at the door after the grass fight, but Three caught me."

Em grinned and relaxed. "What did he say?"

"He said that listening to stuff like that would stunt my growth and it would be my fault if I grew up to be a dwarf. Then he took me out for ice cream."

Em sighed. "I love Three."

"He can be your brother, too," Mel offered. "So what are your mom and dad fighting about?"

Em put her half-eaten Oreo down. "They're not. They don't fight. They don't even talk." She thought hard for a minute. "I don't think they even do it."

Mel shook her head. "You don't know that. They could be really sneaky and wait until you're asleep. Your mom and dad are grown-ups. Mine are *immature*." Her chin went up on the last sentence, and she looked so much like her mother that Em grinned again in spite of her worries. Then Mel, being Mel, went back to the problem at hand. "So if they don't fight, what's the problem?"

"They don't do *anything*." Em thought hard, trying to come up with a reason that would make Mel understand. "Dad bowls a lot and messes with the yard and goes out to work. And Mom works around the house and does her school stuff to get ready for when it starts, and talks to my grandma and your mom, and goes to visit my crazy great-grandma in the nursing home. But they don't do stuff together." She pushed her glasses up the bridge of her nose and frowned at Mel. "I know it doesn't sound bad, but it is. There's something wrong. And my mom is really upset today. I don't know why, but she's acting really unhappy."

Mel sat up. "So they don't, like, hug each other, and make jokes, and pretend to have fights and then laugh, and stuff like that?"

Em tried to imagine her parents doing any of those things. It sounded so wonderful, to have parents that laughed, but she couldn't picture it. Her mom laughed with her and with her aunt Treva, but she couldn't remember her laughing with her dad. She couldn't remember her dad laughing at all. "No," she said. "No, they never do."

Mel's face looked sober. "Maybe they're getting a divorce."

"*No!*" Em pushed the Oreo package away, sick to her stomach. "No, they aren't. They don't fight. Ever. They never fight. They're not getting a divorce."

"You could live here," Mel offered. "My mom loves you and so does my dad. You could be my sister."

"They're not getting a divorce," Em said.

Mel slumped back on the pillows again and stared into space, thinking hard. Em watched, pinning all her hopes on Mel, telling herself that Mel was the idea person in their friendship, that everything would be okay when Mel came up with something.

"We could spy on them," Mel finally offered.

"No," Em said. Mel was the idea person, but sometimes her ideas were really bad, which was why Em got final say. Mel gave up the spy idea and thought again.

"I've got it." She sat up. "You come spend tonight with me, and that'll give them some time alone. That's what my mom says saves their marriage sometimes. She dumps me on my grandma, and once when she didn't know I was listening, she said, 'Thanks, Irma, this is going to save your son's marriage.'"

"I've spent the night with you before," Em pointed out. "I do it all the time."

"Since you started feeling bad about them?" Mel asked.

Em thought back on it. The bad stuff had started last week. They never talked or laughed, but it hadn't bothered her until last week when everything seemed colder and tense. And it hadn't really, really bothered her until today. Until she saw her mom's face when she'd come in from the car. "No," she told Mel. "Not since then."

Mel rolled to her feet and headed for the ladder. "Come on. Let's go *ask*."

Coming to see Treva may not have been the best idea, Maddie reflected. Now that Treva had garnished the sixth pan of manicotti with enough freshly grated Parmesan to blanket Frog Point, she was fixated on the idea of searching Brent's things for evidence. "No," Maddie told her. "We are not going to go through his stuff. No way."

"Sure we are." Treva sat down across from her, happy with her plan. "We'll find stuff that'll tell us what's going on. Letters and things."

"Letters?" Maddie looked at her in disbelief. "Brent won't take a phone message, and you're going to look for love letters?"

"Well, whatever. Is he going to be home tonight?"

Maddie tried to remember what day it was. Thursday. "No. He's bowling with his dad."

Treva brightened, and Maddie felt wary. Treva was too peppy about the whole catastrophe. "That's great. We can search tonight. And I have another idea." Treva leaned forward. "I think you should cheat on him and get even. I even know who you can do it with. Remember that hoody guy who followed you around senior year? He was always fighting somebody. And he was cute in an unstable kind of way. Remember?"

"No." Maddie glared at Treva, a move that had no effect on her whatsoever.

"Sure you do. He had those great eyes and that big old car with a backseat the size of your family room." Treva paused for effect. "C. L. Sturgis."

Maddie put her chin in her hand and tried to look uninterested. "Vaguely. I remember him vaguely."

"Well, I saw him with Sheila Bankhead this morning in front of the police station. And he's looking *much* better. The hoody part's gone. Of course, he still looks unstable, but at thirty-eight that's exciting."

"Seven."

"What?"

"He's thirty-seven. He's a year younger than us. What does C. L. Sturgis have to do with my divorcing Brent?" There. It was easier saying it that time.

"I told you. Pay Brent back first by having an affair of your own. With C. L. Sturgis."

"Have sex with C. L. Sturgis?" Maddie began to laugh and just kept on going.

Treva was patient, but she finally broke in. "Why not?"

Maddie stopped laughing and met her eyes. "Because I never make the same mistake twice, that's why."

"You had sex with C. L. Sturgis?"

The back door slammed. Mel stomped in and yelled, "Mom? Can we—"

"Out!" Treva said without turning around, and waited until the door slammed again before she leaned across the table to Maddie and said, "You had sex with C. L. Sturgis? *And you didn't tell me?"*

"It never came up." Maddie rubbed her forehead and tried not to think too much about that night, laughing and warm in the backseat with C.L. It had been a mistake then and it would be a mistake now.

Treva was still marveling. "This is amazing. I didn't think you could keep a secret from me for twenty minutes, let alone twenty years. And your mother never found out?"

"No, thank God." Maddie sat up straighter, galvanized by the thought. "I never told anybody. Can you imagine what would have happened if that got out? I never told *anybody*."

"Yeah, but he didn't, either," Treva said. "That must have taken some self-control."

"I never thought about that," Maddie said, surprised. "That was pretty sweet of him." She tried to remember what she had thought about. "I worried myself sick about it for a couple of weeks, but nobody said anything, and I got my period, and there was a lot going on. It was near the end of senior year, and right after it happened you and Howie got married and there was that flap, and then there was graduation, and everything happened at once. And then I left for college, and the next year he graduated and left town forever, and I sort of forgot until he turned up today. He said he wanted to talk to Brent."

"Brent? What about?"

Maddie blinked at her. "You know, I didn't ask. I didn't care." She drew a deep breath and asked the question she'd been dreading. "Treva, you've got to tell me. Does everybody know about this already? Am I the last to find out? Because I don't think I can—"

Em stuck her head in through the back door, and Maddie cracked her face into a smile. "Hi, baby."

"Hi." Em came in and leaned on the table, and Maddie could see the tension in her face. "Aunt Treva, can I come stay at your house tonight? Mel and I need to compare our school lists so we can share some things and save you money."

"How thrifty of you," Treva told her without taking her eyes off Maddie. "Of course you can stay."

"Cool." Em slipped out the door again, and they heard her yell, "Hey, Mel!"

"Are you okay with that?" Maddie said. "Were you going out tonight? I don't want to dump her on you."

"Forget that," Treva said. "You need time alone to scream at Brent. Three can sit them if I can't. They're the least of our problems."

Maddie slumped back. "Em's the most of mine. I'm having nightmares about what happens when she finds out what everybody knows."

"I don't know what everybody knows. I only know what I know, and to answer your question, I didn't know about this." Treva put her hand over Maddie's. "Forget Em for a minute. What do you want? If Em weren't in the picture, what would you want?"

"I think I'd leave him," Maddie said. "Except then there's my mother, having to face the town with the first Martindale divorce. And his parents coming after me. And Brent isn't going to take a divorce sitting down, he fought like hell the last time. And—"

Treva tightened her hand. "Will you forget everybody else for a minute? What do *you* want?"

Maddie blinked at her. "I don't know." She tried to push away the guilt of not thinking about everybody else first. "I think I'd like to be on my own. In fact, I think I'd love it. Just doing what I want, not worrying about what the neighbors think—that would be wonderful." She sat back, and Treva's hand slipped away. "You know my naked-in-front-of-the-bank fantasy? I have another one, about being alone on a desert island with a lot of chocolate and books. Just me and Esther Price Hand-dipped Nuts and Caramels and the complete works of everybody. No neighbors."

"I have that one, too," Treva said. "It used to be a lot of chocolate and Harrison Ford. And then one day I thought, *Why is Harrison here? If he wasn't, I wouldn't have to do these damn sit-ups.*"

"I'd just like the aloneness of it," Maddie said. "Nobody to keep happy. Nobody to feel guilty about. Just me forever."

"Forever?" Treva lifted an eyebrow. "Two weeks, maybe, but then I'd want my family back. Even Howie, even if he is a guy."

"I'd like forever," Maddie said, and then she straightened in her chair. "Except I wouldn't because I'd die without Em. And it's a fantasy. I have to live in this town, and my mother deserves me taking care of her, and Em definitely deserves me taking care of her, and I was the one who promised Brent I'd be there for better or worse, so forget the desert island." She shook her head. "I don't know what I want. I think I'd better just concentrate on what I can have."

"You can have a divorce," Treva said. "Leave him."

"What if he isn't cheating?" Maddie said. "What if there's an explanation? There might be. It's possible."

Treva rolled her eyes. "Fine. Then talk to him. But *do it.*"

Talk to him. Say, *Brent I'm going to leave you.* Say, *I'm taking Em and leaving you.* Five years disappeared with blinding speed. She'd been here before and it had been horrible. Maddie felt her eyes grow hot and steeled herself. She was not going to cry. She was not going to sit in her best friend's kitchen and be pathetic. She stood up, needing to escape before the tears came. "Right. I know you're right. I do. But I have to go now."

"All right." Treva sat back. "Sure. Later. Whatever you want. Are you sure you're all right?"

"Just peachy," Maddie said, and went to get her daughter.

The heat was so thick that the air weighed Maddie down as she walked Em home down Linden Street. She must have walked down Linden a million times in her life. She'd lived with her mother in the old yellow house two blocks down from Treva's place, and Treva had lived where she and Howie lived now, taking the house over from her mom and dad when they'd moved to the condos by the river. All Maddie's life, Linden had meant running up a block to see Treva, breathless with plans or news, just as it meant walking down three blocks to see her now.

And it had meant Brent, coming by to pick her up and drop her off on dates and school days, Brent who'd bought her a house on Linden because she loved the street and wanted to be close to Treva, Brent who could be so sweet and who was probably cheating on her now.

Do you hate him? Treva had asked. It was possible to love someone and hate him at the same time; she'd felt that way about him once, after Beth. But now all she felt was rage and dread and lethal exasperation; there wasn't any love left to counteract anything anymore. And that was her marriage. To her horror, she found she couldn't stop the tears. Em would see. "Race you to the car," she said, and pounded down the last block to collapse in the driver's seat of her aged Civic, winded but not weeping.

Em got in and slammed the car door behind her a minute later. "No fair. You got a head start. Where are we going? Why can't we take Dad's car? It's better."

Because I'm never getting in that car again. Maddie put the car in gear. "This one's fine. Let's go see your dad."

Em grew still. "Okay."

Maddie met her eyes and smiled, straining every muscle in her face to make it do what it didn't want to do. "We'll just ask him what he wants for dinner. That'll be fun."

"Okay," Em said again, but the cautious look stayed in her eyes.

Maddie backed out of the drive while Em hunched down so no one would see her in a rustmobile. The Civic, at least, was one battle Maddie had won in her marriage. She gripped the steering wheel harder as she thought about it. Brent had pushed her to trade it in for the new car he wanted to buy her and had even sent a tow truck to drag it away, but she'd thrown herself across the hood of the car at the last minute, and the guy in the tow truck had gone off without it. "I love this car," she'd told Brent. "I paid for it myself, it never stalls, and I understand it. It takes years to learn a car like I know this one. I wanted to be buried in this car." Brent had stopped nagging her then, but he'd looked at her as if she were demented. Maybe that's why he was cheating: the shame of her car, complicated by her dementia, drove him to it.

He was cheating. All her arguments to Treva aside, there wasn't going to be another explanation. Treva had been right to roll her eyes. He was cheating.

Maddie turned on a country station and drove through the center of town toward her husband and the end of her marriage, listening to the Mavericks as she tried to ignore her mangled life. People smiled and waved at her, and she waved back and felt approved of. People in Frog Point liked her. She was nice. That's who she was, Nice. That was a hell of a thing to be, Nice, but it was what she was, maybe all that she was. A terrible thought struck her that maybe the reason she was fighting the idea of divorce was that divorce wasn't Nice. That would be stupid. Except that if she wasn't Nice, she wasn't sure she'd still exist.

She distracted herself with better thoughts. Old Frog Point was beautiful in late summer, its streets canopied by huge old elms and oaks in full leaf, their branches rubbing together over the street, and Maddie felt sheltered as she drove through their dappled shade. Their roots pushed up gray slabs of concrete sidewalk into cracked and rolling waves, crusted with moss in the shady parts. When she and Treva had been little on Linden, they'd pretended the slabs were mountains and made up stories about them and roller-skated up and down them and played hopscotch. Em and Mel did the same things now, safe away from all the ugly things that happened to little kids in bigger towns. Whatever its drawbacks, and they were legion, Frog Point was home. It had wrapped itself around her for thirty-eight years and kept her warm while it watched every move she made. If it hadn't been for Brent, she could have lived with that. Even with Brent, she was going to have to live with that. She belonged to Frog Point.

The Mavericks finished, and Patsy Cline started in on "Walking After Midnight." Patsy had had her man problems, which was some comfort; if a class act like Patsy could be a fool over men, too, maybe Maddie wasn't a complete loss. An ancient brown Datsun came zooming up behind them and braked at the last minute before beginning to tailgate them. The Datsun was even older than her Civic, so old that it looked like something that C. L. Sturgis might have wrecked in his glory days. Maddie thought about C.L. back then, cocky and crackling with nervous energy, and just for a minute, she wished she were back there, back before she'd made all her mistakes, able to choose C.L. instead. But that would mean no Em, and Em was worth everything, even this, so she let go of C.L. and the memories and kept going toward her husband.

The squeal of brakes brought the Datsun back to mind. It had come up behind her too fast again and stopped at the last minute, almost skidding into her.

"What are you *doing?*" Maddie said to the Datsun in her rearview mirror, and the driver peeled off down a side street, evidently disgusted at how poky she was being. Well, nobody rushed to their own disasters, especially when they had their kids in the passenger seat. Maddie drew a deep breath. This was going to hurt Em so much; that was the worst part, the absolute worst. That was what she'd never forgive Brent for, that he'd hurt Em when she loved him so much.

But she couldn't forgive him for what he'd done to her, either, and driving slowly through the cool green shade, she let her anger seep into her bones. He'd made a fool of her again. If she left him, she'd be crawling away into the sympathetic, scornful arms of the town with no way to fight back. Treva was right; somehow, she should be able to get even. C.L. came to mind again, this time a recent memory, standing in her doorway, broad and smiling and solid and possible and pretty damn attractive as an adult.

No. Absolutely not. She had enough problems without committing adultery. Aside from the fact that it was wrong, adultery in Frog Point got you your own miniseries on the grapevine.

Still, the thought of revenge was lovely. And, she was surprised to realize, the thought of confounding the town by not being a good girl was pretty attractive, too, as long as all she did was think about it, not do it.

Reba McEntire took over the radio from Patsy, and Maddie turned a corner only to brake a good ten feet short of the next stop sign for a little multicolor mutt. It was sitting in the middle of her lane, scratching an ear, unimpressed with her car. "No hurry," she told it, and Em relaxed and laughed.

Then Em became very still and turned to her mother, her eyes wide with innocence behind her glasses. "I bet that dog doesn't have a home. Maybe we should adopt it."

Maddie peered at the dog over the steering wheel. It was wearing a red collar, and its tags jingled as it scratched. "It belongs to somebody, Em. It's probably on its way home."

"Well, then," Em said. "Maybe we could go buy a dog and give it a home. As a good deed."

Maddie leaned back. *Angel Daughter cashes in,* she thought. *Finally.* "Okay, spill it. What's up?"

Em gave up and slumped back on the seat. "I want a dog. I want one really, really bad. And I've been good. And my birthday's coming up."

"Your birthday's in January," Maddie said.

Em groaned. "I *knew* you'd say that. Listen, we really need a dog, Mom. We do."

"This is because of 'Frasier,' isn't it?" Maddie said. "Em, it's not as easy as it looks on TV. You have to take care of a dog—"

"I know," Em said with such satisfaction that Maddie knew she'd been had. Em crawled around the seat and brought up a batch of library books. "I've been studying."

Maddie looked at the books. *Caring for Your Puppy. The Complete Book of Dog Care. Dog Lore. No Bad Dogs.* There were others in Em's lap.

"I read them all, even the hard ones," Em said. "I can do it. *Please.*"

Maddie's first impulse was to say no, that she had too much to deal with already, but Em was so earnest. And Brent would hate having a dog, which was a major selling point. And a dog might distract Em if there was a divorce coming up, something she could hold on to while the rest of her world fell apart.

Em looked at Maddie as if her entire life depended on what Maddie said next.

"All right," Maddie said. "We'll go to the pound when we get back from Daddy's."

"Yes!" Em bounced on the seat.

"But you'll take care of it—"

"Yes, I will, I know how to, I will, I will, I love you, Mom!" Em bounced and bounced, her grin swallowing her face.

The mutt stopped scratching and yawned, and Em laughed again, and the world seemed a good place for a moment. *Maybe I won't go up to the company to see Brent*, Maddie thought. *Maybe we'll go get a dog instead. Or maybe I'll just stay here parked in the middle of the street.* Maybe if she never got to the corner, things wouldn't change.

Then she glanced in the rearview mirror and saw the ancient Datsun hurtling around the corner toward them.

She turned in panic to warn Em, but her voice was lost in the scream of peeling tires and slammed-on brakes and the gut-wrenching scrunch of pleated metal. She felt the blow of the impact on her back, and her head jerked forward as the seat gave beneath her and slid and the radio cracked into silence, and then her head whipped back and smacked sickeningly into the headrest behind her.

Chapter
Three

E m," Maddie said, when everything stopped moving.

Em—short, relaxed, and wrapped in her seat belt—sat unhurt, her eyes wide behind her glasses. "I'm okay, Mom. Wow."

"Are you sure? Does your neck hurt?" Maddie's neck hurt.

"I'm okay. Boy, he really hit us."

Maddie pushed her car door free of the buckled frame, and small metal things tinkled onto the ground. She got out, and the world looped around her. *Slow here.* Everything seemed at once brighter and less clear. With meticulous care, she picked her way back to the other car. Broken glass scrunched underfoot as she went. The radio blared out something obscene, and Maddie wished she could, too, but it wasn't a possibility because it would hurt too much.

The driver sat there, holding his head and moaning, and she bent to see if he was all right. He was a kid from the high school, a pale, weedy blond she recognized without putting a name to him, not one of the kids she'd had in class.

"Are you all right?" she said. "Did you hit your head? Was your seat belt on?"

"My car. I hit you hard. *My car.*"

"Your radio works." *You moron.* All the anger she'd been repressing came flooding back, and she almost screamed at him before she remembered that he'd been in an accident, too, and there was no point in making him even more miserable even if he was a reckless degenerate. At least C.L.'s accidents had always involved guardrails and ditches, not other people. The kid moaned again and refused to meet her eyes. She straightened and went back to look at her car.

It was dead. The hatchback was mashed up into the backseat, both taillights crushed into powder. Knowing nothing about cars, she knew that no one would fix this one. It was too old.

She should have screamed at the kid after all. Three times he'd come at her.

Em got out. "Boy."

My car.

"Does this mean we get a new car?" Em asked.

The kid joined them. "Do you think your insurance will cover this?"

Maddie turned to look at him. *I could kill you where you stand.* She began to walk back to her car, taking careful, measured steps.

The boy followed her, and then the police pulled up.

She sank back into her car and rested her head on the steering wheel. The officer, a boy who'd failed her senior art class five years ago, asked for her driver's license, and Em fished it out of her bag for him. He was polite, but he asked too many questions, and she got confused, and he asked if she was all right.

"I was going to be buried in this car," she said, and he radioed for an ambulance for a possible concussion.

Brent met her at the emergency room, tall, dark, rough-hewn, and in control. *I was looking for you*, she wanted to tell him, but he spoke first.

"I'll take care of everything." Then he turned away from her to talk in deep, serious tones to the young doctor and the even younger nurse. *I hate you*, Maddie thought, but it didn't seem like the time to mention it with Em right there. The room reeked of disinfectant and alcohol, and she tasted metal from the medication they'd given her. She was cold and the examining table was too high, and she wanted to go home, but Brent was still talking to the doctor.

She watched her husband. Would another woman want him? He was getting a little pudgy, but he was still good looking in a big, boyish, beefy sort of way. That dark lock of hair that always fell in his eyes. That endearing cowlick at the crown of his head. Those dimples. That cocky smile. That bastard. He walked toward her with his shoulders back, and the nurse appreciated it. Maddie pulled away as he came near.

He was saying something to her, and she focused in on him from very far away.

"Don't worry, it wasn't your fault," he was saying, his arm around Em, who leaned on him lovingly.

"I know."

"The kid wasn't insured, but our insurance will cover it."

"I know."

His hand tightened on Em. "And Emily's all right, thank God."

"I know."

"You don't even have a concussion. Just pulled muscles in your neck. Tylenol Three is all you need."

"I know."

Brent sighed, his solicitude morphing into exasperation before her eyes. "We can go now."

"I know."

The nurse gave him a glowing smile and Maddie's painkillers, and he walked them out to the Cadillac, putting Em in the backseat before he turned to Maddie, who was looking at the car, trying to figure how it had gotten from the driveway where it had betrayed her all the way to the hospital.

"I was cleaning this car," she told him. "It was in the driveway."

"Howie dropped me off so I could pick it up. Your car's in back of Leo's. I called while the doctor was with you. Leo says it's totaled. You'll have to get a new car now."

Her car was dead in the weeds in back of a service station. Normally that would have depressed her, but she was too dazed to care. "I know." She got in the car and tried to remember what normal life felt like. Yesterday.

He got in beside her and patted her knee, and she moved it away. "Just relax, Mad," he told her. "You're going to be fine."

She nodded once, but a knife went into her neck, so she stopped. "I know."

Brent exhaled through his teeth. "Could you please say something besides 'I know'?"

How about, your expressions of sympathy touch my heart? How about, could we have a moment of silence for my car, which was just brutally murdered by a teenaged moron? How about, are you

*having an affair and if so with whom, you rotten lying son of a
bitch?*

"Maddie?"

Em was in the car. "Thank you for coming to get us."

He sighed and put the car in gear, and a thousand years
later, they pulled into the driveway. Maddie sat and stared out
the window, knowing she had to say something. Soon.

"Maddie, we're here." Brent reached over and unbuckled her
seat belt. "Mad?" He put his hand on her shoulder. It felt like
a lead weight.

Right. They were here. She almost felt sorry for Brent. It
couldn't be easy talking to her like this; she realized that.
She sympathized. She watched him walk around the front of
the car and open her door. That was nice of him.

"Maddie, get out of the car. You're not hurt that bad. The
doctor said so."

Right again. She got out of the car. Her shoes stuck to the
melting tar in the driveway, and she concentrated with great
effort to pull her feet free. They were so far away. Brent was
too close.

"Mom?"

Em's voice had an echoey quality to it. Maddie focused
on her face and smiled. "I'm fine, baby. Let's go inside." The
creosote smelled nice and clean, and she concentrated on that
for a moment to keep from screaming at her husband.

"Emily, are you sure you're okay?" Brent got down on his
knees on the sidewalk beside her and looked into her eyes. He
looked so sweet on his knees, holding on to their daughter,
clean and earnest with that cowlick at the crown of his head.
The bastard.

Em nodded, keeping an eye on Maddie. "I'm fine, Daddy.
Really."

"Okay." He hugged her and kissed her on the cheek and then stood up and watched her as she headed for the porch before he looked at Maddie. "You, too, Mad. I'll be late tonight. Order pizza and take it easy. Don't wait for me."

Maddie moved by him, and he tried to pat her shoulder, big clumsy thuds that slid over the top of her arm. *Don't touch me*, she thought, and the spurt of anger was fresh and clean after all the murky dithering she'd been doing. She stopped and waited until Em was a couple of yards away, going up the porch steps, and then she met his eyes.

"Maddie, come on." He put his hand on her arm to guide her toward the porch, and she shook it off with such ferocity that he stepped back.

"What's going on, Brent?" she whispered at him, clenching her teeth to keep from screaming. Her hands curled into fists and came up in front of her. "What are you doing? What the *hell* are you doing?"

"What?" Brent stared at her, stricken. "What are you talking about?"

Maddie moved closer to him, toe to toe, and spoke under her breath. "I found some other woman's underwear under your front seat, damn you. Who are you seeing? Is it Beth again?" She shook her head at him even though it made her skull scream, and pressed her fists against her chest to keep from hitting him, needing to make it clear to him, needing to make it clear to herself. "I'm not doing this again, Brent. I won't do this again. I won't. If you're cheating, I'll leave you, I *swear* I'll leave you this time."

Brent glanced at Em, who had stopped on the porch and was watching them. "Nothing's wrong," he said, and his voice was too loud. "You're confused. You just hit your head." He dropped his voice. "You're upsetting Emily. Knock it off."

"I found underpants," she said to him under her breath.

"Black lace crotchless underpants. You tell me *now*, you explain that."

Em said, "Mommy?"

"Just a minute, honey," Brent called back to her. He lowered his voice again. "You know I wouldn't cheat on you. I promised you. How long are you going to make me pay for Beth?"

Maddie took a step back, confused. He was so rational. "What about the pants?"

"I don't know." Brent's exasperation made his voice rise. "Somebody's idea of a joke."

"It's not funny," Maddie said.

"It sure as hell isn't." He stepped away from her and went to the porch to Em. "Mommy's feeling bad," he told her, and when Maddie followed him to the porch and said, *"Wait a minute,"* he said, "Not now," and turned back to take Em's hand. "Mommy needs a nap. Come on, Em, I'll take you to Aunt Treva's so Mommy can rest."

Em looked close to tears. "Mom?"

Maddie drew a deep breath. She'd never wanted to scream at anybody more, but not in front of Em. Never in front of Em. "Daddy's right. You go stay with Mel tonight. Stay all night. I'll be okay."

Em swallowed. "Are you sure? I could take care of you."

Maddie blinked back tears. "Thank you, honey, but I'm just going to take my pills and go to sleep. Honest. You go with Daddy."

Em nodded, her head wobbly on her neck. "Okay, but I'm not staying all night. I'm coming home tonight so I can help you when you wake up."

Maddie put her arms around her and pulled her close, feeling how stiff Em's body was against her. "I'm all right, Em. You can stay with Mel."

"No." Em's voice cracked and Maddie held her tighter.

"All right." Maddie patted her back and rocked her a little, as if she were a baby again. "All right. Daddy can bring you home later, after bowling. Everything's going to be all right."

Maddie watched as Em went down the walk to the car, her face turned back to look at Maddie, her hand in Brent's hand. Brent, the son of a bitch who was using their daughter as an excuse to escape. She wanted to scream at him, *You come back here and talk to me*, but instead she waved as he backed the car out of the drive. Then she took a deep breath and went inside.

She took a painkiller and put the pill bottle on the kitchen windowsill so that the light made it glow amber. Pretty. Then she sat down for a moment so her head could clear, trying not to think about Em or black lace or divorce or her car or anything else that was confusing her.

It was so nice that she didn't have a concussion. What the hell did she have? She looked around her. Well, she had an ugly kitchen. They'd put gray linoleum in because Brent had gotten a deal on it, but she was the one who'd painted the walls yellow. Yessir, that was her choice. They certainly were yellow. She felt as if she were trapped in a pound cake.

At least the black lace had cut through the yellow.

She got up carefully and moved into the hall. The hall was white. Boring but not offensive. Sort of like Brent. Until today. Today he was offensive and unbearable. She pulled herself up the stairs using the banister, and the strain made her dizzy, so she leaned on the wall until she got to the bedroom. Peach. Why had she thought peach would be a good idea? The quilted headboard was especially ugly. When you got right down to it, she hated the whole room. The whole damn house. It was time to move. Maybe that's what she'd do, she'd move and not tell Brent. But then somebody else would. This was Frog Point. You couldn't get away with anything in Frog Point.

Maddie eased herself down onto the bed. It was heaven to

close her eyes. It meant her eyeballs weren't going to fall out. But the rest of the pain, the pain everywhere else, pressed down on her so that she sank into the mattress to get away from it. *The thing is,* she thought, *I hate him. So it shouldn't matter whether he's cheating or not. But I hurt all over, and I hate the thought of facing this damn town with all this mess to handle, and I can't stand what this is going to do to Em. So I think I'll think about this later.*

I'll have to think about it later.

At seven that evening, C.L. leaned against the back door of his uncle's farmhouse and listened to the crickets tuning up. They had about an hour to go before dark, but a few of them started early, and their creak blended with the faint wash of the river that ran past the farm a couple of hundred yards away, and with the birds making the most of the last of the hot August day. It was the kind of evening that made a man want to crawl into a hammock with a cold beer and a warm woman, but the woman he was trying not to think about was married and had slammed a door in his face. So much for hammock fantasies. It was probably impossible to make love in a hammock anyway, although if Maddie had been the one in the hammock, he would sure as hell have been willing to try. This thought led to others, none of which he should have been thinking and all of which made him jump a foot in guilt when his aunt spoke behind him.

"Did you wash your hands, C.L.?"

C.L. jerked around to see Anna loading the kitchen table with dinner, covering the red and white checked oilcloth with thick white china plates and bowls full of steaming ham and potatoes and God knew what else. The smell registered on him, and his mouth watered at the thought of the salt and juice in the local-cured ham and the cream and the cheese that the potatoes bubbled in.

"I have died and gone to heaven," he told her, and she said, "Not unless you've washed your hands, you haven't."

Her voice was tart, but she looked just as warm and sure as she had when Henry'd brought him home to her twenty-seven years ago. His mother had told him for the last time how worthless he was and that this time she was going to send him to a home for delinquents because that's what he was, and he'd run off to sleep in the park, acting as if that was what all ten-year-olds did. Then Henry had pulled up beside him just as he was heading for the picnic house, and said, "Get in, kid." C.L. had wanted to say no, that he could take care of himself, but even back then, you didn't argue with Henry. So he'd climbed in the car, and Henry had taken him out to Anna, who'd said, "You'll stay with us, C.L.," and then he *had* said, "No. I can take care of myself," because he knew what happened when people did you favors: they made you pay forever. His mother was still making him pay for giving birth to him. He didn't want any more of that.

But then Anna had said, "Why, we know that, C.L., but who's going to take care of us? We're getting on, you know. We could use somebody young and strong around the house." C.L. grinned now at the memory. Henry must have been in his forties about then, strong enough to bench-press a cow. And Anna had never had a feeble day in her life. But it had made sense to a ten-year-old who wanted to be needed, and taking care of them didn't seem to have any strings attached to it, in fact they'd owe him, so he'd said, "Well, all right, as long as you know I'm just doin' it for you." And Anna had taken him upstairs to a big bed with soft white sheets and told him he'd have pancakes for breakfast.

It had taken him twenty years to figure out that the obligations you had to people who took care of you were nothing compared to the obligations you had to the people you wanted to take care of. You could pay back the people who took care of you, but the ones you had to keep safe, well, they were with you forever. Which meant that even though he wanted nothing more than to never see Frog Point again, he had to come back to see Anna. He looked at her now with love that went bone-deep, and thought about how much she still looked like the brisk blonde woman who had saved his life so long ago. Her apron was new, something trendy in stripes instead of her usual flowers, but her now white hair was still parted in the center and wound into a knot at the nape of her neck, as smooth and neat as ever, and her blue eyes hadn't changed at all. Nothing important about Anna ever changed.

He grinned at her. "Yes, ma'am, I certainly have washed my hands. You trained me right." He walked around her to his place at the side of the table and squeezed her waist as he went.

She sniffed. "I know you're grown, C.L., but you're my boy still."

"You bet." C.L. dropped into his seat and held up his hands for inspection, palms out. "See? Clean."

Anna set another steaming bowl in front of him, green beans this time. "You clean your plate tonight, too. No argument."

C.L. looked out over the spread: sugar-cured ham, biscuits and butter and Anna's raspberry jam, green beans with bacon, cheese-sauced potatoes, homemade pickles, chunky hand-cut cole slaw with red peppers. Anna's food, one of the miracles of life. "Yes, ma'am."

The screen door slapped and Henry came in from the porch, not as gigantic as he'd seemed when C.L. was a boy but still plenty big and broad, his hair white now instead of dark but still thick and springy. He washed his hands at the sink and said,

"Smells real good, Anna," and she said, "Thank you, Henry," and C.L. thought, *I have heard them say that to each other before every meal I've ever had here.* And not for the first time, he sent silent thanks to his mother for throwing him out. It was the best thing she'd ever done for him.

Henry sat down at the head of the table, and C.L. folded his hands while Anna dropped into her chair and bowed her head. Henry said, "Lord, thank you for this food, Amen." Anna and C.L. echoed, "Amen," and then Henry reached for the ham and Anna passed the biscuits to him, and C.L. scooped up a ladle of potatoes. "Don't eat all of those, boy," Henry said, and C.L. looked at the huge bowl and said, "Well, I don't know, Henry. I'm hungry tonight."

"Worked up an appetite asking questions all over town, did you?" Henry stared at him from under furry white eyebrows, and Anna said, "Henry, the boy's eating."

C.L. grinned at his uncle and shoved the potatoes across the shiny oilcloth. "I was just looking for Brent Faraday. Didn't anybody tell you that?"

"About twenty people," Henry growled. "You up to something?"

"Nope." C.L. forked a piece of ham the size of Florida onto his plate. "Just doing one last favor for Sheila."

Anna hesitated, her fork frozen over her plate. "Sheila?"

Too late, C.L. remembered that Sheila was not one of his aunt's favorite people. "It's all right. She just called and asked me to check into some things. She's getting married to Stan Sawyer. Don't worry."

"I'm not worrying," Anna said, but she put her fork down.

"It's all right," C.L. said. "It's just a favor, that's all. She said if I did this for her, she'd sign away the rest of the alimony. This is all about money." He reached over and patted her hand. "It's all right. Eat."

Anna gave a small humph sound and picked up her fork.

Henry picked up the attack. "So what does Sheila have to do with Brent Faraday?"

C.L. stifled a sigh and turned back to his uncle. There was no use fighting it. Henry was going to get all he knew sooner or later anyway. "Stan's doing some kind of business deal with Brent. Sheila figured since she had an accountant for an ex-husband, I might as well make myself useful and look at the books. It'll only take an hour or so, and I'll be back in Columbus by Monday. This is no big deal." C.L. looked from Henry to Anna, seeing that neither one was buying it. Time for a distraction or he'd spend the whole meal talking about Sheila and Brent. "Mrs. Banister called the cops on me for staring today. What's the world coming to when I get busted by Vince Baker?"

Anna sniffed. "Thelma Banister doesn't have a brain in her head." Then she cocked an eye at C.L. "I'm not surprised Sheila asked you to see about Brent Faraday. Sheila never was a stupid girl when it came to money."

C.L. blinked at the acid in her voice when she said, "Brent Faraday."

"Brent Faraday." Henry scooped up some potatoes. "Interesting."

C.L. put his fork down and surveyed both of them. "You're kidding me. You mean this town finally caught on to Faraday?"

"Maybe not the whole town," Henry said, and Anna murmured, "He was always such a loud boy."

Cheered, C.L. sat back in his chair. "Well, I'll be damned—no, sorry, Anna—darned. What did he do?"

Henry kept on eating, shooting his sentences out between bites. "Why don't you tell me? You're the one chasing him down. Heard you talked to his wife."

"I stopped by the house looking for Brent. He wasn't there."

C.L. had nothing to feel guilty about aside from a few hammock fantasies, but somehow the look Henry gave him made him uneasy. "I didn't even go in the house, Henry. I just asked for Brent."

"You had such a crush on her," Anna said. "I remember when you came home from school that one day and told me about her. You couldn't have been much more than ten because you hadn't been with us long. Eleven maybe. Such a nice girl."

"I swear I spent five minutes on her front porch. That's it." C.L. tried to look innocent since he was, but Henry was still glaring. "I swear, Henry."

"She's married," Henry said.

C.L. held his hands up. "Henry, I'm innocent. She slammed the door in my face. I was looking for Brent, not Maddie."

"Why?" Henry said, and threw C.L. off track again.

"Well, Brent appears to have sold him a quarter partnership in the construction company. That would be half of his half, so they'd each have a quarter, and Howie would have the controlling interest. Sheila isn't too happy about that."

"Howie Basset is a nice boy," Anna said. "He wouldn't do anything crooked."

C.L. sighed. Maddie was a nice girl, Howie was a nice boy, and the fact that they were both pushing forty and could have stopped being nice over the years was irrelevant to Anna. She should know better. After all, *he* had changed. He was responsible now. He hadn't wrecked a car since 1983. And he hadn't hit anybody since high school. Of course, Howie really was a nice guy, so Anna wasn't far off the mark, but still—

Henry reached for the biscuits. "So why are you chasing Brent Faraday?"

"I want to look at the books. And I need his permission to do it. He almost has to give it to me since I'm acting as Sheila's accountant, but—"

Henry stabbed some green beans. "How's Stan feel about Sheila worrying about his money before it's hers?"

"It wouldn't be just the money," Anna said. "C.L., you're not eating. Henry, you be quiet now until he eats."

C.L. obediently picked up his fork again. "What do you mean, it's not just the money?"

Anna pointed at his plate, and he cut into the ham before she answered him. "Well, she's not going to want him looking like a fool in front of the whole town."

Henry snorted.

C.L. grinned at him. "Not a fan of Stan's?" Anna pointed at him again, and he ate some ham.

Henry shook his head in disgust. "Woman would have to be a damn fool to think he's a better catch than you."

C.L. stopped chewing and swallowed his ham whole in surprise. "Me?"

Henry glowered at him. "You've done real well, C.L. We're proud."

C.L.'s chest went tight and for an awful moment he thought he was going to tear up. Of course, Henry would disown him if he did, so he didn't, but it was touch and go there for a minute. "Oh," he said. "Thanks."

Anna picked up the bread basket. "You need a biscuit, C.L." She put two on his plate.

C.L. nodded, his head still wobbling from the shock of Henry's spoken approval.

"You don't eat enough in the city," Anna went on, passing him the butter. "You're just thin, that's all there is to it."

C.L. buttered a biscuit and bit into it to oblige her.

"If you were here more often, I'd fatten you up," Anna went on. "You know, Frog Point only has one accountant."

C.L. choked on his biscuit.

"Leave the boy alone, Anna," Henry said.

"Just thought I'd mention it." Anna picked up the bowl of green beans. "Be real nice to have him home again. Beans, C.L.?"

C.L. swallowed the last of his biscuit, took the bowl, and changed the subject. "You know I never did find Brent. Did he leave town while I wasn't looking?"

Henry speared himself another slice of ham. "Nope. Spent the afternoon at the hospital."

C.L. tried not to grin. "Somebody get as fed up with him as I am?"

"Nope." Henry sat back and began to carve into the ham. "His wife was in an accident."

C.L. lost his grin while Anna made a soft sound of distress and said, "Not that nice Maddie. Is she all right?"

"Hit her head pretty hard." Henry stabbed his fork into his ham. "The little girl is fine. That dumbass Webster kid came around a corner and rear-ended them. She was stopped in the middle of the street. Said she stopped for a dog."

"That's Maddie, all right," Anna said. "Wouldn't hurt a soul. I'll make her some cookies."

"I think she likes brownies," C.L. heard himself say. "I'll take them to her."

Henry shot him a sharp glance. "Thought you were looking for Brent."

"Just being neighborly," C.L. said, kicking himself. "Somebody should make sure she's all right. You planning on eating the rest of those potatoes, Henry, or you just keeping an eye on them down there?"

"Oh, mercy." Anna stood to pass the potatoes. "Henry, the boy's hungry."

"That's what I'm afraid of," Henry said.

C.L. ignored him and ate. He was going back to town later

that night to find Brent, but he had no intention of telling Henry that because Henry had a dirty mind.

"Drive careful when you go back to town tonight," Henry said.

"Yes, sir," C.L. said.

"We're getting a dog," Em told Mel when they were both on Mel's couch with pretzels and hot dogs, Three's idea of a balanced meal.

Mel popped her eyes open in approval. "You asked? Cool."

Em nodded. "I forgot to ask my dad, but my mom said yes." She remembered her mother's face as they'd left and felt her breath clutch a little. "Before the accident," she added, and her voice sounded funny, even to her.

"She's going to be all right," Mel said. "Your dad said so. Think about the dog."

"We'll go to the pound," Em said, thinking *puppy puppy puppy* to keep the bad thoughts away. "We'll save a puppy that way. It'll be better."

Mel nodded. "That's a good idea. Can I come?"

Em nodded. "Sure." They could all go, she and Mel and Aunt Treva and her mom. She thought of her mother and the dazed look in her eyes and the way she'd stood so close to her dad, shaking, and the way they'd looked at each other, like they hated each other. *Puppy puppy puppy.* She swallowed. "When my mom's better, we'll go." Her mom was going to be better. Everybody said so. "She'll be okay. Her pills make her dopey, but she'll be okay."

"This could be *really* good," Mel said, moving into her cheery mode. Mel's cheery mode could be pretty exhausting, but Em was grateful for the effort. "Because, like, now that she's *hurt,* your dad will remember how much he *loves* her and he'll take *care* of her, and it'll be all right."

"He's going bowling," Em said, and ate a pretzel rather than look at Mel.

"Oh," Mel said.

Puppy puppy puppy puppy puppy . . .

Chapter Four

The pain was better when Maddie woke up at nine. It had localized in her head, which gave her a body part to hold. She groped her way downstairs, but the phone rang while she was trying to read the label on her medication, and she lurched for it before it could ring again and liquefy her brain.

"Maddie, it's Mama. Are you all right?"

"Yes, Mom." *Don't shout like that.*

"Anna Henley called to see if you were all right, and that's how I found out about the accident." Her mother's tone said that she wasn't amused about that. "Are you all right?"

"Yes, Mom." Her head was coming off, and her neck didn't move.

"She said you hit your head. She said it wasn't your fault, it was that Webster boy's, but then you know how those Websters are anyway, all of them. Thank goodness it wasn't your fault. I can't believe you didn't call me. Are you all right? Do you want me to come over?"

Maddie winced under the onslaught. "No. I'm fine. Don't worry. I'm fine."

"Are you going to be all right to go visit Gran on Sunday? You know how she is. I understand if you can't go."

"I can go," Maddie said. Assuming she was off the phone by then.

"You don't sound good. I can come over right now—"

"No. Although I may need to borrow your car later this week."

"Any time. You want me to drop it off now? It's not dark yet. I can just run it over—"

"No." Maddie pressed her hand to her forehead. If her mother came over, she'd have to kill her. Time for a diversion. "What's all this about Gloria Meyer getting divorced?"

"It's true." Her mother's voice sank down on "true," so Maddie knew the story was going to be a good one. Of course, Maddie's story would be a beauty, too, when it got out. *Maybe Brent's not cheating*, she told herself. *Maybe he's telling the truth and it's all just a bad joke.*

"Her husband says she won't sleep with him," Maddie's mother went on. "Can you imagine?"

Maddie thought about Barry Meyer. Treva had once called him a weedy little warthog. "Yes, I can. Easily. Plus he never mows the lawn."

"Well, that's what she said. He never does anything around the house. I guess he's just worthless. But"—her mother's voice sank lower—"I've also heard he thinks she's seeing someone else."

"Gloria?" Maddie tried to picture Gloria and Brent together.

Gloria in crotchless panties? "Must have been the ChemLawn man."

"I don't know who, but I was *very* surprised."

"Me, too," Maddie said. "I can well believe Gloria doesn't have sex with her husband because I can't believe Gloria has sex with anybody." She sat down on the stool by the telephone, watching the second hand on the clock. If she listened for another two minutes, it would be obvious that she was fine and then she could hang up without worrying her mother. She could do another two minutes before her head fell off.

"People are surprising," her mother said. "Just when you think you really know somebody, they'll up and do something like this."

"Like what? Divorce?" *I'm going to be sick.*

"No, like Gloria having an affair."

"Well, get off this phone and go find out who it is," Maddie said, praying it wouldn't be Brent. "I can't believe you're wasting time with me."

"Maddie, how on earth would I find that out?"

"How did you find out she wasn't sleeping with Barry?"

"He told his brother who told his wife who told Esther's daughter."

Maddie closed her eyes. "Right. How is Esther?"

"She's fine. Are you sure your head's all right?"

So much for distracting her mother. "Let's talk about Gloria instead, please."

"There isn't anything left to say about Gloria, although if you ask me, she was like this all along. Remember back in high school when she got hysterical when they didn't induct her into National Honor Society as a junior? Hyperventilated right there in gym."

"I missed that." Maddie tried to remember Gloria back in high school. She'd been even paler then, walking down the halls close to the lockers. The only time Maddie had ever seen any color in Gloria's face was when Brent went by, the big football player, the high school hero. She should have let Gloria have him then. "She was three years younger. I was in college when she was a junior."

"Well, she was a spectacle, let me tell you. Just held her breath and turned blue, not that you could tell since she's always been kind of blue anyway. That woman doesn't eat right. But she's the kind who always gets what she wants. Those pale little wispy things that look like they'd blow away like dandelions, those are the ones to watch for."

"Right," Maddie said, storing this away for future use.

"Just look at Candace at the bank."

Maddie thought about Candace at the bank, a healthy, intelligent, sensible, down-to-earth, gym-toned blonde who could probably arm wrestle half her clientele to the ground. "I never thought of Candace as wispy."

"Well, no, there's all that German blood in her, but you know she just smiles and smiles and yet there she is, bank manager."

"Okay," Maddie said, not understanding at all. "I don't get it."

"Well, where did she come from? Not money." Maddie's mother sniffed. "She was a Lowery, for heaven's sake. And yet there she is, just about in charge of the whole bank because you know Harold Whitehead is useless. They just bring him and prop him up in that chair for looks. *She* runs the place."

Maddie thought of Candace back in high school, wearing clothes that weren't quite right, studying her butt off for a scholarship, moving quietly through the confusion. Candace hadn't let the town define her or defeat her. Maybe she should use Candace as a role model. "Mama, Candace has worked like crazy to get where she is."

"I know that. But you'd never know it to look at her, would you? Butter wouldn't melt in her mouth."

"I thought you liked Candace."

"I *do* like Candace," her mother said. "She's a lovely person. I'm just amazed a Lowery is running the bank."

"This is too confusing," Maddie said. "I've got to go. Call me back when you have some good stuff on Gloria."

"She's got Wilbur Carter to handle the divorce," her mother said. "If you can believe it. That woman must be dumb as dirt. Any fool knows you go to Lima if you want a decent divorce attorney."

Maddie made a mental note to get a Lima phone directory. It was going to be bad enough that she was getting a divorce, she was not going to be dumb as dirt, too. Her mother had a reputation to defend.

"I'm going to go back to bed now, Mom," Maddie said. "Take care of yourself and don't worry."

"Well, I'll worry anyway," her mother said. "I'm going to stay right by this phone, so if you need anything, you call."

"Thank you, Mama," Maddie said. "I love you."

"I love you, too, Maddie. Get some rest."

I should be nicer to that woman, Maddie thought as she hung up. She went back to the kitchen and filled a glass with water and swallowed two more pain pills. Then she went out to the porch and sank into one of the big wicker chairs to inhale the summer air, but all she could smell was tar from the driveway. The porch needed honeysuckle. Lots of honeysuckle. In her mind she decorated the porch rails with pale yellow-bellflowered vines while she tried to remember the scent. And tried to forget about her mother and Em and Brent, the only man she'd been with since high school.

High school. Glory days. Like the day Howie took the rap for flooding the rest rooms so Brent could pitch the first Big

Game. Where he dropped the ball, and kissed Margaret Erlen-meyer afterward. She should have taken that as a clue back then. But she'd gone for revenge instead and ended up in the back of C.L.'s Chevy at the Point, looking for a payback and finding . . . what? Well, not great sex, but not a bad time. What she remembered most was laughing with him. Good old C.L. Maybe Treva was right. She could sleep with C.L. and pay Brent back again.

She conjured up C.L.'s face, the real C.L. she'd seen that afternoon, not the fuzzy high school memory. He looked centered and sure of himself and . . . solid. C. L. Sturgis as a solid citizen. That was a good one. Well, no matter how solid he was, she was not going to sleep with him again. C.L. prob-ably wasn't as desperate these days as he'd been at seventeen, and then there was the fact that adultery was not her style. Her style was being good. Nice. Adultery was a bad idea. She hoped C.L. left town soon; she had enough problems.

The painkiller had kicked in, making her numb, but numb-ness was a nice change from the earlier part of her day. Maybe now she could look on the bright side. Where the hell was the bright side?

Well, at least Brent carried his own weight at the construc-tion company. He was a good salesman. And he was a good father. He was also very possibly a cheating son of a bitch, but how could she leave him? How could she send Em's father away, except for one night a week and every other weekend? Especially since he bowled so much. She had a sudden vi-sion of Em in very small bowling shoes, searching for her father in a crowd of potbellied men with advertising on their shirts. Not good.

Except maybe he wasn't bowling so much. Maybe Treva was right and he wasn't bowling tonight at all. After some scattered, sliding thought, she went in the house and called

Treva to borrow her car since she didn't want to deal with her mother again so soon. She got Three instead.

"I'm baby-sitting the munchkins," he told her. "Mom went out."

"Never mind, it's not important," she said, and dialed her mother after all. "I need to borrow your car for a little while," she told her. "I won't be long." She stonewalled until her mother gave up asking questions, and then she left, waving to Mrs. Crosby as she turned down the walk.

Ten minutes later, Maddie parked her mother's gray Accord at the edge of the bowling alley and walked through the parking lot. She made the round trip twice because she was a little rocky from the painkillers, but Brent's Caddy was not there. Treva's little yellow Sunbird was out in front, which threw Maddie a little, and Howie's gold Saturn was tucked in a corner around in back close to a shiny red convertible that looked a lot like the one C.L. had been driving, but Brent's car was nowhere to be seen. Fine. So he'd lied. Well, *there* was a surprise.

"Maddie?"

She swung around and peered through the dusky lot. Mr. Scott, the owner of the bowling alley, stood outside the front door to the alley. "I saw your mother's car," he told her. "Do you need anything? Are you all right? I heard about the accident. Can I help you?"

"I'm fine, Mr. Scott," she lied. "Thank you for asking, but I'm fine." She got back into the Accord before he or anyone else could ask what she was doing. Going undercover in Frog Point was not a possibility. There was no cover, and the night had a thousand eyes.

Inside the alley. C.L. sat at one end of the curved orange plastic padded bar with Vince and watched the finale of a drama he'd have found interesting if it hadn't been making two people he liked unhappy. Across the curve of the bar, Howie Basset, a great little shortstop C.L. remembered with a lot of respect, was sitting one seat away from his wife, Treva Hanes, a great little cheerleader C.L. remembered as Maddie's best friend, and they were both so clearly miserable that the entire town would be debating their divorce by morning.

"I'm real unhappy about this," Vince said into his beer. "Howie's a good guy."

"Score another one for Brent Faraday," C.L. said, and Vince nodded and said, "Jackass."

After a day of methodically trying every place Brent should have been, C.L. had found him through pure dumb luck, bowling on the alley next to Vince's with his father, Norman Faraday, the former honorable mayor of Frog Point. Brent had looked startled to see him. C.L. had waved and settled down to watch Vince try to pick up a succession of spares since there was no point in trying to ask Brent questions with Norman around to butt in, and the bastard wasn't going anywhere until his game was over anyway. Three different women C.L. had known in high school offered to buy him a beer to welcome him home, and after the third one went away, Vince said, "You're startin' to make me feel envious, boy."

"Not my type," C.L. said, keeping Brent in view from the corner of his eye.

"We all know your type," Vince said. "She's married."

C.L. ignored him to watch Brent and his dad. For the next half hour, Norman called people over and talked loudly about what a treat his son would be as Frog Point's next mayor. Brent shook hands, but he also shook his head at every suggestion. "No," C.L. heard him say more than once, "no, I'm not interested in running, thanks anyway." Impervious, Norman waved him off and called over another guy to discuss his son, the next mayor. If C.L. hadn't disliked Brent so much, he'd have felt sorry for him.

When Brent and his father retreated to the bar at the end of the game, C.L. grabbed Vince and followed. Over beers, they watched the discussion the Faradays had, Brent growing more heated as he shook his head, and Norman growing more oblivious as all Brent's denials rolled off him.

"Just what we need, another Faraday for mayor," Vince said. "Jackasses, father and son."

"Brent doesn't seem to think he wants it," C.L. said.

"Norman thinks he should have it," Vince said. "And you can bet Helena thinks so, too. If they both want it, Brent gets it. He'll be mayor. The jackass."

Then Norman moved away and C.L. got up to make his move, only to sit down to watch again when Howie Basset got up from a seat in the corner and sat next to Brent.

"This might be good," Vince said. "I've heard rumors."

"You and everybody else in this town. This place lives on rumors." C.L. tried to take the high road, but curiosity got the better of him. After all, he was supposed to be investigating this stuff. Investigating was not gossiping. "What rumors?"

"Problems at the construction company," Vince said. "Something's funny with the money. Or so I've heard. And if it's true, it's not Howie that's up to something."

"No, it wouldn't be." C.L. had played baseball with Howie without ever getting to know him well, but Howie had played hard and fair. And he was mad as hell now, grilling Brent. C.L. watched the emotions chase themselves across Brent's face as he tried to bluster, then reason with, then withdraw from Howie. Howie kept his voice low, but his intensity was enough to draw a few looks.

Then Howie's wife came into the bar and poked Brent in the back and said with some venom, "I've been *looking* for you," and more heads turned to watch her go sheet white when Brent moved and she saw her husband sitting behind him.

"Well, now that you've found me, you can talk to your husband instead," Brent had said, and tossed a few bills on the bar before he left. "Have fun."

Treva sagged into the closest seat, leaving an empty space between her and Howie.

"Oh, crap," Vince said, and C.L. had watched them in horrified sympathy for a few seconds before he deserted them to find Brent.

He didn't. The parking lot surrounded the alley on all four sides, and though C.L. made a circuit around the building, he'd evidently started in the wrong direction. Brent must have hightailed it out of the lot, and with Norman and Howie and Treva on his butt, C.L. could understand why.

What C.L. couldn't understand was how he could have searched for Brent for an entire day in Frog Point and not found him. It was as if Brent knew C.L. was looking for him and was ducking confrontation. Which didn't bode well for the future of Sheila's fiancé's investment.

C.L. went back inside and sat down next to Vince again.

"D'you find him?" Vince asked, and C.L. said, "Who?"

"Brent," Vince said with heavy patience. "The guy you've been chasing all over town. Did you find him?"

"No," C.L. said. "Tell me what's going on at the construction company."

"Henry knows you're asking this stuff, right?" Vince's freckled face looked wary. "This isn't something you're doing just to annoy that jackass, is it? Because if it is, I'll help, but I'll have to lay low on it because Henry wouldn't like it."

"Henry knows." C.L. watched Treva lean toward Howie, pleading with him. Her face was enough to break any man's heart, unless she was screwing Howie over with Brent Faraday, in which case she could fry for all he cared. "What's Brent up to?" he asked Vince.

"Dottie Wylie says the company ripped her off on the house they built for her last year."

C.L. transferred his full attention to Vince. "What? The house wasn't good?"

"Nah." Vince frowned. "Howie builds good houses. He built mine. Dottie says she paid too much. And the money part of the company is Brent. He estimates 'em, sells 'em, does the paperwork. Howie's a builder, but Brent—" Vince's eyes narrowed as he searched for the right word. "Brent's a dealer. Wouldn't want to buy a used car from him. A house Howie built, sure, but a used car, no."

C.L. tried to make the information fit with Sheila's problem. The company wasn't crooked because Howie was there, and the product was good because Howie built it. But anything to do with money was Brent's, and Sheila's Stan was about to hand over two hundred and eighty grand to somebody Vince didn't trust. If Vince didn't trust him, there was something wrong. Considering Henry and Anna's comments at dinner, C.L. knew he'd found out enough. All he had to do now was call Sheila and tell her to stop Stan.

But not yet. It would only be fair to talk to Howie first. Sheila had been against that, telling him the deal was between Stan and Brent, but Howie deserved to know what was going on since it was his company, too. Howie was a reasonable man, he'd look into things, and Brent would be stopped, maybe even shown up for the bastard he was.

Except at the moment, Howie didn't look reasonable. He looked like a maddened mule.

"I need to talk to Howie Basset," C.L. said, and Vince said, "I think I'd try that tomorrow."

Across from them, Treva leaned toward Howie, her face

drawn, and C.L. felt a surge of sympathy for them. When Treva gave up and walked out, C.L. felt worse. They were such nice people. They shouldn't be looking the way they did. That was something else Brent Faraday would have to pay for. Something else besides whatever it was he had done to make Maddie so grim.

But mostly, C.L. thought, he was going to pay for Maddie.

Maddie drove around town for another hour, cruising the parking lots of the local bars and Frog Point's one motel to find Brent's Caddy, feeling like the cliché of a cheated wife. Finally she pulled over to the side of the road and told herself, *Think*. Where would she go if she wanted to be alone with somebody who wasn't Brent? It would have to be somewhere nobody in Frog Point would see. She'd been stupid to drive by the bars; that would be the last place Brent would go. He must have been really careful since nobody in Frog Point had noticed he was cheating. It would have to be somewhere nobody else could get to.

Which could only mean the Point. She'd almost forgotten that once upon a time everybody had gone to the Point to get laid, because they didn't anymore; Brent and Howie had barricaded the road when they'd built the construction company at the base of the hill, and just a month ago they'd posted a night guard. That meant that the Point as open-air orgy was history for everyone.

Everyone but Brent. Bailey, the night guard, would chase away any would-be neckers, but he'd recognize Brent's car and let it go past. Bailey wouldn't recognize her mother's Accord, though. He'd stop her and then try to talk her out of going up there, and the next day the whole town would know that Maddie had tried to hunt Brent down at the Point.

She'd have to find another way to get up there.

She drove out of town until she was a hundred yards past the drive to the company and pulled off the bumpy road to park under the heavy, creaking branches of the elms that lined the ditch there. The woods between the road and the Point were tangled and thick, but they weren't impenetrable. She'd gone mushrooming there with her grandparents when she was little. She'd gotten most of her leaf collection for her high school biology class there when she was a teenager. She could catch her husband committing adultery there now. She felt cold at the thought even though the heat still pressed in on her. *I have to know,* she thought. *I have to know for sure before I screw up Em's life.*

The bad thing about how thick the woods were was that she had to push through a lot of brush, and it tended to spring back and slap her, cutting at her hands and tangling in her hair. The good thing was that there was always something to lean on. The ground was spongy, full of leaf mold that smelled peaty as she scuffed through it, and the tread on her running shoes clogged fast, making her slip in places. The crickets chirped frantically, the heat spurring them to record rhythms, and as she got closer to the Point, the breeze stirred the wild-flowers, and the sweet smell of the honeysuckle took Maddie back twenty years. She remembered the honeysuckle and the crickets and the heat, and there had been a moon. And most of all there had been C.L. in the backseat of his Chevy, his arms wrapped around her, making her laugh while he fumbled with her bra.

She reached the end of the woods and stopped, one tree in, to stare out at the open graveled space of Frog Point.

Brent's car was there.

Maddie leaned on a tree, all her energy gone with her un-certainty. So much for Brent's panties-as-bad-joke theory. The moon was waxing and cast a feeble light into the front seat, and she could see Brent's head nodding toward whoever was in the passenger side. She could tell from the way he moved that he was talking, arguing, and she leaned forward to try to see better. The head across from him stopped moving as if the person had seen something beyond Brent, outside the car, and Maddie stepped back again in case the something had been her.

Brent opened his door. His passenger did, too, and Maddie caught a glimpse of pale hair over the top of the car before they both climbed into the dark backseat. Not Beth the redhead, so he'd moved on to somebody new. Whoever it was couldn't have seen her or she'd have told Brent. Now Maddie could barely see the blobs of their two heads, and then she couldn't see them at all, and she realized they were down on the seat.

The son of a bitch.

What would happen if she just walked over there and opened the door? Just walked over there and opened the door and said something rude like, "You want to explain that underpants joke to me again?" It was what Treva would do. But Treva would never have to. Treva was married to Howie, the perfect husband. Maddie was the one stuck with Brent. *Damn him.* She thought of the look on his face if she wrenched open that door, of the look on the woman's face, whoever she was. At least if she walked across that clearing and opened the door, she'd know who those disgusting pants belonged to. This was not a situation that called for politeness, damn it.

Do it, she told herself, and took a step toward the car. Then something moved in the trees across the way, and she stepped back again and squinted into the darkness. Maybe a deer. Whatever it was had been tall. She leaned forward a little, waiting until she saw the movement again. Definitely tall. Bigfoot, maybe, or that serial killer she'd thought about before she'd opened the door to C.L. Both were impossible in Frog Point, but so was the rest of the day she'd had, especially the moment she was having right now.

She waited a full minute, until she was almost sure that she'd imagined it, and then, just as she was about to move again, a man stepped out into the clearing and edged toward the car, peering inside as he kept his distance. Bailey, the night guard. She slumped back against the tree, too tired to laugh or cry. Of course Bailey would come up to watch. What else was there to do around here at night? And if he'd just stayed in his woods another minute or so, he could have watched her jerk open Brent's car door and throw the fit heard round Frog Point. And it would have been heard round Frog Point by the time Bailey got through with it.

Fine, she'd wait until they got out again.

The shadows in the backseat began to move, and Maddie closed her eyes. They were having sex while Bailey watched and she waited. It was too damn much. She turned her back and slid down to sit at the base of the tree she'd been leaning against. She just wanted a good look, she just wanted Bailey to leave, she just wanted to go home. She was sitting in leaf mold while her husband had sex with another woman, and the thought made her ill. What difference did it make, anyway, who it was? She'd know soon enough when she left Brent. And she was leaving him. That was all that mattered. She was going to leave him.

The hell with it. Maddie stood up. She'd had enough for one day without entertaining Bailey, too. Brent would have to come home sooner or later, and then she could have her fit in private. The important thing was, now she knew. Now it didn't matter how dumb he made her feel with his stupid explanations. Now she knew.

She began to pick her way back down to the car. The way down was much faster, although she slipped again in the leaf mold. When she was back at the car, she took her muddy shoes off and put them on the floor of the backseat on the newspaper her mother kept there for umbrellas and anything else that might make a mess. The least she could do was try not to make a mess for her mother. Then she climbed in the front seat and let herself slump back, her head throbbing as the painkiller wore off.

Oh, hell, she thought, *just hell.* And then she put the car in gear and drove back home.

C.L. was half-asleep, his car parked across the tree-lined street from Maddie's house, when she drove into her driveway at eleven-thirty. He disliked her house—it was a nice color of blue with white shutters and a wide porch, but Brent lived there—and the neighborhood was so Frog Point that he'd caught several neighbors peering through windows at him earlier. By the time a car pulled in, he was ready to snarl. Then he watched Maddie ease herself out of the car, and his snarl evaporated. The light from the streetlamps made her front yard dim instead of dark, but he couldn't see her face at all as she sagged against the car.

He almost went to her. If there was anybody in the world who shouldn't be hurt and alone, it was Maddie. Unbidden, the memory of elementary school Anna had dredged up earlier came flooding back, clear and sharp still.

It had been the last week of school at the end of fifth grade, on the dusty playground at Harold G. Troop Elementary School. C.L. could taste the dust in the air, remembering, and the blood in his mouth. He'd just finished walloping Pete Murphy for calling him a creep, and he was on the lam, sure that Mrs. Widdington was going to nail him but running anyway on the slim hope that she'd forget about it before the noon bell. He'd rounded the corner to hide out in the black iron fire escapes and come face-to-face with Maddie Martindale, one of the dumb girls in the sixth grade who thought they were such big stuff. He started to duck away and then stayed, caught in spite of himself.

She was sitting about six steps up on one of the fire escapes, and she looked like something out of the Sears catalog. Her brown hair had been tied back in a glossy ponytail with a big red bow, and she was wearing a red plaid dress with a wide white collar, so white that it glowed in the sun. C.L. remembered wiping the blood from his mouth with the back of his hand, his other hand going up to his ripped shirt, trying to brush some of the dust off. His hands had been so dirty from the fight that they'd made his shirt worse, and he'd looked from them to her hands, her fingertips polished with the same bright red as her dress. That's when he'd known something was wrong because she was chipping the paint off her right thumbnail, leaving it pink-stained and blotchy.

"What's wrong with you?" he'd demanded, wiping his hands again, this time on his pants, embarrassed by his own dirt and enraged that he was embarrassed.

She'd raised dry, swollen eyes to his and said, "My daddy died."

Even for C.L., the king of I-Don't-Care, this was significant. Of course, his daddy was dead, too, a long time ago, long before he could remember. "When?" he demanded, and she said, "Tuesday."

He counted back. It was Monday. Six days. "That's bad," he told her, and then feeling that something more might be needed, he added, "Sorry."

She nodded and went back to chipping her nail polish, and

he was seized with the need to do more. She was so shiny and bright that somebody should make her feel better. He jammed his hands in his pockets, but all he could come up with was a broken stick of gum. Juicy Fruit. Even the yellow wrapper was dirty.

He looked up to see her watching him. "Here," he said, and gave her the gum.

She took it carefully, and it seemed so dirty in her fingers that he almost grabbed it back and ran. But before he could move, she unwrapped it, first the yellow paper and then the foil, peeling it gently from the sticky gum. Then she pulled the stick apart at the break and offered him half.

He swallowed the lump that had somehow clogged his throat and took it, and when she moved over on the fire escape he sat down beside her, careful not to let his dirty shirt touch her sleeve. They chewed the gum together in the sunlight.

It was possibly the best moment of his ten-year-old life.

Then Mrs. Widdington came round the fire escape, and yelled, "C. L. Sturgis—" only to break off when she saw who he was with. "Hello, Madeline," she said, nice and soft. "How are you?"

"I'm fine," Maddie said.

"Well, good. That's good." Old Widdy had looked foolish for the moment, and then she turned back to him. "Come with me, young man," she said with the murder back in her voice.

He thought about running and discarded the thought. Maddie was watching. He stood up, still careful not to brush against her, and went down the steps to his doom.

Widdy grabbed him by the collar and started to march him off, but she stopped after a few steps and turned back to Maddie, her fist jammed up under his ear as she talked. "Is there anything you need, Madeline? Anything you want?"

He'd looked back over his shoulder, caught in Widdy's grip, and Maddie had nodded.

"Yes," she'd said. "I want that boy to stay with me."

After a moment's surprise, Widdy had said she was sorry, but no, he was bad, and had dragged him off to the principal where he'd gotten paddled to teach him not to hit others, but it hadn't mattered at all because Maddie had said, "I want that boy to stay with me."

Then he got expelled for a week, and then school was out, and the next year she was at the junior high, and even when he got there, she was in the smart classes and he was in the dumb ones because he was a behavior problem, so he didn't see much of her. He didn't have to. All he had to do was close his eyes and she was there, saying, "I want that boy to stay with me."

But she wasn't saying it now. He watched her walk slowly, carefully, from the car to the porch, and he wanted to go to her. She shouldn't be alone. But she shouldn't be alone with him, either. People would talk; they were probably watching now. And Henry would have his hide. He was considering going out to the farm for Anna when Maddie leaned against the porch rail as if she just couldn't move anymore, and he got out of the car.

"Maddie?" he called, and she turned as he came up the walk. "I was waiting for Brent. Are you all right?"

"Oh." Her voice sounded thin and flat. "I thought you might be stalking me. It's been that kind of a day."

"Well, it's almost over," he said, trying to sound hearty. "Half an hour to midnight." She wavered for a moment. He reached out to put his hand under her elbow to support her and noticed for the first time that she was barefoot, and her vulnerability laid him low. "Are you all right?" he said, moving to help her to the porch, but she leaned into him instead, so he slid his arm around her shoulders to hold her up and felt his heart kick even faster. This was bad. "Maddie, do you want me to call a doctor?"

She shook her head once, her forehead against his chest, and her curls brushed his chin. They were so soft that he gave up and put both arms around her and held her, wanting to keep her safe and also, treacherously, just plain wanting her. "I'm sorry, Mad. I don't know what this is about, but I hate it. What can I do?"

She drew a long shuddery breath. "Well, don't be nice to me for starters or I'll cry all over you."

"That's okay," he said, even though he hated women crying. It was okay. She could wipe snot all over his shirt if she wanted, as long as he could hold her. "Go ahead. Howl."

She clutched him closer for a moment, and he held her tighter in response; then she said in a voice that was almost normal, "Do you realize we're standing in the middle of my yard? The whole street can see." She lifted her head, and he saw a watery smile, and his heart lurched. "This is going to ruin your reputation."

"Oh, damn," he said, trying to keep his voice light. "And up to now I've been so appreciated."

"I appreciate you," she said, and he forgot to breathe for a moment. Then she took that moment to step away from him, and he felt emptier than he could have imagined. "Thanks, C.L.," she said. "I needed to not feel alone there for a minute."

"You're not alone." He thought about kidnapping her and taking her out to Anna and making sure she was never this unhappy again. But there was Brent in the way, and she had a kid, a daughter, he thought, and it was too late for them. "Take care of yourself, Mad," he said as he turned to go. "Yell if you need anything." Her soft "Thank you" followed him down the path, and by the time he was back in his car, she was inside the house.

He sat and watched the lights go out in her house and tried to think unexciting thoughts while his mind and body ached for her. He had to get out of there.

C.L. put the car in gear. Tomorrow he'd find Brent. The son of a bitch couldn't hide from him forever. And then he was going to leave, no matter how much Frog Point needed an accountant.

Friday morning came too early. Maddie rolled over and regretted it. Her head throbbed and the thought of opening her eyes was unbearable, but she pried them open anyway. The sun did a number on her brain, so it took her a minute before she could squint at Brent's side of the bed. It had been slept in, so he'd come and gone while she'd slept off the double dose of painkillers she'd taken before bed. She could hear the sound of Em's radio down the hall, so he'd brought her home last night, probably fast asleep, just as he'd promised. But Brent was gone. The Great Avoider.

Well, at least she could depend on him to never be around. There was a lot to be said for dependability. She'd read somewhere that abused wives and children could take almost anything as long as the abuse was consistent. It was unpatterned abuse that was impossible to withstand. Now, Brent was consistent. If she stayed with him, she knew he'd cheat on her, but she also knew he wouldn't leave her. Lots of women lived with that.

The future stretched out before her, tight with suppressed anger, rigid with unspoken pain, lonely forever, with no chance of ever feeling warm again. She closed her eyes and thought of C.L. with his arms around her the night before, telling her he hated it that she was unhappy. He was almost a stranger, and yet she'd gotten more comfort from him than she had from Brent in the last five years. And that was the rest of her life if she stayed.

The hell with that, she thought, and got up to fight.

Chapter Five

Maddie stood in the sunshine in her kitchen and popped her morning pain pills. Her whole body hurt, and not just from the accident. She'd been tense for—she glanced at the clock and did some fast arithmetic—twenty-two hours now, since she'd found that damn underwear. Twenty-two hours of bracing herself for the inevitable. Well, the inevitable was here, and there was no point in standing around bracing herself anymore.

She needed a divorce lawyer.

But nobody from Frog Point. Nobody was going to call her dumb as dirt. The problem was getting a name in Lima. She knew people who were divorced, but not how they'd gotten that way. And besides, she didn't want just any divorce lawyer, she wanted a shark, somebody who would make sure she got custody of Em, sure that she didn't come out a fool. Who did she know that had done well with a divorce? Nobody. Nobody did well with a divorce. She thought of Em, and closed her eyes, and told herself, *Think.*

Her mother had said that Sheila Bankhead had taken C.L. for everything he had. He hadn't looked poverty-stricken when he'd shown up at her door, in fact he'd looked supremely successful, but they'd been divorced for years. Maybe he'd had time to recover.

She pulled the Frog Point phone book from the drawer under the phone in the kitchen and flipped through the *B*s, watching the pages tremble as she turned them. *Knock it off,* she told her shaking hands, and then she found Sheila's number and dialed, taking deep breaths until Sheila answered.

"Sheila? This is Maddie Faraday." There was no answer, so Maddie tried again. "Sheila?"

"I'm sorry." Sheila's voice came through the wire, cautious. "Maddie Faraday?"

"We were in high school together." Maddie felt like a fool. "I'm—"

"I know who you are," Sheila said. "I'm just . . . surprised."

Maddie pulled a chair away from the kitchen table and sat down because standing up was taking too much energy away from the phone call. "I know, we're not close, and I wouldn't bother you, but I need your advice."

"*My* advice?" Sheila's voice went up a notch. "You need *my* advice?"

Maddie gave up on tact since it only seemed to be confusing the issue. "I need the name of a good divorce lawyer, Sheila. Do you know a good one?"

"*You're getting divorced?*" Sheila practically hit high C.

"Oh, no," Maddie said. "This is for my next-door neighbor."

"Oh, right. Gloria Meyer. I thought she had Wilbur Carter."

"My mother said that wasn't a good idea," Maddie said, pleased to be telling the truth finally.

"Your mother's right," Sheila said. "Tell Gloria she wants Jane Henries. She was great with my divorce. C.L. never knew what hit him. She's in Lima. Wait. I think I still have the number."

Twenty minutes later, Maddie had a lawyer.

"Maddie Faraday?" Jane said. "Your husband owns that construction company in Frog Point."

"Well, part of it," Maddie began.

"I have family near you. You had my nephew in your art class. And you want a divorce?"

"Yes, thank you." Maddie wasn't sure of the connection between art and divorce, but she was in too deep to back out. "Can you help me, Mrs. Henries?"

"Hell, yes." Maddie heard her laugh. "Call me Jane. I'm booked today, but you can come in on Monday—"

"Monday is fine—"

"—and in the meantime, you gather up all the financial records you can find so I know what we're going after—"

"I just want custody—"

"—so we don't miss anything. We're talking irreconcilable differences, I gather?"

"Oh, yes," Maddie said. "They're irreconcilable. I want him dead."

Jane Henries laughed again. "That I can't help you with, but get me the records and I can make him broke for you. Sometimes that's better."

"I don't want him broke—" Maddie began.

"Sure you do. You've got a kid with college coming up. He gets married again and starts another family, and then where's your daughter going to be?"

"He wouldn't—"

"Sure he would. Get me those records."

Brent wouldn't stop taking care of Em. He wouldn't. Would he? "All right," Maddie said. "Whatever you say."

"Good," Jane said. "Keep thinking that way."

When Em came down the stairs fifteen minutes later, Maddie was pouring milk into a Flintstones glass, measuring it with her eyes until it was an inch and a half from the rim, enough to give Em a fair amount of calcium without giving her a more than fair chance of spilling it all over the table. It was something to concentrate on besides financial records and lawyers and divorce and wondering how she was going to put Em through college if Brent was raising a new set of kids with some woman in black lace underwear, so she gave it all her attention.

Em slid into her chair and looked at Maddie over the rims of her glasses, her eyes watchful. "How are you feeling?"

"Just fine," Maddie said as cheerfully as she could. Breakfast was not the time to tell a kid she was about to become a child of divorce. "I'm great."

"Does your head still hurt?"

"Nope," Maddie lied. "The pills take care of it all."

Em let her breath out in relief and let her shoulders slump back. "That's good. I'm hungry."

Maddie put her milk in front of her. "So how was last night?"

"We watched movies." Em scooted her chair up to the table. "We think Mrs. Meyer is a vampire."

Maddie lifted an eyebrow at her. Gloria, a vampire? "Not a chance. How do you want your eggs?"

"Poached with cheese, please."

Maddie turned to the microwave and stopped. "It's broken. I forgot. We'll get a new one later today. Second choice?"

"Scrambled." Em's eyes narrowed. "It's not just the teeth. It's her fingernails. And her eyes. They look like grapes. And she's real pale 'cause she never stays out very long during the day. Just at night."

Maddie took a blue mixing bowl from the cupboard and two eggs from the refrigerator, admiring how pretty their blue and white roundness looked against the yellow counter. Much better than the black. She broke the eggs into the bowl and stirred them with a fork while she thought about Gloria. Of all the people in the world for Em and Mel to pick for a vampire game, Gloria was the least likely, but then Gloria was turning out to be the iceberg of Frog Point, nine-tenths below the surface.

Still, sucking blood was out. From what she'd heard yesterday, the chances of Gloria sucking anything were nil. "I can't see it, Em." She reached for the milk and tipped some into the bowl before she began to stir again.

Em reached for her glass. "I bet there are no mirrors in her house. She's always out at night, and I know who she's looking for. Dad."

Maddie stopped stirring. "What?"

Em nodded, her eyes on Maddie. "Dad. She goes out at night and waits for him to come out in the yard. Then she calls his name. Sometimes he stops, but he doesn't look happy. He knows she's a vampire." Em stuck her finger in her milk and swirled it around, making blue-white whirlpools, but she didn't take her eyes off her mother. "But don't worry, I know how to handle it. Garlic, holy water, and a stake through the heart."

Maddie heated a pan on the stove and poured the eggs in, waiting until the translucent goop became creamy yellow before she spoke again. "I think all we have is garlic powder."

Em considered. "I could dissolve it in holy water."

"We don't have any holy water." When the eggs were cooked through, she tipped them onto a plate and stood admiring the delicate yellow next to the blue china. Pretty. If the Other

Woman was Gloria, she was going to poison her grass. "What video did you see last night?"

"*The Lost Boys*. Maybe Mrs. Meyer will explode when I sprinkle the holy water on her."

Maddie put the plate in front of Em. "Throwing water on the neighbors is not a good idea. I forgot to put your toast in. That's what you get for distracting me."

"I'll do it." Em got up and fished two slices of bread from the bag and dropped them into the toaster.

It couldn't be Gloria. The whole idea of Gloria in black lace crotchless underwear was ludicrous. Em's toast popped, and the nutty, yeasty smell made Maddie hungry, so she dropped in two slices for herself.

Em sat and slathered globs of butter and jam on her hot toast. There had to be at least three thousand calories on that bread, all of which Em would burn off by running upstairs once. When Maddie's toast popped, she spread it with a thin glaze of jam. If she was going to be single, she wasn't going to be fat, too. Time to start dieting. The Divorced Woman's Diet. No fat, no salt, no money, no sex. Oh, hell.

Meanwhile, Em's thoughts had bounced on. "You really do feel okay?"

"I feel fine," Maddie said. "Stop worrying."

"Then can I spend the night at Mel's?" Em bit a corner off her toast. "I was supposed to stay last night, remember? I came home so you wouldn't be here alone, but you look pretty good now. If you're all right, can I stay tonight?" She stopped, anxious. "If you're not, I'll stay with you. I don't mind at all."

"Oh." Maddie swallowed. "Have I mentioned that you're the perfect child?"

"Thank you. Can I stay with Mel?"

"Did you ask Aunt Treva?" Maddie bit into her toast carefully and chewed. Her head didn't come off in pain. So far, so good.

Em shook her head. "No, Mel's going to. Can I?"

"Call and find out."

Em scraped her chair back.

"After breakfast."

Em bent over the table and shoveled her eggs onto the jam-and-buttered toast, making the breakfast sandwich from hell. "I'll eat this on the phone," she said, and took off for the family room, dripping butter. "Thanks, Mom."

Maddie mopped the butter from the floor with a towel and straightened, encouraged that the toast was staying down even though she'd gotten reckless enough to bend over. *Good*, she thought. *I'm going to live.* Things were looking up.

Em shrieked from the family room, "Aunt Treva wants to talk to you," and Maddie picked up the extension.

Treva's voice was cautious. "How are you?"

"Em, are you off the extension?" Maddie called.

"I heard her hang up," Treva said. "How are you? Did you talk to him?"

"No."

"Oh, hell, Maddie—"

Maddie cut her off. "Wait a minute, he didn't come home until I was asleep, and he was gone when I got up, but I called a lawyer. I'm filing on Monday. I'm doing it, Treva. I'm going to do it as quietly as I can, but I called her. It's done."

"Yes," Treva breathed into the phone. "Oh, yes, yes, yes. Oh, good for you."

Maddie leaned against the wall. "I don't know. This is going to be awful. She says I should have financial records."

"She who?"

"The lawyer. Jane Henries from Lima."

"Ooooh, she's good." Treva's voice sounded hysterical with happiness. "I've heard she takes everything but their socks. Where are you getting financial records?"

"I already have them. I do the taxes every year, so I have all the records in the closet. It's no big deal."

"What about the office? I think we should search his office."

Maddie almost dropped the phone. "Have you lost your mind? I want the divorce, not the scandal. I told you, I'm going to do this very quietly, and if I search Brent's office, people will not be quiet."

"He's scum, Maddie." Treva's voice was so intense she was snarling. "He deserves to get taken to the cleaners. Don't you want to see what he has squirreled away at work? I sure as hell do, and I bet Jane Henries does, too. We're going to the office. We go all the time, nobody will think anything of it. I'll pick you up in fifteen minutes. Three can watch the girls."

"Treva, I don't think he'd have stuff hidden at work. Why would he—"

"Where else would he hide it?" Treva said. "If you won't do it for yourself, do it for me. I've had a bad week. I'd like to pass it on to somebody else, Brent if possible. Besides, what else do you have to do today?"

Treva, as usual, had a point. If Maddie didn't search the office, she'd be pretty much stuck sitting at home, waiting for Brent to walk in so she could divorce him. She really didn't think there was anything there, but then she really hadn't thought there was another woman, either.

"Oh, come on over," Maddie said.

The phone rang again as soon as Maddie hung up, and she put her head against the cool wall, trying to find her place in the world. What she wanted was to have a nice nervous breakdown, but she wasn't ever going to have the time because she'd be on the phone. When hers rang again, she picked it up and said, "Hello?" and her mother said, "Maddie, honey, it's Mama."

Maddie winced. Her mother had heard about the divorce already. "It's all right, Mom."

"No, it isn't. Lock all your doors."

Maddie frowned at the phone. Not the divorce. Maybe this was about C.L. holding her in the middle of her lawn last night. She'd been trying not to think about that again, but if her mother knew—"Why?"

"There's a prowler loose."

Maddie sagged against the wall, reprieved. "At ten o'clock in the morning?"

"Well, no. Candace saw him last night. She told me this morning."

"What were you doing at the bank again?"

"Cashing a check. Really, Maddie, it's not safe. Especially with Brent out so late like last night."

How did she find out about these things? "Mom, that was one night."

"Well, a prowler only needs one night and there you'll be, murdered in your bed, and you with a head injury already. How's your head?"

"Fine, thank you, Mother." Her mother, the head writer for the Worst Case Scenario. If she only knew.

"Will you lock your doors, please?"

Maddie gave up. "Yes. I promise. I have to go now. Treva and I are going out."

"Wait. What's going on with Treva and Howie?"

"The usual happily married stuff," Maddie said.

"I don't think so," her mother said. "They had a fight at the bowling alley last night."

"At the alley?" Their cars had been in the parking lot. "What were they doing at the alley?"

"Esther says that Lori Winslow says that Mike Winslow was there and said that Howie was talking to Brent and then Treva walked in and there was a ruckus." Her mother's voice was avid. "Didn't she say anything?"

"No," Maddie said. "And I'm not asking her about it, so don't bring it up again. Married people have fights."

Her mother shifted gears. "What was Howie so mad at Brent about? Is there trouble at the company?"

Everywhere but *the company*, Maddie wanted to say, but instead she said, "No. You know how people love to talk. They're blowing things out of proportion."

"Esther said Lori said Mike said Treva looked like three kinds of death."

"Esther needs to get a life. And I have to go now."

"Out with Treva? Should you go out? How's your head? Are you all right?"

"I'm fine," Maddie repeated. "Oh, I've still got your car. We'll drop it off."

"If you need that car, Maddie, you keep it. Walking's good for me."

"I don't need it." Maddie felt torn between guilt and exasperation. Her mother was so nice when she wasn't gossiping; she didn't deserve a daughter who was a lying predivorcée who had sarcastic thoughts. "Treva will take me places."

"Well, that's nice, dear. Have a good time. Let me know what she says. Be careful of your head."

How? Maddie wanted to say, but she didn't, knowing if she pushed her luck, she'd end up tramping through town in a motorcycle helmet. "I will," she said, and went to tell Em to get ready.

C.L. drove down Main Street keeping an eye peeled for Brent Faraday, determined to nail him and forget his wife. Maddie had given him a very nasty night of worries and hot dreams, and now he was groggy and grumpy and a little desperate to get out of town.

And Brent wasn't helping things any. It was past nine, and he wasn't at the construction company, so what kind of businessman was he? Yes, Brent had been in, the blonde secretary had told him. "You just missed him, Mr. Sturgis," she'd chirped, cute as hell. "He left for the bank ten minutes ago. The First National on Main Street. Downtown." As if Frog Point were big enough to have a downtown. "One street and three traffic lights do not make a downtown," he wanted to tell the secretary, but it didn't seem fair to take his annoyance out on her, so he shut up and went to cruise the bank.

There his luck turned. He passed the First National just as Brent came out, dressed in a suit and carrying a gray gym bag. C.L. slowed down to pull over, but the parking spaces on both sides of the street were taken, and the car behind him honked.

"Hey, Brent!" he yelled, and Brent turned and looked taken aback for a minute. Then he waved and kept on walking.

C.L. opened his mouth, and the car behind him honked again, longer. He'd no doubt be hearing about this from Henry later. The hell with it; he'd just have to turn around and follow him. C.L. drove to the next street, turned right into the drive-through circle at the Burger King, earning a glare from the woman at the window, and then turned back onto Main Street on a yellow light, earning more glares and honks from other drivers. Just like old times. He couldn't wait until dinner when Henry ripped a strip off him for rude driving.

He drove down Main Street. Brent was gone. C.L. circled the downtown twice, going behind the shopping district and into the side streets, but Brent had evaporated. C.L. had had people avoid him in the past, but never with the enthusiasm that Brent Faraday was showing. The son of a bitch must be up to something really low.

And sooner or later C.L. would find out what it was. In Frog Point, nobody kept a secret for long.

. . .

An hour after searching Brent's office, Maddie sat at her kitchen table with Treva and stared at the two things they'd found that were interesting.

One was a box of Trojans.

"I thought you were on the pill," Treva had said as she'd pulled them out of Brent's bottom desk drawer.

"I am," Maddie said. "Gee, maybe he's cheating on me."

"I hope he dies," Treva said, and went back to searching, but Maddie came up with the next find, a locked metal box about ten by fourteen inches with "Personal" scrawled across the top in Brent's handwriting. "I want to see inside that box," Treva said, but Brent's secretary, Kristie, came to the door then and asked them to leave.

"You shouldn't be going through Mr. Faraday's desk," Kristie said, her squeaky little voice quavering.

"Well, actually, it's only one quarter his desk," Treva snapped. "Because as it happens, Mrs. Faraday and I each own one quarter of this company, so the desk is half ours, which makes us half your boss, so you can leave now."

"*Treva*," Maddie said, but Kristie had backed out, hurt and confused, and they'd finished searching after that, taking the locked box to open at home and the condoms, as Treva said, to slow Brent down.

But now the locked box sat in the middle of Maddie's kitchen table and sneered at them. The lock had proved impossible to pick and the lid refused to be jimmied off. Maddie considered running over it with her car but decided that would be immature. Also she didn't have a car anymore. Life just kept getting better.

Treva was disgusted. "Christ, what does he have in there? His morals?"

"He'll be home later," Maddie said. "I'll look on his key ring."

"Sure. You can just say, 'Honey, I found this secret box when I burgled your office; could I borrow the key?' That'll work."

Maddie looked at the box doubtfully. "I'm not even sure the key will work anymore. You hammered a screwdriver in there, remember?"

"I was angry," Treva said. "It was defying me."

"Always a bad move."

Treva checked her watch. "Oh, hell, I promised Three I'd be home half an hour ago." She stood up and gestured to the box. "You want me to take that, get it out of your way?"

"No," Maddie said. "Let me work on it some more." She stood, too. "You sure it's okay if Em spends the night tonight?"

Treva nodded. "You and Brent need to have this out in private. Just don't go to sleep this time until you get your hands on him." She looked at the box again. "Forget the box until I can help you. Pry Brent open instead."

"Yeah." Maddie drew a deep breath. "He used her yesterday, Treve. I tried to talk to him, and he went and stood behind her and said, 'Don't upset Em.' And poor Em just stood there, scared to death."

"I hope he *dies*. I really do." Treva came around the table and hugged Maddie hard. "You deserve better. This is good, what you're doing. You're going to start all over again, brand-new. It'll be better this time."

"Right," Maddie said, but when Treva left, she sat down at the table and thought, *Better how?* How was being alone going to be better? How was Em not having a live-in father going to be better? She wanted to cry and scream and behave badly, and she thought about how good it would be to just throw herself at somebody, to feel the impact and let go of all of her anger and frustration. That made her think of C.L., broad and sturdy, holding on to her last night. It had felt so good to have someone to lean on, and he'd said all the right things, bless him, and his chest had been hard against her cheek, and if he'd been there now, she'd have hauled him onto the floor and taken out all of her frustration on him in vengefully enthusiastic sex.

Which would be the last thing she needed. Maddie poked at the box to distract herself. There must be some way into the damn thing. Maybe a can opener. Or an ax. She didn't really think there was anything important in it, but it was better than thinking about Brent. Or C.L. and sex.

It shouldn't be that tough. The round plate for the keyhole stuck out about a quarter of an inch. She should be able to get that off.

She got up and rummaged through the tool drawer and came back with a wood chisel and a hammer. "Brace yourself," she told the box, and jammed the chisel in behind the lock. It took half a dozen blows with the hammer, but the plate came off.

The box stayed locked.

"Well, *screw* you," Maddie said, and smacked the top of the box with the hammer.

The lid flew open and clattered back on the table.

"All right." Maddie sat down. "That's more like it."

She pulled the box to her and took out the stack of papers inside. She thought at first they were all business papers, copies of contracts and invoices, but toward the bottom the contracts became letters. Love letters.

There were twenty-nine of them. Twenty-seven of them were Beth's, all planning a future with Brent, but there were no dates, so it wasn't clear when she'd written them. Maddie read through them, struck by how much Beth loved him and believed in him. Maybe he should have stayed with Beth.

Maybe that's who he was with now.

Maddie put Beth's letters to one side and picked up the last two. Both were unsigned. One on white paper with red daisies in the corner was written in a spiky hand and suggested that they meet in her garage, surely not Gloria since none of the requests she was making had to do with the grass. The other was folded white paper ruled with blue lines, the kind of paper school kids used. It said "Brent" on the outside, and the writing looked as if it might belong to somebody like Kristie, loopy and immature. Now all she needed was a handwriting sample from Kristie, and she could be rude to her without guilt. "Found your pants," she could say. "God, they were tacky." This was such a rational thought that Maddie blinked, surprised at herself. Where was the pain here? She should be furious over all these affairs instead of feeling sarcastic. *This is a good sign*, she thought. *I must be over him. The rat bastard.*

Feeling vaguely cheered, she opened the letter and lost her breath. "You have to meet me at our place," it said. "I know you love Maddie, but I'm pregnant and I don't know what to do."

Maddie dropped the letter on the table. "You son of a bitch," she said out loud.

He'd gotten Kristie pregnant. Well, he'd gotten somebody pregnant. So much for the box of condoms. Kristie or somebody was going to have Em's half brother or sister. That was nice. What the *hell* had Brent been thinking of?

She had to do something. This was going to be worse than she'd ever imagined. And she was the one who would get to explain everything to Em. "You know how much you like Kristie?" she could say. "Well, Daddy liked her a lot, too, and—"

She shoved all the letters but the pregnancy note back in the box and slammed the bent lid shut. Then she looked at the note again. The writing didn't look familiar at all, and the paper was no help. Would Kristie write on notebook paper? It was all too confusing.

She stuffed the note in her purse to compare later with something of Kristie's from the office. Then she put her head down on the table because it had begun to pound. She was a sick woman. She shouldn't be reading stuff like this. She shouldn't be having this life. It was too much. She had to do something about it, but right now her head was killing her.

She took three pills, hoping to obliterate all conscious thought, and went upstairs, taking the box and the condoms with her and hiding all of it under the bed where Em wouldn't trip over it. Then she crawled under the covers and passed out.

"So how's your mom?" Mel said when she and Em were in front of the TV with big plates of manicotti and a bowl of garlic bread. *Ace Ventura* was on for the fiftieth time, but neither one of them was doing more than pretending to watch it anyway.

"She says she's better." Em poked at her manicotti and took a cautious bite. It was good. "She doesn't have that awful look on her face that she had yesterday, like she's going to cry any minute." She stabbed her fork into the manicotti again and took another bite and chewed while she thought about how to say the next part. "My mom and dad had a fight yesterday," she said finally. "A real one."

Mel's eyes widened. "You're kidding."

"Yeah. It was a real quiet one, but it was right in front of me. They looked so mad, Mel." Em turned to her, trying not to cry. "They looked like they hated each other. And then my dad brought me over here and left her all alone. It's awful."

"Why didn't you tell me then? About the fight, I mean."

Mel sounded funny, really tense instead of her usual bouncy self.

"I just couldn't talk about it," Em said. "It's awful when your dad and mom fight. I know you said yours do all the time, but they sound like joke fights. This was real. I didn't even want to think about it. Then my mom was real quiet today, and I didn't see my dad at all. This is bad, Mel."

Mel looked like she wasn't sure she should say what she was going to next. Em got a funny feeling about that because Mel never cared what she said to anybody. "There's something else," Mel said.

"What?" Em said, her throat tight.

Mel swallowed and shifted on the couch. "My mom is pretty mad at your dad. I heard her on the phone this morning and she was yelling at him."

Em sat back. "How do you know it was him?"

"Because she was yelling his name." Mel looked miserable. "It was awful, Em. She told him she'd kill him if he told any-body."

Em swallowed. "About what?"

"I don't know." Mel cut into her manicotti again, trying to look like she didn't care, but Em could tell she did. "It gets worse than that. After she hung up, my dad came in and asked her who she was talking to. She said my grandma." Mel clamped her mouth shut for a minute. "She *lied*. Then they had a real fight, too. They were doing those sharp kind of whis-pers and Mom slammed her hand down on the table and then Dad went out and slammed the door." She stopped and swal-lowed. "After my dad left, my mom started to cry. She never cries. It was awful. I don't even want to talk about it now. I want it to go away."

"I don't think this is going to go away," Em said, remember-ing her mom and dad in the front yard the day before, the way her mom had looked, with her fists up against her chest like that. "Something really, really bad is happening."

Mel stared at the TV. "Maybe Mrs. Meyer bit your dad and made him a vampire, and he bit my mom, and she doesn't want anybody to know."

"Mel, knock it off," Em said. "This is for real."

Mel kept on staring at the TV. "I don't want it to be for real. I want it to go away."

"Me, too," Em said. "But I don't think it's going to."

The screen dissolved into a lot of fizzy snow, and Mel sat up. "I don't believe it." Her voice went high with stress. "*Mom!* This sucks. *Mom!* The cable's screwed up!"

"Language," Aunt Treva said as she came in the room.

"I can't *believe* this," Mel said, while her mom jiggled the cable box. "Everything's screwed up. What happened to it?"

"It looks like it just went out." Aunt Treva straightened. "I'll call them tomorrow and tell them they ruined your life. In the meantime, read something."

"That's a *joke*, right?" Mel said.

"It'll be good practice," Aunt Treva said. "School starts a week from next Tuesday."

"Do *not* remind me," Mel said. "Can we watch videos?"

Aunt Treva shrugged. "Sure. Rot your mind. Whatever."

Mel waited until her mother was gone, and then turned to Em. "Can you *believe* it? Anything we want on *video*? Whatever's wrong is really wrong. My mom's been nuts for over a week now. I couldn't believe she let us watch *The Lost Boys* last night. That's an R. This is bad."

Em thought about it. "You're right. It was about a week ago that my dad got grumpy. Something happened then. What are we going to do?"

"We're going to have to start snooping around," Mel said.

"They're never going to tell us. We're going to have to find out for ourselves."

Em thought about it. Spying had been dumb the day before, but things hadn't been this bad then. "You're right. We have to do something to save them. I just don't know what. I've never snooped before. What do we do?"

"Well, for starters, every time the phone rings, we listen," Mel said. "That's just obvious."

Chapter Six

The doorbell woke Maddie shortly after seven that evening, leaving her groggy and confused. Why was Brent ringing the doorbell? He had his own key. She grumbled her way down the stairs and opened the door.

"I woke you." C.L. leaned in the doorway, his eyes dark with what looked like appreciation but couldn't be since she was rumpled from sleep and wearing cutoffs and a pink plaid shirt that was older than God. He ducked his head at her. "Sorry I got you up."

Maddie closed her eyes against the fact of him as opposed to the idea of him. She'd been thinking about dragging him out of that doorway and having her way with him, and now here he was in the all-too-solid flesh, which unfortunately was looking pretty good, dressed as it was in chambray and old denim. It was embarrassing. She opened her eyes and tried to be polite. "No problem. What do you want?"

"Anna heard about your accident. She sent brownies." He held out a plastic-wrapped plate to her, and she took it, being careful to avoid his eyes. Making eye contact would be bad.

Looking straight ahead gave her a great view of how broad his chest was in his chambray shirt. The shirt looked soft from washing, and Maddie restrained herself from reaching out and touching it. That was the kind of thing that men often misconstrued. She was pretty sure C.L. would misconstrue it. *Get rid of him*, her conscience told her. "Thank you, C.L. Tell Anna I appreciate it."

"I'll do that," he said. "Have you seen Brent lately?"

"No." Maddie smiled past his left ear and tried to close the door, but he was in the doorframe, leaning against it, and there was a lot of him, and he didn't move. "Well, it's been nice seeing you, C.L., but I've got to go eat these brownies now."

His grin widened. "Thanks, it's great to see you, too."

Maddie's heartbeat kicked up a notch. He had to go. She tried to close the door again, but he still didn't move, so she gave up on subtlety. "I'm sorry to be rude, but this is a bad time. Could you come back later?"

"Sure. When?"

She'd forgotten he could be this persistent. His persistence was how she'd ended up in the back of his Chevy twenty years ago, but she'd forgotten how flatfooted he could be about it. "How about September? Things should have settled down by then."

He shook his head. "Can't wait that long. I have to go back to work on Monday."

Maddie smiled brightly at him. "Well, maybe the next time you're in town."

He straightened and lost his grin. "Maddie, it's hot. I'm tired. I just want to talk for a couple of minutes."

Since that was the line he'd used to lure her into his car all those years ago, Maddie winced and shook her head. "C.L., my husband is coming home soon and—"

"Great. Brent's the one I came to see. Can I come in?"

She could see in his eyes that he wasn't leaving until he'd talked to Brent. Maddie sighed and stepped back, and C. L. Sturgis walked past her into her house.

You were supposed to offer a guest a drink, so Maddie grabbed two glasses, a carton of orange juice, and a bottle of Brent's vodka and led C.L. out into the backyard so the neighbors could see they weren't having illicit sex even though C.L's flashy convertible was parked in front of her house like a red light.

"Slam the back door," she called back to him as she led the way. "It's old and it doesn't close right."

She turned and saw him looking at the edge of the door. "You know, you could plane this down a little and it wouldn't stick anymore," he told her, running his hand along the edge. "Only take about five minutes."

She'd asked Brent to do something about it, but he'd been too busy. He built damn houses, but he was too busy to fix his own back door. Maddie's head hurt and anger made it worse. If she'd stuck with C.L. twenty years ago, her back door would work.

"Thank you," she said. "We'll do that."

They sat on the splintered picnic table with the bottle hidden between them and drank the sweet-tart juice laced with vodka and talked awkwardly. C.L. looked great in the twilight, broad and tan and strong and healthy, and Maddie slurped her drink so she wouldn't think of any more adjectives. She was married, even if it was unhappily. Adjectives had no place in her life.

"So how have things been?" C.L. asked her, and Maddie almost laughed. "You and Treva still tight?"

"Yep," Maddie said. "Blood sisters forever."

"And you both have kids." C.L. shook his head. "Hard to believe. I leave town for twenty years and you both lose your heads."

"We just did it to fill in the downtime until you got back," Maddie said.

"So tell me about your life," C.L. said.

It's not really my life. I just live it for the convenience of other people. "I live in Frog Point. My mother calls every day. I visit my grandmother in the retirement home every Sunday so she can yell at me. I teach art with my best friend, who teaches business. I have the perfect child, who wants a dog. My microwave is broken and my car is dead." Maddie drank another slug of screwdriver. "That's about it. Not very interesting."

"Hey," C.L. said. "I'm here. That's interesting."

"Yes, it is," Maddie said. "Thank you for stopping by. Without you, I'd be calling around pricing ovens." *And rehearsing my divorce speech.* "I owe you."

"Good. Don't forget it. Tell me about Treva."

"Treva?" *Treva has a problem she's not sharing.* "Well she has two kids, Melanie, who's eight, and Three, who's twenty."

C.L. frowned at her. "They named the kid Three?"

"No, they named him Howie Junior." Maddie poured herself another orange juice and surreptitiously slopped in some more vodka. The alcohol was loosening her muscles nicely. The hell with Tylenol 3. "Howie didn't care, but Treva insisted and she wouldn't budge. Then Howie's mother—Do you remember Irma Basset?"

"School secretary?" C.L. grinned. "Hell, yes. She saw me at all my worst moments. Not a woman to mess with."

"Well, Irma pointed out that the baby couldn't be a Junior because Howie was a Junior, so he'd have to be Howie the Third. Treva was going to fight her on it until she found out that the only way for the kid to be Howie Junior was for Howie Senior to die, which would make her Howie the Senior and the baby the Junior."

"Only in Frog Point," C.L. said. "I bet it took weeks to work this out and the whole town discussed it."

"Easy guess," Maddie said. "So then they took to calling the baby Howie Three, and eventually they just shortened it to Three and it stuck. And now he's twenty, and I'm middle-aged."

"Beats death," C.L. said.

The alcohol loosened Maddie's muscles and she felt her tension evaporate, but C.L. started every time a car door slammed, and every now and then he checked his watch before asking her another mindless question. *What does he want?* she wondered, and then, *What do I care?* Brent was coming home any minute, and she was leaving him, and her life as she knew it was over, and all her concentration had to go on not making a mess for her mother and Em. C.L. was just a very attractive subplot at *Götterdämmerung.*

An hour and three screwdrivers later, C.L. stopped checking his watch and they'd both relaxed. Frog Point was semi-dark with the thick velvety dusk that comes on hot August evenings. The crickets were vocal but slowing down, probably from exhaustion. Maddie pictured them rubbing their legs together frantically in unison. They must have the thinnest thighs in the insect world. Her glass was empty.

"Let's just pour the vodka into the juice carton and drink from there." She tucked her tongue between her teeth and poured.

C.L. looked at her. "You develop a drinking problem since I saw you last?"

"No." Maddie raised the carton to him in toast. "As a matter of fact, I just started drinking tonight."

C.L. arched an eyebrow at her. "Anything you want to tell me about? Money troubles maybe?" She looked at him sharply, and he added, "Just asking."

"No. There is nothing I want to tell you about. In fact, this will all be over in September, but no, you'll be out of town then." Maddie swished the carton around and took a drink. "If you don't like it, go home."

"No. Hell, I love it. Give me the carton." She passed it over, and C.L. took a healthy swig and choked.

"I know," Maddie said. "We're a little low on orange juice. Em keeps drinking it."

"Healthy little devil." He tipped the rest of the carton into the grass.

"Hey."

"It slipped. What happens in September?"

"You spilled my vodka."

C.L. looked at the screwdriver-soaked grass. "I was thinking maybe we should pace ourselves."

"Come on." Maddie shoved herself off the picnic table. "There's wine in the house."

C.L. followed her. "Why don't we have a Coke? And then you can tell me what's going to happen in September. If it's good, I'll come back and watch."

Maddie picked her way to the house. *I'm a little drunk*, she thought, *but I'm not stupid. This guy is after something.* She leaned against the screen door, and C.L. stopped on the porch step behind her.

"Maddie?"

"I was thinking," she said, and went into the house.

"Bad sign." He followed her, slamming the screen door behind them. "It was you thinking that ended our last relationship."

Maddie headed for the cupboard where they kept the wine Brent's parents gave them every holiday even though they didn't drink wine. "Two hours in the back of a 'sixty-seven Chevrolet is not a relationship."

C.L. leaned against the refrigerator. "Wrong. Two hours in the back of a 'ninety-seven Chevy is not a relationship. You could raise kids in the back of a 'sixty-seven. God, that was a great car. I wonder whatever happened to it."

Maddie pulled a bottle of wine out of the cupboard. "You ran it through the guardrail out on Route 33."

"I mean, I wonder what happened to it after that," C.L. said with dignity. "Somebody might have fixed it up."

Maddie snorted and handed him the wine bottle. "Yeah, into ashtrays. They found pieces of it for years." She began to rummage through the junk drawer looking for the corkscrew. "As a matter of fact, you became a sort of folk hero. Every time somebody'd pick up a piece of scrap iron, they'd say, 'Must have come off of old C.L.'s Chevy. Good old C.L.'" She found the corkscrew and passed it over.

C.L. took it from her and began to screw it into the cork. "Well, that's nice. That's real nice."

"And then they'd snicker."

He stopped twisting at the cork and grinned at her. "You're a hard woman, Maddie Martindale. Good thing I like hard women."

She leaned against the counter and narrowed her eyes at him. He couldn't possibly still be carrying a torch for her after all these years. He couldn't possibly be thinking she'd go to bed with him again. That was out of the question.

Probably.

He looked great, tall and broad, and she was a sucker for tall and broad. Of course, he wasn't as tall and broad as Brent. Well, that was okay. Brent looked like a pretentious biker. C.L. looked like, well, an adult. Actually, what C.L. looked like was a damn good time. And she was due for a damn good time. Just once, she deserved to do something just for herself. Screw Brent.

"Okay," she said. "Let's go."

C.L. popped the cork on the wine and stood there with the bottle in one hand and the corkscrewed cork in the other. "Go where?"

"Up to the Point. The way we did in high school." She smiled, enthused with her idea. This was a plan. This would make her feel better. This was *action*. Revenge, that was the answer. She'd go up to the Point with C.L., and Bailey would tell everybody, and then she wouldn't be the nice little wife being cheated on anymore. It would be like screaming "Fuck" on Main Street, only better. She beamed at C.L.

He did not look enthused. He looked horrified. He put the wine on the counter and said, "Maddie. Honey. You've had enough to drink."

Her smile deflated. "Is this rejection?"

"No, no." C.L. ran his hand through his thick dark hair, looking more distracted than she'd ever seen him. "Well, maybe. You're married. A small point, I know, but—"

Maddie scowled at him. "You coming with me or not?"

"To the Point." He seemed to be having trouble coping with the concept. It seemed clear to Maddie.

Maddie picked up the wine bottle. "Yeah. Re-create our youth." She tried to smile temptingly at him, but it wasn't very good, and he shook his head and took the bottle from her.

"Not a good idea, honey. I was a lot younger, and cars were

a lot bigger then, and you weren't married. You don't want to do this."

Maddie glared at him. "Fine, forget it. You can go now."

"Wait." C.L. put the wine back on the counter and held up his hand. "Let's discuss this."

Maddie crossed her arms over her chest and glared harder. "You don't discuss adultery. You just do it."

"Well, that's a real turn-on." He leaned against the wall and folded his arms, too. "I didn't think it was passion that was driving you into my arms. You know, I'm about two beats behind here, and it's confusing me. What's going on?"

Maddie looked at him, really looked at him this time, leaning there grinning at her, his face all edges and angles, his dark eyes glittering. For the first time in forty-eight hours, she forgot Brent and the anger.

"You've changed," she said. "You're—"

"Older?" He straightened up and took the wine from the counter. "Twenty years, honey. It makes a difference. Got any glasses?"

She got them from the cupboard as she went on. "I suppose. But it's not age. You look good. You really do. You look . . . centered. Sure of yourself."

"Yeah, well, I'm not a junior in high school anymore. Thank God." He looked at the glasses. "You want Pebbles or Bam-Bam?"

"Oh, sorry." She reached for them. "Those are Em's."

He moved them out of her reach. "If you have no preference, I'll take BamBam. Us guys have to stick together." He poured the glasses half-full and pushed hers toward her. "To Em," he said, lifting his glass, and she clinked hers with his.

She drank about half of it and then turned and went into the hall, taking her glass with her, to stand before the mirror in the entryway. "I can't remember what I looked like," she said as he came to stand behind her. He was only four or five inches taller than she was, so he put his head beside her to see. Brent always towered over her; he used to put his chin on her head when people took pictures of them. She hated it, especially the way his chin would dig into her head.

"You looked like this," he said. "Only smoother, sort of un-alive."

She made a face in the mirror. "Unwrinkled is what you're getting at."

"No." He shook his head. "You were sort of unlived-in then. Nobody home yet. You were cute and spunky and sort of sexy in an Ivory Snow sort of way, but you weren't quite there yet. Sort of a pod person. Now you're there."

Maddie took another drink and considered. What thoughts had she had in high school? What passions had she suffered? She was appalled to realize there weren't any; her memories were of what other people had done, what other people had wanted. What Brent had wanted. And it wasn't just high school, either. That was her whole life. If somebody asked her who she was now, she'd say, "Martha Martindale's daughter" or "Brent Faraday's wife" or "Emily Faraday's mother," but she wouldn't be able to say anything that was just Maddie. Even her career depended on her being somebody's teacher. Her whole life was defined by relationships. "That's awful," she said.

"Except for one night," C.L. said close to her ear. "You were there for me one night."

Maddie sighed. "I think all you saw that night was your reflection. I think you're right. I don't think I've been there until now."

"Now?"

"I'm having a very maturing week," she said, and finished her glass. He was very close beside her, and she liked it. She smiled over her shoulder at him. "Want some more?"

He looked thoughtful. "I don't know. Does alcohol still have the same effect on you?"

"What effect is that?"

"As I remember, at stage one, you're tight, and at stage two, you throw up."

"Oh, that's awful." She closed her eyes. "I remember. You were sweet."

"Thank you. Then there's stage three."

"What happens at stage three?"

He tried to look innocent, which on C.L. was a dead giveaway. "I get laid."

"Oh, no." She turned back to the mirror and watched him watch her. "You turned me down once tonight; I don't do multiple humiliation."

"I didn't turn you down," C.L. said. "I said I was too old to do the twist in the back of a convertible at the Point."

"If you'd wanted me bad enough, you'd have said yes."

C.L. looked at her in the mirror and smiled, and she felt a little sizzle start inside her. He passed his glass over to her. "When the offer is serious, I will say yes. In the meantime, thank you, I will have another glass of wine."

The phone rang fifteen minutes later while they were laughing about a high school disaster. *Damn*, Maddie thought. *I don't want to talk to anybody. I feel good.* And she stopped and thought as she picked up the phone, *This is the first good time I've had in years.*

"Maddie?" Brent's voiced snapped over the line, and she gave a guilty start as she looked at C.L. Then she kicked herself. The hell with Brent; she had nothing to feel guilty about. The thought was depressing. She should have something to feel guilty about. Why should he be the only creep in the family?

His voice grew more exasperated, if possible. "Maddie, are you there?"

Behind his voice, Maddie could hear the sounds of balls rolling down wood alleys and hitting pins. For once he was where he was supposed to be, the louse. "What do you want?"

"Listen, I'm going to be late. Something's come up."

I bet it has. Well, something's about to come up here, too.

"Maddie? Howie wants to talk as soon as we're done here. But I want you home when I get there."

"Right. No problem." She looked back at C.L. and made her decision. This was her night. It was a shame to victimize good old C.L., but he'd bear up. "Take your time," she told Brent. "I'll just go to bed." She pressed her lips together to keep from laughing out loud.

"Maddie? Are you laughing?"

"What would I have to laugh about?"

"Maddie, I went to the office before I came out here."

"Oh." She took a drink of wine.

"I want that box back."

I bet you do. "We'll talk."

He started to argue, but she wasn't interested anymore. "Gotta go," she said, and hung up on him. She turned and waved to C.L. "I'll be right back."

She ran up the stairs to the bedroom, where she checked her mirror. Okay, it was time to get serious here. *The man will go to bed with you,* she told herself, *but not here.* There she drew the line. And the one motel in town might as well put its guest register on the front page of the *Frog Point Inquirer,* which would be tacky. That left the Point, the place where Brent had been getting his. But C.L. didn't want to go to the Point. So her job, should she decide to accept it, was to lure him up to the Point and inflame him. Or maybe inflame him here and then lure him.

It was at this point that she realized she was drunk, but she accepted it and moved on. It was unimportant except for the fact that if she weren't drunk, she'd never be doing this at all. So it was good she was drunk. Also, tomorrow morning she could comfort herself with the fact that she'd been drunk. "It wasn't my fault," she could say. "I was drunk." Looked at from this angle, drunkenness was a definite plus. She smiled at herself in the mirror.

Now, the clothes. She took off her shirt and cutoffs and pulled on a pale green sleeveless jersey dress with ten thousand tiny buttons down the front that popped out of their holes easily. That was good; easy on, easy off. She could see the outline of her bra through the thin cotton, so she reached under the skirt, twisting her hands high up to get at the catch. While she fumbled with her bra, she checked out her legs.

I have great legs, she thought, but the white cotton underwear, that had to go. She pulled her bra straps down over her arms and fished the bra out through one of the armholes on her dress. Her breasts slipped down a little but not much, and the soft cotton dress felt wonderful next to her skin. *This is not a bad body*, she thought. *It's not great, but it's nothing to sneer at, C.L., old buddy.*

"Maddie?"

His voice came from the bottom of the stairs. She'd been playing around too long. She stripped off her white cotton underpants and dropped them on the floor. Nobody committed adultery in white cotton underpants. She flounced her skirt a little, distracted by the breeze between her legs. How the hell had Brent's chippie not noticed her underwear was missing? Of course, with crotchless, you'd get a breeze anyway. Did you take off crotchless underpants?

"Maddie? Are you all right?"

"Coming." The last thing she grabbed and shoved in her dress pocket was one of Brent's condoms from the box from his office. It seemed fitting.

C.L. was waiting for her at the bottom of the stairs. Maddie tried to float down, but she tripped on the last step and fell against him, and he caught her, and it wasn't funny anymore. He was very real and very solid, and she didn't have any underwear on so her breasts squashed against him, and he looked distracted enough to have noticed, and she wasn't at all sure she wanted to do this.

"Are you okay?" he asked, and she took a deep breath and said, "Yes. Let's go."

"Where?"

"The Point," she said firmly because she wasn't sure.

"Ah, Maddie." C.L. let go of her and stepped back. "Come off it."

Maddie gritted her teeth in exasperation. "I'm serious. I want to go."

He looked trapped for a minute, and then he said, "Oh, *darn*," and slapped the newel post. "Can't do it. No condoms. Sorry, but—"

She pulled the one from Brent's box out of her pocket and handed it to him.

He looked poleaxed. "You're serious."

"Very." Maddie stared at him wide-eyed, trying to look wholesome and innocent. "We can just talk if that's all you want. But I think we should go for old times' sake."

"Right. Old times." He sighed and put the condom in his pocket. "Okay, let's go talk at the Point. But first we get another car. I don't want to hear any crap from Henry about my car being up at the Point."

"You're thirty-seven years old," Maddie said. "What do you care?"

"We're talking Henry," C.L. said. "I care a lot."

They drove over to get Treva's car and ended up with Brent's Caddy since he'd driven with Howie to the alley. Maddie was delighted; now Bailey would think it was Brent on the Point, and she might get away with both her reputation and the experience of doing the wrong thing. "This is going to be great," she told C.L., and he looked less than enthused, but she didn't care.

Her victim days were over.

Fifteen minutes later, ignoring all his best instincts, C.L. pulled the Cadillac up to the edge of the Point and stopped, jerking on the emergency brake as he shut off the engine.

"Great." Maddie opened her door.

"Where are you going?"

"Backseat." She climbed in the back and closed the door behind her.

Terrific.

He'd known all along he should have stayed out of Frog Point, but he'd come anyway, reasoning that nothing much could happen in forty-eight hours. He'd check on Sheila's little problem, ruin Brent Faraday, shake Henry's hand and kiss Anna good-bye, and be gone. What could possibly go wrong? And now he was in a dark car with the one woman who completely screwed up his head every time he got near her, and she wanted sex. Well, so did he, but they weren't going to have it. He had his pride, and whatever had inspired Maddie to come up here, it wasn't desire. She was mad at Brent, and this was payback time. Well, she could forget it; he'd been in this movie before, and he damn sure wasn't going to be in it again. He'd humored her this far because she'd been drinking and he was pretty sure he could wear her down and get the story of what was going on from her eventually, but he absolutely was not going to do anything else. Absolutely not.

"You know, you weren't this slow twenty years ago," Maddie said. "Come on."

"Gee." C.L. settled down in the driver's seat. "I can't hear the frogs."

"C.L., there haven't been any frogs at Frog Point for forty years. Get back here."

C.L. rested his forehead on the steering wheel for a moment and then turned to look at her. She stared at him with fierce determination, her eyes huge in the darkness, her arms folded under her chest, willing him to get in the backseat. Her breasts were round and loose under the stretchy fabric. He remembered the night before in her front yard and how warm and soft she'd been in his arms. Then he remembered half an hour before at the bottom of her stairs and the lust that had almost flattened him when she'd fallen against him. And she'd handed him a condom. And he'd taken it.

He was pretty sure he wasn't getting into that backseat.

"You have no bra on," he said.

"It's a symbol of my sincerity. I don't have any underpants on, either." She patted the seat beside her. "Come on."

He really shouldn't get into that backseat, especially since he knew she had an ulterior motive. It was a motive he was caring about less and less as his heart pounded harder and harder and all the blood left his brain, but it was there, and he needed to know what it was before he did something stupid. "Maddie, why are you doing this?"

"I can't believe you!" she exploded. "I'm offering you my body, and you want to know why?" She glared at him.

This couldn't be happening to him. It was everything he wanted and everything he didn't want. C.L. groaned and banged his forehead on the steering wheel. Then he started to laugh.

. . .

Maddie had no idea what C.L. was laughing about, but she was patient. Eventually he would get in the backseat. He couldn't possibly have changed that much in twenty years.

"Okay," he said finally. "But just remember, this time it was your idea. You seduced me." He checked the emergency brake, locked the passenger door, and then got out, locking the driver's door behind him. As he climbed in the back, she lost it and laughed.

"What's so funny?" he asked her, his voice grumpy as he settled in beside her.

"You." Maddie jerked her thumb toward the front seat. "The emergency brake. Locking doors. You're so *careful.*"

"Yeah, well, plunging over a cliff in the middle of intercourse is not my idea of a great climax."

Maddie sniffed. "Twenty years ago you wouldn't have thought of that."

"Twenty years ago I didn't have an emergency brake." He peered out the window. "Christ, it's dark."

Maddie was losing patience with him. "Yeah. That's why we're up here instead of on Main Street. You gonna make your move any time soon?"

"Okay. Fine." He grabbed her and made her jump, and then he kissed her hard, smashing her lips against her teeth as he forced her down on the seat. Her shoulder scraped the upholstery and his body was a bulky weight on top of her, and she squirmed under him.

"Wait a minute!" She shoved at him, trying to lever him off with her elbow, but he was too heavy, and his shoulders pinned her to the seat so she couldn't roll away. *"Wait a minute."*

"Isn't this what you wanted? Hot sex in the back of a big car?"

Something in his voice made her stop struggling, and when she did, he pushed himself off her, staying balanced above her on his hands. She couldn't see his face, but whatever he was, he wasn't overcome by passion. "You're laughing at me," she said, fury lacing her voice.

"Damn right, I'm laughing." He didn't sound happy about it. "And you deserve it. What the hell are you playing at?"

She shoved at his chest again. "Let me up."

He pulled her into a sitting position and leaned back in his corner of the car while she straightened her dress, humiliated at her own stupidity. Why had she assumed he wanted her? God, she was dumb.

"Had a fight with old Brent, did we?" C.L. asked. She couldn't see him in the gloom, but she could hear the disgust in his voice.

She jerked on her skirt again. "No, we didn't."

"I was just asking because as I remember, that's how I got lucky the last time." C.L.'s voice eased a little. "Old Brent was fooling around with—"

"Stop calling him 'old Brent.'"

"—Margaret, I think, and he pissed you off, and so you came up here with me."

Maddie slumped back against the seat. The worst part was, he was right. She hadn't dragged him up to the Point because she was overcome with passion for him; she'd dragged him up there for revenge. Twenty years, and she was still working the same game plan. What a fool. "Okay." She sighed. "You got me. Not too bright, that's me." No wonder her husband played around.

"You want to tell me about it?"

Oh, yeah, that was exactly what she wanted to do. "No. I've made enough of a fool of myself tonight."

"Hey, don't think I'm not grateful." C.L. patted her knee.

"Brings back memories, wrestling with you." He laughed. "Boy, was I surprised that night when you went all the way."

"Yeah." Maddie leaned her head back on the seat, too depressed to hold it up anymore. "I was surprised, too. Not my plan at all." *But then nothing works out the way I plan.*

"I never could figure out why you picked me," C.L. went on. "It sure as hell wasn't my technique. Equal parts lust and fear. That couldn't have been pretty."

She rolled her head on the seat to look at him. "You were funny."

C.L. groaned a little. "Oh, thank you."

"No." Maddie shook her head. "I mean, funny on purpose. You made me laugh. I had fun."

"Yeah?" He sounded a little vulnerable still, even though it had been twenty years ago.

"Yeah. You were cute. And nice." She thought for a minute. "You weren't trying to be a big macho stud, you know. You were just really nice and really glad I was there."

"Glad is an understatement. I was in ecstasy."

Maddie laughed in spite of her gloom.

He reached out his arm and touched her shoulder. "Come here and tell me about things."

She stiffened. "What?"

C.L. shook his head at her. "I realize I'm not getting laid, but that doesn't mean I can't cop a cuddle. Come here and let me hold you."

Maddie hesitated and then slid over. He put his arm around her and patted her shoulder, warm and comforting. She took a deep breath and inhaled the honeysuckle and began to feel better. "This place makes me feel good," she said. "Maybe it *was* the good old days when we came up here."

C.L. shook his head again. "Not as I remember it. Life was just one disaster after another."

Maddie craned her neck up. "Including me?"

He tapped her gently on the head. "Especially you. You dumped me and broke my heart."

She leaned closer to him, her cheek brushing the softness of his chambray shirt. "Did you really think I was going to drop Brent for you?"

He was quiet for a minute. "No," he said finally. "But I was still wiped out when you didn't."

Maddie straightened up. "I'm sorry. I'm really sorry. I thought, well, that you were just after One Thing, and when you'd gotten it, that was enough. I never dreamed—"

"Forget it." He pulled her back to him. "That was twenty years ago. A lot of sex has gone under the bridge for both of us."

Maddie snuggled closer, nestling her cheek against the hardness of his chest. She felt much better. Good old C.L. "Yeah, but that was my first time. That makes a difference."

"Mine, too," he said, and she sat straight up, smacking his chin with her head. "Ouch!" he said, and grabbed his jaw.

Maddie gaped at him. "That was your first time, too?"

"Yes." He took his hand away from his chin. "Jesus, woman, be careful. You got a head like a rock."

Maddie sat back. "Well, that explains a lot of things."

"Like what?"

She turned back to him. "Like why when it was all over you said, 'Was that as bad for you as it was for me?'"

C.L. scowled at her. "I never said that."

"You did." She started to laugh. "I thought you were being funny. But it was bad."

C.L. shook his head. "There is no bad sex. Only some that is less good."

"That was bad. It was uncomfortable and awkward and messy, and I felt stupid."

C.L. sighed. "Thank you."

"The second time was better," she offered.

"That must have been Brent. We didn't do it a second time. You never spoke to me again after that night." C.L. slouched down in his seat. "I came to your locker the next morning and you turned away. God, what a comment on my performance."

"It wasn't Brent," Maddie said. "We did it twice that night."

"Oh." C.L. stopped, struck by the memory. "That's right."

Maddie pulled back, outraged. "You didn't remember?"

"Honey, that whole night is just one blur of lust for me. What you took for humor was probably my idea of foreplay. You know." He made his voice high and squeaky. "'That was pretty bad; let's try it again till we get it right, okay?'"

She laughed and he put his arm around her again. "You never sounded like that."

He pulled her closer. "I did inside. God, I was scared."

"Of me?"

"Of you, and the backseat, and not being able to do it right and then of not being able to do it again. Even after that night, for years afterward, every time I had sex I'd think, 'This is it. I'll never have this again. I'll never get another woman to do this again. My life is over—'"

"Stop it," she said, laughing again. "You'll have me in tears."

"In fact, even now . . ."

"Yeah? What about now?" She pulled herself up to look in his eyes, but it was so dark she was almost nose to nose with him before she could see them. "Are you married?"

C.L. blinked at her. "No. I'm divorced. Ten years ago."

His voice was final, but she wanted more. "Why did you get divorced?"

"She liked money. It didn't look like I was ever going to have any. We fought about it, and after a while, we just hated each other. It seemed enough."

Maddie sat up a little in outrage. "She married you for money?"

"No." C.L. shook his head. "No, that wasn't fair. It was more than that. We were screwed up from the beginning."

"What happened in the beginning?"

C.L. frowned at her in the gloom. "What is this?"

"You disappeared from my life," Maddie said. "I want to know what happened. I know the life story of everybody in Frog Point. It's pretty interesting to run into a mystery for a change."

C.L. shrugged. "Not much mystery. I ran into Sheila about twelve years ago when I was home visiting. She'd been working as a secretary for a couple of years after high school, and we looked at each other and saw what we wanted, and then it turned out neither one of us had looked hard enough."

"She wanted money," Maddie said. "And she saw that in you?"

"She saw an older guy who'd gotten out of Frog Point and lived in the city and wore suits to work. Then we got married, and it turned out that I was just me, and she found out she missed Frog Point, and I wouldn't move home, and we didn't have the money to live the high life she wanted, so there was nothing to hold us together." He sighed. "It was an honest mistake. No bad guys, just two fuckups."

Maddie didn't want to ask the next question, but she had to. "What did you see?"

"What?"

"What did you see in Sheila?"

C.L. sat very still for a moment. "I saw a sweet, pretty girl who wanted to be with me."

"And that's all it took?"

"That's a hell of a lot."

"You must have missed her when she left." Maddie bit her lip. "Is divorce . . . hard?"

"It's hell," C.L. said, but there didn't seem to be much pain in his voice. "It feels good when it's over. Takes about a year to come through it if you don't care much. If you love each other, I understand it takes forever."

She was quiet for so long, he bent over her to see if she was asleep.

"Hello?"

"Just thinking."

"Oh?" His voice was light. "Thinking about divorcing old Brent?"

Maddie drew a deep breath. "Well, up till now I was thinking about killing old Brent, but I'm not so mad anymore."

"Why were you mad before?"

"He's cheating on me."

C.L.'s laugh sounded like a snort. "Oh, there's a surprise. And one mystery solved for me."

"What?"

"Why you're up here, doing a remake of The Night We Lost Our Virginity. Revenge, Part Two. And they say history doesn't repeat itself."

"Maybe not," she said.

C.L. leaned back away from her. "Don't try to soft-soap me now. The ugly truth is out."

"That's a joke, right?"

"About half."

"Because I think you're wrong." Maddie stopped for a minute, trying to find the right words. "I mean, I came up here that night to pay him back, but that's not why I stayed. I had a good time. Except for the sex."

C.L. groaned. "God, that makes me feel so much better."

Maddie leaned closer so she could see his face. "Look, you want honesty? The sex was not good. But the holding and the laughing part was great. You were sweet. You made me feel good. I liked you a lot."

"So why did you marry Brent?"

There was sarcasm in his voice, but she answered him seriously. "I don't know. I've been thinking about that a lot. Everybody knew I was going to marry him, and if everybody knew it, it must be true, so I never considered anything else. By the time I came up here with you, we'd picked out a silver pattern. I had spoons. That made everything seem irrevocable. I had an identity. I was going to be Brent Faraday's wife. I know that sounds stupid, but I just never considered anything but marrying Brent."

"I know," C.L. said. "That's the way we all thought back then."

"I still did until yesterday," Maddie said. "That's why I was so mad at him."

"Was?"

She craned her neck a little to look up at him. "You've sort of changed my mind."

"Don't let me do that," C.L. said. "Go back to being mad at him."

"No, I mean it. This is nice. This is the warmest I've felt in a long time. If Brent's just going out to get sweaty with some bimbo, he's slime, but if he's finding this, this *comfort* with someone else, I think I can understand." She snuggled closer and C.L.'s hand closed on her shoulder again. She felt a rush of peace flow through her that was so intense it was physical. "I feel great. You're wonderful."

He patted her shoulder, "Easy there. Let's not lose our grip."

She rubbed her face in his shirt just to feel it against her skin. It smelled like the sun and soap and underneath, faintly, of his sweat. No ugly cologne, nothing but him and the sun. She tipped her face up to his. "Did your aunt wash this shirt? It smells line-dried. It smells wonderful."

He laughed at her, and she met his eyes, dark as night and fringed with those impossible lashes, and his lips smiled down at her, ripe enough to bite into, and he was solid and warm and sweet and confident, and she wanted him so much that her breath went. He stopped laughing, watching her, and after a moment, he bent over her and kissed her, his lips brushing over hers, and made her whole body tighten. He stopped and said, "Maddie?" and she put her hand on the back of his head and drew him down to her, running her hand down his shoulder as he bent into her. His mouth tasted like wine and heat and something more, like him. His arm felt solid under his shirt, solid wrapped around her, and she shuddered as he eased his hand up under her breast and made it swell and harden. The heat was sudden and everywhere, and she twisted closer to him, feeling the brush of his sleeves against her skin and the muscles in his arms pulling her in as the ache spread. His lips moved down her throat and she sighed against him in the dark, drawing in deep breaths of him, and every breath made her want him more, and when his hand finally moved hard over her breast, now tender with heat, she moaned and bit him on the shoulder and pulled him as tightly to her as she could.

"If you're going to say no," he breathed in her ear a few minutes later, "say it fast."

She clenched her teeth to keep from screaming for him. "I want you now. Make love to me *now*."

Chapter Seven

C.L.'s eyes were intense on her in the moonlight, and the weight of his hand made her catch her breath as it slid down the buttons on her dress, popping them one by one as his fingers trailed down her stomach. His face was close to hers, his eyes black with wanting her, and then his head dipped and his lips tickled the hollow of her neck as his hair brushed her cheek. The tickle there made her shake and then it became an itch in her breasts and the hollow of her elbows and the back of her knees and then hotly between her legs, and all the while he moved against her, shirt and skin and heat, smelling of sunshine and sweat and C.L., and she squirmed and scraped her fingertips hard down his back and into his jeans.

"Wait," he whispered into her neck. "Let me unbuckle my belt."

She arched back on the seat as he fumbled with his belt, so alive and needing him so much that she couldn't lie still beneath him, shuddering until she could feel his weight against her again. Then he slid his hands under her dress and along her back, and she clenched her teeth when he pulled her up to him, yanking her dress off her shoulders from inside. She fell against him and felt the roughness of his shirt against her breasts. He felt wonderful, but it wasn't enough, she needed him naked, too, and trying to unbutton his shirt took too long. She banged her head on his collarbone in frustration, and when he jerked her head up and kissed her hard, she ripped his shirt open, flinging buttons everywhere, and pressed against him, the smooth heat of her breasts against the coarse hair of his chest, the tickle and itch that was everywhere now driving any other thought from her mind. She moaned with heat and need, biting his lip until it bled and she tasted the salt of his blood in her mouth.

"Oh, God, Maddie, hold on," he said, and still holding her to him, he slid his hand between her legs, and his fingers felt so impossibly good against her damp thighs and then sliding inside her that she cried out. He pressed her down on the seat, and she wrapped herself around him as his mouth found her breast, and he sucked hard while he stroked her. Then she did lose her mind, clawing at him while he fumbled in his pocket for the condom. He spread her thighs with his, and she arched up at the shock—the itch and the heat fused—as he went hard into her. She pressed her face to his as his body rocked against hers, barely realizing he was kissing her as she gave herself up to the rhythm and incredible satiating, mesmerizing friction of him in her. His hands and lips were everywhere, and she could feel her blood pound and swell in her temples and her breasts and her fingertips and finally, hotly, deep inside her, deeper inside her, tighter, until she broke and came hard, banging her head against the seat, crying out as she felt the spasms take her, and her climax was almost an anticlimax because the sex before had been so excruciatingly good.

Maddie lay there for a moment, tipping her head back and drawing a deep sobbing breath before she looked up at C.L. The clouds had left the moon, and his eyes were hot in the dim light as he stared down at her. She felt herself glow back up at him, transformed. She'd done something bad, something selfish, something just for her. She'd never be the same again, and it was wonderful.

"Come here," he said, and pulled her up so that she straddled him, his back to the seat. He slid his hips under her and pressed her down to him, as close as he could, and when she felt him go hard into her, she clutched at his shoulders, digging into the muscle there.

"How?" she breathed as her head dropped to his shoulder in boneless pleasure.

"It wasn't easy." His voice was thick and husky. "You did go off damn quick." He slid one hand up, lacing his fingers in her hair, and pulled her head back so he could see her face. "But this time it's different. *Look at me.* This time I want you to know who you're with."

"I knew." She traced his lips with her fingers and rocked forward, closing her eyes as she felt him deeper inside her. "I knew all along. I've never had it like this."

"Honey, nobody ever had it like this." He kissed her, his tongue lightly touching hers, running over her lips, her throat, his hands on her breasts, teasing and tickling in counterpoint to the rocking deep inside her, and she felt the pressure well up again, like something great and lovely coming out of hiding, tearing along her veins. She cried out and he pressed harder. "Look at me," he said, and twisted his fingers in her hair to bring her head up again, and she saw him in the moonlight, his eyes glittering, his teeth clenched as the spasm shook him, too, and she thought, *I'm the reason he's feeling this, he wants me, I'm making him lose control, he's coming in me, because of me, oh, God*, and then she lost it, too, drowning as the climax took her again, flexing her swollen fingers and twisting closer to him, coming in his arms as he came in hers.

And as her mind came back, she collapsed against his broad, damp chest and thought, *This isn't anything Maddie Faraday would ever do. This is brand-new, just me, for me.*

I want this again.

C.L. eased himself out of her, and they sat slumped together, entwined and shuddering, then quiet, and finally he breathed in her ear, "We must remember how we did this."

Maddie laughed into his neck.

"I'm serious." C.L.'s voice came back as he held her tighter. "I've had good sex before, but this was nirvana. Was it the car? I'll buy one. I swear."

"No," she whispered. "It was you." *It was me.*

His arms tightened around her again, and he whispered into her hair, "Are you going to refuse to talk to me tomorrow? If I come to your locker, will you turn away?"

"No." She breathed against him, inhaling the sunny, tangy scent of him, dizzy because he was there and because she felt so free. "I don't think I'll ever be able to say no to you again. Not after this." She kissed him, and he took her mouth with such greed that she felt charged because he wanted her so and because the sex had been so very good. *I can do anything.*

She relaxed into him, and he eased her down on the seat to lie beside him, pulling at his clothing while she pulled at hers until they both gave up on modesty and lay locked together in tangled fabric and contentment. Maddie thought she'd never move again. She smelled honeysuckle everywhere, and sweat, and sex, and the sun in his shirt. She licked the salt from him off her lips and savored the tang, and felt him warm and heavy and solid beside her, wrapped around her, and shivered from the bone-deep pleasure of it all. She could see him in the silver light, the gloss of his skin, the dark lace of his eyelashes on his cheeks, the faint smile on his open lips. She traced his mouth again with her fingers, and he kissed them without opening his eyes.

"You have the strangest smile," she said dreamily. "It's like a V."

"Should I change it?" he asked, half asleep.

"No." She traced her fingers over his lips again. "It's very sexy."

He smiled against her fingers, his eyes still closed. "Then it stays."

"In fact, everything about you is sexy."

"Thank you."

She nestled closer. "Do you think I'm sexy?"

He opened one eye. "I think you should be declared a national resource and protected by law. Are you always this chatty after sex?"

"Nope." Maddie smiled at him with her whole face. "Never before. It's just because I'm so happy."

He closed his eyes and snuggled her closer. "Good. Chatter on. I'll listen, I swear." He kissed her on the neck and she shivered at the butterfly touch. "You have a great neck."

She lay next to him and listened to the crickets and his heartbeat, inhaling the honeysuckle and C.L. She ran her fingers down his shoulder and onto his arm, following the contours of his muscles. He had a great body. Everything about him was great.

A sudden cramp in her leg reminded her that he was also heavy. She tried to ease herself into a better position, but there wasn't one. If she didn't straighten that leg out, she was going to be lame for life. "C.L.," she whispered, and he cuddled her closer, sending shooting pains up her thigh. "C.L.," she said out loud, and his eyes shot open.

He lifted his head up. "What?"

"You're squashing me. And my leg is kind of twisted—"

"Oh, sorry." He moved to sit up. "Here—"

"Ouch!"

"Sorry." He pulled her into a sitting position, but she slid off his lap. The blood rushed into her leg and set it on fire with stabbing pinpricks of pain, and her knee cracked as she straightened it out.

"God, I creak."

He patted her knee. "Fortunately, I like older women."

She could hear the exhaustion in his voice. "Take me home. You need sleep."

He put his arm around her and pulled her back against him. "Can I get it with you?"

Maddie shook her head, but she didn't move away. She couldn't; he felt too wonderful against her. "I think Brent would catch on if he caught you actually in the bed."

"Oh, yeah, old Brent." C.L. hesitated. "You got any plans there I should know about?"

"Yes," she said. "I'm getting a divorce. I'm filing Monday. I just haven't told Brent yet."

He sighed and pulled her closer to him, his hand sliding down to touch her breast. "Well, that's one problem off my mind. Tell him tonight so I can sleep over."

Maddie jerked away. "No."

"Hey," he said, "that was a joke."

"You stay a secret until the divorce is final."

C.L. frowned at her. "Why?"

Maddie shivered. "I have a daughter. I don't want him to have custody."

He shook his head at her. "Maddie, no woman loses custody because of an affair, especially if her husband is making it with another woman."

"I don't care. I'm not taking any chances. Not with my kid."

"Okay. I can understand that, I guess." He yawned, taken by exhaustion. "God, I'm tired. When can I see you again?"

Maddie thought about Brent and her happiness faded. "Tuesday night. He fools around after bowling on Tuesdays and Thursdays."

C.L. stopped stretching. "That's four days from now."

"Think of it as foreplay."

"Very funny." He leaned over her and kissed her hard, stroking his hand over her breast, and she felt the heat flare again as she tasted him. He kept his face close to hers and said, "I'm feeling very possessive of you. That's bad."

Maddie brushed his lips with hers and felt his hand tighten on her as he closed his eyes. It was intoxicating being wanted this much. She felt the heat thicken in her. "Why is that bad? I think it's great."

C.L. opened his eyes. "You're married, that's why. Maybe *I'll* kill Brent."

The sudden pounding on the window made them both leap. Maddie pulled her dress shut and sank into the darkness of the far corner, while C.L. blocked her from the window with his body. He rolled the window down, and a voice asked, "Ain't you folks got beds?"

Maddie shrank away as the light from the flashlight blinded her. Bailey. Of course, Bailey. He'd seen the car and come out to watch and got a real bonus: the boss's wife and the town's worst screwup. Maddie closed her eyes and tried not to think about how much trouble she was going to be in. After all, this was what she'd wanted. Revenge. So much for being the Perpetual Virgin of Frog Point.

Her mother was going to kill her.

Meanwhile, C.L. had moved to block the light. "Who the *hell* are you?"

"Well, I'll be damned, C. L. Sturgis. How you doing, C.L.?"

"What?"

"It's me. Bailey." The guard turned the flash so it shone in his own moonlike face, grinning above his security guard's uniform. "Remember me?"

"Bailey? You're a cop now?" C.L.'s voice lost its edge. "Jesus, what's the world coming to?"

Bailey's grin got wider. "Same as ever, it looks like from here. Takes me back twenty years, catching you getting laid in the backseat of a car. Evening, ma'am."

Maddie sank even farther back into the dark.

C.L.'s voice got grim again. "Bailey, old buddy?"

"Yeah, C.L.?"

"Turn the fucking light off."

"Oh, right." The light went out. "You really do got to get out of here, though, C.L. It's private now."

"I'm going." Maddie could hear C.L. fumbling his shirt together as he climbed out of the backseat and slammed the door behind him, still shielding Maddie. "Nice seeing you again, Bailey," he said, and Maddie watched as he grabbed the guard's arm and pushed him away from the car. "Go away now."

"I'll go down the hill first, old buddy, but I'll wait for you at the bottom."

"Good, good, Bailey, you do that. Now get back in your car." C.L. lifted the little guard onto his toes as he marched him toward his car.

"Aw, c'mon, C.L., are you with who I think you're with? This town ain't had any real good gossip for months." Bailey craned his head back over his shoulder, trying to look back.

"Cops don't gossip, Bailey, not even rent-a-cops. And I'm alone." C.L. opened the door to his car and shoved him in. "You will not mention this to anyone, hear me?"

"You're alone in the back of Brent Faraday's car on the Point? Now pull the other one. Besides, I seen somebody in there."

Maddie could see C.L. leaning over the car door. "Bailey," he said. "Go away and keep your mouth shut or I will beat the crap out of you."

Bailey laughed, but he started the car. "You wouldn't hit me, C.L. And you should know you can't keep a secret in this town. You ought to know that."

"No, but I can damn well try," Maddie heard him say under his breath as he got into the driver's seat. "Keep down," he told her, and turned the ignition key.

Maddie watched Bailey's taillights disappear down the road. Everyone would know tomorrow. "I feel like a whore."

C.L. let his breath out in a rush. "Maddie, ease up, please." He put the car in gear.

"He ruined it."

"Only if you let him."

Maddie thought about it as the car began to move. She'd just had the best evening of her entire life. She was going to regret it tomorrow; she was going to have a thousand things to regret tomorrow, but tonight she was gloriously in the dark with C.L. "Okay," she said, and climbed over the seat to join him.

"I don't seem to have any buttons on my shirt." C.L. frowned at her in the light from the dash as he made the turn off the Point. "What did you do, bite them off when I wasn't looking?"

"Next time pay attention," she said, and stuck her tongue in his ear.

He swerved, but he got the car back under control before they ran off the road. "Don't do that. At least not while I'm driving. Of course, in my car, this won't be a problem. The shift will keep you on your own side."

Maddie moved back to the passenger seat. "I liked your old car better. I could sit right beside you."

"You still can. You'll just have to put one leg on each side of the shift. It'll give a whole new meaning to fourth gear."

Maddie laughed. "You make me feel like I'm eighteen again."

He took his hand off the stick shift to pat her knee. "I noticed you were pretty spry getting over the seat. No creak at all."

"You should see me going the other way."

C.L. turned to her, and Maddie could see him in the light from the dash, smiling at her with calm possession. "I intend to," he said, and she settled back in her seat, wrapped in afterglow, ignoring tomorrow.

C.L. drove his worst enemy's Cadillac through the dark in a daze of sated lust and wonder. He couldn't decide if his luck had turned golden or if this was the universe playing its usual joke because the last thing he needed was to get involved with a married woman in Frog Point. But the woman was Maddie, and she was getting a divorce, and his mind was tapioca, but he was pretty sure he was the happiest he'd been in a long time. Maybe ever.

He had Maddie back.

She slid out of the car when he parked it behind Treva's house, and he said, "Hey!" and she came around and kissed him through the car window, over and over, laughing low. It really was Maddie, finally, her round face and full lips and hot eyes, and she laughed and kissed *him*, and he thought, *What the hell, I don't care about anything but this.* He got out of the car and tried to pull her to him, but she moved away.

"I have to go home," she said, backing away. "I'll walk it. Somebody might see us if you drop me off."

Thunder rolled in the distance, and the wind picked up as he watched her leave him. "Tomorrow," he said. "I'll call you. I want to see you tomorrow."

She was fading away, walking backward in the direction of her own house. "I'll try. You don't know how hard I'll try."

She turned and ran down the alley, and he put the keys to the Caddy on the dash and walked to his own car. Two hours in a backseat and his life was brand-new.

The storm kicked in as he started the Mustang, and he drove out to Henry's in the rain, his mind a kaleidoscope of Maddie moving to Columbus with him (could she leave Frog Point?), Maddie's kid (what did he know about kids?), Anna's face when he'd tell her (she'd be happy, especially about the kid), Henry's face when he'd tell him (inscrutable), Maddie's face when he'd suggest moving to Columbus (no way), Anna's face when she remembered Maddie was married (oh, hell), and Frog Point's faces when they'd realize he was going to be her husband (stunned), all of which led to thoughts of the extra land next to Henry's farmhouse ("nice piece of land to build on," he'd told C.L. when he'd married Sheila) and the chance to see Anna and Henry every day, and under it all, clouding any rational thought processes, Maddie's heat and softness moving against him in the dark, her low moans, her eyes when she'd looked in his and come, and the way she'd curled in to him and clung when it was all over.

This time he'd gotten it right.

A small sane part of him said that two hours of car sex did not make a future, but the rest of him glowed with knowledge that this time they'd both get it right.

Right in front of everybody in Frog Point.

Maddie slipped through her back door, wet from the rain, trying to hold on to the glow of the evening, but her happiness faded with the house. Great sex was not going to make her problems go away. Great sex—

"Where the *hell* have you been?"

Brent's voice came out of the darkness and she started, and then he turned the kitchen light on and blinded her.

"Brent?" Her voice quavered as she played for time. Was her dress buttoned right? She didn't have a bra on.

"I said where in the hell have you been?" He ran the words together like a curse, sweating and shaking and breathing hard, one hand braced on the counter, and his eyebrows made a black slash across his forehead as he glared at her, his head down like a wounded bull.

"Brent, I'm okay." She went toward him, trying to reassure him. "I took the Cadillac to go for a ride. Don't worry about me."

He grabbed her arm. "I'm not worried about you—" He broke off and shook her arm a little. "When I tell you to be home, I expect to find you *home*. Do you understand?"

"No," Maddie said, guilt and anger scrambling her thoughts. "Why are you acting like this?" She wrenched her arm away. "This isn't like you. What are you so mad about? What difference does it make?"

"It makes a difference because I say so." He leaned over her to trap her against the sink. He reeked of sweat and beer and he was so close that the pores of his skin looked like craters. "I'm your husband."

She shook her head at him. *No more. I don't need you anymore. I'm free of you.* "That's crap." She pushed away from him.

He put his head down again, moving toward her, glaring at her under his brows. "I want to know where you've been."

"Why?" she asked, backing up. "I don't ask where you've been. I don't ask"—she took a deep breath—"because I know."

He stopped. "What?"

"I know all about your slimy little secrets. I got that damn box open. I know it all." She turned away to the rain-spattered window because she couldn't stand to look at him anymore, but she saw him reflected there. He was standing dumbstruck, his arms dangling at his sides. Big dumb cluck. Her neck hurt, and she reached for her pills. She'd take them without water. She didn't want to lose the taste of C.L. in her mouth. "Who the hell do you think you are?" she went on as she shook the pills into her hand. "Did you really think you'd get away with this stuff forever just because you're Brent Faraday? Well, you're not going to. If you think I'm buying that crap, you're even dumber than—"

She was turning to confront him when he hit her, back-handing her with his fist across her eye. She stumbled, and then tripped backward, hitting the wall as she fell, spilling pills across the floor. *Thank God Em's not here*, she thought as she slid down the wall to the floor. *Poor baby.*

Then her sense of self-preservation kicked in, and she scrambled to her feet as he came after her. She ran into the hall, screaming, "Don't touch me!" and when he didn't follow her, she stumbled into the living room to lean against the edge of the couch, trembling and breathless, still gripping the bottle of pills.

Her head hurt, almost beyond pain. So this was what it felt like to get beat up. Battered. This was going to be another good one for the neighbors. She felt the side of her head, and her hand came away with blood on it. His ring must have cut her. She'd have to explain to Em tomorrow. To her mother. To the town. Her knees went out on her and she sank down onto the couch.

And they'd know about C.L. because Bailey would tell. What the hell had she been thinking of? She'd sold her life down the tubes for two hours of absolute happiness. It might not have been a bad price if it had just been for her, but she'd sold Em and her mother, too. She was a selfish bitch and there was no way she could save things now. She'd really done it this time.

She couldn't do this anymore. She couldn't fix things anymore. She couldn't be the good girl anymore. She just couldn't. She tried to focus her eyes and saw the bottle of wine she and C.L. had shared on the table, nearly empty, just a couple of inches left. She was so tired, and her head hurt, and she was never going to be happy again.

Three Tylenol had sent her into oblivion that afternoon. Most of her pills were scattered all over the kitchen, but there were still seven when she dumped the bottle into her palm. Oblivion was still within reach. She dropped the pills into the wine bottle one at a time, and then swished it to make the pills dissolve.

"Maddie."

Brent was slumped in the doorway, still wearing his bowling shirt. God, he looked stupid. It wasn't the shirt. C.L. would look great in that shirt. It was Brent.

She looked at the bottle and set it down with a crack on the table. Brent was the problem, not her. She had to stop drinking. She'd almost committed suicide there, or at the very least,

serious illness. And that self-pity had to go, too. She definitely
had to stop drinking. "So," she said, feeling the side of her
head again. "Bad day?"

Brent closed his eyes. "I'm sorry. I'm sorry I hit you. I love
you. You know that. I'm sorry."

"I know you're sorry," Maddie said. "I know." He'd never
hit her before, and it almost didn't matter now. It just made it
easier for her to leave him. She'd be almost glad he'd hit her
if it hadn't hurt so much and there wouldn't be so much hell
to pay later for it. All the people she was going to have to explain it to, all the people who were going to think he'd hit her
because of C.L., and while she was explaining, Brent would
go on his careless way. The bastard.

"You went through my stuff at work," Brent's voice was
heavy. "You went through my office."

"Oh, yeah." Maddie was surprised. Somehow that seemed
like another day. Another century. "I had a reason."

"I want that box back."

"Later."

"I want it back *now*. And I want to know where you've
been. Who have you been talking to?"

Maddie was tired. Battered, bone-dead, after-sex, I-don't-
want-to-have-this-conversation-now tired. "Let's talk tomorrow."

"Now."

"Great," she flared at him as she rose to her feet. "You first.
Where the hell have *you* been? And don't tell me bowling,
you bastard. I can't believe what a liar you are. I'm never going
to believe anything you tell me again."

Brent seemed to swell before her eyes. "*Shut up*," he said.
"This isn't about me. Where—"

"The hell it isn't about you," Maddie told him. "This is all
about you being the big man, isn't it?"

"Shut up," Brent said.

"Good old Brent Faraday, can get any woman he wants, most likely to succeed, that's it, isn't it?" She moved around the coffee table and headed for the hall, sick of the conversation. "Well, I'm not playing that game anymore. I'm leaving."

"No, you're not," Brent said, shaking. "You're not going anywhere."

"I know what you are—" Maddie said.

"*Shut up!*"

"—and it's not much, so don't—"

She passed him while she was still talking, and he said, "*Shut up!*" again and swung at her again, his fist hitting the side of her face with a dull thud that made the inside of her head sound hollow, inches below where he'd hit her the first time.

She staggered backward and righted herself, blinking back automatic tears. Then she said, "*No more,*" and shoved past him, knocking him back and then to the floor as she stumbled toward the stairs. He fumbled to his feet and she ran, flinging chairs behind her to slow him down. She heard the hall table fall and wood splinter as he fell over it, but she didn't turn back, making it to their bedroom and slamming and locking the door behind her just before his body thudded against it. She shoved the heavy vanity in front of it and then she spoke to him in bursts, trying to catch her breath, swallowing her tears. "Get out. Get out of the house. I'm calling the police. You're drunk. Or crazy. I don't know what you are. But I know what you've been up to, and I know the kind of man you are, and it's over. *Get out.*"

She heard him sag against the door. "Maddie," he said, and she thought he might be crying except that Brent never cried. "I'm sorry. I didn't mean to hit you. It just happened. Where were you tonight? Just tell me. I just need to know what you know. I need to know who you told."

"I was with C. L. Sturgis," she said. "All night. I'm filing for divorce on Monday. I know everything, all about your blonde, everything, but hitting me was the worst. Hitting me *twice*. Go away. You're not my husband anymore."

"What did you tell him?" Brent said, and she could see the door move under the pressure of his body, but she leaned against the bureau, and the lock held. "Jesus, Maddie, what did you say?"

"Go away," Maddie said. "Just go away."

After a long silence, she heard him going down the stairs, hitting each tread like a punching bag. *This is it*, she thought. *This is the end of that life. That's gone. I'm glad he hit me. That was the bottom. I could never take him back now. Not for Em, not for my mother, not for anybody.*

She heard him moving around downstairs between the breaks in the thunder outside, and then, after a while, she heard him talking. She sat on the bed and eased up the receiver on the bedroom extension, but all she heard was Brent saying drunkenly, "I still don't believe there's any goddamn prowler, but I'll bring it. But that's it. Then it's over." A woman's voice said, "Fine," and then Brent slammed the phone back on the hook and Maddie heard the hall phone crash to the floor. He walked around for a good fifteen minutes while she sat on the edge of the bed, her head throbbing, but then she heard the jangle of his keys as he went out the front door, and she fell back onto the bed.

She began to cry from the pain and exhaustion and fear and confusion and her lost marriage, all tied up with a couple of good punches to the head. As tired as she was, she couldn't sleep. All the things she had to take care of—Em and Kristie's baby and her mother and the puppy and the divorce and Treva and her car and even the microwave—all of it jumbled in her head with the pain and the tears while the storm picked up speed outside and she thought she'd go mad from all of it. And she wished C.L. were there to hold her, to make Brent stay away, to make everything right again.

It wasn't until almost four when the storm ended that she drifted to sleep, and it was then, right on the edge of unconsciousness, that she realized it wasn't the beating alone that had ended everything for her, although that would have been enough. It was the reason behind it. He wasn't afraid she'd been cheating on him; he was afraid she'd been spying on him, that she'd caught him at his slimy little game and the whole town would find out what a creep he was. "I just need to know what you know," he'd said, and she could smell the sour fear on him, the fear that he might not be the great Brent Faraday anymore.

At least I'm not afraid, she told herself. *At least I'm ready to be who I really am.* She thought of her mother then, and the town, and Bailey telling everybody everything, and that was bad. And then she was too tired to think anymore and sank into sleep.

Somebody called her name, and Maddie sat up too soon. The side of her head throbbed until she felt blinded by the pain. *I've got to stop waking up like this*, she thought. *What did I do last night?*

The she remembered.

She heard her name again. Treva. Treva was downstairs with the girls. She pulled the vanity away from the door and stumbled down the stairs. Treva, Mel, and Em stood in the hall, staring at her in shocked silence.

"What's wrong?" Maddie asked.

"We tried to call," Em said politely, looking more than a little scared, "but we got a busy signal." She looked at the floor. "I guess that's why."

Maddie turned. Two chairs and the hall table lay on their sides, one chair leg broken where Brent must have crushed it chasing her. The phone from the table was strung across the floor, the receiver complaining in a nasal monotone. Em stepped around her mother and replaced the receiver. It began to ring, and she answered it and then said, "Just a moment, please." She turned to her mother. "It's for you."

"Em, honey," Maddie began, desperate for an explanation that might get that look off her daughter's face. "Listen. I had too much to drink last night, and I fell over some furniture on my way to bed. That's when I hit my face." Her head throbbed harder; she must look like hell. "I'm sorry. You know I don't drink, but there was a good movie on cable and I had a little wine and . . ." She shrugged.

"How about some breakfast, girls," Treva said brightly. "Pop-Tarts. Something that will rot your teeth."

Em handed the phone to her mother and turned in to the kitchen. Mel looked at Maddie in fear and amazement and followed.

"Not a good lie," Treva told Maddie. "The cable went out last night. We had to watch videos."

"Oh, God." Maddie turned to the mirror. "Oh, *God!*" Her black eye started on her cheekbone and went up to her eyebrow, broken in two places by gashes where Brent's ring had cut her. "Emily," she whispered. "Em saw this."

"Hell." Treva peered over her shoulder to survey the damage in the mirror. "I saw it and I want to throw up. What happened?"

"Brent hit me," Maddie whispered, and then, as Treva sagged against the wall, her mouth open in shock, she finally answered the phone. "Hello?"

"What's going on over there? Has Brent left yet?" C.L.'s voice was happy, full of sunlight and sex. "I've been trying to call you since ten. You've been on the phone with Treva, right?"

"No," she said, staring in the mirror at her face. Then to her horror, she started to cry.

"I'll be right there," C.L. said. "Wait. Don't cry. I'll be right there."

Chapter Eight

N o," Maddie said. That was all she needed, a lover in her house, something else to explain to Em and her mother and the neighbors and—"It's all right," she told him. "I'm all right. Treva's here. The kids are here."

"Look, I'm at my uncle's. I can come over anytime. I'll stay by the phone. Call me when I can come over. What happened? I'm coming over."

"No," she said, "I'll phone you later," and hung up while he was still arguing. C.L. was important, but how important, she wasn't sure. Em's importance, she knew for sure. She turned to Treva. "What am I going to do about Em?"

Treva was still staring. "How many times did he hit you?"

"Twice. I locked myself in the bedroom." Maddie looked at herself in the mirror again and winced. It was still horrible.

"Dear God," Treva said. "Go on upstairs and fix yourself up. I'll distract the kids. Use lots of makeup. And you'll have to wear sunglasses."

Makeup and sunglasses weren't going to work. Em had already seen her. "What do I tell Em?"

Treva sighed. "I don't know. How about the truth?"

Hi, honey. Daddy beat me up last night. Maddie shook her head. "I can't. He's her father."

"Yeah, and he hit her mother."

"Would you tell Mel if it was Howie?"

"I don't know. Howie wouldn't." Treva sounded as close as she'd ever gotten to tears in public. "Get yourself cleaned up. What a mess."

Half an hour later, dressed in an old work shirt and jeans, her face covered in makeup, her eyes hidden behind sunglasses, Maddie faced her daughter in the kitchen.

"You drank a bunch of wine last night," Em said.

"Yep. Dumb me." Maddie sat down.

"Why did you use two glasses?" Mel asked, not bothering to conceal her interest.

"Em's Daddy had one," Maddie lied. "He came home late and had one glass."

"Mel, we've got to go," Treva said, and then to Maddie, "Call me later." She bustled her daughter out the door and into the car before Mel could make any other bright observations.

Maddie held out her arms. "Come here, baby."

Em moved around the table and let herself be pulled into her mother's lap. Then she began to cry.

Maddie cradled her and rocked her. "Talk to me, honey."

"I was scared," Em sobbed. "Everything's been so awful, and everybody's fighting, and then I saw your face and I was scared."

"I know." Maddie held her tighter. "It looks awful. I was scared when I saw it myself, but it happened before. Remember when I joined the health club and tried to lift too much weight and the blood vessels broke in my eye?"

Em stopped crying. "Yes." She sniffed. "I'd forgotten that. But your face didn't get all beat up."

"That's because I didn't drop the weight on my face then," Maddie said, inspired.

Em looked at her with lowered brows. "You dropped the weight on your face?"

"Yep. One of Daddy's in the basement. I'd had a couple of glasses of wine, and I let it slip. Not too bright, huh?"

Em didn't look like she was buying the story, but at least she'd stopped crying.

"I felt stupid," Maddie went on embroidering. "I didn't even know it was this bad until I looked in the mirror after you got here."

Em pulled away and slid to her feet, suddenly remote. "You should see a doctor." She wiped the last of her tears away with the back of her hand. "You could have brained yourself. Or have a concussion."

"Maybe later," Maddie said, relieved that the immediate crisis was over. Em would remember the furniture in the hall eventually and the lack of cable, but she was going to get hit with a zinger very shortly, her parents' divorce. After that, smashed furniture would be the least of her problems.

The phone rang before she could clean or call Treva.

"Maddie, honey, it's Mama."

Maddie sat down at the kitchen table and tried to sound uninjured. "Hi, Mom."

"I called earlier, but I got a busy signal."

"I left the phone off the hook and got some sleep."

"Well, that's good. How's that nice Sturgis boy?"

"What?" Her mother couldn't possibly have heard already unless Bailey—

"I saw Gloria Meyer at Revco. She said you sat in the backyard with him for hours last night. Drinking orange juice and vodka."

Maddie closed her eyes. Eagle-eye Gloria had even spotted the vodka. She must have used binoculars. "He's fine, Mom."

"What does he do for a living?"

"I don't know. Why?"

"Just wondering. Why did he come to see you?"

"He came to see Brent." That was something she'd lost her grasp on in all the excitement: what had C.L. wanted with Brent? Maybe it had just been a cover story to get to her. If so, good for C.L.

"Is he building a house here?"

Maddie sighed. "I don't know, Mother. I don't think so. I think he's just visiting. He said he'd be here a week. He's staying with his uncle Henry. He's divorced. There were no children. He lives in Columbus. He drives a red Mustang convertible. That's it. That's all I know."

"Well, really, Maddie. I just wondered what the man did for a living."

"I'll find out."

"It's not important, dear. They still haven't caught the prowler."

"Well, I'm sure Henry's working on it. Don't worry."

"You know, I just thought. Gloria Meyer's getting that divorce. Maybe if the Sturgis boy stays in town, you could introduce them."

It'll never work. He likes sex. "Sure."

"Gloria's very upset."

"Why?" Maddie asked obligingly.

"Because somebody told Wilbur Carter she was getting a

divorce attorney from Lima—which, really, Maddie, is the only sensible thing she could do—and Wilbur got very upset because he is her mother's cousin and family and all."

Oh, hell. "How do you know all this?"

"Because Wilbur ran into Gloria on Main Street, right in front of the bank, just as Margaret Erlenmeyer was coming out of Revco, and he asked her about it, so Margaret stopped and pretended to look in the window, and Gloria denied it, so he's still doing her divorce."

"Interesting," Maddie said, trying to sound not interested. "Wonder how that rumor got started."

"I have no idea, but I'd heard she was getting Jane Henries. She's very good, you know."

"So I'd heard."

"And then Gloria goes and stays with Wilbur." Her mother's tone implied *dumb as a rock*. "But then that's Gloria. No more sense than a goose. Did you talk to Treva?"

"Treva is fine," Maddie said.

"All right, dear. It's just that that bowling-alley story seems to be true. How's Emily?"

"Fine. Listen, Mom, I've got to go."

"Of course, dear. I'll be over to pick up Emily tomorrow morning. If you're still going."

Maddie sagged against the wall. All this and she had to see her grandmother tomorrow, too. "Of course I'm still going. Has there ever been a Sunday that I didn't see Gran?"

Her mother's voice was glum. "No, but I'm always afraid you'll decide not to one day."

And this would be the Sunday to do it. "I will not decide not to."

"You're a good daughter, Maddie. I'll see you tomorrow. Take care of yourself. Lock your doors."

"You bet. I love you, Mom."

"I love you, too, dear. Get some rest."

Maddie checked her makeup—still awful but better than the mess it covered—and went upstairs to look in on Em. She was curled up on Maddie's bed with a book in her hands, but the telephone beside the bed was crooked, as if she'd just shoved it over.

"Grandma called," Maddie told Em.

"That's nice," Em said politely.

Had she been listening on the extension? Maddie tried to remember if she'd said anything Em shouldn't hear, but it seemed unlikely. She'd been talking to her mother, after all. Now, if it had been Treva . . . She saw Em steal a sideways glance at the phone and then back at her.

What was she supposed to do? Ask Em if she'd been listening in?

Em snuggled farther down in her bed and raised her book a little. So fine, she didn't want to talk. Maddie took the coward's way out.

"I'm going to straighten up the downstairs and call Aunt Treva and then we'll have lunch, all right?"

"All right," Em said, uninterested.

Downstairs, she picked up some of the debris until her head started to throb again. Then she dialed Treva's number, listening to hear if anyone else picked up a receiver on the line. When Treva picked up the phone, Maddie said, "Is this a bad time?" and Treva's voice exploded across the line.

"Are you out of your fucking mind? I've been sitting here *waiting*—"

In the background, Maddie heard a click. "Do you hear anybody else on this line?"

"No." Treva sounded a little stunned. "Why?"

"I think Em may be listening in on the phone."

"Trying to find out what the hell is going on at her house?" Treva snorted. "I don't blame her. Is she listening now?"

Maddie stretched the phone cord to the bottom of the stairs. "Em!"

Seconds later, Em stuck her head out Maddie's bedroom door. "What?"

"Go read outside," Maddie said. "Get some sun and fresh air."

Em didn't look happy, but she nodded and went back in the bedroom and then came down the stairs with her book. Maddie ran upstairs and picked up the bedroom extension so she could watch Em in the backyard while she talked. "Okay, she's outside and I can see her. Did my eye upset Mel?"

"Not as much as it upset me," Treva said. "What happened?"

"I'm not sure. I was drinking last night."

"With Brent?"

C.L.'s face came to mind, and she wished he were there with her, to lean on and to laugh with and to just unload on. "Uh, no, not with Brent."

"Was that why he hit you? Child bride turns out to be secret drinker? Found in love nest?"

"He found me coming in the back door. And I told him I knew about the other woman and he hit me."

Long silence. "Well, it's not my way of apologizing."

Maddie screwed up her face as she tried to think, and her bruised skin screamed back at her. So much for thinking. "Treva, I think he hit me because I found out. I mean, I think he was scared, not mad. Or scared and mad. It was weird. It wasn't right."

"Well, that we can agree on. He shouldn't have hit you. So is hitting something new or have you been keeping this from me, too?"

"No, never. Ever. He yells, he gets sarcastic, he leaves and doesn't call, but he's never hit me. Or Em. He's never even paddled Em. He—" The doorbell rang downstairs and she stopped to listen to Em tramp through the house to get it. "Somebody's here. I have to go."

"Wait a minute. Where did you go in the Caddy last night?"

Em called from downstairs. "Mom, there's some guy here to see you."

"Hold on, Treva." Maddie put down the phone and went to the top of the stairs. "What?"

"There's somebody here." Em moved aside so that C.L. could step forward and look up at her. He was smiling, and then he wasn't, anger chasing horror across his face.

"Jesus fucking Christ," he said. "What happened to you?" His concern and anger wrapped around her, and she was treacherously glad he was there.

"I'll be right back." She ran back to the phone. "I'll call you later," she said to Treva, "I've got company." She hung up while Treva was saying, *"Wait a minute."*

Downstairs she could hear C.L. say, "Hey, sorry about the profanity, kid. I just wasn't ready for your mom's face."

"Me neither," Em said. "You were better than I was. I cried."

It took Maddie a while to get rid of Em without seeming to get rid of her, especially since Em and C.L. had bonded over their collective disapproval of her face. Eventually Em wandered back up to Maddie's bedroom with her book, and Maddie and C.L. stopped smiling.

"Nice kid," C.L. said.

Maddie kept her voice light. "I like her."

"She said you dropped a weight on your face."

Maddie sat down on the stairs, too tired to be upbeat anymore. "It's a story that sounds better if you're eight years old."

C.L.'s jaw got more rigid. "How did it happen?"

Maddie shrugged. "Accident."

"Crap." C.L. sat beside her. "He hit you."

She let herself lean on him a little, and he put his arm around her. "Once," she lied. She pulled his arm from around her shoulder but held on to his hand. "I love the way your arm feels around me," she whispered, "but Em is upstairs. And I'm fine. Really, he only hit me once."

"Once was evidently enough." C.L.'s voice was grim, but his other hand was gentle when he put it under her chin. "Look at me."

"I'm fine."

He leaned closer, close enough to kiss. "Look at me, damn it, I want to see your eyes."

"I'm okay." Maddie pulled away a little. "Treva checked them. No concussion."

"Headache?"

"Hell, yes."

"Dizziness?"

"No."

"Nausea?"

"No. Not even a hangover." She tried to grin, to defuse him. "I'm okay."

C.L. took a deep breath and his hand tightened on hers. "Maybe you are, but I'm not. I let you walk into that."

Maddie shot a glance up the stairs to make sure the hall was still empty. "It wasn't about you," she whispered. "He was mad because I'd been spying on him."

"That's why he hit you?"

Maddie pulled away a little. "Can we talk about something else? This is the second instant replay I've done. It makes me sick."

"Second? Oh, Treva." He paused. "So what did you find out about Brent?"

"That he was having an affair. I know, I know, big surprise. I was surprised."

"Is that all?"

"Isn't that enough?"

"It would be enough for me." C.L. leaned his shoulder into hers, and the weight and the warmth felt wonderful. "God, you look awful. Damn it, I should have come in with you."

"No, it's all right," she said, and felt herself start to cry. *Stop it*, she told herself. *All you do is cry.*

C.L. tried to put his arms around her and she stiffened. "No. Em is just upstairs."

"Right." He took her hand and pulled her to her feet. "Come here for a minute." He pulled her down the hall, out of the sight line of anybody upstairs, and cupped her face in his hands. "I'm worried about you," he said, and kissed her so gently that his kiss was a whisper on her lips. "I want you safe." He kissed her again, slower and firmer this time, and she leaned into him, savoring the taste of him, as his arms went around her and pulled her close. She felt so safe. She shouldn't be doing this, but she felt so safe, and his kiss made her warm all over. She wanted to spend the rest of her life in that kiss.

When C.L. pulled away, he looked as dizzy as she felt. "I have to go right now, or we'll be on the floor, but I will definitely be back. Keep the door bolted."

"What do you mean, keep the door bolted?" Maddie followed him down the hall to the front door, still distracted from the kiss, wanting him against her. "Is this about the prowler?"

"There is no prowler." C.L. opened the front door and turned to her. "Henry's investigated. Nobody's seen anything. Don't worry about some phantom prowler when you have real trouble on your hands."

"What do you mean?"

C.L. shot a glance upstairs and then leaned closer to her and whispered, "I mean I don't think it would be a good idea to let Brent in."

Maddie felt incredulous. "He's Em's father. How can I keep him out?"

"Picture him hitting Em. That should do it."

"He wouldn't."

"How do you know? He hit you." C.L. craned his neck for another look upstairs. "I don't think she's watching, but we'd better not chance it." He touched her lips with his finger. "Consider yourself kissed good-bye until I can do it right. I'll be back later. Bolt the door behind me."

Maddie watched him start down the walk. "Where are you going?"

"To find your husband," C.L. said.

When he was gone, she felt deserted, but she closed and bolted the door.

Em bounced a little on her mom's bed, waiting for Mel to pick up the phone. At least she hoped it was going to be Mel. They really needed their own phones. They were eight, that was old enough. Richelle Tandy had her own—

"Hello?" Mel said.

"Did you listen in when my mom called your mom?"

"No," Mel said. "I was outside. I didn't even know they *called*. Did you listen?"

"My mom caught on," Em said. "She made me go out in the backyard while they talked. And there's more. There's some guy here. I've never seen him before, but Mom knows him."

"What's he doing?"

Em craned her neck to see down the hall without being seen. "They're just sitting on the stairs talking. You should have been here. He said, 'Jesus fucking Christ' when he saw my mom's face."

"He's going to hell," Mel said.

"My mom said she dropped a weight on her face." Em tried to make her voice sound fair, but she didn't believe it, so it was hard. "I think that's a lie."

"Maybe," Mel said. "Hey, maybe this guy is why your mom and dad are fighting. Maybe your dad was *jealous*."

"I don't think so," Em said. "My mom was mad at my dad, not the other way around. Besides, he just showed up today."

"For all you know, he could've been around for *years*," Mel said.

"In this town?" Em stopped, hearing her mother's voice in hers. "C'mon, Mel. Get real."

"You never saw him before?"

"Nope."

"What's he look like?"

Em squinted down the hall again. "He's kind of tall, but not tall like my dad. And he's got real dark hair. And he's wearing a blue plaid shirt and jeans."

"That could be anybody," Mel said. "He could've been here for years and nobody saw him."

"No," Em said. "You would notice this guy. What's going on at your house?"

"My mom is *really* mad about your mom's face," Mel said. "She's cooking. I think she's gonna yell at your dad again."

"He's not here," Em said. "I don't know where he is. And my mom talked to my grandma, but she didn't tell her about any accident with a weight."

"This *sucks*," Mel said. "This really, really *sucks*."

"I gotta go listen," Em said. "I'll call you later and we'll make a plan."

"I bet it's about this guy," Mel said. "I just *bet* you he's the trouble."

C.L. ran up the flight of steps to his uncle's office, nodded at chubby old Esther Wingate at the phone desk, and went in without knocking.

"What the hell?" Henry said, jerking his head up.

"I want to report a crime," C.L. said grimly. "Domestic abuse."

Out on the landing, Esther picked up her head, all ears.

"Close the damn door," Henry said, and C.L. did. "Now, what the hell are you talking about?"

"Brent Faraday beat up his wife last night," C.L. said. "Arrest him."

Henry looked at him steadily. "Is she pressing charges?"

"She doesn't have to," C.L. said. "It's domestic abuse. I'm pressing them."

"No, you are not," Henry said. "Sit down."

C.L. sat. "Henry, her face is a mess. He hit her at least twice, because there are two ring cuts on her face." The memory of those gashes came back to him, and he took a deep breath before he went on. "He hurt her. I want him hurt, too. Arrest him."

"You better talk to Maddie about this," Henry said. "She might not thank you."

"The hell—"

"C.L.," his uncle roared over him. "Shut up. She has to live in this town. People like to take care of their own problems. If she handles it, nobody needs to know what happened."

"You're kidding me." C.L.'s rage made his voice thick. "You are fucking *kidding me.* You're going to let him do it again. You're going to—"

"I didn't say that," Henry said. "I'll have a talk with Brent Faraday. It won't happen again. It never happened before, if that's what you're thinking, because I'd know. He won't do it again."

"He sure as hell won't." C.L. got to his feet.

Henry said, "*Sit down*," and C.L. sat.

"Just what is this woman to you?" Henry said. "I'm starting to get a bad feeling about this."

"Henry, I'd be upset about any woman who got hit," C.L. said.

"Not like this," Henry said. "If I didn't know better, I'd think you were going out looking for Brent Faraday to maybe beat him up a little."

C.L. sat back. "It was part of my plan."

Henry glared at him. "Well, make it not part because if he shows up with so much as a hangnail, I'm putting you in jail."

"Oh." C.L. nodded. "That's real good, Henry. He's the beater, and I get jailed."

"He's the jackass and you know better," Henry said. "Besides, Maddie wouldn't like it. People would think there was more between the two of you than there was, and there'd be talk. You let me handle it quiet."

"Henry—"

"Go do something else," Henry said. "I don't give a damn what as long as you're not hitting anybody or hanging around a married woman. Go do something nice for somebody. Surprise people."

"Thank you very much," C.L. said, and got up to go.

"And one other thing," Henry said.

C.L. stopped.

"You stay away from that woman," Henry said. "She's got neighbors. She doesn't need you sniffing around."

"Thank you, Henry." C.L. tried to sound offended. Henry and his X-ray mind. "I do not sniff."

He stomped out of the office, frustrated and guilty and crazy to do something. Henry was right, he couldn't go back to Maddie's and just hang around, and Henry would make sure Brent never swung on her again. He wanted to go see her again and touch her again, but there were the neighbors. If he didn't do something soon, he would have to go find Brent and smack him, and that wouldn't be good, so—

Lost in thought, he headed for the Mustang. He had to do something to help Maddie or he'd be even crazier than he was now.

Maddie was hauling the last of the broken furniture out of the hall when the phone rang. *I'm going to have this thing taken out*, she thought. *Other people have lives; I have phone conversations.*

It was Candace at the bank. "I'm terribly sorry, Maddie, but your account is overdrawn."

Maddie dropped the chair leg she'd been holding. "What?"

Candace's voice was heavy with sympathy. "I can just return the checks, but I thought if you'd run in and make a deposit, we could save you the returned-check charge."

Not to mention the hoo-ra when the town found out she'd been bouncing checks. Her mother would have a fit. Maddie pressed her hand to her forehead, trying to think. They couldn't possibly be overdrawn. She'd just balanced the checkbook when the statement had come last week. Something was wrong, but she didn't feel like arguing about it now. At least she'd finally come up with a problem she could solve. "Why don't you just transfer over some from the savings? I can authorize that on the phone, can't I?"

"Your savings account is empty, too."

Maddie sat down hard on the stairs. "What do you mean, empty?"

"Five dollars and sixty-three cents." Candace sounded apologetic, which was pretty decent of her, considering it wasn't her screwup.

"Right. Thanks, Candace. Give me a minute." She rubbed her head with her fingertips. The throbbing there was turning into pounding. Where was the money in their accounts? Brent must have pulled everything out this morning. Why? And where was she going to get money now? Her automatic paycheck deposit wasn't for another week.

"Let me think for a minute," she stalled Candace. She could ask her mother, but her mother would want to know why. Maybe Treva—

"Is there anything in your safe-deposit box?" Candace suggested. "You're only going to need about two hundred and forty to cover the checks so far."

There were a couple of CDs in there. There would probably be a penalty for cashing one in early, but penalties were the least of her problems right now.

"I'll be right there," she said. "Thanks, Candace."

She went to the little spindle-legged desk her grandfather had left her for the key. The small middle drawer was pushed in crooked, and all the anger she'd felt for Brent spurted up. *Damn him.* He knew you had to push the drawers in gently or they sat crooked. He knew—

She was going to scream or cry, and either one was a bad idea. The desk drawers didn't matter, even if they did pretty much sum up Brent: he knew better, but he didn't care.

She pulled out the right-hand drawer where they kept the safe-deposit key, but it wasn't there. Brent must have taken it. What was he doing with all their money? The possibilities weren't good, and she searched the rest of the desk for the key, desperate to be proven wrong.

It turned up in the little middle drawer after all, pushed to the back.

Thank God, Maddie thought, and called up to Em to tell her they were going to the bank, but when they went outside, there were no cars. Brent had taken the Caddy the night before, and her Civic was dead, towed to its semifinal resting place at Leo's Garage. She could walk the mile to get to uptown, but not everything from now on was going to be that easy. She felt trapped. Somebody had murdered her car and now she was trapped.

Mrs. Crosby came out on her porch.

"Hello, Mrs. Crosby." Maddie waved at her, self-conscious about her face until she remembered Mrs. Crosby couldn't see beans.

"Goin' for a walk?" Mrs. Crosby called, and Em said, "Sheesh" under her breath.

"Just downtown," Maddie called back, and then she heard the phone ring inside. *Damn.* Em rolled her eyes and sat down on the porch step while Maddie went back in and grabbed it.

"Mrs. Faraday?"

"Yes?"

"This is John Albrech, about your Civic?"

All this and insurance agents, too.

"It may be a while before we can settle on your car—"

Maddie's temper broke. "No, it will not be a while. It will be immediately. I have paid premiums on that car for twelve years, right on time. I want this settled on Monday. Is that clear?"

"I don't think you understand, Mrs. Faraday—"

"I understand perfectly. I either want that car fixed at Leo's or a check to replace it. By Monday."

"Well, fixing it is out of the question, it's—"

"Fine. A check will be fine. I need a car. Either my old one back or a new one, but I need a car." She heard her voice rising hysterically.

"Now, just be calm, Mrs. Faraday. A rental—"

"I will *not* be calm!"

"I'll be back in touch on Monday," he said, and hung up.

She went back out to Em. "We'll walk."

Em took this philosophically, and Maddie was glad. She didn't feel like extolling the virtues of exercise at the moment. Her head hurt and it took all of her energy to keep walking. And thinking. Something was going to have to be done about Em since all hell was breaking loose and she knew it. And what did Em think about C.L.? And there was something wrong with Treva, and she was going to have to find that out and help. And then there was Kristie's baby, if it was Kristie's baby. And why was their checking account bouncing all over the place? And where was Brent anyway? Hard at work in his bowling clothes? And what was C.L. doing? Belatedly she remembered that C.L. had had a small violence problem in high school, and wondered if he was someplace beating up her husband. He might still have the same violence problem. He still had the same sex drive.

Her life was too small in a town that was too small to have this many loose cannons rolling around. Maybe she should call a meeting. She could have everybody gather in the living room and tell them to sit down and shut up until she got her bearings.

It was only a twenty-minute walk, and she and Em did it in record time, each of them lost in her own thoughts. She saw several people she knew, and they stared at her face, so she figured her makeup was less than successful. "Ran into a door," she said cheerfully. Everyone seemed to accept it; it must have sounded like something she'd do.

The bank was cool and dark inside, and she had to take her sunglasses off to find her way to a teller's window. "I need my safe-deposit box," she said, showing her driver's license. "What do I do?"

The girl, who was all of twenty, looked at her face, obviously dying to ask what had happened. "You wait right here, Mrs. Faraday," she said, patting Maddie's hand. "I'll get someone to help you."

Who the hell is she? Maddie thought, not in a mood to be patronized. The nameplate by the window said *June Webster*. Maybe June was Brent's extracurricular activity. She looked like she might be expensive.

Harold Whitehead came out of his office and crossed the floor to Candace's desk, nodding to Maddie as he went by her. He must have missed her face entirely because he didn't react. That was like Harold.

When he went back to his office, Candace looked up and smiled at her. Then her eyes widened. She came across the floor to them, cool in her beige and pale gold suit, and whispered, "Are you okay?"

Maddie smiled. "Ran into a door."

Candace didn't look convinced, but she didn't push it, either. "What did you decide to do about the checking?"

"Safe-deposit box." Maddie held up her key. "And could you print me out a statement of my account so I can see where we went wrong?"

"Sure." Candace held out her hand to Em. "I've got some ink stamps you can play with while your mom goes downstairs, Emily. Want to stamp some paper?"

"Thank you," Em said politely, and took her hand without

much enthusiasm. Em's tolerance for adults was evidently on the wane.

"Mrs. Faraday?"

The infant teller stood waiting. "Here's Mr. Webster to help you."

Another Webster? They looked like brother and sister, pale and blond and patronizing. Mr. Webster was older, middle twenties tops, but he was serious, very serious. He frowned at her face and then took her through the formalities of signing for her box and led her to a cubicle.

"I'll leave you alone," he said, making Maddie feel conspiratorial.

"Good idea," she said. "That way I won't be able to drag you down with me when they find out."

Mr. Webster looked blank. "Pardon?"

"Joke. Never mind. Thank you."

He left so she could have some privacy, and it was so quiet, Maddie thought about spending the rest of her life there. No phones. She opened the box, and then blinked.

It was full of hundred-dollar bills.

"Oh, my *God*," she said, and Mr. Webster came back to the cubicle.

"Are you all right?" he asked, and then his eyes fell on the cash.

"Fine," Maddie said weakly, waving her hand at him. "You can go."

Mr. Webster looked at her uncertainly, and then he faded away.

She took a quick inventory of the box. Her grandmother's jewelry was there under the money, and Em's college bonds, and the CDs, but mostly the box was full of bills wrapped in packages, a hundred bills to a wrap in the package she counted, ten thousand dollars each. She counted twenty-eight packages. Two hundred and eighty thousand dollars. No cents. It was more money than she'd ever seen in her life, and she was quite sure it wasn't possible for them to have that much. Not legally, anyway.

Think, she told herself, but it was hard because there was so much money right there in front of her.

Obviously Brent had been doing something besides having an affair. Unless he'd been charging for his services. And if so, there was still something wrong because no one would ever pay Brent that much for sex. He just wasn't that good.

This was going to be bad. She should tell somebody. Henry Henley or somebody. Except she didn't know where the money came from. What if it was honest somehow? What if Brent really had this much money, and she turned him in to the police? Frog Point would love that one. No. She'd have to talk to Brent first. "Excuse me, but after I found the underwear, I found a lot of money, and I'm getting upset. Are you a thief and an adulterer, or just an adulterer? My divorce attorney will want to know."

It was too confusing. She started to shut the box, and then thought again. With the way things had been going, better to empty the whole box and make sure there wasn't anything else appalling in there. She pulled out Emily's bonds and her jewelry cases and the money, and underneath them all she found a manila envelope.

I don't want to open that, she thought, but how much worse could things get? Her husband was an adulterous wife beater who was also quite probably a thief, and her car was dead. She'd pretty much hit bottom. It was just an envelope. *Get a grip*, she told herself, and opened the envelope and dumped the contents out: two airplane tickets and two passports.

The tickets were to Rio on Monday, August 19, the day after tomorrow. He was going to South America with somebody.

Two days ago that would have shocked her. Now all she thought was how much easier it was going to be to divorce him if he was out of the country. If you looked at it just right, it was semigood news. He could send Em postcards and she could collect the stamps.

Then the significance of the two passports hit. At last she'd know the identity of the blonde. The first passport she opened was Brent's, and she threw it back in the box. Then she opened the second passport and went cold. There was a rushing noise and she thought, *I have head injuries. I must keep calm. Now, let's keep our perspective here.*

The good news was, he wasn't taking some bimbo to South America with him.

The bad news was, the second passport was Emily's.

Chapter
Nine

Maddie felt dizzy again. *Deep breaths*, she told herself, but there wasn't enough oxygen in the world.

Brent was going to take Emily to Brazil. He'd gone out and gotten her a passport and now he was taking her to Brazil.

She dropped everything but Em's passport back in the box and slammed the lid. Outside the cubicle, she shoved past Mr. Webster and ran up the stairs to the bank lobby.

No Em.

Brent had found her. Maddie's breath came shorter as the panic hit her. He'd come into the bank and he'd found Em and—

"Mom?" Em came out from behind Candace's counter, her fingers smeared with stamp-pad ink. "Candace has some really neat stamps."

Maddie stopped herself from grabbing Em and running from the bank. "We have to go now. Thank you, Candace." She took Em's hand, and the warmth of Em's grasp made her drop to her knees. "I love you, Em," she said, and hugged her daughter tightly.

"I love you, too, Mom." Em's tone added, *You're acting weird*.

Maddie stood up, ignoring Candace's startled face. "Let's get lunch, okay?" Brent couldn't walk into a restaurant and take Em. That was public. Sooner or later, they were going to have to go home, but right now, later was better. Later meant she could think. "Burger King."

They crossed the street, and Maddie ripped pages out of Em's passport as she went, throwing them in two different trash cans as they walked. The case was too tough to rip, so she threw that in the Dumpster behind the restaurant. She was pretty sure that a ripped passport wasn't valid, but if it was, Brent was going to have to dive in three different bins to reconstruct it.

He'd gone behind her back and gotten their child a passport and now he was going to take her away.

The hell he was.

She kept Em's picture, stashing it in her purse. He wasn't taking Em.

Through it all, Em was silent.

"I know I'm acting weird," Maddie told her when they were in the restaurant. "I think I need to lie down again."

Em nodded and ate her cheeseburger and fries in silence, watching her mother's every move. The silence was good; it gave Maddie a chance to reassure herself that Brent couldn't take Em, to calm down so she could pretend to be sane. All she had to do was get Em home, chain the door so Brent couldn't get in, and wait until Monday. If she just held on to Em and sanity until Monday, Brent would have to go to Rio alone, and she could divorce him in absentia.

Somehow, divorce didn't seem nearly the trauma it had the day before.

Once they were home, Maddie locked, bolted, and chained the front and back doors and then searched the house to make sure Brent wasn't hiding there, waiting to jump out at her like Freddy Krueger. Then she sat on the stairs and put her head between her knees. It wasn't fair that she should have head injuries at a time like this. She hurt all over. Someone should be holding her and saying, "Poor baby." C.L. would be good at that.

"Mom?"

Maddie lifted her head and smiled at Em as best she could. "It's my head again, sweetie. Go and watch some mindless rot on TV. It's bad for you, but I'll take you to a museum another day."

Em nodded warily and took off down the hall, and Maddie walked into the living room and sat down, staring at the coffee table and the two empty glasses and the wine bottle. She heard Em dialing the hall phone. Probably to talk to Mel. "My mother's a weirdo," she'd say. "El weirdo. Daddy's been teaching me Spanish."

This couldn't be happening, but as long as she stayed calm and kept the doors chained, there was nothing to worry about. Maddie lay down on the couch and stared at the coffee table some more. She should be cleaning. Empty wine bottles on a coffee table looked cheap.

In the background, she heard Em talking to somebody in her polite voice. She couldn't be calling Mel. Who was she calling?

"Em? Who are you calling?"

"Daddy, at work."

Maddie sat up fast, a mistake because her head almost exploded. *"Why?"*

"I think you should go back to the hospital. You're still sick."

She tried to keep her voice normal, but panic made it tight. "What did he say?"

"I don't know. Uncle Howie said he wasn't there."

"Oh." Maddie started to breathe again. One more crisis and she'd have a heart attack right there on the couch.

"Should I call Aunt Treva?"

"No, no, that's okay." Maddie lay back down again. It felt so good she decided to never get up again.

"How about that C.L. guy? He could take you."

He took me last night, she thought, and for a minute, she felt good about that. But only for a minute. Then the panic came back. "No, baby," she told Em. "I'll just rest." *Until Monday. We're going to do a lot of resting until Monday.*

"Okay. Yell if you feel funny."

Em went upstairs, and Maddie let herself relax a little. Everything was going to be all right. They were locked in the house with the chains on. Brent couldn't get in. Visions of Brent breaking through the chains rose before her. She could push furniture in front of the doors, but Em was already suspicious as it was. Best to act as normal as possible. No furniture. Maybe—

The phone rang. Em answered it upstairs and yelled, "Mom!" and Maddie got up. It couldn't be Brent, Em would still be talking to him.

Brent was not taking Emily. After that nothing else mattered.

She picked up the downstairs line and said, "Yes?"

"Maddie?" The voice was a strange one, gravelly and tentative. "This is Bailey."

"Bailey?" The rent-a-cop from the Point. Not someone on her regular phone list.

Bailey's voice grated over the line. "I just wanted to tell you that I haven't told anybody about what I seen last night."

"Thank you," Maddie said.

"C.L. and me go back a long ways," Bailey said. "I wouldn't never do anything to hurt C.L."

"That's good," Maddie said. "I'm sure he appreciates it."

"I was kind of hoping you'd appreciate it, too." Bailey's voice got as whiny as a gravelly voice could. "You know what I mean?"

"I haven't a clue," Maddie said, almost relieved now that Bailey was getting somewhere. "What do you want?"

"How about a hundred dollars?"

"What?" Maddie was so surprised she almost dropped the phone. "You're blackmailing me?"

"No, no," Bailey said, frantic. "I wouldn't do a thing like that. That's illegal. I just thought you might want to show your appreciation."

Her appreciation. "And if I don't?"

"Well, it's a damn good story," Bailey said. "It'd be a real shame to waste it."

She wanted to say, *Bailey, you idiot, that's blackmail*, but he wasn't going to get it, and she didn't care. "You know, Bailey, any other week this would be upsetting—"

"Now, Maddie—"

"—but this week you're just part of the scenery." Okay, she wasn't going to pay blackmail, but she was going to have to stop him. That meant calling Henry. Which meant stringing Bailey along for a while. "How do you want me to get this hundred to you?"

"I could stop by," Bailey said.

As blackmailers went, Bailey was almost endearing in his

ineptitude. "Things are pretty hectic here right now," she told him. "Let me get back to you on this."

"Well, don't wait too long," Bailey said. "It's an awful good story."

"I'll get back to you," Maddie said, and hung up. The hits just kept on coming.

She picked up the phone to call Henry and remembered that C.L. didn't want his uncle to know he was sleeping with a married woman at the Point. "Oh, hell," she said, and put the phone back. So she'd talk to C.L. first. Whatever. She went back to the living room and lay down on the couch and tried to remember what she'd been thinking before Em had taken ten years off her life with a phone call to her father and Bailey had gotten delusions of grandeur. Oh yes, sloppy housekeeping. The wine bottle. Empty.

Maddie frowned at the bottle. Empty? It should have wine in it. Wine and enough painkillers to kill a horse. Or at least relax it into a coma.

What had happened to the doped wine?

Maddie sat up. Somebody had drunk the wine with the pills in it. Treva hated wine. C.L. hadn't been in the living room. Em knew better than to drink alcohol.

Only one person could have finished the wine.

Oh my God, Maddie thought. *I've killed my husband.*

"My mom just got a really weird phone call," Em told Mel, having called her from Maddie's bedroom. "Some guy's blackmailing her."

"Cool," Mel said. "Just like in the movies."

"No, it's not cool." Em let her voice go sharp with exasperation. "This is my mom. He wants a hundred dollars."

"That's not much," Mel pointed out. "In the movies, it's always millions."

"He said it was about last night. I bet it's about what happened to her face."

"Wow." Mel was silent for a moment. "Is she going to do it?"

"She told him she'd call him back. And, Mel, the guy knows that C.L. guy who was here today."

"Did he say anything about my mom and dad?"

"No. This is just about my mom and whatever happened last night. I wish my dad was here. He could fix it."

"Where is he?"

"I don't know." Em swallowed. "I don't know anything. What are we going to do?"

"We can't find out any more about the guy on the phone if we don't know who he is," Mel said. "So that leaves this C.L. guy. You'll have to grill him."

"Right," Em said. "Get real."

"Grown-ups like to talk to kids," Mel said. "It makes them feel like they can relate."

"They can't." Em's voice was firm.

"Well, don't tell this C.L. guy that. Be sweet and ask him questions and maybe he'll tell you what you need to know so you'll like him."

Em thought about sucking up to a stranger. "That makes me gag."

"Okay, big critic, what's your plan?"

Em thought for a couple of minutes. There didn't seem to be anything else she could do. "Okay, I'll do it," she told Mel. "But it's going to be yucky."

. . .

The living room was cool and dark with the drapes pulled. Maddie put a cold cloth over her eyes, stretched out on the couch, and tried to be rational.

Maybe Brent wasn't dead.

Right. She'd poisoned the wine. It wasn't spilled, and he was the only one around to drink it.

And he was now missing.

Worst-case scenario: suppose he'd drunk the wine and got in the car and drove off a cliff.

What cliff? Frog Point had no real cliffs.

Just a Point. Hardly a cliff. More like a shelf above a ditch. A high shelf. A deep ditch. Okay, a cliff.

Maddie groaned. At least if he'd driven off the Point, she could stop worrying about him kidnapping Emily.

They'd find his body full of her painkillers. She'd go to prison. Her mother would have to raise Em. Oh, God, no, she'd turn out like Maddie. Insane. Treva's kids were turning out well. Maybe Treva could raise Em.

Maddie went to the hall, picked up the phone, and heard Em say to Mel, "It's going to be yucky."

"Mel, go get your mom," Maddie said, and she heard Em say, "Mom?" and Mel drop the receiver with a clunk and then after a minute, Treva said, "Hello?"

"Treva? Get over here right away."

"What happened? Are you all right?"

"No. Get over here. I need you now."

Maddie kicked Em out of the bedroom so she could lie down again, giving her instructions to unchain the door only for Treva and no one else, and ten minutes later, Treva knocked on the bedroom door and came in. "What's going on? Why is it so dark?"

"Don't open the drapes. My head is killing me."

Maddie heard Treva move through the dark room to sit on the edge of the bed. "What's wrong?"

"I killed Brent."

"What?"

Maddie's head began to pound harder. "The wine's gone. I put my pills in the wine bottle because I was upset, and now it's empty."

"He drank it?"

"Well, I didn't. He must have." Maddie took the cloth off her eyes and peered through the gloom at her best friend. "Treva, he's missing. He's not at work. He's not here. He'd be somewhere. He's dead. I killed him."

Treva's voice was unsure in the dark. "You're panicking. You couldn't have killed Brent. It's too bizarre. Don't panic."

Maddie put the cloth back on her eyes. "Good. I won't. Will you raise Em until I get out of prison?"

"You don't go to prison for accidentally poisoning your husband."

"Who's going to believe it's an accident? He's cheating on me, and everybody in town knows it." Then Maddie remembered the night before and groaned. "Plus, last night I got picked up by a rent-a-cop in the backseat of my husband's car at the Point with another man, and now he's blackmailing me, and when I don't come across with the money, he's going to tell everybody."

"What?"

"And then Brent picks last night of all nights to beat me up." *And he was going to steal my kid and take her to South America with a lot of very suspicious money.* She had to do something about that money. Later. She took the cloth off her eyes again and looked up at Treva. "Really, the motives are just all over the place. The police won't even have to bend over to pick them up."

"Forget the motives, go back to the part about the Point. The cops picked you up with who?"

"Not cops, Bailey. I was making love with C. L. Sturgis."

Treva's voice went up a notch. "In the back of Brent's car?"

"You think that was tacky?"

Treva started to laugh. "No, no, I think it's great. Oh, God, I wish I'd been there."

"I wish you had, too," Maddie said, still panicked but a little cheered by Treva's attitude. "That'd be one less motive for me."

"So how was it?"

Maddie propped herself up against the quilted headboard. "I tell you I just killed my husband, and I'm being blackmailed, and I'm going to be arrested at any moment, and you ask me, 'How was it?'"

"You didn't kill your husband." Treva waved that theory away with her hand. "Think about it. A couple of Tylenol Three in a little wine isn't fatal. He's not dead. I think you took a crack on the head in a car accident and then got punched twice last night—for which I hope your husband rots in hell—and I think you're not thinking straight, as who would be? Lie back down again."

Maddie slid back into the bed. "You're right. I'm not well."

Treva pushed herself up farther onto the bed and sat cross-legged. "So, before you die, tell me. How was it?"

"You're a ghoul."

"No. I'm only a ghoul if you had sex with a corpse. Was it that bad?"

Maddie started to smile. She couldn't help it.

"What?" Treva pounced. "It wasn't bad? It was great?"

"It was cosmic."

"What?"

Maddie's smile widened. "He's been practicing. I've never

had anything like it in my life. We're going to move into the backseat of the Cadillac."

Treva laughed out loud. "This is wonderful. This is great. Wait until I tell Howie."

Maddie sat up. "No!" Then her head throbbed and she added, "Ouch," and lay back down again. "No, you will not tell Howie."

"Oh, come on. He's going to find out anyway when you move into the car."

"You tell *nobody*."

"Why?"

"Because I'm married!"

Treva's grin faded. "Oh, yeah. I forgot."

"I'm getting the divorce," Maddie said. "But until then I have to be careful."

"That reminds me," Treva said. "That box we found in the office—"

Downstairs the doorbell rang.

"*Brent.*" Maddie scrambled out of bed. "He's come for Em!"

"Ringing his own doorbell?" Treva said, but then Em's voice shrieked up the stairs.

"Mom! That C.L. man's here again. And you should see what he's got!"

Maddie was so relieved, she sagged against the doorway. As long as it wasn't Brent, she didn't care.

It was a short-legged, wobbly, black and white and tan puppy with huge paws and a nose like a bullet, and Em and Mel were already in love.

"Meet Phoebe," C.L. said.

Treva started to laugh.

Maddie leaned against the wall. "Phoebe?"

"Em just named her," C.L. said. "I was thinking Hilda. Doesn't she look like a Hilda?"

"Oh, yeah," Treva said, and went off into laughter again.

Em was in ecstasy. "Isn't she perfect?"

"She's perfect!" Mel echoed.

Perfect, Phoebe wasn't. She looked vaguely off, a fun-house puppy whose proportions weren't quite kosher. She was too long to be a beagle and too short to be a dachshund and too fat to be either, and then there were those spots: Phoebe's back had regular big brown beagle spots, but her sides and legs were spattered with little black dalmatian spots.

"She's a stretch beagle," Treva said.

"She's a guard dog," C.L. said. "She's here to protect you."

The guard dog wobbled over and flopped down next to Em and put its little head in her lap.

C.L. shrugged. "Well, she's vicious if you're attacked."

"She looks like she weighs about five pounds," Maddie said. "If we get attacked by anything larger than a squirrel, we're going to be in real trouble."

"Yes, but she's going to get a lot bigger."

"What?"

"She's just a pup."

Maddie pictured her already rocky future with the addition of a huge mutant beagle in the house. It was more than she could take. "C.L., it's very nice for you to arrange to *loan* us this dog, but—"

C.L. grinned at her. "Oh, it's not a loan. It's forever."

"I *love* you!" Em shrieked at C.L., and hugged the puppy, and Treva sat down on the steps because she was laughing too hard to stand.

Maddie gave up. "How much bigger?"

"Lots. She's part beagle and part dachshund and part setter

and part dalmatian." C.L. looked down at the puppy. "And a few other things, I think. She's a very American dog."

"And how big do these American parts get?"

C.L. shrugged. "Don't know. Never seen one before."

Maddie sat down on the stairs beside Treva. At least the new disaster didn't involve money, adultery, blackmail, kidnapping, or divorce. This was just what she needed: G-rated trauma. "What was this anyway? Some kind of genetic engineering at the pound?"

"No. A friend of Henry's had a beagle mix that met this incredibly aggressive dachshund mix. Sort of like us last night."

Treva sputtered with laughter again, and Maddie ignored her. "Very funny."

C.L. looked her straight in the eye, and this time he was serious. "You need this dog, Mad." He moved his head infinitesimally toward Em, and Maddie really looked at her daughter for the first time since she'd come downstairs. Em's face was relaxed and happy, shining happy.

"You're right," she said. "I need this dog."

"I didn't forget you, either, cookie," C.L. said. "There's a microwave in the trunk. We'll go get you a rental car later. Full service, that's me."

"That's what I heard," Treva said, and Maddie said, "Shut up, Treva," but C.L. just laughed.

"Come on, Mel." Treva stood up in spite of her daughter's protests. "We'll come back later. These people have company."

"I am not company," C.L. said, but they left anyway, and Em took Phoebe out to the back porch, ecstatic over her every wobble while C.L. brought the new microwave in.

Maddie watched Em through the kitchen window. "This is great," Maddie said, not taking her eyes off Em. "But you didn't have to—"

"Yes, I did." C.L. craned his neck to see where Em was, and

then he bent and kissed her, the same soft, mind-melting kiss he always gave her, and she let herself relax against him for a minute.

"You do that well," she murmured.

"I do other things well, too," he said. "I have an idea."

"I bet you do, but my kid's in the backyard, so forget it." Maddie turned back to the window. She wanted to call Em to come in, but she didn't want her to think anything was wrong. *Come inside, honey. Daddy might kidnap you.*

C.L. tried to look dignified and failed. "It wasn't that idea, although that's a good one, too. I think you and Em should come out to the farm for a while."

Maddie blinked. "To Anna?"

"You've had a rough time," C.L. said. "I looked all over for Brent and couldn't find him, but that doesn't mean he won't be home tonight." He moved closer. "I hate having you alone here where I can't take care of you. Come stay with us where you'll be safe."

Safe. If she took Em out to the farm, Brent would never find her. And even if he did, he'd have to go through Henry and C.L. to get her. It was the perfect solution.

Except that everybody in Frog Point would be talking about it by church tomorrow morning.

She had a choice: she could stay home so people wouldn't talk, or she could keep her daughter safe.

"I know you're worrying about what people will think," C.L. was saying, "but—"

"We'd love to come," Maddie said. "I'll pack. You go talk to Em. Go out there and keep an eye on her."

"She's fine," C.L. said.

"Humor me," Maddie said, and he looked confused but he went.

. . .

Em sat on the back porch steps with her arms around Phoebe's warm, sweaty little body and concentrated on the miracle C.L. had given her so she wouldn't have to think about anything else. Phoebe was wonderful, squirming against her to lick her face, and when C.L. came out and sat with her, she was wiping away puppy spit.

"You okay, kid?" he asked her, scratching behind Phoebe's ears.

"Of course she's okay," Em told him. "She's *wonderful*."

"No, I mean you."

His voice sounded serious, although it was hard to tell since she didn't know him at all. Em looked up at him sideways. He had a nice face, the kind of face that looked like it grinned a lot even though it wasn't grinning now, and if the world hadn't been in such a mess, Em might have liked him, especially since he'd given her Phoebe. And now she had to grill him. "I love her," she told him. "Thank you so much."

Phoebe's squirming got more violent, so Em let her go and watched while she trotted across the yard and peed on the sidewalk.

"Okay, so we have some work to do," C.L. said, and Em laughed in spite of herself at the way he said it, sort of cheery like her first grade teacher, but making fun, too. "The grass is too high," he went on. "It tickles her tummy, and it's hard to pee with something tickling, right?"

"Right." Em had her eyes back on Phoebe, who was investigating the edge of the driveway. "Come here, Phoebe!" she called, terrified that the puppy would disappear down the street, that there would be the same screech of brakes that she'd heard two days before, that Phoebe would be squashed and dead in the middle of the street—

Phoebe came bounding back and wriggled in between them on the steps, and Em clutched the puppy to her side, holding on to all her warmth and life.

"We need to fence in the rest of the yard." C.L. scooted over a little to give Phoebe more room. "Just that open space between the driveway and the house. We'll put in a gate so you can still get to the car. And I'll cut the grass so the tickle thing won't be a problem."

Em felt cold all of a sudden. "My daddy cuts the grass." She looked up at him sideways again. She wanted to like him, but she wasn't sure what he was doing in her life, so maybe he shouldn't be there. And then there was the blackmailer. If she didn't grill him, Mel would kill her. Em set her jaw. *Are you in love with my mom?* didn't seem to be a good start. Maybe something almost like that, but not quite. "Do you know my daddy?"

She saw him draw back a little and thought, *He's going to lie*, and then he said, "I knew your mom and dad back in high school. I haven't been in town much since then because I moved away, so I haven't talked to your dad in a long time."

Em considered his answer. He had good eyes, they looked right at her, so he probably wasn't lying. And he talked to her the same way he talked to her mother, like an adult, except that he sounded more serious with her than he did with her mom. "That's the truth, isn't it?" she asked him, still suspicious, letting Phoebe slip squirming through her fingers again.

"Of course it's the truth."

He sounded sort of mad, so she said, "Sorry. Sometimes people say stuff to make me feel better."

"Well, I'm not going to lie, even if it makes you feel lousy,"

C.L. said. "All lying does is get you in trouble anyway. You forget what you said in the lie, and then somebody catches you, and then there's hell to pay. Might as well tell the truth and get it over with."

He sounded sort of grouchy, like he was talking about something that had happened to him, and Em grinned, her troubles and the grilling forgotten for a minute. "Somebody caught you, huh?"

C.L. grinned back. "My uncle. I swear, he can read minds."

"I wouldn't like that." Em thought back over some of the things she had to hide, like the fact that she didn't believe her mother.

"I didn't, either," C.L. said. "But I learned to live with it. Hey, Phoebe, get your butt back here." As the puppy trotted back to them again, he added, "You know, we could use a chain to keep Phoebe in the yard."

Em nodded. "And a bowl and some food and a collar and a leash." She stood up. "I'll go get some paper for a list."

"I brought puppy chow," C.L. told her. "And you don't need paper for the rest. Sit down, I'll teach you a trick."

Em sat down. Tricks sounded good.

"It's called a memory picture," he told her as Phoebe burrowed between them and up onto her lap again. "My uncle taught me this. Okay, how many things do we have to remember?"

Em counted them in her mind. "Four. No, five, we need puppy biscuits, too."

"Okay, close your eyes," C.L. said, and she did. "Now, picture Phoebe wearing her collar, with the leash attached, and—What else was there?"

"A chain," Em said with her eyes still closed, "attached to the leash."

"You've got it, kid," C.L. said. "Smart. What's next?"

"She's eating puppy biscuits out of the bowl," Em said, putting the picture together.

"Look at it hard." C.L.'s voice was nice beside her, not pushy or loud, just sort of laid-back. "Got it?"

In Em's mind, Phoebe ate brown biscuits from a red dish, a blue collar around her neck and a bright green leash attached to that, and attached to that, a huge, heavy silver chain—

"The chain's too big," she told C.L., and then felt stupid because she was the one who'd made it up, hadn't she?

"Then make it smaller," he told her, and there wasn't anything in his voice that sounded like he thought she was dumb. "You imagined it big because you don't like the idea of Phoebe chained up. But we'll finish the fence soon and then we won't use it anymore. It's just to keep Phoebe safe until we get the rest of the fence up."

The chain shrank to a reasonable size, and Em knew she should ask why he thought he was going to be finishing the fence and not her daddy, but Phoebe's nose was cold and wet against her hand, and she had a memory picture of all the things she needed, a new trick to show Mel, not to mention all the information she'd already gotten from one good question. She didn't need to ask any more. Grilling wasn't her thing even if she was pretty good at it.

"Okay," she said. "I've got it. And maybe a ball and a Frisbee."

"Where are they?"

"The white Frisbee's under the dish, and the purple ball's on Phoebe's head." Em giggled at the picture. "That's seven things, right?"

"Right," C.L. said. "And I bet you don't forget one of them."

I don't forget anything, Em wanted to say, but she patted Phoebe instead and memorized the picture again. It was something to think about besides her mom's face and the blackmailer and why C.L. was talking about finishing the fence instead of her dad.

"How about we take Phoebe out to my uncle's farm?" C.L. said, and Em tensed again because he sounded fake relaxed for the first time. "Okay," he said, in his normal voice. "Here's the story. I think your mom needs somebody to take care of her for a while, and my aunt Anna takes care of people better than anybody I know. And the farm will be a good place for Phoebe to play. Maybe you and I can go fishing. Just take some time off. What do you think?"

I think you and Mom already decided we're going, Em thought, *so what do you care what I think?* But all she said was, "All right."

Maddie watched C.L. put Em in the front seat for the ride out to the farm, relegating Maddie to riding swathed in a scarf in the backseat, fighting the wind. He talked to Em all the way there, telling her about the farm and the river and fishing and how much Phoebe was going to love it, and his voice was so tender, Maddie fell for him all over again.

About halfway there, near the deserted Drake farm, Em spoke for the first time. "How far is it?"

"About fifteen miles," C.L. told her. "Your street to Route 31. Then right on Porch Road, and right again on Hickory. Thirty-one people on the Porch eating Hickory nuts."

Maddie said, "What?" but Em grinned, and Maddie didn't care that she wasn't in on the joke as long as Em was happy. And safe.

C.L. finished his answer. "It's about twenty-five minutes if you drive carefully."

Far away from Brent. Maddie relaxed for the first time since she'd found Em's passport. "Which means with you driving, we'll be there in ten," she told C.L.

"Hey, I've changed," C.L. called back to her. "I'm a responsible citizen with a future in this place. I never speed anymore."

She laughed, and he shoved in a cassette and called back, "Remember this?" Bruce Springsteen howled out "Born to Run." *This is so* not *my song*, Maddie thought. Too bad Bruce never recorded anything like "Born to Be Cautious and Good." She could have used a theme to explain her life.

"I like country," she called to him. "Got any Patsy Cline?" "Crazy" would also explain her life.

C.L. shook his head. Ten minutes later he turned down the lane, and Maddie saw Henry's little white farmhouse and the lawn behind it running for about a hundred yards right down to the river. There were trees down there, and a dilapidated dock, just as C.L. had promised. She hadn't been here in years, but it looked like yesterday.

C.L.'s aunt Anna came out on the porch as they got out of the car. "Hello, Maddie, honey," she said, doing a fairly good job of not staring at the bruising on Maddie's face.

"Hello, Anna." Maddie walked toward the porch, holding Em's hand. "Thank you for having us."

"Stay here, Em." C.L. started for the garage. "I'll get the fishing poles."

"Our pleasure." Anna smiled at Em. "This must be Emily. Haven't seen her since she was a toddler."

"How do you do," Em said politely, her little face solemn as she bent to pat the puppy that waddled beside her. "This is Phoebe. C.L. gave her to me."

Anna's eyes widened a little in surprise. "That was thoughtful of C.L." She glanced at Maddie, and Maddie smiled.

"Very thoughtful," she said, and Anna looked relieved.

"Fishing poles, Em," C.L. said, coming around the house. "We'll have fish for dinner."

"That's as may be," Anna said, "but I'm making pot roast just in case."

"Good," said C.L. "That'll take the pressure off." He jerked his head toward the river, and Em went to stand beside him, Phoebe tumbling behind her.

"Don't you let that child fall in the river now," Anna warned him.

C.L. rolled his eyes. "Come on, Em, they're cramping our style."

Anna and Maddie watched them walk off to the dock, C.L. going slowly so as not to lose Em, both followed by a meandering Phoebe.

"That's a lovely child, Maddie." Anna held the screen door open for her.

"I like her." Maddie followed Anna inside the house. "And now you're going to spoil her with real food. Are we having mashed potatoes?"

An hour later, the potatoes were peeled, and Maddie and Anna had swapped all the gossip they knew, although Maddie had kept any of her own news out of the conversation since, by some miracle, it wasn't gossip yet.

"Gloria Meyer." Anna shook her head. "Well, she should have known that wouldn't last."

"Sometimes you don't know," Maddie said, trying to be fair. "Sometimes it's all right in the beginning, and then things just go wrong."

Anna took the bowl to the sink and ran water over the naked potatoes.

"I'm getting a divorce," Maddie blurted, and felt like a fool. She braced herself for a lecture.

Anna dried her hands on a dish towel and put the potatoes on to boil. "Sometimes you have to. No shame in it. That child's going to get a sunburn out there." She went out the screen door and called from the porch, "Emily, come in and we'll make some cookies now. And, C.L., that grass needs to be mowed before your uncle gets home."

When she came back in, Maddie said, "I don't know why I told you that," and Anna said, "Eases my mind some. Thank you."

Maddie felt a little dizzy from trying to cope with everything that wasn't being said. "You're welcome," she said, and then spent the next hour watching Anna bend over Em as she dropped cookie dough on the sheets, while Phoebe slept exhausted in the corner.

Anna wants grandkids, Maddie thought, and since C.L. was being slow in that department, Anna was more than happy to take Em. Maddie wanted to say, *Listen, don't get ideas about C.L. and us*, but it would be cruel and unnecessary to say anything right now. Let Anna have her time with Em.

She turned to look out the window. C.L. had taken his shirt off and was pushing an old hand mower up and down the riverbank. He looked hot and sweaty and broad and strong and really good. She could use some time with C.L. *Don't think about it*. Anna was standing right there, for heaven's sake. Maddie turned away from the window and went to help finish dinner.

Henry came home half an hour later. "Glad you're here," he told her gruffly, and took Em out on the porch to teach her to play checkers. A little while later, C.L. broke off his mowing for dinner, and the five of them sat around Anna's big round table and passed platters of stringy tender beef, and bowls of potatoes whipped in cream, and gravy the color of mahogany, and tiny new peas, and biscuits that bled with butter. Em ate with great concentration while Maddie watched her, smiling in spite of the mess her life was in. Em had never had food like this. This food would clog her arteries and she'd have a heart attack at nine. But she'd go having tasted paradise.

Toward the end of dinner when the serious eating slowed, Henry and C.L. had a heated and technical discussion about gas-powered mowers, and Anna and Emily discussed future cookies.

Henry pointed his fork at C.L. "That push mower is as good as the day I bought it."

Beside him, Anna bent near Em. "You just roll some dough into a ball and then roll it in the cinnamon."

C.L. shook his head. "Hell, Henry, I lost ten pounds today just doing the back half of the lawn. You'll have a heart attack someday."

"With my fingers?" Em asked.

"City living," Henry said darkly.

Anna nodded. "Yep, with your fingers. Then you squash it down on the cookie sheet."

C.L. shrugged off the implied insult. "I can finish the lawn after dinner. I would have finished it before, but I didn't want to miss dinner. And Emily's cookies."

"We'll make cinnamon cookies the next time I come back," Em whispered to him.

"I can't wait," C.L. said.

Henry harrumphed to get C.L.'s attention back. "You never complained about that mower when you were a kid."

Anna stood up. "Anybody want some of Emily's chocolate chip cookies?"

C.L. tried to look superior. "That's because I was a good kid."

Both Anna and Henry looked at him in silence.

"I want some of Emily's cookies," C.L. said to change the subject.

"I'll get them." Em slid from her chair.

"What are you looking at me like that for?" C.L. said to his aunt and uncle. "I wasn't a delinquent."

"You were a pain in the ass," Henry said.

"I think I'll go out and finish the mowing." C.L. took some cookies off the plate Em had grabbed from the counter. "Thank you, Em."

"Was he a handful?" Maddie asked Anna as they washed the dishes while Em and Henry went out on the porch for one last game of checkers.

"Lord, yes," Anna said. "That's why we raised him. My sister Susan wanted him put in a home for delinquents, but we took him out here instead. I thought for a while he was going to be the death of Henry, but it worked out. He's a good boy," Anna said, rinsing the roast platter. "He just needed somebody to love him. And to tan his hide when he did wrong. He just needed to learn."

This was a side of C.L. Maddie had never thought about, C.L. as a kid. Like Em. "What did he do?"

"Fighting mostly. He was a terrible fighter. Really tried to hurt people." Anna stopped and stared into the distance, a puzzled look on her face. "I never did understand that, 'cause he was always so sweet with me. And gentle with animals? You should have seen him with animals. We thought for a while he might be a vet, he was that good with them. And with little kids. And then he'd go out and break somebody's jaw." Anna shook her head. "He always had a reason. Always said somebody was pickin' on somebody else or had done something evil, and everything would go red and he'd just hit."

Maddie swallowed. "But you said it worked out."

"Well, it did seem as if it took him longer than it would have other boys." Anna pulled the plug out of the sink drain and stared out the window as the water glugged down the drain. "I remember one time, Henry sent him into town to get us a couple of those galvanized trash cans." Anna wrung out her dishrag and draped it over the faucet. "He took them right out there," she said, pointing out the kitchen window, "but they were stacked, and they wouldn't come apart. I stood here and watched him get madder and madder, and then he stomped off to his car and got his baseball bat and came back and just beat those cans to pieces till there was nothing left but scrap."

"What did you do?" Maddie asked, suddenly cold. Could C.L. have gone after Brent? She tried to remember everything about C.L. since she'd seen Brent. He'd been happy when he'd come back to see her, until he saw her face, and then he'd gone off to find Brent. He said he hadn't, but—

Anna was answering her. "I just watched. Then he got back in the car and went off to town and came back with two more cans that he'd paid for with his own money. Not stacked. And that was the end of it."

"Dear Lord."

Anna turned to her and smiled reassuringly. "He eventually mellowed out some. And you know him now. Just as sweet as he can be. But I do think sometimes part of the old C.L. is still there. You know, he always was stubborn as a boy, and he still is. If he wants something bad enough, he gets it. Did then, does now."

Maybe not, Maddie thought.

Em came into the kitchen from the porch, looking over her shoulder to watch Phoebe waddle in behind. The mower had been silent for several minutes, and it was growing dark outside. Anna handed Maddie a couple of beers. "Take this out to C.L. Em and I'll watch television till bedtime." She smiled at Em. "You're going to sleep in C.L.'s old room."

"Phoebe, too?" Em said, her voice suddenly tense.

"Phoebe, too," Anna said, and Em went docilely off to watch

TV with a glass of milk, a plate of cookies, and her very own dog.

"She's never going to want to go home," Maddie said.

"Fine by me," Anna said, and went in to watch "The Simpsons" for the first time in her life while Maddie went out to meet C.L.

Chapter Ten

Maddie had to go clear down to the river and around the trees to find C.L. since he'd collapsed into a hammock down there. "I lied to Henry," he told her when she ducked under a branch to get to him. "That fucking machine isn't going to kill him; it's going to kill me."

Maddie handed him the beers. "Drink. You'll be okay."

He popped the top on the first beer and drank half of it down. "Come here and sit beside me."

His voice was low and went straight into her spine. Twenty-four hours ago, they'd been in the backseat. Maddie shivered a little at the memory. Now they were only a hundred yards from Em. "No, thank you." Maddie looked around at the dark landscape and the starry sky to distract her thoughts. "This is pretty down here."

"I have this hammock fantasy about us," C.L. said. "Come over here. I need TLC."

Maddie sat down on the ground, out of arm's reach, far enough away that she couldn't accidentally lean into him because it would feel so good. "Anna said you stole things when you were ten."

"If you're going to throw my past in my face, you can go now."

This was a good idea. The last thing she needed was to be out here in the dark with C.L. Maddie got up to go, and he leaned out of the hammock and caught at the hem of her shorts. "I lied. Don't go. Sit down and have a beer. I'll share."

He tugged on her shorts again, and she felt his fingers warm on the back of her thigh. It felt wonderful, which was a bad idea, so she pried his hand off the hem and then off her hand and sat on the ground again, her skin still tingling from his touch, changing the subject before she lost her mind and jumped him. "Was it nice growing up here?"

C.L. relaxed back into the hammock. "Mostly. Anna had a hard time with me. She was so sad when I screwed up. I couldn't stand that."

"My mom used guilt trips." Maddie leaned back in the cool grass. "Still does. She says, 'The neighbors will think I didn't raise you right.' Sometimes I think my whole life has been spent proving to the neighbors that my mother raised me right."

"She raised you right," C.L. said. "You're damn near perfect."

No, I'm not. That was the other Maddie, the one who'd been pretending for thirty-eight years, and Maddie felt a spurt of irritation that C.L. was still fixated on the fake instead of the real Maddie. Dreams must die really hard for him if he still thought she was a Good Girl after all the screaming they'd done the night before in the backseat.

Which reminded her of Bailey. "Not that perfect," she said. "I'm being blackmailed." C.L. sat up in the hammock and Maddie went on. "Bailey wants a hundred dollars to keep his mouth shut."

"What an idiot." C.L. relaxed back into the hammock. "I'll take care of him. He didn't upset you, did he?"

"Are you kidding? With everything else, Bailey is comic relief. But yes, I would appreciate it if you'd take care of him."

"My pleasure, ma'am. Rescues are my specialty. Want a beer?"

Maddie peered at him through the dark. "Are you trying to get me drunk?"

"No. I'm too wiped out by that damn mower to have ulterior motives. Christ, I must have mowed a thousand acres. Come here and comfort me."

"You are a man among men," Maddie said, searching for a topic to distract herself. "What's C.L. stand for?"

"Nothing."

"What do you mean, nothing? Your mother named you C.L.? Just the initials?"

"No," C.L. said. "My mother named me Wilson. It's a family name. Is this going to be a big deal?"

"Wilson Sturgis." She started to giggle and let it grow into a full-blown laugh. "So what does C.L. stand for?"

"Chopped Liver."

Maddie snorted in disbelief, and he explained. "One day I came home, I was about seven or eight, and my mother was talking to some old neighborhood lady about my sister, and it was, Denise can do this, and Denise can do that, and Denise is just too wonderful for words. So I said, 'Hey, what am I, Chopped Liver?' Denise called me Chopped Liver for a couple of weeks after that and then she shortened it to C.L. and it stuck."

Maddie sat stunned. "Did you mind?"

"Hell, it was better than Wilson." He sipped his beer. "I kind of liked naming myself, you know? I got to be whatever I wanted, no matter what my mom thought."

That sounded good, naming yourself, becoming whatever you wanted to be. Impractical, but good. Maddie leaned back in the grass to think about it and saw the moon, high and beautiful and spooky white. "It really is beautiful here."

"We really are going to make love in this hammock some-day," C.L. said.

All Maddie's peace went up in flames as desire slammed into her again. "Stop it." She stood up. "I think you're terrific, and I'm more grateful than I can ever tell you for what you've done for Em, and yes, I do really, really want you." She stopped for a moment at the thought. "But—"

"Not now," C.L. finished for her as he sat up in the hammock. "I know, Henry and Anna are just up the lawn and you're not divorced yet. I can wait, it's all right. And the things I do for Em are because I like Em, not for you, so you don't need to be grateful. Em and I do all right on our own."

Maddie stood caught by what he'd said. "Em and I," he'd said, as if he knew Em, as if she was somebody apart from the daughter of the woman he'd slept with. As if he was thinking of her as a person he knew, somebody he cared about in her own right. It was so far from any idea she had of what C.L. was that it took her breath away and made her want to fold into him, crawl into his arms and let him absorb her and Em and everything.

"I have to go in," she said. "Anna and Henry will be wonder-ing." She walked away from him then, as fast as she could, back toward the house and her daughter, and with every step she wanted to turn back more. When she reached the porch, she turned and saw him watching her in the moonlight, and that made everything even harder.

C.L. woke up early on his makeshift bed on the couch and joined Henry at a breakfast table crowded with plates of pancakes and strawberries and hash browns, and butter that shone in the sunlight, and syrup so thick it poured in ropes. "Want me to shout upstairs for Em and Maddie?" he asked, and Henry answered before Anna could. "Let them sleep. I need to talk to you. Isn't it about time you went back to the city?"

"Henry!" Anna came to sit with them, putting a jug full of foamy milk in front of C.L. "He can stay as long as he wants, the longer the better." She patted C.L.'s hand. "He's home where he belongs."

"He needs a vacation to cool off," Henry said. "He can come back home later."

"I've been thinking about that," C.L. said. "Coming home, I mean. Is that offer for the land next to the house still open?"

"Oh, C.L.," Anna said, and Henry scowled.

"You go back to the city and think about it," he told C.L. "You calm down first."

"That land's yours any time you want it, C.L.," Anna said. "You just say the word."

"I thought I might talk to Howie Basset sometime about a house," C.L. said to Henry. "Might be a good idea to have me next door. That way, we could go fishing a lot easier when you retire."

Anna nodded and smiled and undoubtedly kicked Henry on the ankle because C.L. saw him wince.

Henry looked torn. He said, "C.L., I am warning you," but

he said it without any force, and Anna broke in and said, "You go see Howie today. Bring him out here. He should start soon if you want to get in before Christmas. He could build it before Christmas, couldn't he, Henry?"

Henry shot C.L. a dirty look and picked up his fork. "If C.L. doesn't cool himself down here, he'll have it built by the weekend." He pointed his fork at C.L. "You always were a hothead, and it always got you in trouble, and it's doing the same thing now. You slow down and stay away from—" He broke off after a quick look at Anna. "You stay out of trouble," he finished.

Anna passed the hash browns to C.L. "You go see Howie today. It's Sunday, so he'll have the time."

"Yes, ma'am," C.L. said, and heaped potatoes on his plate while he ducked Henry's glare. He was going to move slow. But Anna was right, if he wanted Maddie and Em in a house with him any time soon, he'd have to see Howie today.

Right after he saw Brent.

"I'm warning you, C.L.," Henry said over his pancakes.

"I'm hearing you, Henry," C.L. said, and thought about Maddie and Em safe in a new house next door.

Maddie called her mother from the upstairs phone before she went down to breakfast. "Mom, this is Maddie. Don't come to the house to sit Em this morning, she's staying at the farm with Anna Henley."

"Well, what in the world is she doing out there?"

"We're both out here." Maddie tried to sound positive and truthful as she started into the story she'd rehearsed the night before. "Things have been hectic at home, so we came out here for a break."

Her mother's voice was sharp. "Where's Brent?"

"I don't know."

"Maddie, what's going on?"

Maddie took a deep breath. "I'm leaving him, Mom. I'm filing for divorce tomorrow."

The long silence told Maddie her marital trouble wasn't news to her mother. If it had been, she'd have said, "Oh, no, you can't," or something else off the top of her head. The silence meant she was choosing her strategy. *Forget it, Mother,* Maddie wanted to say. *You can't change my mind.* The problem was, her mother usually could. Of course, that was before the New Maddie. The one who slept with other men and poisoned her husband.

When her mother's voice came again, it was soothing. "Now, Maddie, I know he's a problem, but don't be hasty."

You have no idea how much of a problem, Mother. "I'm not being hasty. I've thought about it, and I know what I'm doing. I called a divorce lawyer."

"Oh, no, not Wilbur Carter."

"Jane Henries in Lima."

"Well, that's good. Anybody but Wilbur Carter." Her mother caught herself and went back to the fight. "Although I think you should think about this. Divorce, Maddie. I know your generation thinks it's nothing—"

"My generation does not think it's nothing."

"—but it's a terrible thing. Think of Emily."

I am thinking of Emily. She'd hate Rio. "Mom, I know what I'm doing."

"Well, there's no need to rush, is there? You don't need a divorce tomorrow, do you?"

Come to think of it, she didn't. With Brent safe in Brazil, she could take decades to get a divorce if she wanted. "No, Mother, I don't. I won't rush."

"That's all I ask."

For now, Maddie thought.

"And if you change your mind about Em, I'll be here." Her mother's tone implied that she was always where she was supposed to be, something her daughter certainly couldn't claim. "Are you sure you feel well enough to visit Gran?"

"As well as I ever feel when I'm visiting Gran," Maddie said. "Oh, and Em has a dog."

"What?"

"C. L. Sturgis gave her a puppy yesterday. They cannot be parted."

"Maddie, have you been seeing that man?"

Maddie closed her eyes and took a gamble. "Mother, have you heard that I've been seeing that man?"

Her mother's voice was doubtful when she answered. "No."

Maddie let out her pent-up breath. Bailey had kept his mouth shut. "Don't you think you would have heard if I had been?"

"Gloria said you sat on your picnic table with him for hours. Drinking."

"Gloria also hired Wilbur Carter. What does she know?"

"Well, I suppose you're right. What did you say this Sturgis boy does for a living?"

"I didn't. I don't know. I have to go."

"Call me when you get back from Gran's," her mother said, and Maddie hung up.

Em sat across the breakfast table from her mom and reached down for Phoebe, more to make sure she was with her than to pat her, but since her hand was down there and Phoebe expected pats every few minutes, she stroked her soft puppy head anyway. "I love Phoebe."

"I know. I like her pretty much, too."

Em went back to her breakfast pancakes, keeping one eye on her mother. "I like C.L., too."

Her mom sort of jumped, nervous, which was not good. Usually her mom was so calm she was boring. "He's a good guy," her mom said. "You need some more syrup?"

"So you like him, too?"

"He's an old friend. We were in high school together."

Her mom passed her the syrup. Em put it on the table beside her. Food wasn't what she was interested in, even though Anna's food was something else. "Was he in school with Dad, too?"

"Yes." Her mom cut into her pancakes and forked up a huge bite. "With Dad and Aunt Treva and Uncle Howie and a bunch of other people. Just like the friends you and Mel have." She popped the bite in her mouth, and Em leaned back to wait while she chewed so she could ask her another question. Her mother never took big bites. It was unhealthy. She must be stalling.

The high school thing was an interesting side trail, the idea that someday she and Mel would be grown-up and so would all their friends, and some of them would go away and come back. She wondered what Jason Norris would come back like. Maybe like Doug on *ER*. And he'd stop by to see her, like C.L. had.

Em frowned as her mother swallowed. "Were you like boyfriend and girlfriend?"

"Nope." Her mother passed her the strawberries, and Em put them next to the syrup. "The only boyfriend I ever had was your daddy. Boring, huh?"

"Maybe." Em swallowed and asked the question she didn't want to ask. "Where's Dad?"

Her mother blinked and looked peppy again. "Uh, well, I think he's working on something for the company."

Em felt cold. She was pretty sure that was a lie, or at least a cover-up. It didn't sound right. Something for the company didn't sound right. Not the way her mom said it.

Anna came back in the kitchen then and said, "Em, do you need anything?" and Em knew she had to shut up about her dad.

"No, thank you," she said. "This is delicious." It was, too; she just didn't want to eat. She wanted to know what was going on.

"It's Sunday, so I have to go see Great-Grandma today," her mom said, real peppy. "You're going to stay out here with Anna so Phoebe can run around. Is that okay?"

"I guess so," Em said.

"Anna said something about making strawberry pie," her mom said. "That sounds pretty good, doesn't it?"

"I guess so," Em said.

"We'll have a real good time," Anna said firmly.

"Wait'll you see the necklace I have for Great-Grandma," her mom said, and her voice sounded a little desperate.

Em gave up. "Let me see it."

Her mom dug the necklace out of her bag, and it was really ugly, a big gob of red glass hanging from a fake gold chain.

Em nodded. "She'll really like it. You're not wearing anything else, are you?"

"Nothing I want." Her mom sounded better again, but Anna was looking at them funny, so her mom said, "My grandmother has a way of taking whatever you have that she wants. So we distract her with stuff we don't want." She turned back to Em. "Right, Em?"

Her mom sounded like she really wanted Em to agree, like what Em said really mattered even though it didn't. Em just nodded.

Her mom put on the necklace and kissed Em good-bye. "Have a good time with Anna and Phoebe. Help with the dishes."

"Don't tell Great-Grandma about Phoebe," Em called as her mother went out the door. "She'll make me give her to her."

Anna had loaned Maddie her old station wagon ("I'm not going anywhere, you just take it"), and it was amazing how much better Maddie felt when she had a car again. It wasn't that Frog Point was so huge that a car was necessary, it was more that having one gave her the illusion she could escape if she had to. She couldn't, but at least the car made the idea plausible.

She definitely couldn't escape her grandmother.

Grandma Lucille sat swathed in bilious sea green chiffon under peach-pink sheets in her pale peach-pink room, looking like a bad parody of the flapper she'd once been. Her shoe-polish black bob framed her withered pixie face where only her sharp little black eyes were the same as they'd once been, tiny, shrewd, and hard as obsidian. Maddie hadn't inherited any of her gran's advantages, she'd been told a thousand times sitting in this room, not her pretty face, not her adventurous spirit, not her kick-ass spunk. But since Gran had long ago become the biggest pain in the butt the family had ever known, Maddie wasn't unduly upset by this lack of genetic similarity. "You wouldn't believe how it was when I was growing up, Maddie," her mother used to tell her when she was little. "She *humiliated* me. I would never do that to you."

Looking at Gran now, Maddie sent a silent thank-you to her mother and renewed her determination to pass the same lack of scandal onto her daughter. The last thing she wanted to be was the Gran of her generation.

Although traits were supposed to skip a generation. And there was C.L. and the Point. If she kept on the way she was going, she'd definitely be the Gran of the nineties. She had to get a grip on her life. But first she had to get this visit over with. She crossed the room, ignoring her grandmother's snarls that Maddie was putting on weight and looking her age, and parted the peach-pink linen-look drapes that led to her grandmother's small terrace.

"Too much light." Gran's voice was scratchy and sharp. "Bad for my skin. Yours, too, but you're hopeless."

Maddie compromised on half-closed drapes, knowing if she'd left them closed, her grandmother would have moaned that there wasn't enough light.

"So, Gran," Maddie said brightly as she came to sit beside the bed. "How are you?"

"I'm ninety-five, how do you think I am?" her grandmother snapped.

You're eighty-three, Maddie wanted to tell her, but she fought the impulse. Getting into an argument with Gran was the personal equivalent of a land war in Asia. "Well, I'm hoping you're doing fine," Maddie said. "You look wonderful."

"That's because I don't go around sitting in bright sunlight like some people I know." Gran leaned forward. "That Janet Biedemeyer next door? The woman's a wreck. She looks like alligator luggage. Put a handle on that woman's back, she could fly cargo. And she's twenty years younger than I am if she's a day. If I'd—" Gran stopped and squinted at Maddie. "What the hell happened to you?"

Maddie stifled a sigh. "I ran into a door, Gran. It's fine."

"Ha!" Gran leaned back against her pillows, delighted. "Hit you, did he? I thought he looked the type."

"No, Gran," Maddie said as sternly as she could fake. "Brent did not hit me. I tripped and fell against the edge of an open door."

"Sure. That's why there's those cuts on your cheek from his

ring," Gran said, and Maddie sat up a little. "Oh, yes, now you'll pay attention. Well, you've come to the right place for help." *Oh no, I haven't,* Maddie thought, but her grandmother went on. "I've been there myself. Now, here's what you do—"

"Grandpa *never* hit you," Maddie said, forgetting to be diplomatic in her outrage. "I don't believe it. You should be ashamed—"

"Not your grandpa," Gran broke in, exasperated. "He never lifted a hand to me." Gran grimaced, as if there was something about his lack of violence that still annoyed her. "I'm talking about my first husband."

Maddie sat back. "I thought he was your first husband."

"Nope." Her grandmother sat back, too, now in control. "My first was that worthless fathead Buck Fletcher."

Maddie tried not to grin. "Buck? You married somebody named Buck?"

"Beats Brent," her grandmother sneered back. "What a world with a name like that in it."

Don't get her started, Maddie told herself, and ducked the argument. "I can't believe you were married before and nobody ever told me."

Her grandmother shrugged. "He died before you were born. I didn't mourn much, I can tell you." Her grandmother cackled and then zeroed back in on Maddie's face. "You can't use makeup for squat, child."

"Thank you, Gran," Maddie said, wishing she could follow Gran down the attractive side trail of Buck-the-secret-first-husband but pretty sure it would lead to shared reminiscences of abuse, just what she didn't need. "I brought you candy." She leaned over to open her bag and let the red glass pendant swing forward.

"Thank you," her grandmother said automatically, one claw stretched out to take the gold box Maddie fished from her bag. "Esther Price. Good." She tore the red ribbon off the box of hand-dipped chocolates. "Small box."

"I'll bring another next week," Maddie told her. "I always do."

"You're a good girl, Maddie." Gran bit into the milk chocolate turtle that sat on the top of the box. That was another irritating thing about Gran: she always took the turtles and then spit the nuts out. One went sailing across the room even as Maddie had the thought. "Good," her grandmother said, and then she refocused on the pendant. "Pretty necklace."

"This?" Maddie held up the red glass slab. "It's a family heirloom. From Brent's family." She tried to look enthused about it. "It's one of my favorite pieces. I—"

"I'm not going to be with you much longer, you know," Gran said weakly, sinking back against the pillows, the box of chocolates in one hand, the mutilated turtle in the other. "I'm old."

No kidding, Maddie wanted to say, but she nodded instead, working to look sympathetic. "Well, you certainly don't look old," she lied. "You look better than I do." Unfortunately with the current condition of her eye, that one was marginally true.

Gran sniffed. "I could go anytime." She put the half-eaten turtle back in the box and put her free hand over her heart. "Anytime."

"Oh, gee, Gran," Maddie said. "Is there anything I can do?"

"That necklace would go good with this nightie." Gran patted the bilious green chiffon.

The red glass would look ghastly with that nightie, but then, so did Gran. "Well, I don't know, Gran," Maddie said. "It was Brent's mother's—"

"*That* woman." Gran forgot to look fragile as she sneered. "Helena Faraday never had a well-dressed day in her life." Gran snorted at the thought and then remembered she was at the point of death and sank back against the pillows again. "I'm sure she won't mind if you loan the necklace to your dying gran, Maddie. After all—" here Gran paused to look pious, giving, and beatific, all of which were beyond her "—you'll get everything when I go."

"Well, if you think it will make you feel better," Maddie said, having had enough Sarah Bernhardt for one visit. She pulled the necklace over her head and passed it across to her grandmother, who strung it around her own neck and went back to eviscerating the turtle.

Maddie stood up. "Well, you're looking much better, Gran, so—"

"Sit down," her grandmother ordered, all weakness gone. "I haven't told you the news."

Maddie sat down, looking longingly at the Esther Price. If she had to listen to nursing-home scandal, she should at least be eating chocolate, but her grandmother would do her bodily injury if she tried.

"Mickey Norton is flashing again." Gran put down the half-eaten turtle and picked up a chocolate cream. "Abigail Rock two doors down gets all upset, but at least Mickey's still trying. That Ed Keating down at the end of the hall doesn't even get out of bed anymore. It's terrible the way men fall apart as they age."

"Oh, I don't know," Maddie said, thinking of C.L. "Some of them get better."

Gran snorted again. "Like your husband?"

"I've really got to go, Gran," Maddie said, standing up, and Gran said, "Sit down," and she did, listening to all the scandal her grandmother had stored up for a week. Fortunately Gran had a machine-gun delivery, so she could do the week in half an hour.

"And now there's you," she finished. "Look at you, all beat up. Everybody in this place knows you're my granddaughter. There goes my good name." She looked forlorn for a moment, and then picked up another cream.

"It's not your name," Maddie pointed out. "It's Brent's. It's a Faraday scandal or a Martindale scandal. They'd have to go back three generations to make it a Barclay scandal."

Her grandmother leaned forward, incensed. *"And you think they won't?"*

Maddie drew back a little. For the people in this home, three generations was yesterday. "You're right. Sorry about the eye, Gran. I shouldn't have come. I won't come back until it's all healed."

"Ha!" her grandmother shouted. "You think they won't notice that, too? You come back here next Sunday, just like always. Learn to use makeup by then. The scandal. Ha!"

Maddie stood up to go.

"Sit down!" her grandmother said.

"Can't." Maddie began her sideways shuffle to the door. "Gotta go. Next week, I promise. 'Bye, Gran."

"I'll be dead by next weekend." Her grandmother picked up another cream, this one with a walnut on top.

"You look great in that necklace, Gran," Maddie said, and closed the door behind her. As she turned away, she heard the walnut bounce off it.

The back door was ajar when Maddie got home.

She stood on the back porch, her key in her hand, and stared stupidly at the open door. The door routinely popped open if it wasn't slammed shut, but she'd locked everything before she'd left.

Brent.

She nudged the door with her hand. It swung open the rest of the way, and she walked tentatively across the threshold.

Everything looked the same. Maybe she hadn't locked the door after all. She remembered slamming it to make sure it had closed—no, she had locked it. She was sure she had locked it.

"Brent?" she called, her voice quavering a little. She put her purse on the counter and went into the living room. Everything there looked the same, too, except for the desk.

The drawers were crooked, just a little, all of them a little off center. Maddie went through all of them. The safe-deposit key was gone.

Brent had come to get the safe-deposit key. And Em. He'd come back tonight and take her unless she stopped him.

She went to the hall and picked up the phone and dialed the police station. "I'm not sure," she said, when the dispatcher asked her what was wrong. "But I think the prowler was here."

The police dusted the drawer for fingerprints and found only hers, and asked her questions she couldn't answer ("I have no idea why the prowler would want our safe-deposit key"), and seemed skeptical until she said, "Listen, will you watch the house tonight? I'm afraid," and some of her real fear must have seeped into her voice because they told her they'd keep a squad car out in front. If she could keep Brent out of the house for one more night, she could put her life back together.

If she could convince Em to stay at the farm one more night, they'd be even safer.

It didn't seem like too much to ask.

When the police left, she searched the house, looking for more evidence that Brent had been there. He was everywhere, having lived there for so long, his magazines and his work shoes and his pocket change, and she wanted him out, completely out, now. It was time. She dragged a couple of cardboard boxes from the garage and began to pack his things.

Three hours and several boxes later, she was down to his closet in their bedroom. She opened the last two boxes and dumped his clothes in, not bothering to fold them. Some things were missing as she packed: his favorite cotton shirts, his jeans, a lightweight suit, his bowling shoes. He'd packed, she realized as she pulled his things off the hanger. He'd already taken what he wanted. She pushed the last of the clothes into the boxes and dragged the boxes out to the open garage with the rest of his stuff. Then she went back upstairs to clean his sports junk out of the back of the closet.

His baseball bat, she put to one side. She could use it on Brent if he came back. The bastard had *packed* already. She'd known he was going to leave her, but somehow knowing he'd packed made her madder. She yanked out his golf bag and it tipped over. A dozen golf balls rolled across the floor and the clubs clattered out. Not her day.

Maddie propped the bag up and tried to stuff the clubs back in, but they wouldn't go all the way, so she dumped them out and then wrestled the bag upside down to see what was stuck in the bottom. A small package fell out.

For a while she just sat on the edge of the bed and looked at the package on the floor. God knew what was in it. Pornography? Cocaine? At this rate, it could be Jimmy Hoffa's ashes and she wouldn't be surprised. Nothing could surprise her anymore.

When she unwrapped it, it was money, four packages of hundred-dollar bills. Forty thousand dollars. It was like Monopoly money, only it was real.

"What the hell has he been doing?" she said out loud, and then thought, *Get-away money.*

The sound of someone pounding on the door downstairs woke her out of her stupor. She pushed the four bundles of money under the mattress, threw the wrapping in the trash, and ran downstairs.

"What took you so long?" C.L. asked when she opened the door. "I thought you were dead." He sounded half-serious.

"I was thinking."

"I warned you about that." He pushed his way in and tilted her chin up to look at her. "Your face looks better. Sort of."

"What do you do for a living?"

"I'm an accountant." He shut the door behind him. "Em's still at the farm, right?"

"Right—" Maddie began, and then he kissed her, shutting off all speech, his lips warm on hers, his arms squashing her against him. She leaned into him to prolong the kiss because it felt so good and so few things had felt good lately and because for all her highfalutin' speeches about waiting to avoid the scandal, she'd missed him. It was hell being smart when what she wanted to be was Gran.

Then his hands moved down her back and she broke the kiss and moved away before he got her in more trouble. "Stop that. Somebody will look through a window and see."

C.L. drew her into the living room. "You and I need some time alone. Henry said you had a prowler."

Maddie tried to remember where they'd been before the kiss. "You're an accountant?"

C.L. sighed. "What's wrong with being an accountant?"

"Nothing. I just hadn't pictured you as an accountant." Maddie thought about it. "Actually, I hadn't pictured you employed."

C.L. leaned back away from her. "Thank you very much. Now, about your prowler—"

"Why are you so interested in this prowler?"

C.L. looked exasperated. "A stranger breaks into the house of the woman I love, and you're surprised I'm interested?"

"He might not have been a stranger," Maddie said, ignoring the "woman I love" bit as a complication she wasn't ready to deal with. "I locked the doors last night, so whoever got in either knows how to pick locks or had a key."

C.L. sat up again, interested. "Who has keys?"

"My mother, Treva, and Brent."

He met her eyes. "My money would be on Brent."

Maddie nodded. "Mine, too."

"What would he be looking for?"

"I went to the bank yesterday," she said. "I looked in our safe-deposit box."

"Go on." C.L. seemed tense, as if he were listening very hard.

"There are two tickets to Rio in there and two passports."

C.L. whistled. "Ducking out on you, is he?"

Maddie nodded. "The tickets are for Monday. The other passport was Em's."

He winced. "That must have been a shock."

"I took Em's passport out and ripped it up. He might have come back to look for it. And the safe-deposit key is gone." She thought about the clothes he'd packed. "And so is he, I hope."

"Hold that thought," he said, and leaned down and kissed her, brushing his lips across her so lightly he made her shiver.

"I like it when you do that," she whispered, and he said, "Good. I'll do it all the time." He kissed her again, slower, and just as she was feeling very warm, a car door slammed outside and he started. "This town," he said, and pulled away from her to look out her window. "Not your mom. Some washed-out blonde next door."

"Gloria." She hated it that he'd pulled away, but she was re-lieved at the same time. "I think she might be the one Brent's sleeping with."

C.L. squinted out the window. "Jesus, why?"

"You always say the right thing," she said, but he'd moved on.

"You stay here with the chain on. I'll go check with Henry to make sure he knows to watch that safe-deposit box."

"Hey," Maddie said. "Don't screw this up. I want him out of here."

"You and I may, babe," C.L. said as he headed for the door, "but there are a lot of people who want him to stay and explain a few things. It'll be easier for all of us if he does."

Maddie followed him. "C.L., there's something going on here I don't know about, isn't there?"

"Don't ask me," he said. "I'm a stranger here myself." He kissed her again, hard this time, making her clutch at him, but he glanced guiltily over his shoulder after he did it. Then he was gone before she could ask him anything else.

Maddie watched him drive away, and thought, *Later for you, buddy.* She'd use her womanly wiles on him, and he'd tell her everything. Once she got past her own struck-dumb-by-lust part.

She went back upstairs and counted the money under the mattress again. Forty thousand dollars. Why hadn't he taken it last night? He'd have to come back for it. He couldn't have forgotten it.

What if the prowler wasn't Brent?

It made no sense. It had to be Brent; nobody else could use the safe deposit key.

Just go away, she thought. *I want you out of my life.* Then she remembered the pills. Had she already gotten him out per-manently? Oh, hell.

She stuffed the money back under the mattress and grabbed her bag. It was only a mile to the pharmacy. She could make it before they closed.

At Revco, Maddie showed the pharmacist the empty bottle of pain killers.

"How dangerous are these?" she asked. "I mean, if I took too many. Say seven."

The pharmacist gave her a lecture on abusing prescription drugs and then told her that seven probably wouldn't hurt anyone permanently. "They would impair judgment and probably cause unconsciousness." He looked at her sternly. "Exceeding the recommended dosage is a very bad idea."

"I couldn't agree more," Maddie said, and let go of the fear that she was a murderer; as far as she was concerned, Brent's judgment had always been impaired and he probably needed the sleep anyway. She asked for a refill, which the pharmacist gave her, scowling with suspicion, and then she went home to finish cleaning Brent out of her life. "While you were sleeping," she could tell him, "you moved."

She put the last of his things—including his golf bag with the money—in the garage. Whatever he needed to get to Rio, he could pick up in the garage.

While she was closing the garage door, a car drove up.

It was a late-model Ford, and Maddie had never seen the woman who got out before. She was sharp-eyed but pleasant-looking, and she was a redhead, so she wasn't Brent's latest, but Maddie braced herself anyway, waiting for the worst. This was one of Brent's ex-lovers. This was somebody Brent had cheated. This was C.L.'s secret wife. She winced on the last one and tried to be calm as the woman came up to her.

"You closing up a garage sale?" the woman asked.

Maddie blinked at her. "Pardon?"

"It's Sunday," the woman said. "People close up garage sales cheap on Sunday." She took a step back and looked around. "I thought you might be having one. I guess not. Sorry."

"A garage sale," Maddie heard herself say. She yanked the garage door up again. "Sure. It's just men's clothes. And some sports stuff." She remembered the money and said, "But not the golf clubs."

The woman's eyes narrowed. "What size clothes?"

It was probably wrong to sell Brent's stuff to a total stranger, but he should have thought of her before he'd cleaned out their checking and savings accounts. She had to sell his stuff. She was out of money.

"Mostly extralarge," Maddie said. "Make me an offer."

Ten minutes later, the woman drove off with a great deal on everything but Brent's golf clubs, and Maddie went back upstairs. She moved her clothes over to fill up the closet and tossed some of her underwear and sweaters in the empty drawers. When she was done, she'd reclaimed the entire room as hers.

She should have felt guilty, but she didn't. She felt free. She looked around it and thought, *I hate this place. I have to get out of here. It's ugly.*

The peach quilted headboard was especially ugly. Brent had picked it out. It should go, too.

Maddie got a screwdriver, unscrewed the brackets at the bottom, and pulled the headboard free. Then she dragged it down the stairs and threw it in the garage.

Gloria Meyer came out to watch her. "Is that *your* bed?"

"Spring cleaning." Maddie looked at Gloria and thought, *Vampire, huh?* and went back inside to do battle with whatever came after her next.

. . .

Brent wasn't hiding at the company when C.L. got there, but Howie was there, even though it was Sunday.

"Seven-day week?" C.L. said when Howie came down to open the door, looking the same solid, steady guy he'd been in high school, with less hair.

"Just the man I wanted to see." Howie waved him in.

"I was looking for Brent," C.L. began, and Howie said, "He's gone to ground somewhere. Forget him. I want you to look at our books."

"You're kidding." C.L. followed him into his office. "I've been hunting for Brent for three days trying to get permission to do just that."

Howie's computer was on, and his desk was slathered in printouts. "He wouldn't have given it to you." Howie motioned him to a chair and sat down in front of his computer. "He was embezzling. I know he was, I just can't find it."

"Sheila was right then." C.L. pulled his chair closer to the computer. "She always did know money. What have you got?"

"A mess," Howie said. "Brent handled the sales and the books, and I did the plans and the construction. It worked great until about a year ago when we started selling more houses and making less money."

"Ouch," C.L. said.

Howie nodded. "Then Dottie Wylie started complaining. She's selling the house we built for her last year. I thought Brent had underbid it, which wasn't like him. He always wanted the bids jacked up. That house was worth two hundred easy, and he bid it at one eighty."

C.L.'s eyes narrowed. "So why's Dottie complaining?"

"She says she's taking a loss on the house. And she's asking two ten. I went over and talked to her, and she showed me the paperwork to prove it." Howie looked tired. "She paid two twenty."

"Brent took the other forty thousand," C.L. said. "Jesus, he was screwing everybody."

"And the whole town knows it, thanks to Dottie." Howie rubbed his forehead.

C.L. frowned. "If that was the case, why the hell did Stan buy in?"

"Buy in what?" Howie said.

"The company," C.L. said. "Stan bought half of Brent's half for two hundred and eighty thousand, and Sheila's having a fit."

The look on Howie's face told C.L. this was all news to him. "Brent doesn't have half," Howie said. "He has a quarter. So do I. Treva and Maddie have the other two quarters."

"He sold out completely?" C.L. said, and Howie met his eyes.

"He's gone then." Howie settled back. "He's sold out, which he can't do without offering the three of us first refusal, so the whole deal is illegal." He shook his head. "What does Maddie think about all this?"

C.L. slumped down a little in his chair. "Hard to tell. I'm not even sure she knows about it. She thinks he's leaving because there's another woman, but there's more to it than that. She's still protecting him." C.L. stopped there because that part hurt. "She doesn't want us watching his safe-deposit box or trying to stop him from leaving."

"Can't blame her there," Howie said. "If I was married to Brent, I'd want him gone, too. Dumb bastard. He was talking the other night about how much he hated Frog Point and being Brent Faraday and running for mayor. Looks like he finally did something about it."

C.L. tried not to grin at the news. Em was safe, Maddie was free, and he was coming home to both of them. "Good for Brent. The dumb bastard finally did something I like."

"Well, I'm not happy about it." Howie sighed and then jerked his thumb at the numbers on his computer screen. "I hear you're an accountant. I could use an accountant."

"Now, there's a coincidence," C.L. said. "I could use a house."

Howie blinked at him. "Here? In Frog Point?"

"Yeah," C.L. said. "Surprised me, too. Let me use your phone to tell Sheila that Stan just got taken for a ride, and then we'll work something out."

Em called from the farm half an hour after Maddie had the house cleaned. "Phoebe and I want to come home," Em said, and there were undertones of hysteria in her voice. "I want to see Daddy."

"I don't know if Daddy's going to be home tonight," Maddie said. "Why don't we wait until—"

"*I want to come home,*" Em said, and Maddie said, "I'll be out in an hour. Hang on."

Okay, Em needed to be home, so she'd come home. But she needed to be safe, too. C.L. could keep her safe, but he couldn't stay the night. If he couldn't stay the night, Maddie wasn't sure she could keep her safe, even with the police out front.

Her head hurt.

While she was struggling with her options, the phone rang.

"Maddie?" Treva said. "You had a prowler last night?"

"How did—"

"Howie ran into C.L. Are you okay?"

"I'm fine." Maddie checked her reflection in the vanity mirror. She wasn't fine. If anything, her bruise looked worse, the purple seeping into dirty yellow around the edges. "I look like hell, but I'm fine."

"Howie said C.L. is worried about you. He said he's serious about you."

"Forget C.L.," Maddie said. "I have a problem. I think Brent might be going to try to take Em."

"Take her?" Treva's voice was shocked. "Kidnap her?"

"Things are bad here," Maddie said. "I just have to keep her safe one more night. I took her out to the Henley farm last night, but she won't stay out there anymore. She hasn't seen Brent since day before yesterday. She's scared." Maddie's voice shook on the last word. "So am I."

"We'll come over," Treva said. "All of us. He can't take her if there's a crowd there."

"You can't stay all night," Maddie said. "I don't know what to do."

"Well, we can stay until we figure out what to do," Treva said. "Are you going out to get her now? We'll meet you when you get home. We'll tell the kids we're having a pizza party. They'll buy it."

Maddie leaned against the wall, reprieved again for a few hours. "I owe you, Treve."

"No, you don't," Treva said, and her voice sounded grim. "You don't owe me a damn thing. Listen, I called to find out if you wanted any help opening the box from Brent's office."

The box of letters. Kristie's baby. "I don't care anymore," Maddie said, trying to sound uninterested so Treva wouldn't get curious. "I think I'll just pitch the whole thing."

"Better not. There might be something in there the company needs. I'll come get it and see if I can open it."

Maddie frowned. "I'll just give it to you tonight. That'll be easier. It's no big deal, Treva."

"Fine," Treva said. "And don't worry about that box. There's probably nothing in it."

"Right." Maddie hung up and thought, *What does Treva think is in that box?*

Treva had a key to the house. And she'd known about the prowler. Why would C.L. be talking to Howie today? He'd sounded like he'd be making a beeline from her to Henry. If he hadn't told Howie, how did Treva know about the prowler? Unless she'd been the prowler. She hadn't even asked if anything was taken.

No. Maddie shook her head as she got up. She was getting paranoid. Treva was her best friend. C.L. was protecting her. Next she'd suspect her mother. *Forget it and order dinner,* she told herself, and called in an order for three large pizzas, two deluxe and one vegetarian, to be delivered at eight.

She went out to drive back to the farm and closed the garage door before Mrs. Crosby noticed how slovenly she'd been, stacking boxes in her garage and leaving them there for the whole street to see. Twilight seeped in, and somebody pulled up in front of the house in a pickup.

When the driver got out and started up the drive, she recognized Stan Sawyer.

It wasn't Brent. Nothing else mattered, as long as it wasn't Brent.

"Maddie?"

"Hi, Stan." Maddie tried to sound as cordial as she could, but her voice must have communicated *What the hell do you want?* because he stopped and stood there, shifting his rangy body from foot to foot. "Uh, is Brent around?"

"No," Maddie said. "Can I have him call you when he gets home?"

"He was supposed to meet with me yesterday morning, but he never showed. I need to talk to him real soon. *Real* soon." Stan came closer, and Maddie began to feel uneasy, which was stupid. She was in Frog Point. He couldn't hurt her; the whole block was watching. "You sure he's not here?"

"Howie's coming over any minute," Maddie offered. "He probably knows anything Brent knows."

"No." Stan edged a little closer. "I think Brent's up to no good. I think he's running away."

So do I, she thought, *but I don't want to hear it from you.* "I don't know anything about it." Maddie turned toward the house.

He grabbed her arm. "You gotta hear this. He's got my money."

She tried to pull away, but he held on, jerking her elbow up to her shoulder to hold her. "You're in as much trouble as he is," Stan said, and then they were blinded by the lights of a car turning in the drive.

"This better be Brent," Stan said.

The car stopped, the lights dimmed, and C.L. got out. "Let go of her," he said, coming toward them, his face grim.

Chapter Eleven

This has nothing to do with you, C.L.," Stan said. "This is between me and the Faradays."

"Let go of her."

Maddie tried to pull away from Stan, but he held on to her arm. C.L. looked like murder, like she'd never seen him. "Wait a minute, C.L.—"

Stan ignored her and spoke straight to C.L. "You're the one who started all this, coming back here. Butt out and let me finish it." Stan let go of Maddie, and she stumbled back a little as he stepped forward. "If I'd known Sh—"

C.L. swung at Stan, and Maddie winced at the sound of knuckles clumsily hitting flesh. Stan lost his balance and went down on the creosote, landing on his butt, swearing.

"Don't touch Maddie," C.L. said. "Ever."

Mrs. Crosby came out on her porch. "Maddie," she yelled. "What's going on?"

"What are you doing?" Maddie said to C.L. "Are you out of your mind?"

"Maddie?" Mrs. Crosby bellowed again.

"It's nothing, Mrs. Crosby," Maddie yelled over to her. "Stan just lost his balance. We're fine."

Mrs. Crosby didn't move.

C.L. nursed his hand without looking at her. "Go in the house, Maddie." He nodded to Stan. "C'mon. You've been wanting to do this for a while. Let's go."

"No." Maddie pushed in front of him. "Absolutely not. What's wrong with you guys? You're not sixteen anymore. Stop this."

C.L. tried to move her to one side. "Maddie—"

"No." She turned to C.L. "No more hitting."

He stood rigid for a moment, and then she felt his body relax, and he put his arms around her and gathered her in close. She thought, *Mrs. Crosby should love this*, but she almost didn't care, it felt so good to have him touch her again.

C.L. sighed. "Okay. You're right. This is dumb." He looked at Stan on the ground. "I'm sorry. Just don't lean on Maddie anymore. She doesn't know anything about anything."

"Well, I'll be damned." Stan eased himself up to a sitting position and felt his jaw for a moment. Evidently nothing was broken, because he rested his arms on his knees and laughed. "You and Maddie. Brent know about this?"

C.L. glared at him, and Maddie tightened her hold on him just in case he had any more brilliant ideas about hitting people in the middle of the street.

"You want your teeth?" C.L. said to Stan.

Stan laughed again. "This is a good one." He got up and brushed himself off. "God, does Brent deserve this." He grinned at C.L. "Hell, C.L. I don't have to hit you. Brent'll do it for me. He'll kill you. Both of you."

"Wait a minute, you don't underst—" Maddie began, but C.L. overrode her.

"Looking forward to that, are you?" he asked Stan, but there wasn't any animosity in his voice.

Maddie glanced up at him. All the rage was gone, like magic. If it hadn't been so frightening, it would have been amazing.

Stan shook his head. "God, this is gonna be good. Wait till I tell Sheila." He walked down the drive, still laughing.

"I should have hit him harder." C.L. watched him go. "In the old days, he wouldn't have been able to talk."

Oh, great. So now it was the good old days. She glared up at him and moved away, hating how the warmth went when she wasn't close to him. "What the hell was that all about?"

"I'm not real sure. It's probably got something to do with him marrying my ex-wife." C.L. slung his arm around her shoulders again and turned toward the house, bringing her with him. "I doubt Sheila's told him I'm a real good guy."

"Maddie?" Mrs. Crosby called again.

"Good night, Mrs. Crosby," Maddie called back, and then she shook her head at C.L. even as she leaned closer to him. "It was something about Brent. And what did he mean, you started it? And what did you mean, I don't know anything about anything?"

"I don't know, Mad." C.L. looked sober in the twilight. "There's something wrong out at the company, and it's not good. A lot of people want to see your husband, and they're not happy."

"What did Stan mean when he said you started it?"

"I don't know," he said again. "So, you got anything to eat in there? Hitting people makes me hungry."

He pulled her toward the back door, and she went with him up the back walk to continue the conversation. "This is not over," she said.

"Don't I know it," C.L. said, and held the kitchen door open for her.

C.L. went out and brought Em and Phoebe in from the farm. Treva and her family showed up shortly after they walked in the back door, followed by Maddie's mother, who'd gotten tired of waiting for a phone call that never came, followed by the pizzas, which Maddie's mother insisted on paying for, and the eight of them decamped into the family room, the adults surrounding Em like a cocoon.

"Do you have the box from the office?" Treva whispered to her in the hall.

"Yes, and I got it open," Maddie said in equally low tones. "You're not going to believe what was in there."

"Oh?" Treva spilled her Coke and bent to mop it up with a napkin. "Good stuff?"

"Love letters. Dozens. The ones from Beth are really sad."

Treva looked up at her. "You're taking this awfully well."

"Well, I still loathe Beth for sleeping with my husband, but I don't like my husband much and she does. It's very confusing." Maddie bit into her pizza, feeling her teeth sink through the chewy cheese.

"What else was in there?" Treva asked, but then Phoebe gobbled her fortieth piece of pepperoni and threw up and there was general chaos until the kids took Phoebe outside.

"*Wait*," Maddie said as Em got up to go, but Three said, "I'm on it, Aunt Maddie, it's cool," and stayed close to Em as they went outside.

Maddie moved to sit by the window so she could watch

them. Three stuck to Em like glue, keeping an eye on the driveway.

"He's a good kid," Treva said next to her. "She'll be fine."

"He is a good kid," Maddie said. "Thanks."

"Maddie, what is going on here?" her mother asked, and Treva said, "Hey, you tell us. What's new? Is Gloria really getting that divorce?"

Gloria's divorce was good for ten minutes, and Maddie took it all in while she watched C.L. He sat on the floor, his broad shoulders leaning against her couch, his long legs stretched across her family room rug, and she felt herself go warm just watching him move, a thick glow that moved out from her solar plexus and settled anywhere there were nerve endings. She couldn't have him tonight—there was no way with Em there—but she could enjoy looking at him, listening to his low voice and laughter. *I could listen to him forever,* she thought, and then jerked her mind back to the conversation before she had any other dumb thoughts.

The talk turned to Mrs. Crosby's daughter, who was on a liquid diet, and Margaret Erlenmeyer, who was pregnant again, and Harold Whitehead, who had taken Candace Lowery to dinner even though his wife had only been dead two months. "Said it was a business dinner," Maddie's mother said, and sniffed. "I don't think so."

The kids came back in, Mel talking loudly about dessert, and Maddie's mother stood and said, "It's late, I must be going."

Maddie followed her mother to the front door, casting one glance back at C.L., who grinned at her and made her breath go.

"How was Gran?" her mother asked when they reached the porch. "Do you think she's happy?"

That woman's never had a happy day in her life and she likes it like that, Maddie wanted to tell her, but instead she said, "She's in clover. Mickey Whosis is flashing again, and somebody in the next room has terrible skin." Maddie watched her mother's face. "I didn't know she'd been married before Grandpa."

Her mother turned away and crossed the porch. "It was a long, long time ago. It doesn't matter now. That was very nice of that Sturgis boy to buy Em such a nice little dog."

Counterattack, Maddie thought. *Nice job, Mom.* "Yes, wasn't it? Drive carefully on your way home."

"It's nice that you have such nice friends," her mother went on, not going down the steps.

"I'm a lucky woman," Maddie said. "Make sure you put your lights on."

"Well, Maddie, of course I'll put my lights on. It's pitch dark." Her mother frowned at her. "Madeline, is there anything going on with that man that I should know about?"

Maddie thought about everything that had gone on with that man. There wasn't nearly enough of it, and the tension and need that had been simmering all night became more insistent. "No, Mother."

Her mother turned to go down the steps. "Well, don't do anything foolish just because you think you might be divorcing Brent. Where is Brent tonight? Em is worried."

Maddie leaned in the doorway. "I have no idea. I assume with the woman he's been having the affair with."

Her mother stood motionless in the porch light. "You didn't tell me that."

"I'm surprised you didn't know," Maddie said. "You really hadn't heard anything?"

"No more than usual." Her mother slumped a little. "I guess it really is over then, isn't it?"

"Yes, Mother." Maddie felt sorrier for her mother than she did for herself. She was going to be free and make love with C.L.—*quiet*, she told her libido—and Em would be safe, but her mother would have a divorce in the family.

"Whatever you need, Maddie, you call me. Anything."

Maddie bit her lip. Just when she got to feeling superior, her mother would pull something like this and make Maddie realize how much she loved her. "Thank you, Mom. I will."

"I wish it wasn't happening." Her mother's voice broke a little, and Maddie went down the steps to comfort her.

"We're going to be better," she said, putting her arms around her mother. "I haven't been happy in a long time, but I wasn't unhappy, either, so there wasn't a reason to leave. Now I can figure out how to be happy."

"That's all I've ever wanted," her mother said. "For you to be happy." She straightened. "The town's going to have a field day, that's for sure."

"Well, it was about our turn," Maddie said. "They haven't had a go at our family since Gran was married to Buck."

Her mother scowled at her. "Don't listen to that woman. She makes things up to make herself interesting."

"Gran doesn't need to make things up to be interesting," Maddie said. "She's a one-woman show just sitting there with her mouth closed."

"Oh, dear. I know."

"Go home, Mom," Maddie said. "Things will be fine tomorrow. I'll file for divorce, the town will discuss it and decide that since Brent cheated he deserves it, everybody will be sorry for us for a couple of weeks because we're so nice, and then somebody else will do something stupid and they'll all talk about that. We're the good guys in this one. We'll be okay."

"All right." Her mother patted her arm. "I love you. Take care of Em. It's going to be so hard for her."

"I know." Maddie was about at her limit. "I know. I'm watching out for her."

"All right." Her mother patted her again and started down the walk to the car. Then she stopped and turned back.

"Madeline, you shouldn't be seeing so much of that Sturgis man right now. It's going to look very bad."

That Sturgis man. C.L.'s hot eyes and hot hands in the backseat, in her hall, her kitchen, her living room, on her, sliding under her T-shirt, under her skirt, everywhere—

She had to stop thinking about it. "I know, Mom." She was going to have to stay away from C.L. Thank God he was going back to Columbus.

Her body shivered at the thought. She wanted him near her, holding her, keeping her warm. The way he had in the backseat. Maddie swallowed and wrapped her arms around herself. She wanted him naked and wrapped around her, keeping her hot. Maddie told herself not to think about C.L. naked, but her mind betrayed her and her skin prickled. She shouldn't be having thoughts like this in front of her mother, but now that the idea was there, it was all she could think of.

Maybe she could start going to the city on shopping trips. Three or four times a week. She pictured C.L.'s apartment, furnished with a huge bed, and C.L., naked and hard, on top of her, inside her.

Her mother was still talking. "Wait for a while. Wait a year at least."

Maddie blinked. A year? She wasn't sure she could make it through the next fifteen minutes, and her mother wanted her to wait a year?

"You know people," her mother finished.

"Yes, Mother," Maddie said, and escaped back into the house as soon as her mother's car pulled away. A year. She was definitely going to be doing a lot of shopping in Columbus.

When she went back to the family room, the other three were sitting on the floor with beers, discussing Bailey. C.L. still leaned back against the couch, his shirtsleeves rolled to his elbows over his strong, tanned arms, his jeans-clad legs stretched out in front of him, ankles crossed. He had great thighs, something she hadn't noticed before. If she was to the point where she was ogling thighs, she was in big trouble.

C.L. looked up at her and grinned, and then he must have seen the heat in her eyes because his grin faded just a little, and his eyes narrowed.

Yes, thank you, I would like to, Maddie thought, and wondered how long it would be before she could have him again. With Em there, and Brent in the offing, it could be days, weeks. She sat down across from him, stretching her legs out beside his, and he put his beer down on the floor so that the back of his hand grazed her calf.

The heat shot through her, and she shuddered.

C.L.'s lips parted, and his eyes were hot on hers. She deliberately looked away to concentrate on what Howie was saying. If she and C.L. didn't knock it off, they'd be rolling on the carpet, which sounded so wonderful, she closed her eyes.

C.L. shifted until his leg touched hers, rough denim against her calf, and her mind slid into corners it shouldn't have, urging her to stretch against him, too, to climb across his legs, straddle him hard, press him into the carpet, take his mouth with hers—

Knock it off, she told herself, and tried to concentrate on Howie and Treva.

"After he got fired from the bank, he took payoffs from the casino in the back of the Roadhouse," Howie was saying. "That's why Henry couldn't recommend him as a rent-a-cop anymore."

Treva shook her head. "What I've never understood is why he did a dumb thing like that."

"Because he's a little hazy about the fine points of the law," Howie said. "Bailey's just a nice, dumb good ol' boy. He figured nobody was getting hurt by the gambling, so why not take the money?"

C.L.'s little finger tickled her ankle. Maddie closed her eyes for a moment. Never had a tickle been so cataclysmic. If he kept it up for another minute or so, she might even come. She'd definitely come if he put his hands on her. Anywhere.

"And so now he's a security guard for the company," Treva said. "Sounds like Bailey's not the only dumb good ol' boy around here."

Howie shrugged. "That was Brent's idea, not mine." His voice was cool, and Treva shut up and sat back, and Maddie was jolted out of her heat wave by Treva's obvious unhappiness and the mention of Brent's name.

"Why did Brent want him?" Maddie said.

Howie shoved the pizza box away. "He came in about a month ago and said there were kids up at the Point again in spite of the barricade and we were going to get sued if one of them got hurt. So he hired Bailey." He took a sip of beer while Maddie and Treva exchanged glances. "Hey, it wasn't a bad idea. Now we've got somebody to look after things at night."

Treva said, "This is the guy you just said was a little hazy about the law, right?"

Howie shook his head. "He won't steal from the company. Bailey's loyal."

"He is," C.L. said. He shifted again, closer to her, putting his beer down on the outside of her legs this time, trapping her ankles between his wrist and his hip, talking the whole time to distract Howie and Treva. "He was always getting the crap beat out of him in high school because he wouldn't rat on his friends." He frowned. "Actually, he was always getting the crap beat out of him, period. He was such a beatable little guy."

"Are you speaking from experience?" Maddie asked, pressing her ankle into his hip. *Make love to me.*

Howie laughed. "Hell, half the fights C.L. got into in high school were paybacks to somebody for roughing up Bailey. Bailey thinks C.L. is God."

"They were always people I wanted to hit anyway," C.L. said, smiling his Satan smile at Maddie. *Anytime.*

Howie leveled his eyes at C.L. "Like Brent."

Maddie sat up a little.

"You're the only person Brent ever backed down from," Howie went on. "And that was over Bailey."

"Brent beat up Bailey?" Maddie asked. *C.L. beat up Brent?*

"Only once," Howie said. "And Brent didn't really beat Bailey. He just pushed him around a little. And then C.L. told him to stop, and he did."

Maddie looked at C.L. "Just like that."

C.L. shook his head. "As I recall, I was holding a baseball bat at the time. I wasn't all that tough."

"Did you go armed often in high school?" Maddie asked.

"No, we were playing baseball," C.L. said. "Brent and me were teammates. Buddies."

"Oh, yeah." Howie laughed. "You were buddies."

"We shared some experiences," C.L. said, and let his hand fall carelessly over Maddie's calf.

Higher, she thought, and tried to look bright and interested in the conversation.

"Heard about that," Howie said, and Treva kicked him.

C.L. laughed and Maddie watched the best friends she had and thought, *He fits in. It's like he never left.* And the thought made her hotter yet. *Think of something else.*

She remembered them all back in high school: Howie serious behind his glasses; and Treva bouncing around in her cheerleader skirt with bows on her ponytails, flirting with everybody; and Brent in his letter sweater, looking cool; and C.L. with his shirt out, looking cooler. There'd been others— Margaret Erlenmeyer and her amazing collection of Pendleton skirts; Candace, sober and driven; Stan, always one step behind and bluffing to catch up; Gloria, a pale little nobody of a freshman watching them all, especially Brent—but it was the people in this room who'd meant the most to her. These people and Brent. When she looked at them now, they were an odd group without much in common except shared good humor and history, but that was a lot.

C.L.'s fingers stroked over her calf and her mind went blank with lust.

The kids came in with Phoebe and the room returned to general chaos. Em edged close to her mother

"Where's Daddy?" she whispered.

Guilt made Maddie pull her legs up under her. "I'm not sure, honey. I guess still out on business."

Em's face was worried. "Is he coming back tonight?"

Maddie ached to reassure her. "Probably. Probably really late, like usual."

"Hey, Em," Three called. "Mel and I are going for Dairy Queen. Want to come?"

Maddie wanted to say no, but Em said, "Can I?" and she thought, *This is a distraction, and Brent won't find her if she goes.*

"Yes," Maddie said.

"Can Phoebe come?" Mel asked. "Phoebe's never seen our house."

"Which is why there are no dog-vomit stains on your carpet," Maddie pointed out.

Treva looked at Maddie and then at C.L. "I think Phoebe

should spend the night," she said brightly. "Em can come, too, if she wants."

"*Really?*" Mel said on an exhale of delight, while Howie looked at his wife as if she were demented.

"Really," Treva said. "Go get Em's pajamas."

Em seemed taken aback, but Mel was tugging her along out of the room, and Phoebe romped beside her, so Em went along, casting one confused look back over her shoulder at her mother.

This was not a good idea, she should be keeping Em close, but the thought of being alone with C.L. soon, naked, moving against him, him moving inside her—

But there was Em.

She had to keep Em with her. She couldn't choose sex with C.L. over her daughter. "Treva," Maddie said, and Treva said, "It would be good for Em to spend the night at our house, what with *the prowler* and all. Howie and Three can protect her."

"Oh," Howie said.

"What?" C.L. said.

Treva nodded. "And you need some time to yourself. Selves. Somebody should stay with you in case the prowler comes back."

Pretty heavy-handed, Treve, Maddie wanted to say, but the thought of having C.L. was too overwhelming.

"I like you," C.L. said to Treva. "I have always liked you."

"Maddie?" Treva said.

All right, she was a bad mother. But Em would be safer if she was at Treva's. And she wanted C.L. so much she was screaming with it. "Good idea," Maddie said. "About taking Em for the night."

While Maddie waved them all good-bye from the front porch, C.L. went around the house, checking window and door locks, and met her in the front hall in time to lock and chain the front door. "How are you doing?" he asked, moving closer to her. "You've had a rough couple of days here."

He looked wonderful standing there, strong and sure, broad shoulders and hot eyes and great hands, and the closer he got, the shallower her breath came. *As long as you're here, I'm fine.* "I'm pretty good," she said. "I sold all of Brent's clothes in a garage sale today."

C.L. started to laugh. "Remind me to never piss you off. You're ruthless." He put his arms around her, and Maddie felt her breath go completely and leaned into him, trying not to moan as she finally felt him tight against her. She was not going to take him seriously, she was definitely, finally, going to be free, and there were a hell of a lot of questions he hadn't answered yet, but she did love the way he looked and moved and the way she felt right now, pressing closer to him. Asking him a bunch of questions that would make him move away seemed like a bad idea. Later for questions.

He spoke into her hair. "I suppose this is the part where you throw me out."

Take me right now on the floor. His car was in the driveway, screaming sex while it stood there, and she should throw him out, but she wanted him—

"You're thinking again," C.L. said. "I have warned you and warned you about that." He bent and kissed her slowly, his tongue tickling her mouth, and his hands moved under the back of her T-shirt, his fingers stroking her closer, and the heat flared so high in her she almost screamed. "You need me to protect you, honey," he whispered. "I better stay all night."

His arms tightened around her and he kissed her on the neck, making her speechless as her hands closed on him convulsively. She closed her eyes to imagine him naked against her, moving inside her. It was a terrible thought to have, given her situation, but she was ready to explode, and Treva had just kidnapped her child so she could do just that. And tomorrow Frog Point would know about the divorce anyway.

We'll be the good guys, she'd told her mother, but tonight she didn't want to be good. She wanted to be the way she'd been in the backseat at the Point: powerful and defiant and triumphant and and savage and satisfied. The new Maddie wouldn't be good. She'd take it all, even if it was just for one night.

"Yes," she told him, and his fingers dug into her. "You can stay." She swallowed. "But you have to go out and act like you're leaving and park your car down a couple of blocks and come in the back way."

"You're kidding," C.L. said.

Hurry up, she wanted to scream at him, but she made her voice calm to say, "You want Henry to know?" and he winced.

"All right." He let go of her and stepped back and she almost reached for him. "I'll go move the car, but you'd better be naked when I get back."

"You bet," Maddie said, and when he left, she ran upstairs to take her clothes off in the spare bedroom. It was a good compromise, she thought as she climbed into the bed, shaking against the cool sheets. Naked but not in the bedroom she'd shared with Brent.

Hurry up, she thought again, and slid a little farther down in the bed and thought about C.L.'s hands.

C.L. found her because she'd closed the door to the other bedrooms and left the light on in the guest room. It was a pretty room—he had vague peripheral impressions of pale blue walls and a lot of white fluffy stuff along the windows—but all he really saw was Maddie's round body curled under the thin sheet, her breasts and hips mounded like ice cream under the white fabric, her bare shoulders pale in the lamplight, and her face, shadowed from the bruising Brent had given her, but beautiful, all hot dark eyes and wide smiling lush mouth. He stripped off his clothes as he walked toward the bed.

"Took you long enough," Maddie said as she moved over a little, and his mind clouded with the way her voice was warm with laughter and husky with what he hoped was desire, and the way her body shifted under the sheet.

He sat on the edge of the bed to shuck off his pants, and his weight bounced her a little toward him. "Parking in Columbus was your idea," he said, his voice trembling a little, and then free of all his clothing, he rolled into bed next to her and pulled her close and forgot how to breathe. She was so soft and round everywhere, cool against his heat, tender against his roughness, and her body tensed and shivered against him, muscle and nerve moving infinitesimally so that he had to touch her everywhere just to feel her shudder.

Steady, he told himself. His cheek traced down her shoulder to the slope of her breast, and her skin smelled of flowers and, strangely enough, of Anna's kitchen. "You smell like cookies," he said, his voice thick with wanting her, and she sighed and said, "Vanilla."

He moved up and caught her mouth while it was open from the word, letting his tongue take her softly, pressing her down gently onto creamy pillows that gave like marshmallows under them. He stretched against her and felt her hands trail down his back, her tongue on his collarbone before she nipped his skin with her teeth, and he shuddered and tightened and wanted to take her then, to go hard into her, to pound them both into oblivion, but that wasn't right for Maddie. Not here, it wasn't.

It was something about the house, Maddie's house, a Frog Point settled-kind-of-family house. He'd basked in the warmth and the family feeling of being with everybody all night, and the house and especially this bedroom seemed as if it belonged to another era. Maddie moved against him, and he ached for her, but in the back of his mind while he moved slowly over her—discovering her centimeter by centimeter while stomping on every animal urge he had and reciting the occasional baseball statistic when stomping didn't do it—he felt the house and especially this pretty blue room slowing him down. It was an innocent, civilized, married kind of room, the kind of room he and Maddie would be sleeping in forever once this mess was over. For the rest of his life, he could pull her down onto creamy cool sheets and feel her hot, round body stretch against him and wrap around him, and he could rock them both into settled satisfaction, careful and slow and secure.

Maddie pulsed under him again, and the old desire slammed into him so that he had to stop moving, stop touching her, while he fought down the need to lay rough hands on her and plunge into her hot, slick wetness and drive her to the kind of screaming cataclysm they'd both barely survived in the backseat two nights before. *Jesus, don't even think about it,* he told himself as his whole body throbbed. That's not what they were now, theirs was a different kind of passion, a Frog Point–approved, married, serious, controlled kind of passion, which had never had much appeal before, and didn't have much now, to tell the truth. But if it kept Maddie sighing beneath him in large cool beds, then it was all he wanted.

Beneath him, Maddie was having second thoughts.

She had everything she wanted: privacy, safety, room to maneuver, no worries about Em, and C.L., big and broad and gorgeous and hot and crazy for her, reaching for her with so much lust in his eyes she'd almost come just from being wanted that much.

And then everything had slowed down. It wasn't that she wasn't a huge fan of foreplay, but she'd been thinking about him all weekend and especially all night—his hot dark eyes with those thick lashes that should not have been wasted on a man but were devastating on C.L., and that firm mouth she lusted to bite into, and those hands, oh God those hands, hard on her, all over—so she'd done the extended foreplay thing already without him. It was past time for that. *Way* past time.

She moved against him, but he hesitated, so she kept herself still so he wouldn't stop. It wasn't that the things that C.L. was doing so slowly with his hands and his mouth and his body weren't great, because she was feeling very warm, thank you. It was more that if things were going so well, why was she having time to analyze it? She arched up a little, rocking against him to speed things up, and his hands clenched hard on her hips, but just as she was bracing herself for the kind of sex that would set her free again, he let go and moved away.

"C.L.?" she said, and he said, "Shhh," and kissed her softly.

Well, terrific. There was a time and a place for soft kisses, but hot and naked wasn't one of them, damn it. He pulled her close gently, and the part where her body hit his and felt muscle and bone and heat was incredible, but the gently part was out.

All right, think, she told herself, which was only a little difficult since at the moment he seemed to be memorizing her shoulder with his mouth, nice enough, but not a major erogenous zone. She had at least a minute before he worked his way to the hollow of her neck and hit some good stuff.

The problem was not C.L. Any man who could do to her what he'd done to her in the back of a car was obviously capable of even greater heights in a bed. The problem was his approach. This respectful, slow-motion stuff had to go because she wanted him inside her *now*.

However, telling him that was not a good idea. From sixteen years of marriage to Brent, she knew that critiquing a guy's performance *in media res* only led to grief. So grabbing C.L. by the ears, and screaming, "Will you please just fuck me?" was not going to work, even if she could bring herself to talk dirty.

It would be fun to do that, to demand what she wanted, to scream it all out. But he'd be shocked. He was still working on the theory that she was Maddie the Perpetual Virgin, which might explain why he was worshiping at her shrine instead of blowing her mind. And the last thing she needed was C.L. turned off. He'd move even slower.

C.L. stopped to put on a condom, and Maddie felt a spark of hope. His lips were warm on her neck, and she let herself sink into the sizzle he was sparking there, shivering a little against him. This was more like it. She was being too hard on him; she was being passive, too, with all this thinking. His hands smoothed up her back and she bit her lip. The hell with thinking.

She twisted against him as the tickle of his lips against her neck percolated to her breasts and stomach and thighs, and then it went deeper, and she scraped her nails lightly down his back.

C.L. exhaled and pulled away, taking the sizzle with him, leaving her so frustrated she wanted to scream.

Hell.

Okay, he didn't like aggressive women who clawed at his back. He returned to her neck, and Maddie settled into the glow he was re-creating there. Too bad she was past glow and into inferno. She felt his mouth move to her breast, and she arched closer to him with anticipation, wanting the mind-bending pressure that was so close to pain, but he was gentle there, too. She moaned with frustration, and he must have taken it for encouragement because he went slower.

Maddie gave up. If that's the way it had to be, that's the way it had to be. It wasn't as if she hadn't had boring sex before; she'd been married to Brent. *Fantasize*, she told herself, and conjured up a vision of the sexiest man she could think of, but this time instead of getting Dennis Quaid or George Clooney, she got C.L., hard against her in the backseat, his fingers wound in her hair, jerking her head up to meet his hot, hot eyes while he thrust deeper into her and made her writhe, his mouth bruising hers, his hands rough on her breasts, rougher on her hips while he clamped her to him and rocked hard into her, hard, hard, hard—

She opened her eyes and saw C.L. above her, gorgeous as ever, looking abstracted, thinking about something else so he wouldn't lose control, *the dumb ass*, and she screamed with frustration.

C.L. stopped stroking her breast and said, "Maddie?" and she propped herself up on her elbows until she was nose to nose with him and said, "Listen, it's not that I don't appreciate the attention, but will you please stop screwing around and just *fuck my brains out now?*"

"What?" C.L. said, and then before she could take it back, he said, "We need to talk about this, *later*," and jerked her hips down to meet his, throwing her back onto the pillows as he moved into her slickly, so hard and fast she cried out.

"No?" he said, stopping, and she said, "Oh, God, *yes*," and arched up to bite his shoulder, and after that it was only the hot bulk of his body, and the wetness inside her as he went into her fast and hard, and his shoulders against her fingernails as he bore down on her, and his mouth savaging hers. He felt so wonderful she almost wept with gratitude. His hand clenched in her sweat-damp hair, his mouth tortured her breast, his fingers marked her hips as he held her down, and she moved to meet him, wanting all of him, all C.L. hot against her, thick inside her.

Her body shuddered each time he moved into her, each shudder a surge in her blood, and the rhythm took over and left her nothing but sensation and C.L. and the shattering conviction that he could never stop or she'd die. "Don't ever stop," she said, and then she saw his eyes, so black with lust they looked blank, and she realized he couldn't hear her, that he was lost in her, out of control with wanting her, and that made her shudder more. She arched harder into him, clenching her teeth because he felt so good, and he pressed her tighter against him, going higher into her, making all the need she felt for him twist into one tight, hot spiral, and then everything broke and she jerked, caught in spasms that left her writhing against him while he pinned her to the bed with his shuddering weight, mindless in his own climax, the best fantasy she'd ever had.

"Jesus," C.L. said when he got his mind back. "I didn't know you could do that in Frog Point."

"You can't," Maddie said against his shoulder. "Thank you." His hands closed on her convulsively, claiming her, loving her, wanting her again. She moaned a little and he let go.

"Did I hurt you?" he said, and she snuggled closer.

"Just enough," she said. "Just exactly enough."

Desire slammed into him again, and the only thing that kept him sane was the knowledge that she was his, that they were permanent, that as soon as they found Brent and filed for divorce, they'd get married and be together forever.

"I love you," he whispered against her skin, and then because it had all happened so fast, too fast to pay attention, he started over again.

Maddie stretched against him, loving everything about him and herself and the way they'd made love. She'd never felt freer. *Why did I ever get married?* she thought. As soon as Brent got to South America, she was filing for divorce, and then she'd be free forever. It was such a lush thought that it took her a moment to realize that C.L. was moving, his hair brushing her breasts as he kissed his way down her stomach. Everything inside her that had settled down into afterglow blazed up again. She wound her fingers through his hair to stop him. "I don't think I can stand to come like that again," she said, trying to slide down beside him. "I'll lose my mind and die."

He smiled up at her, his mouth bruised from fulfilling all her fantasies, and said, "Then don't come." His cheek stroked down her stomach, and his hands slid between her legs, and she felt his weight on her thighs before he licked inside her, and her last rational thought was that C. L. Sturgis was a hard man to say no to when you were naked.

Em wasn't happy. Any other night, she'd have been glad to be sharing Phoebe with Mel, glad they'd had ice cream, glad she was staying over in Mel's big double bed. But tonight she wanted her dad. She hadn't seen him for two days, and she wanted to see him again, just to make sure everything was all right.

"That C.L. is really *cool*," Mel said. "Like Jason Norris. A little."

Phoebe begged to be up on the bed, so they hauled her up,

too, and hid her under the covers in case somebody came in to do a last-minute bed check.

"He even gave you a *dog*," Mel said.

"Yeah." Em hugged Phoebe tighter.

Mel pushed harder. "So don't you like him?"

"No, he's okay." Em buried her face in Phoebe's neck.

"You don't sound like it."

"No, I do like him." Em sat up, too miserable to pretend. "It's just that the stuff at my house—"

"I know." Mel nodded. "Your mom's face. That's bad." She leaned over the edge of the bed and almost fell off as she rustled underneath for something, and then she sat up again, all red-faced, with a box of Hostess Cupcakes. "I swiped them from the kitchen. Don't let Phoebe have any or she'll throw up on my bed."

Em wasn't sure that, after the pizza and the Dairy Queen, *she* wouldn't throw up on Mel's bed, but she took a cupcake anyway when Mel handed one over.

"Where's your dad?" Mel asked when they'd both taken a bite of cake and licked the cream out of the center.

Em felt sick. "Away. On business."

"Is that what your mom said?"

Em nodded.

Mel shrugged. "Okay."

She doesn't believe that, either, Em thought, and the thought made her say, "They're not getting a divorce. C.L. is just somebody that everybody knew back in high school. Even your mom and dad. The only boyfriend my mom ever had was my dad."

"Same way with my mom and dad." Mel shook her head at how boring parents could be and took a huge bite of cake. "I wonder who C.L.'s girlfriend was."

For some reason, that wasn't a good thought, either. "Maybe he didn't have one," Em said.

"He had one." Mel sounded sure. "He's cute. And funny. He had one. Bet he still has one." She squinted at Em. "He smiles at your mom a lot."

"They're old friends," Em said. "He smiles at your mom, too. And your dad."

Mel nodded. "You know, if this was a movie—"

"It's not a movie," Em said. "Nothing ever happens to people like us."

"Right," Mel said. "We're really boring. Hey, Phoebe's eating your cupcake!"

"*Phoebe!*" Em jerked her mostly eaten cupcake away and laughed in spite of herself at the white cream on Phoebe's nose. She got up to throw the rest of the cake away, cheered a little. Nothing ever happened to people like her and her mom. And her dad. Em's heart clutched a little at the thought of her dad. Nothing happened to them. Ever. They were all really boring. All of them. Except C.L. She got back in bed. "Hey, guess what. C.L. taught me this great trick. It's called a memory picture and you—"

Mel bent forward to listen, and Em pushed everything else out of her mind except what C.L. had taught her.

The phone rang early. Maddie struggled up from the depths of sleep, aching a little deep inside with pleasure she wasn't quite clear on and confused because she wasn't in her usual bed. C.L., half asleep himself, picked it up before she could stop him.

"H'lo."

"*Who is this?*" The answering bellow was so loud Maddie could hear it.

"Give me the phone," she hissed, but C.L. had already leaned over to answer, and he had great naked shoulders which fogged her mind further, so she gave up and listened.

"Henry?"

"C.L., what the *hell* are you doing there?"

"Visiting," C.L. said weakly.

"It's seven o'clock in the morning, boy."

"I know, Henry." C.L. sat up and passed his hand over his eyes, trying to wake up and think fast. "What do you want?"

"I want Maddie Faraday, you shit-for-brains moron. What are you *doing* there?"

Maddie leaned back on the pillows and tried not to laugh. It wasn't good that Henry knew, and C.L. was so unhappy about the whole mess that it wasn't fair to enjoy it, but she felt so good from the night before, her body still soft with pleasure and satisfaction, and he looked so great naked in her guest bed, that it was hard not to grin even while her life slid further down the tubes. Besides, Henry had the tightest lips in Frog Point. He wasn't likely to pass this on.

"I'll see if she's here," C.L. said, and covered the receiver with his hand. "This is my uncle," he explained to Maddie. "It might be a good idea to try to, uh—"

"Cover up the fact we're sleeping together?" Maddie grinned. "Can't be done. I bet he even knows we're both naked."

"Well, try to fake it," C.L. said, irritated. "You always this chipper in the morning?"

"Only after a lot of great sex the night before." She pulled him down to her, kissing him slowly and thoroughly, remembering him with every cell in her body while she ran her hand down his arm.

C.L. detached himself and uncovered the receiver. "Henry? Can we call you back? Something's come up here—"

Henry had stopped yelling and Maddie couldn't hear what

he was saying, but it was something important because C.L. sat all the way up away from her. He listened for a moment and then said, "We'll be right there."

"What?" Maddie asked as he hung up the phone. "Why will we be right there? What happened to 'something came up'?"

"They found Brent," C.L. said, and got out of bed.

His voice was grim and Maddie sat up, too. They'd found Brent. "I didn't know he was lost," she said, trying to sound chipper again, but she felt buried. Brent would never get to South America now. She was stuck.

"He's not lost." C.L. zipped up his jeans and came back to sit on the side of the bed. He took her hand and said, "This is bad. He's dead. Somebody shot him at the Point."

Maddie stared at him. "What? What? What are you talking about?"

"Somebody shot Brent," C.L. repeated, and Maddie ran the words through her mind, but they were meaningless.

Somebody had shot Brent. Brent was dead. This was impossible. Somebody had shot Brent. After a moment, she looked at C.L. and said, "Who?"

"I don't know," C.L. said, getting up to put his shirt on. "I sure hope Henry does, though, because we just gave him a bitch of a motive."

Chapter Twelve

It took a while for the full impact to sink in. Brent was dead. He wasn't going to South America, he was dead. She wasn't going to divorce him, he was dead. He wasn't going to kidnap Em, he was dead. It was horrible, but remote, as if it had happened to somebody else. Brent couldn't be dead. Bad things never happened to Brent.

Brent was dead.

Em would be devastated. She had to get to Em.

"Maddie?" C.L. said, and she shook her head and climbed out of bed.

"Em," she said. "I have to tell Em."

"Wait. You have to talk to Henry first. Tell Em later." C.L. looked miserable as he said her name. "Tell her when you can stay with her."

Maddie stopped and thought of Em, alone and knowing. "You're right." *Em.* "I can't believe this." She picked up her clothes from the chair where she'd tossed them. "Henry was sure?"

"Henry doesn't make mistakes like is it Brent and is he dead," C.L. said. "That's not an oops-I'm-sorry kind of announcement. He was sure."

"I can't believe this," Maddie said, and went to get dressed.

They showed her Brent on a closed-circuit TV screen, and the hole in his head was under his ear and neat, as far as she could see. The other side was covered, so evidently that wasn't as neat. She'd read someplace about exit wounds being big, so she didn't ask them to move the cover. She didn't need to. It was Brent, puffy and much too pale and a strange color, but Brent. "Is there something wrong with the color on this TV?" she asked, and C.L. said, "No," and she was sorry she'd asked. *That's my husband*, she thought, and her knees almost went. He'd held her and loved her and cheated on her and hit her and now he was dead.

"Maddie?" Henry said, and she took a deep breath.

"That's him," she said, and turned and walked away from the screen before she passed out. C.L. and Henry followed her out into the corridor, and Maddie leaned against the wall.

"Are you all right?" C.L. took her arm. "Sit down for a minute."

"I'm fine," Maddie lied. "Let's get this over with so I can get to Em."

Henry gestured to the stairs and they followed him up the two flights to his office.

"Who shot him, Henry?" C.L. asked when they were inside.

"We don't know as yet." Henry got them both coffee from

the pot on the file cabinet, and when they were both seated, he looked at Maddie. "You got any ideas about this, Maddie?"

Ideas. She wasn't even up to regular thoughts yet and he wanted ideas. "Well, he was sleeping with another woman. That might have upset somebody besides me."

"You weren't that upset," C.L. said.

"How did you feel about him?" Henry asked.

"Henry," C.L. began, but Maddie answered him.

"I didn't like him," she said. "I was going to file for divorce today. I'd called Jane Henries in Lima."

C.L. let his breath out between his teeth. "Mad, maybe you shouldn't say anything else without a lawyer."

"Why?" She looked at him astonished. "You can't believe that I'd do this. Besides, I was with you all night."

Henry glared at C.L., and C.L. sat back and looked at the ceiling. Henry turned back to her. "We're not interested in last night."

Maddie blinked. "But when—"

"We won't know for sure until the coroner's report, but we're figuring sometime Friday night, Saturday morning."

"Friday?" That was more than two days ago. He'd been dead for that long? While she and Em had gone to the bank and had Burger King, he'd been dead at the Point? It was impossible. And she'd sold his clothes and he'd been dead, and they'd eaten pizza and he'd been dead, and she and C.L.—

Maddie put her face in her hands. It was too much.

Henry's voice brought her back. "What were you doing Friday night, Maddie?"

"Friday." What was she doing Friday night? Her self-preservation instincts kicked in. Oh, Lord. She'd been coming all over Frog Point with C.L. Getting slapped around by her husband. Locking herself in her room. This wasn't good. "He wasn't dead Friday night," she told him. "He was home until a little after one on Saturday morning. That was the last time I saw him." He'd left the house and went off to get shot, just like that. "Dear God."

C.L. stood up. "Henry, let me take her home. She's had a shock. You can ask questions later."

"You feel you're in shock, Maddie?" Henry asked.

Maddie did feel wobbly. "I feel sort of stunned, but I don't think that's shock. My head hurts."

Henry leaned forward a little. "You look like someone's been hitting you."

"*Henry,*" C.L. began, "this is not what I expect from you," and his uncle zeroed in on him.

"Well, I wasn't *expecting* to call a woman whose husband has just been murdered and find you in her bed, either."

C.L.'s exasperation evaporated. "I can explain that," he said, and Maddie looked at him with gloomy interest. *This should be good,* she thought. *I'm not sure I can explain it myself.*

Henry leaned back. "I'm waiting."

C.L. did his imitation of virtue. "Well, with the prowler and everything, I didn't think Maddie should be alone."

Henry didn't look impressed. "That's right neighborly of you, boy. What were you doing in her bed?"

"We'd sort of spent the weekend together." C.L. was not enjoying this. "I was looking for Brent Friday night, and since he wasn't home, Maddie and I got to talking."

"That's it? Talking?"

C.L. sat back down again. "Well, see, Henry, she was thinking about a divorce, and we . . . discussed it."

Henry lowered his head. "C.L., if you think I'm going—"

"We made love at the Point Friday night, Henry," Maddie said. "And then C.L. dropped me off at home about one. And Brent was there, and he was mad, and he hit me, and I told him I wanted a divorce and locked myself in the bedroom. And then he left. And I'd already called Jane Henries and told her I wanted a divorce and she'd said to come in today." Maddie stopped, taken by a thought. "I guess I don't need her after all."

"Don't be too sure," C.L. said grimly. He stood up. "We're going."

"About one A.M." Henry glared at C.L. again. "Did you see Brent Faraday when you dropped Maddie off?"

"No. Unfortunately, no."

"Why unfortunately?"

"Because that's when he hit her," C.L. exploded. "Goddammit, Henry—"

"Sit down, C.L." Henry turned his big head to Maddie, ignoring his nephew, who sat down. "Where did he go when he left you?"

"I don't know." Maddie slumped back in her chair and told Henry everything she knew about that night. "She only said that one word," she finished. "'Fine.' She sounded mad, but then he'd just told her it was over, so that's understandable. But I couldn't tell much from one word."

"And there wasn't anything else that seemed strange to you," Henry said. "Everything else was normal."

"Well, there was the two hundred and eighty thousand dollars I found in the safe-deposit box on Saturday, and the forty thousand I found in the golf bag on Sunday," Maddie said. "That upset me some."

C.L. turned his glare from Henry to her. "*What?* And you didn't tell me?"

"I didn't tell anybody," Maddie said. "I thought he needed it to get to Rio."

Fifteen minutes later, Henry had his head in his hands. "So the money in the safe deposit came from Stan," he said. "And the forty thousand in the golf bag—"

"I don't know," Maddie said.

"And you left everything in the box—"

"Except for Em's passport," Maddie finished. "I thought Brent had come back for the key on Saturday night because whoever it was had a key to the house and went right to the desk." She stopped, appalled by a new thought. "But Brent was dead by Saturday night. So whoever killed him took his house key and came looking for something."

"Not necessarily," Henry began, and C.L. announced, "We are changing all the locks today."

Henry shook his head. "It didn't need to be somebody with a key. The burglary report said your locks could be popped with a credit card. Still, I think you're right, C.L. Better change the locks." He smiled at Maddie. "We want to keep you safe."

"Thank you," Maddie said, beginning to feel very uneasy. Henry wasn't the smiling type.

"You don't happen to own a gun, do you?" Henry said, still smiling.

"Henry, that's about enough," C.L. said.

"Because there doesn't appear to be one registered to you or Brent, but we'd be real understanding if you just turned one in."

"I don't own a gun," Maddie said at the same time C.L. stood up and said, "We're going."

"C.L.," Henry said. "You don't seem to understand the situation. What I got here are two people with great motives and no alibis."

"Henry," C.L. said with exaggerated patience. "Why would we shoot him when she could get a divorce?"

"More money if she's a widow."

"She owns a quarter of the company," C.L. said.

Maddie jerked her head up. How did he know that?

"And I'm doing very well, thanks," C.L. went on. "A divorce would have been fine."

Henry sighed. "You just better pray nothing else turns up against you."

"Nothing will," C.L. said.

"I just have a few more questions—" Henry said.

"No you don't." C.L. grabbed Maddie's hand and hauled her to her feet. "I don't like the way this conversation is going. She doesn't answer anything else without a lawyer."

Henry scowled at him. "Whose side are you on, boy?"

"Hers," C.L. said. "First, last, and always. And she has to go tell her kid her father's dead while I get her some new locks and a lawyer. You don't need her now. Hell, it's not like she's going anyplace."

"Neither one of you is going anyplace," Henry said. "Don't even think about leaving town. You, too, C.L."

Maddie had to fight back a laugh. Leave Frog Point? "Where would I go?" she asked him.

"There will be no problem with my staying," C.L. said with dignity. "I have no intention of leaving Maddie while you're thinking dumb thoughts. I assume I can still have the back bedroom?"

"Yeah, and you be there tonight," Henry said. "It's too damn early to be consoling widows."

She was a widow now. Everything was surreal, and she was a widow. C.L. tugged her toward the door.

"We'll call you when we get the lawyer," C.L. said to Henry, and then he pushed her out the door.

C.L. watched Maddie from the corner of his eye while he drove her home. She looked poleaxed, which was about right under the circumstances, and miserable, which—considering she was going to have to tell Em she'd just lost a father—was also about right.

"I'm sorry, honey," he said, reaching for her hand. "I wanted him out of the picture, but not like this."

"It's going to be so awful for Em," she said, curling her fingers around his and making him feel much better than the situation deserved. "Poor baby."

"I'll help," C.L. said, tightening his grip on her hand. "I'll do anything."

Maddie slid her hand away. "The best thing you can do is disappear. You're going to make me look very suspicious, hanging around."

The thought made him cold. *I'll do anything but that*, C.L. wanted to say, but then they got home and her mother met them at the door.

"Esther called me and I came over," she said to Maddie. "She was working the phone desk at the station, and I couldn't wait until you called. What if Em came home? This is so terrible." She looked past Maddie and saw C.L. and her face became rigid.

What did I do? he thought, and then remembered. He'd spent the night with her daughter having gloriously sinful sex, something Esther at the police station had undoubtedly passed on. Mrs. Martindale looked like she was concentrating on the sinful part.

"You remember C.L.," Maddie said brightly.

"Yes," her mother said. "I assume he's going now."

"Nice to see you again, ma'am." C.L. took a step backward. "I'll go get the locks now," he told Maddie. "How many outside doors do you have?"

Maddie looked from him to her mother and back. "Two, front and back."

Her mother's coolness thawed. "What locks?"

"The prowler has a key to the house, Mom," Maddie said. "We think he might be the guy who shot Brent. And now he can get in anytime, and we'll be helpless."

All the blood drained from her mother's face, and she reached out to steady herself on the doorframe. "Merciful heavens, Madeline!"

C.L. put his hand under her arm and helped her to a porch chair. "It's going to be all right, Mrs. Martindale," he told her, trying to sound as soothing as possible. "I'm going out to get new locks, better locks, unpickable locks, and I'll have them up before noon. Nothing to worry about. Maddie, get your mother a glass of water."

Maddie's mother flapped her hand at him. "No, no, I'm fine. Do you need money for the locks? Good locks must be expensive. Where's my purse?"

"No, no." C.L. backed away again. "My treat. I insist. The stores won't be open for another hour or so, but I'll go home and get Henry's tools and as soon as I've got the locks, I'll be back."

"Oh, yes. Good heavens." Maddie's mother patted the air where he'd been, all disapproval gone. "Be careful. Good heavens."

Maddie followed him to the car, and he was careful not to touch her. "What's the big idea?" he whispered to her. "Your mother almost had a heart attack."

Maddie leaned against the car. "C.L., she knows about this morning. Esther must have told her everything when she called her. Didn't you notice the frost when we came in?"

"Yeah, but . . ."

"Well, now she thinks you're all that's standing between me and death. She likes you." She smiled at him, a woeful smile but a smile, and he felt the heat spread again, the way it always did when he was close to her. He got in the car and slammed the door before he did something stupid like dragging her to the ground and having his way with her in the grass while her mother watched.

"Keep telling your mother great things about me," he said. "She's going to be seeing a lot of me."

She shook her head, not willing to play along. "Go get the locks. I have to call Treva. She's got Em."

Em. Poor kid. He didn't have much time for kids in general, but he liked Em. He nodded his sympathy since he couldn't hold her. "Good luck," he said, and backed out of the driveway.

He needed to get locks, but he needed to go back and talk to Henry, too, before he got any stupid ideas like arresting his future niece-in-law.

"Something's really wrong," Mel whispered to Em as they spied through the stair rails, but Em already knew that. Aunt Treva's face was white, and she leaned against the wall and breathed hard. She looked like she was going to cry, and then she said, "Are you sure?" and her face broke and she started to laugh instead, but it was awful laughter.

Mel stood up and said, "Mom?" and Aunt Treva stopped laughing and straightened and saw them and looked awful again.

"I have to go; they're here. Hurry," she said into the receiver and hung up, and then she walked over to the stairs.

Mel went down the steps and put her arms around her mother's waist, asking questions, but Em stayed where she was. The trouble had come on the telephone, which meant the trouble wasn't here at Mel's house, but she already knew that. She'd known all along the trouble was at her house. Her throat caught, and she swallowed a hot lump before she asked, "Is my mom all right?"

Aunt Treva jerked her head up. "Yes. Yes, yes, she's all right, she's fine. That was her on the phone."

"What's wrong?" Mel demanded. "Nobody tells us anything. What's wrong?"

Em's voice went on automatically. "Is my dad all right?"

Aunt Treva looked desperate. "Your mom's coming right over, baby. She'll—"

"What's wrong with my dad?" Fear made her cold, and even Phoebe slumping down the steps to sit beside her didn't make her warmer. "Is he hurt?"

Aunt Treva came closer and took her hand through the stair rail. "Your mom will be here right away, baby."

Aunt Treva never called her baby, ever. "Is he hurt?"

"Is he dead?" Mel asked, and Aunt Treva jerked her hand away, and Em felt cold all over. The cold pressed in on her chest, and she tried hard to breathe.

"Go upstairs," Aunt Treva told Mel. "Go upstairs right now."

"He's not dead," Em said around the cold. "He's hurt, right?"

"Your mom—" Aunt Treva began again, and Em said, "He's not dead," and her not-for-real aunt's head wobbled, not a nod or a shake but a wobble, and Em thought, *My daddy's dead* and she said, "No."

Aunt Treva said, "I'm sorry, baby, your mama's coming over," and then she came up the stairs and put her arm around Em and hugged her close, and Em sat there on the stairs with Phoebe on one side and Aunt Treva on the other until her mother came through the front door and looked up at her.

"He's not dead," she told her mother, and her mother scrambled up the stairs to hold her, and then Em started to cry, because saying it didn't make it so, and he was.

. . .

Somehow Maddie got Em home, holding Em's hand while she drove, making meaningless comfort sounds while Em sat wobbly-necked and cried hopelessly, and Phoebe licked at her tears.

"God bless C.L. for giving her this dog," Maddie whispered to her mother when she had Em in the house and could hold her. "Phoebe may get her through this better than we can."

Her mother nodded and looked miserable. "Maybe it's not good for her to cry like this," she whispered back.

"Better to let it out," Maddie said, conscious that she hadn't cried yet. Could she cry for Brent? There had been good things about him. Lots of good things. When he was in a good mood, they'd had fun. He'd loved Em. She supposed he'd loved her, too, in his own way. When she'd asked for a divorce after Beth, he'd sworn it would never happen again. "I can't live without you, Maddie," he'd said, and he'd fought like crazy to keep her, wearing her down until she'd just given up and stayed. She didn't want him dead, but it was going to be hard to cry for him. Maybe she could cry for Em instead.

She put her cheek on her daughter's hair and rocked her back and forth until Em's crying eased. "I love you, baby. I love you and love you."

Em drew a long sobbing breath and held Maddie tightly.

Maddie's mother came in the room with a tray. "I brought you cocoa, Emmy. And cookies. And here's some dog cookies for Phoebe. She looks very hungry."

Em didn't move her head from her mother's shoulder.

The phone rang and Maddie's mother went to answer it while Maddie watched Phoebe try to climb up her leg to get to Em. She hooked her hand under the puppy's rear end and scooped her up into Em's lap, and Em's arms let go of Maddie to keep the puppy safe. Phoebe snuggled down in Em's lap, and Em's breathing slowed a little bit, still ragged but not sobbing. *Thank God for this puppy*, Maddie thought. If C.L. never did another thing for her, she'd owe him forever for this dog.

Her mother came to stand in the doorway to the living room, looking helpless. "Maddie, it's Leo at the service station. I've told them it's not a good time, but he's insisting."

"On what?" Maddie said, but she eased Em and Phoebe off her lap and onto the couch and went to the phone. Her mother took her place beside Em.

Leo was short and to the point. "You gotta empty out this car because the insurance guy is coming in an hour to get it towed. Anything in this car you want?"

The Civic. That had been a thousand years ago. Four days and a thousand years ago.

Leo kept on talking. "The insurance guy said you wanted it done today, so they're coming today, but there's stuff in it. So is there anything in this car you want, because if you do, you gotta come get it now."

"Let me think." Maddie pulled the phone back to the living room doorway. "Em, did you leave anything in the Civic?"

Em nodded, her head wobbling. "My Barbies and my dog books from the l-library."

"It's okay," Maddie said. "I'll go get them right now."

"Mommy's going to go get them," her mother said, but Em started to cry again anyway.

"I'll be right over," Maddie told Leo. "Don't let them take that car until I get there."

She grabbed her big old leather bag from the closet shelf and Em's Barbie duffel bag from the closet floor.

"Be careful, dear." Her mother rocked Em, who keened hopelessly in her arms.

"I love you, Emmy." Maddie kissed her daughter's forehead

and smoothed her hair back. "I'll be right back here and I'll hold you again."

"Go," her mother said. "Hurry."

The car was behind Leo's, sitting in the weeds at the far back of the lot. It looked deserted and lonely. And dead. Maddie felt the tears start at the sight of it and was appalled. She could cry for a dead car, but not a dead husband? What kind of woman was she?

Maybe she was crying for a dead car because of a dead husband.

"I'm really sorry about this," she told the car. "Really." Then, feeling stupid talking to a car, she pulled up the crumpled hatchback. Half a dozen Barbies stared back at her in mascaraed apathy; the trunk looked like a tornado had hit a home for anorexics. She piled them into the duffel bag and then pulled back the carpet over the tire well to see if any had fallen underneath.

There weren't any Barbies, but there was a whole lot of money, packages of one-hundred-dollar bills, all over the place. "Oh, *hell*," Maddie said, and slammed down the hatchback and sat on the edge of it.

If she looked at it just right, this whole money thing could be pretty funny. There was so much of it, it almost didn't count as real money. It was like Monopoly money. And at the rate she was going, she could afford both Boardwalk and Park Place. Pretty funny.

Except her husband was dead.

Maddie put her head on her knees and tried to think. She had to take the money to Henry. She'd just take it to him and tell him where she'd found it.

You two just better pray nothing else turns up against you, he'd said. Well, this wouldn't count. This was Brent's stash. He must have put it here. He'd have known the car was going to be stuck here for a while. Really, it was the perfect place to hide money.

Really, this wasn't going to look good.

"You okay, Mrs. Faraday?"

Maddie jerked her head up. Leo stood in front of her in his oil-stained dungarees, looking sympathetic and pressed for time. "Yes, Leo, I'm fine."

He nodded at her. "You about done?"

"Almost." She smiled as brightly as she could and then remembered she was a widow and let the smile die. "I'll be right there. Just another minute, honest."

She watched him walk back to the station, and then she yanked open the hatchback and dumped the Barbies out of the duffel, stuffing it with the money instead, as fast as she could, counting the packages as she stuffed it in. Two hundred thirty of them. It didn't matter, what mattered was getting it out of here. She zipped the duffel shut and let her mind go numb walking through the rest of the cleanup. The Barbies went in her leather bag. She went to the passenger side and checked under the seats, pulling out Em's library books and shoving them in the leather bag, too. Then, almost as an afterthought, she emptied the glove compartment into her bag: first aid kit, maps, gum, sunglasses, gun.

"Oh, hell," she said for the second time, looking at the gun in her hand. And now it had her fingerprints on it. They were all in the wrong places, but that wasn't much comfort. She wiped the gun clean with the tail of her T-shirt and dropped it in with the money in the duffel bag. Brent wouldn't have put the gun in the glove compartment. He'd probably been killed with that gun. She had to get some time to think before she told anybody anything because she was pretty sure this looked very bad. Henry would think this was something else against her. She could go to jail, and she couldn't go to jail because she had a baby on the edge of collapse already because her daddy was gone. Thank God for Em's Barbie dolls and library books because otherwise somebody else would have found the gun and called the police, and then Em would have come apart.

Maddie slammed the door of her Civic for the last time and thought of Em, and her lost car, and Em's tearstained face, and somebody out to get her, and Em's hopeless little moans, and then she put her head on the edge of the car and began to cry, for Brent, and for herself, but mostly for Em, fragile little Em, who was not going to lose a mother, too, not if Maddie had to lie to everyone in town.

C.L. was putting the lock on the back door when Maddie pulled in the driveway in Anna's station wagon, and she waved and parked beside his car, thinking hard. She put the Barbie duffel bag with the money and the gun in the backseat, but it couldn't stay there; Anna would have a heart attack if she found it, or the gun would go off and kill somebody when Anna hit a pothole. That was about as far as she got in clear thinking before she had to move and pretend everything was fine.

Except Brent was dead. *You're a widow*, she told herself. *Remember that.* At least she looked the part from crying at the service station.

Em and Phoebe were watching C.L. work, Em handing him tools, wiping at her tearstained face with the back of her grimy hand. "This one's almost done," he said, smiling at her. "It's going fast because Emily's helping."

Em nodded and squeezed her eyes shut, but a tear rolled

from each eye anyway, and she smeared them away again. C.L. ignored them and kept on working, while Maddie dropped a kiss on the top of her head.

"I love you, baby," she said to Em, and Em sniffed.

"Em's a great helper," C.L. said. "She always knows what I need." He looked up at Maddie. "You okay?" he asked, and she thought, *No, my baby's in pain, and somebody's trying to get me.*

She should tell him about the money. She should tell somebody about the money. "Oh, look," she could say. "I just found almost a quarter of a million dollars in the back of my Civic. No, I don't know a thing about it. Why?"

She had to think this through.

Maddie nodded to C.L. and said, "Fine," and thought fast.

There was no place in the house to hide that much money. Whoever had put it in the Civic had the right idea. Car trunks. But not her trunk because she didn't have one, and not Anna's or her mother's.

She went in the kitchen where her mother was cooking and leaned against the sink to look out the window to the driveway. C.L.'s bright red Mustang winked back at her from beyond Anna's station wagon.

It wasn't the best of all possible places, but it was a place.

"Did you get it taken care of?" her mother said, and Maddie said, "Just about." She moved to leave and kissed her mother's cheek. "What are you making?"

"Soup," her mother said. "People will stop by. Esther and Irma already brought casseroles. Oh, and that nice Vince came by to pick up some money. I didn't know anything about it, so he's coming back later."

"Money?" Maddie's heart lurched. How had Henry found out about the—Oh, right, the forty thousand in the golf bag. "Right," Maddie said. "It was something of Brent's."

"Is that why he was killed?" Her mother's voice trembled on the last word. "Money?"

"I truly do not know, Mother," Maddie said. "Try not to think about it." Then she went out to the car.

Anna's station wagon blocked C.L.'s car from the back porch. Maddie reached over his driver door and popped his trunk lid and then went around and shoved all the junk— his jack, jumper cables, blanket, flashlights—off the top of his spare. She flipped the cover back, pulled the spare out, and threw it in the back of her mother's car. Then she took the Barbie duffel full of money from her mother's trunk and emptied it into C.L.'s wheel well, putting the gun back in the duffel when it fell out. Then she threw the cover back over it. She scattered his junk across it again, slammed his trunk lid, and took the duffel with the gun to the house.

Her hands were shaking. The whole thing had taken less than five minutes, but it had also taken five years off her life.

"You okay?" C.L. said as she went past.

"Hard day," Maddie said, and went back inside.

The phone rang, and when Maddie picked it up in the hall, it was Henry asking for C.L. C.L. came in and said, "Right. I'm coming." He hung up, took a quick look around for her mother or Em, and kissed her. "Gotta go. I'll be back later to put the lock on the front."

"Wait a minute," Maddie said. "Take the money in the golf bag. That way Vince won't have to come back with it."

"Forty thousand in a golf bag." He shook his head. "In the future, we'll be investing differently." He kissed her again, lingering a little this time, and then went out the back door, and she heard him say something to Em before he went down the steps.

Well, there went the money. Easy come, easy go.

Maddie turned and saw her mother looking at her from the kitchen door. "What?"

Her mother tried to look stern, but she was too upset. "Maddie, how long have you been carrying on with that man?"

Maddie sighed. "I kissed him for the first time in twenty years on Friday night. If you can call three days 'carrying on,' that's how long it's been."

Her mother's face sagged. "Maddie, that's awful."

"I'm sorry, Mom," she said, moving toward the back door and Em. "We should have waited until I got the divorce."

"Is he why Brent hit you?"

Maddie tried to look outraged. "Mother! I told you. I ran into a door."

Her mother turned back in to the kitchen. "I'm not as dumb as I look, Maddie. I knew you didn't run into a door. Everybody in town knew you didn't run into a door."

She was going to have to do something about her mother, but Em came first. Maddie went out the back door just as Phoebe scrambled out of Em's lap and ran off into the yard. Em followed her, her shoulders sagging. Maddie followed, too, and sat on the picnic table to watch them.

Three days ago she'd sat here with C.L. Brent had been alive. Her life had been a mess, but not like this, not with her daughter brokenhearted. Em came trailing back, her face lost, and Maddie realized that if Em had taken the divorce like this, she could never have gone through with it. She could never have done this to her child. "Come here, baby," she said, and Em crawled up beside her on the table. "I got your dog books and your Barbies. Everything's in the house."

"Thank you," Em said, and burst into tears.

Maddie pulled her into her lap and rocked her back and forth. "Just cry," she said. "Cry and cry. I'll hold you."

"I was scared last night," Em sobbed. "I knew something was wrong. I want my daddy back."

Guilt flooded over Maddie; while her child had been afraid, she'd been laughing in bed. *No good time ever goes unpunished*, she thought. She should have known being that happy in Frog Point was a sin. And even that wouldn't be bad if she'd been the one paying for it. But it was Em who'd suffered alone, Em who had been afraid and hadn't had her mother to comfort her.

"I don't want to stay at Mel's anymore," Em said.

"You don't have to," Maddie said.

"I don't want to go out to the farm anymore."

"We won't."

"I just want to be here. With you."

"I won't leave you again," she whispered into Em's hair. "I'll always be there for you, I swear. I'm so sorry, Emmy. I'll always be there, I promise."

C.L. was history. He had to be. She couldn't have Em hearing rumors along with everything else she was going to hear. Em had to come first. Maddie and C.L. were adults, they'd survive if they didn't have each other, but Em couldn't make it without her mother. Maddie was all Em had now. C.L. had to go.

"Oh, Em," Maddie said, and began to cry, too.

Chapter Thirteen

I got the new locks on the back door, Henry," C.L. said when he'd climbed the stairs to Henry's office again. "Now get the bastard so they're not necessary."

"Sit down, C.L.," Henry said, and C.L. knew that what was coming wasn't good.

"She didn't do it, Henry," he said. "She did not do it."

"He was shot at the Point in his own car," Henry said. "Her fingerprints are all over it—" he held up his hand as C.L. started to protest—"which they would be since it's her car, too. His are there, and a lot of smeared ones that aren't going to do us much good, and then there's one other set, on the steering wheel and on the front and back door handles, that we're looking at, so that could be a suspect, too."

C.L. sat down. "Or it could be me. We took the Caddy to

the Point Friday night. Did you find a lot of buttons in the backseat?"

"As a matter of fact, we did."

"Those are mine," C.L. said. "It's these cheap city shirts. They just fall off."

Henry looked grim. "C.L., this isn't funny. If those prints are yours, then we only got three people in that car."

"Or three people who are careless and one person planning a murder," C.L. said.

"Then where did that person go?" Henry said. "Bailey swears nobody drove or walked by the company that night after Brent drove up."

"And you believe him?" C.L. shook his head. "Anybody with five bucks can buy Bailey. Which reminds me, he was blackmailing Maddie about being at the Point with me. You might want to mention that the next time you talk to him."

"That fool," Henry said, dismissing Bailey. "There aren't any footprints in the mud of the road. That drive gets soaked. It was raining when the Caddy pulled up to the Point because we've got tire marks. But there aren't any footprints going down the drive."

"So the shooter walked along the gravel sides," C.L. said.

"Bailey didn't see anybody," Henry repeated.

"Or through the woods," C.L. said. "Big deal. It's an easy walk."

"The only footprints there are small. Probably a woman's. We're going to have to look at Maddie's tennis shoes."

"Great," C.L. said. "Do it. She's innocent. Her tennies will be as clean as her conscience. Then you can start looking for the real—"

Henry picked up a report and slapped it down on his desk with a crack that must have made Esther prick up her ears outside the door. "C.L., will you pay attention here? We got a man who was cheating on his wife, and beating her up, and stashing a hell of a lot of cash in a safe-deposit box. Then he gets killed, and when I call to tell the widow she's a widow, she's in bed with another man. Now you tell me, who do you think did it?"

"You're forgetting it's Maddie," C.L. said.

"Listen to yourself, will you?" Henry said. "That woman's got you so twisted you don't know which way is up."

"I know she didn't kill her damn husband," C.L. said, stung by the accusation because it was the truth. "If you're so sure, why aren't you arresting her?"

"Because I don't have a murder weapon," Henry said. "And I don't have any proof she walked down that hill. And I still don't know why a big healthy guy like Brent Faraday let somebody put a gun behind his ear and shoot him without making any kind of a fuss. There's a whole hell of a lot more I don't have, but for right now, she's the best I've got."

"What about the mistress?" C.L. said, grasping at straws. "He was going to leave her, too. And what about his embezzling partner? He was going to leave him holding the bag. Hell, Henry, you've barely started. You go after the real bad guy and stay away from Maddie."

He got up to go and Henry scowled at him. "Never mind me, you stay away from that woman. She's dangerous."

C.L. sighed in exasperation. "Henry, she is not going to shoot me. She didn't shoot her husband and she's not going to shoot me."

"I'm not talking about that," Henry said, "although it's a damn good thing to keep in mind. I'm talking about the way you've been acting around her. You keep your pants zipped and your mind clear, you hear me?"

C.L. leaned forward, speaking very clearly so Henry would understand he was serious. "Henry, I am going to marry her.

We're going to live next door with Em. She's family now. Stop worrying about her and start worrying about the creep who killed Brent."

"You haven't learned a damn thing about women since you were ten years old," Henry said, clearly disgusted.

"The hell I haven't," C.L. said, fervently hoping he had.

An hour later, Maddie carried an exhausted Em upstairs and sat beside her until she fell asleep. Treva called and wanted to come over, but Maddie put her off until later, needing Em to get some sleep, needing time for herself to sort things out.

Em had to be kept safe, which meant Maddie had to be above reproach; no more C.L. and no getting arrested.

But staying out of jail wasn't going to be easy if somebody was out to get her. Somebody had planted the money and the gun in her car. What could anybody gain from seeing her arrested? Anything she would inherit from Brent would just go to Em, so it couldn't be money. She'd lose Em if she went to jail; could it be that? Maddie entertained a brief fantasy of Helena Faraday framing her for Brent's murder so she could raise Em and take control of Brent's estate, but it was ridiculous. First of all, Helena would have to have known about the money, and Maddie was sure that was something Brent hadn't shared with his parents. Then Helena would have had to fight Maddie's mother for custody of Em, and anybody's money would have been on the Martindale side. Helena was vicious when it came to money and power, but she couldn't hold a candle to Martha Martindale when it came to hanging on to family members. It couldn't be Helena.

So it was somebody outside the family, but somebody who knew them well enough to know Maddie's car had been wrecked and was in back of Leo's. Which meant most of Frog

Point. And the only general reason to frame Maddie was to point suspicion away from the real killer.

So it probably wasn't anything personal. That was some comfort.

Maddie put her face in her hands. She didn't know enough. She didn't know where the money had come from or whose gun it was or anything. Did that mean she should turn it over to Henry? "Do not tell that man anything else," C.L. had said to her when he'd come back with the locks. "He has the extremely dumb idea in his head that you might have killed Brent. We're calling a lawyer, and you say *nothing* to Henry until then."

It was a toss-up. Saying nothing was easy, but carrying the knowledge around was hard. *What's best for Em?* Maddie thought, and decided that if the money meant there was even a slim chance of Em losing her right now, it wasn't worth it. She'd think about it later.

But she had to think about the gun now. She had to hide that damn gun.

Double-checking to make sure her mother was resting in the living room, Maddie took the duffel bag into the kitchen, and opened the refrigerator. Two casseroles rested on the bottom shelf, and she picked out the sleazier one because it was in a deeper dish. She took a Ziploc bag out of her drawer, got the gun out of the duffel using a paper towel, and zipped it into the bag. Then she grabbed a big spoon and scooped out the center of the casserole. It was Spam and whole wheat noodles.

Maddie looked at it in disbelief. Somebody thought this would be a comfort? Although, actually, it was, since nobody in their right mind would ever try to eat any of this glop. It was a perfect hiding place. She dropped the gun into the scooped-out place and covered it with the stiff top layer of crunchy noodles and burnt Spam. She patted the potato chips back into place, stuck the whole thing in the refrigerator, and then closed the door and shoved the extra casserole down the garbage disposal.

She could give the casserole to Treva later with several other dishes to freeze for her. Freezing wouldn't hurt the gun, and having the gun out of the house meant it couldn't hurt her. Relieved of that worry, she went upstairs and crawled into bed next to Em.

"It's all right, baby," she said to her sleeping daughter. "I'm not going anywhere."

At six, after more than a dozen phone calls, and two more casseroles, all of which her mother handled, Maddie heard a car door slam out front and opened the door to the Bassets. Treva had brought everybody—Howie, Three, and Mel—and half a dozen loaves of bakery French bread, which she passed into the hands of Maddie's mother, who came out of the kitchen to say hello and then disappeared again.

Em was sitting on the couch, clutching Phoebe. She had the dazed look of a child who had cried too much and needed to cry again but couldn't find the energy. Mel looked at her wide-eyed and then sat down and put her arm around her. "I love you, Emily," she whispered, and Em put her head on Mel's shoulder for a moment.

Three knelt down before her. "Hi, kid," he said. "You okay?"

Em shook her head. "No," she said softly. "My daddy's dead."

"I know, honey," he said. "I'm really sorry."

She nodded and clutched Phoebe closer, and the puppy yipped.

"Phoebe looks like she needs to go out," he said. "Let's take her out in the backyard."

Em nodded and Three led her and Mel out into the hall with Phoebe padding anxiously along behind, and Maddie almost said, *"No,"* until she remembered she didn't have to worry about Em being kidnapped anymore. Brent was dead.

"So how are you?" Treva said, pulling her down onto the couch. "You okay?"

"No." Maddie leaned back. It seemed too great a chore to do anything else. There was too much here for her to handle. "This is awful."

"Let me get you a drink." Howie backed out into the hall.

"You have his sympathies," Treva told her. "He just hates stuff like this."

"Who doesn't?" Maddie said. "I wish Brent wasn't dead. A divorce would have been better."

"Shhhh!" Treva grabbed her arm. "Are you crazy? Your husband has just been murdered. Do *not* talk about divorce."

Maddie nodded. "I know. You'd think I'd be all caught up in how awful this is. But actually, it's the details of the situation that—well, there's just so much to take care of." Maddie looked at her friend. "You have no idea how complicated my life is."

Howie came back in the room with a tray and three glasses. "All I could find was Scotch."

"Good," Treva said. "Give it all to Maddie."

The doorbell rang, and Howie put down the Scotch and went to answer it, his relief at getting away obvious and great. It was Gloria from next door with a casserole. She came into the living room and stood there, red-eyed and defeated in her best blue Laura Ashley, clutching her Pyrex before her.

"Maddie, I just heard," she said. "If there's anything I can do—" She broke off in obvious distress.

"Thank you, Gloria," Maddie said. "It's sweet of you to come.

And a casserole, too. Really . . ." She led Gloria and the casserole into the kitchen and dumped them both on her mother.

"I'm going to say that a thousand times in the next couple of days," she told Treva when she came back. "I should have cards printed."

"What was wrong with that woman?" Treva said.

"I think she had plans for Brent," Maddie told her. Could it have been Gloria? Gloria in crotchless panties? Gloria shooting Brent in the head?

The doorbell rang and Treva said, "Casseroles freeze well."

"Good idea," Maddie said. "Can you take some of them home with you?"

Three casseroles and two cakes later, Helena and Norman Faraday showed up and the day really went to hell.

Norman looked shattered, his pop eyes even more startling than usual because of the red rims. Maddie had never thought him a handsome man, but he'd radiated power and that had camouflaged his physical shortcomings. Now she watched him as he tottered into the living room, all that power gone now that all his dreams of living through his son were gone. He was just a little potbellied guy in his sixties, slumping in his Sansabelt slacks, looking lost and ineffectual. For the first time since she met him, Maddie felt sorry for him.

"I'm sorry, Norman," she said, and he said, "You didn't do right by my boy," but there was no venom in his voice.

Helena had enough venom for both of them. There was no slump to Helena; her hard straight body was even harder and straighter now that she was rigid with rage and loss. She looked straight into Maddie's eyes with such loathing that Maddie took a step back and then remembered that morning. By now, thanks to Esther at the police station, they'd have heard about C.L. being in bed with her when Henry called. For a moment,

Maddie felt sympathy for both of them. If somebody had betrayed Em, she'd be just as merciless.

Of course, Brent had betrayed her first, but now that he was dead, the point seemed moot. She'd cheated on her dead husband and now her mother-in-law hated her and was going to punish her forever.

"Hello, Helena," Maddie said.

"I have *nothing* to say to you," Helena said, and went to sit with Em.

"I'll take that Scotch now," Maddie said to Howie, and Helena sucked in her breath through her teeth and glared at her as she bent closer to Em.

Em couldn't think. Every time she tried to, she remembered her daddy was dead, and that was awful, that was the worst, she couldn't stand that, so she just stopped thinking. Mel and Three left for ice cream, pleading with her to go and promising to bring her some back when she refused, and she sat in her living room, feeling like lead, just heavy all over, while people came and went, carrying dishes, saying quiet things and looking at her like they were sorry for her. She wanted to go out in the backyard with Phoebe, she wanted to crawl into her mother's lap, she wanted to see her daddy, but he was dead, so she had to sit there.

Then her grandmother Helena came from where she'd been talking to Em's mother and sat beside her, and Em wished she'd gone to the backyard anyway.

"You must never forget your father, Emily," Grandma Helena said, and Em wondered what she was talking about. How could she ever forget her daddy?

"You must remember him for the very important and very good man he was," Grandma Helena went on, taking her hand.

Grandma Helena always smelled like perfume, but like chemicals, not flowers, and Em felt sicker as Grandma Helena leaned closer. "He was a very important man in this town. Always remember that you are his daughter, and don't let him down."

Em nodded. It was easier than explaining that she didn't care if her dad was important or not. She just wanted him back. She tried to scoot away a little, but Grandma Helena held her hand tighter.

"Always remember that you are Brent Faraday's daughter," Grandma Helena went on. "Never forget."

Em looked up at her. "How could I forget my daddy?"

"Not just your daddy," Grandma Helena said, leaning forward more, and Em pulled away a little again. "He was a Faraday. And so are you."

"And so is my mom," Em said, trying to make sense of what was going on.

"*No.*" Grandma's voice was quiet, but it felt like she'd yelled. "Your mother is a Martindale, which is quite a different thing altogether." Em watched as her grandmother looked at her mom across the room. *She doesn't like my mom*, Em thought, and she jerked her hand away and stood up.

"I won't forget my daddy," she said. "Excuse me."

Grandma Helena started to say something else, but Em walked away from her grandmother, something she'd never done before because it was rude to walk away from adults when they were talking to you, but she had to get away.

She went down the hall, ignoring her grandmother when she called after her, and then her mother when she called, too. Phoebe was sitting by the back door, and she wagged her tail when she saw Em.

"Come on," Em said to her, and held the door open for her. Phoebe bounded out, and Em followed her to sit on the porch steps and think.

How could Grandma Helena think she'd forget her dad? Grandma Helena wasn't the nicest person Em knew, but she'd never seemed dumb before. Em would never forget her daddy, ever.

Except even now it was harder to remember *exactly* how he'd looked and sounded, *exactly* as if he were going to come walking through the door any minute. Em squeezed her eyes tight shut. He was tall and he had dark brown hair and he always smiled at her because he loved her. She tried to capture memories of him teaching her to ride her bike, but he'd had to go away before she got the hang of it, so her mom had come out and shown her and stayed with her until she got it. He hadn't been there for Brownies either, or for the school play when she was a bell ringer because he'd had to be at work, but he'd come to some of her softball games, he'd seen her hit one out of the park.

That was it. Em focused on the way he'd looked when he'd come out on the field to hug her. He shouldn't have, the game wasn't over yet, but it was so good to have him there, and he was smiling and he was so proud. That was the moment she was going to keep, her dad smiling at her. She struggled to think of the other things that made him special, the way he hugged her and the way he loved butter pecan ice cream, and the way he said "Emily"—all of it, not just "Em"—and the way he put his head back when he laughed, and she put it all in the memory picture, her dad, with her Little League cap on his head so she'd remember the exact moment, and he'd be hugging her with one arm and holding ice cream with the other hand, and he'd be laughing with his head thrown back, and she put it all in the picture and closed her eyes hard, memorizing it, just the way C.L. had taught her.

And when her mom came out and said, "Em?" she had it, and she opened her eyes and said, "I'm fine," and followed her mother back into the house, calling Phoebe to come with them. She went in and sat down next to her grandma Helena, and took her hand, and said, "I won't ever forget him," and her grandmother squeezed her hand, and said, "You're a good girl. You're a good Faraday."

Then her grandmother gave her mother another dirty look.

Several casseroles later, C.L. came back, and Howie brought him into the living room, now crowded with sympathizers and the Faradays. "Maddie, you remember C. L. Sturgis, don't you?" Howie began in a pathetic attempt to short-circuit gossip, but C.L. circled around him, grabbed her arm, and pulled her up toward the hall.

"Excuse us," he said, and dragged her through the hall and into the family room, closing the door behind him.

"What are you doing?" Maddie asked, outraged. "Do you know who's out there?"

"Henry got a warrant and opened your safe-deposit box," C.L. said. "The money's gone. Know anything about that?"

She gaped at him. "Brent must have taken it out," she said, and then stopped. She'd seen it Saturday afternoon. Brent had been dead by then. It wasn't Brent.

"You and Brent are the only ones who opened that box in the past two weeks," C.L. said. "And you were the last one in there. They keep records of that. And I have to tell you, I'm not real happy with you right now since I just stood in front of Henry and swore you'd told him the truth about everything. What did you do with it?"

Could it be the money from the car? It wasn't the right amount, but— Then the impact of what he said hit her. "I'm not a liar," she said hotly. "I didn't take the money. I left the money and the tickets and Brent's passport all there. The only thing I took was Em's passport. I swear."

C.L. looked confused, as if he wanted to believe her but didn't. "Jesus, Maddie, this is scaring me. If you know anything about this, come clean. I don't want to lose you to some dumb mistake Henry's going to make because he thinks you're out to get me."

"*What?*" Maddie said, and then Treva came through the door.

"Whatever you're doing," Treva whispered, "stop it and get out here. This looks very funny, and the Faradays aren't laughing."

Maddie pushed past C.L. and went back to the living room to join her mother and Em on the couch. Gloria was sitting next to Helena, and they both glared as she went by. Just what she needed, Helena and Gloria bonding.

She picked up Em's hand and held it tightly. Forget Helena and Gloria. Somebody had stolen her safe-deposit key and taken the money. She wasn't even sure that was possible to do, but somebody had done it. And nobody was going to believe her, especially if she suddenly handed over two hundred thirty thousand dollars. People would think she'd stolen the other fifty thousand. Henry would arrest her.

She had to turn that money over to Henry.

Em curled up beside her and put her head into Maddie's lap.

She couldn't turn that money over to Henry.

"We need that other lock on," she heard her mother tell C.L. when he followed her into the living room, oblivious to the Faraday glares, and he nodded and said, "Come help, Em," and held out his hand. Em straightened and sniffed and went to help him.

"They've had the prowler here," Maddie's mother explained,

and everyone tried to look more sympathetic than they had before with the exception of the Faradays, especially Helena, who seethed with uncontained malevolence.

It was a long afternoon, longer after C.L. left and Vince from the police department showed up asking for her running shoes. She'd left them in the back of her mother's car, and he asked if he could take them and went to find them. Even if she'd cared, she couldn't have said no, and she didn't care. She just wanted away from everybody but Em, and Em safe and not crying. At nine her mother shooed everyone out the door and helped her get Em into bed with Phoebe close beside her, and then her mother left and Maddie got ready for bed, too. Tomorrow would be another day full of casseroles and kindness, and the day after would be the funeral. It was too much to contemplate and Maddie shrugged herself into a pink Care Bears sleep shirt that was so old it was softer than her skin, and crawled into bed.

Comfort clothes, she thought, as the ragged hem brushed against her thighs. Almost as good as comfort food. Now, if she only had a teddy bear. C.L. sprang to mind and she tried to shove him away. Em had to come first.

But it would have felt so good to just tell him everything and then let him make love to her until she was mindless. She let herself think about it once and then pushed the thought away. It wasn't going to happen. There was no point in even thinking about it. She fell asleep carefully not thinking about C.L., tall beside her, hard inside her.

It was much later when Maddie heard something and woke up. She went to check on Em and Phoebe, the one asleep after a last crying fit, the other drowsing and making rabbit-chasing noises, and when she saw they were fine, she relaxed and realized she was hungry. She hadn't eaten all day, and there were a thousand casseroles in her refrigerator and at least two cakes she knew of. The clock said two A.M., but her stomach said now.

She tiptoed down the stairs and was in the living room before something moved in the dark and she realized she wasn't alone. She gasped, and a hand clamped over her mouth while an arm pulled her back against a hard body.

"Shut up," C.L. whispered. "You'll wake up Em."

Maddie bit down hard.

He swore under his breath and let go. "What the hell?" His voice rasped at her in the dark. "Jesus, that hurt. Have you had your shots?"

Maddie turned on him, whispering, too. "What are you doing here? You broke into my house!"

"I did not. I have a key." He held it up in front of her in the gloom. "I installed the locks, remember?"

She grabbed the key. "You're looking for the money, aren't you? I don't believe this. I told you, *I left the money in the box.*"

C.L. exhaled in exasperation. He grabbed her hand and whispered, "Come here," and pulled her into the kitchen, and she went, partly because she didn't want to wake up Em and partly because even if he was a louse, his hand felt good in hers. "Maddie," he said in a low but normal voice when they were in the dim kitchen, outlined by the glow of the night-light by the sink, "if Henry finds you with that money, you're dead. I'm trying to save you, damn it. Tell me where it is, and I'll find a way to get it to Henry without you in the middle."

"Listen," she told him as quietly as she could. "I left the money in the box. I swear to you on my mother's life, I left the money there."

C.L. looked relieved but still suspicious. He dropped her hand and put his hands on her waist, pulling her a little closer, which he had no business doing, but his hands felt so good, hot and sure even through her soft shirt, that she couldn't pull away. He ducked his head down to look into her eyes while he held her close. "So if Henry searches here, we have nothing to worry about, right?"

As long as he doesn't look in your car. Maddie tried to step back, but C.L. held her in place.

"I ask because your shoes match the only footprints coming down from the Point," he said. "You didn't tell me you'd walked up there."

"That was Thursday night." Maddie tried again to step away without making a production of it, but C.L.'s grip on her waist was firm. "I walked up, and I saw Brent up there with a blonde, and then I walked down and came home and met you. I left my muddy shoes in the car. I was in my bare feet, remember?"

"Right." C.L. relaxed his grip a little. "You were in your bare feet. I can tell Henry that. Can I also tell him he won't find anything else if he searches here?"

"He won't find the two hundred and eighty thousand," she told him. "I left it in the box."

C.L.'s hands tightened on her waist. "So what *will* Henry find if he searches?"

"A lot of dust," Maddie stalled. "I haven't had much time to clean, what with murderers and blackmailers and all. Which reminds me, did you talk to Bailey? Because if he talks, we can both kiss what little we have left of our reputations good-bye. Did you—"

"No," C.L. said. "I told Henry to handle him. Tomorrow—"

"Will be too late." Maddie put her hand on his shoulder to turn him toward the door. "Go. Find him."

"It's the middle of the night." C.L. moved closer again, making her hand slip up to his neck, and his arms went around her to pull her close. "Maddie, we have to talk about the money." He kissed the top of her head, and she thought, *Move away now.*

"I don't know about any money." She tried to take a step back. "All I know is my kid is upstairs, so you can let go now. She's not walking in and catching us. You can't stay here."

"We'll hear Phoebe barking before Em hits the stairs," C.L. said in her ear. "Tell me everything you know about the money so I can figure out what to do." He moved his hands over her back, and she shivered, and then he moved them down farther and she forgot why he was a bad idea. "God, you feel good," he said as he pressed her hips to his. "Tell me about the damn money so we can make love."

"We can't do that anymore," she said, and he slipped his hands under her shirt and moved them up her bare back. "No." She pushed him away. "Em is upstairs. There is no way in hell. I don't even want to have to explain why you're in the kitchen, let alone in me. *Out*."

"Good idea," he said, and opened the back door. While she was trying to feel relieved, he grabbed her hand and yanked her out the door onto the dark back porch with him.

"Hey," she said, and he said, "Not even Frog Point can see us in this dark." He caught her to him as she tripped barefoot down the steps. "Come here."

"No," she said, and then his mouth was on hers and she wrapped her arms around his neck and kissed him just one more time because he tasted like heat and safety. She stood on the bottom step, which made her mouth level with his when he stood on the ground, and it brought a new angle to their kiss that had advantages, but they were outside, and that was stupid, so that was going to be it. "Thank you," she said breathlessly when he finally broke the kiss. "I enjoyed that. Goodbye."

He pulled her down with him to the sidewalk and wrapped his arms around her. "I can't let you go. I have to save you. Even if you don't want me to, I have to. I thought I could just ride into town and nail Brent and ride out again, but I can't leave you. I love you."

Maddie drew back. "What do you mean, nail Brent? Is that what Stan was talking about?"

C.L. pulled her close again. "That's why I came to the house Friday night. Brent sold Stan his quarter of the company . . ." C.L. went on explaining the deal he'd made with Sheila while he held on to her, and Maddie stared out into the dark.

He hadn't come back to see her. She'd forced an unwilling man to the Point while he'd been trying to pump her for information about her embezzling husband. "I can't believe this," she said. "You're telling me I raped you at the Point?"

C.L. stopped in midsentence and squinted down at her. "Are you nuts? Did you hear me screaming for mercy in that backseat? Didn't you notice the way I just dragged you out of your house because I can't stand not touching you? Get a grip, woman."

"You didn't come for me at all." Maddie felt stupid. "This whole thing started because of money. And you never told me. You slept with me, and you never told me."

"What difference does it make why I showed up to begin with?" C.L. said. "All that matters is now. Once we're married—"

"What?" Maddie jerked her head up. "Once we're what?"

"Married." C.L. kissed her forehead. "I talked to Anna and she said you should wait a year, so this time next year should be good. That'll give me time to get the house done—"

"What house?" Maddie asked, numb. "What are you talking about?"

"Howie's building us a house next to Henry and Anna, on that piece of land close to the river." C.L. held her tighter. "I was going to surprise you, but—"

"I'm surprised." Maddie pulled away from him. "I don't want to get married. I've been married. I didn't like it."

"You weren't married to me," C.L. said. "We'll be different. We—"

"C.L., there isn't any we." Maddie made her voice as firm as she could so he'd listen. "Everything I do right now has to be for Em. I can't be with you. I can't even be near you. You have to go."

"No." He kissed her cheek, and then the corner of her mouth, and then her mouth, and she fell into him the way she always did, for just one last time, she promised herself, into the rich darkness of his kiss that took her no matter what she was feeling at the time. Then she pulled away, and this time he let her go. "No. No more. You have to go. I can't believe you made all these plans—"

"What did you think?" C.L. said, losing his temper. "That I was sleeping with you just for the sex?"

"Yes," Maddie said, and then remembered the tenderness in the way he held her and kissed her and worried about her. "No. I don't know. I sure didn't think you'd build a damn house after two nights with me. What were you thinking of?"

"Us," C.L. said, his voice tight. "I was thinking of us. The same damn thing I've been thinking of since high school. This is the same thing all over again, isn't it? I'm looking at the future and you're turning away."

Maddie turned to him, amazed. "I haven't seen you in twenty years, and you come to town for one weekend, and you think that's it? That's all you know of me, high school and two nights of sex, and you're ready to make a life commitment?"

He was quiet for so long that she looked closer to see if he was all right. "I have loved you all my life," he said, and she closed her eyes at the pain in his voice. "I never stopped.

Sheila told me once that I'd married her because I thought she was like you. She said one of the reasons she left was because she couldn't be you for me. I thought she was just making excuses, but now I think she was right."

"I don't want to hear this," Maddie said, hugging herself. "I have all I can handle right now. Don't give me any more. Don't make me handle this, too."

"I love you," he said, and she said, "No, you don't, you love somebody you think you knew in high school. That's not me. I don't think it ever was me, but it's definitely not me now."

"I know who you are," C.L. said, quiet and intense. "I know exactly who you are."

"Then you know more than I do," Maddie said, "because all I know right now is that I have a baby who's heartbroken, and I have to stay out of jail to take care of her. And every time you walk into my living room, you remind Frog Point that I had a reason to kill my husband." Maddie stepped back. "You have to stay away. Forever."

C.L. sighed. "All right. If you need me to keep my distance for a while, I understand. But don't make it forever." He stepped toward her and put his arms around her, and she hesitated. "Don't do this to me again," he whispered. "Don't turn away from me. I need to know you're still mine." He kissed her hard, desperately, and she tried not to kiss him back. Then he just held her, his cheek against her hair, as if she were his lifeline.

If I come to your locker, will you turn away? he'd asked her that night in the car, and Maddie ached to tell him she loved him, but Em came first. "C.L., I'm not who I was in high school. I'm not even who I was yesterday. I can't see you anymore. I have to keep Em safe now, and the talk—I can't see you."

He said, "For a while," and held her tighter. "I'll stay away for Em's sake. But only for a while."

Maddie knew she should argue, but she didn't have the energy. When he was gone, she went inside and locked and chained the door and crawled in bed with Em and Phoebe, regretting having sent him away even while she knew that she had to. Em stirred beside her and said, "Mommy?" and she said, "Right here, Emmy. It's just us," and held Em's hand until she fell back asleep.

"How are you?" Treva asked when she picked Maddie up the next morning to do funeral arrangements. "I mean, really."

"Tired," Maddie said. *Last night I sent away the second best thing that ever happened to me so I could protect the first best thing.* "My life is full of people I have to be careful around. You're the only person I don't have to pretend in front of. You're a good friend, Treve."

Treva sighed. "I try, kid. Which means I get to give you the bad news."

Maddie looked at her in disbelief. "That's a joke, right? How much worse can things get?"

Treva slid down in her seat. "You are now the hottest thing on the Frog Point grapevine. You want to know about this or not?"

"Oh, hell." Maddie shut her eyes. "Tell me."

Chapter Fourteen

Treva took a deep breath. "Well, most think you shot your husband, but opinion is divided as to whether or not you should pay for it. The majority think it was a shame that Brent hit you and cheated on you, and that you should get off, you being such a nice person up to now and all."

"Well, that's good to know." Maddie let her head rest against the back of the seat.

"However, there is a small but vocal contingent led by Helena Faraday in cahoots with Gloria Meyer. They think you should fry. They're gaining some support as it becomes known, thanks to Esther, that you were sleeping with C.L. when the word came down that you were a widow. Also Leona Crosby has been keeping tabs on C.L.'s Mustang. Couldn't he drive a quieter-looking car?"

"Not C.L."

"Then there are the fringe theorists." Treva's voice got a little cheerier. "There's healthy speculation that Stan and C.L. were fighting over you in your driveway Saturday night. Did that happen, or has Kellie Crosby been hitting the cough syrup again?"

"C.L. hit him while Leona Crosby watched," Maddie said. "The rest is cough syrup."

"Well, that's made some people think C.L. might have killed him. Except he was shot, not beaten up, so that leads people back to you again."

"Good," Maddie said. "Dear God, my poor mother."

"Your mother's holding her own," Treva said. "She's said some cutting things about Esther's reliability, and since she and Esther have been tighter than ticks up till now, she's making some headway. And she's up to speed on the Faradays, too. Helena's in for a bumpy ride."

Maddie straightened. "Don't tell me this."

"Did you really have to hospitalize Helena once for drinking cologne?"

"Oh, *Mother*." Maddie put her face in her hands. "The only thing I can do now is move, and Henry won't let me leave town."

"I've also heard rumors that Henry is out to get you because of C.L.," Treva said. "But that doesn't sound like Henry."

"You know, what makes me nuts is that none of these rumors are about Brent," Maddie said. "He cheats on me and embezzles, but nobody knows anything about that. How can that be?"

"Oh, there are rumors," Treva said. "He was embezzling from the company, he was dealing drugs to get the money to buy votes for mayor, he cheated on his bowling scores— Brent's doing just fine. I have not heard that he was cheating on you, however. Either Brent finally got some discretion, or his honey is the invisible woman." Treva peered at her. "How are you with all this?"

"Lousy," Maddie said. "Mourning is the pits. People have been dropping food off all morning. If I see one more damn casserole, I'm going to spit."

"Mine's in the backseat," Treva said, starting the car.

Maddie focused on the one problem in her life that wasn't heartbreaking. "There must be a real potato chip shortage in town, too. What's wrong with bread crumbs on top of casseroles?"

Treva checked the street and pulled out into her lane. "You must have been reading those fascist yuppie Democrat cookbooks again."

"For that matter, what's wrong with naked casseroles? For that matter, what's wrong with unchopped food?"

"We appear to be losing our grip here."

"Okay," Maddie sighed. "What kind of casserole did you make? Manicotti, right?"

"I was kidding. It's fudge brownies with chocolate chips and cashews."

"God sent you to be my friend," Maddie said, "because She knew I needed you."

Six brownies later, they pulled into the funeral home driveway. Maddie looked up at the beautiful old Victorian and said, "Why are all the best old houses in town funeral parlors?"

"Because Frog Point won't let anybody open a whorehouse." Treva looked at the house doubtfully. "Are you sure you're ready for this?"

"I am never going to be ready for this," Maddie said, and got out of the car.

. . .

The little man at the funeral home was oily and dry at once, like old parchment.

"The undead," Treva whispered. "They walk."

"Shut up," Maddie said.

He looked at them with a mixture of condescension and consolation and led them to a large room full of caskets. "Here's our selection. All fine, fine pieces. I'm sure you'll be pleased, and that your, ah, husband would be also."

Maddie looked at him, appalled. Yeah, Brent would be thrilled.

"Could we be alone for a while?" Treva asked.

"Of course." He nodded and faded out the door while Maddie looked at the caskets helplessly. There were so many and they all looked like bad reproduction coffee tables, too much wood and brass. Too much everything. She started to shake and thought, *Not in front of Em*, and then realized that Em wasn't there.

She had to pull herself together and buy a casket and get back to Em. "What do you think?" she asked Treva.

"Get a Hefty bag," Treva said. "That's all he deserves."

Brent in a Hefty bag. For some reason, that was the thought that did it; Maddie began to laugh and cry at the same time.

"Maddie, I'm sorry." Treva sat her down on the nearest casket. "Here." She groped in her purse. "Have a Kleenex. I thought you didn't love him."

"I didn't," Maddie sobbed, grateful at last to be crying for him. "But the son of a bitch is dead."

Treva sat down and put her arm around her. "Maddie, the man slept with other women, he beat you up, and he was going to desert you." She patted Maddie on the shoulder. "Pull yourself together. The man was roadkill. A Hefty bag is too good. We'll get a generic leaf bag."

Maddie looked around the grim room and almost lost it again. "Treva, I can't handle this. I'm not ready for funerals."

"I suppose Howie and I could clean out the freezer chest till you're ready," Treva said dubiously, "but I really think it's better to get it over with."

"Um. Mrs. Faraday?"

Maddie and Treva both jumped and then turned to look at the little man who had crept up behind them.

"Have you made your choice? Can I, ah, help in any way?" He looked pointedly at their choice of seating.

They stood up, and Maddie looked from him to Treva and back again to him. "I don't know."

"I do," Treva said. "What's the cheapest thing you've got?"

When Treva dropped Maddie off after stops at the florist, church, funeral home, and stationers, her mother told her in a voice two steps away from panic that she was wanted at the police station.

Henry was waiting for her, but so were C.L. and a pleasant-faced middle-aged woman who introduced herself as Jane Henries. "I'm just standing in until Mr. Sturgis can get somebody tougher from Columbus," she said cheerfully. "Now, if you ever want to divorce anybody, you can just stick with me all the way through."

Maddie felt like flinging herself into Jane's arms. She was the first person who seemed to think everything was going to be fine. Then she noticed the lines around Jane's mouth and the glint in her eyes, and realized that around Jane Henries, everything was going to be fine *or else*.

"Now, Maddie," Henry told her when they were all sitting down. "I want you to know we're all on your side. This town knows what a good person you are, and even if we go to trial with you as defendant, they'll be understanding."

"They'll be a lot more understanding when she doesn't go to trial," Jane said.

Henry ignored her. "So I want you to know that if you've got anything to tell me, I'll listen and understand."

"She doesn't have anything to tell you," Jane said. "Can we go?"

"Well, I have a few things to tell her," Henry said, exasperated. "And since you're her attorney, you'd better listen, too."

Jane smiled serenely at him, and Maddie relaxed. C.L. had been right. She needed a lawyer.

Henry ticked off his points on his fingers. "First, you have motive. By your own admission, your husband was cheating on you; by Howie Basset's evidence, he was embezzling from a company you owned one quarter of; and by your admission, he was going to take your little girl from you."

"From what I've heard about Brent Faraday," Jane said to nobody in particular, "half the people in this town had motive."

"Plus you told John Webster at the bank you were guilty," Henry went on.

"I did not," Maddie said, stung into speaking.

"According to him, you told him that he should leave you alone with the box because you didn't want to incriminate him."

Maddie looked at him, amazed. "I what?"

"He said your words were that you didn't want to drag him down with you."

Maddie closed her eyes. "That was a joke."

"Never joke with banks or the police," Jane said, still serene. "They have no sense of humor. That's evidence of nothing, Sheriff, and you know it."

"Plus you've been hiding evidence," Henry said.

He found the money. Maddie tried to look innocent.

"You took a box from your husband's office and didn't tell me about it. Why?"

"Oh, hell," Maddie said. "I forgot about it. Jane told me to get financial evidence, so Treva and I took it when we couldn't open it there."

"I did tell her to gather up everything she could find," Jane said. "Her action was on the advice of her attorney."

"I'm going to need that box," Henry said, and Maddie slumped back in her chair and nodded.

"Then there's your suspicious behavior," Henry went on, and Maddie thought of C.L. and winced. "Why didn't you report your husband missing? He was killed Friday night and not found until Monday morning. You never reported him missing. And then there's Mrs. Ivory Blanchard."

Maddie blinked. "Who?"

"You sold her all of your husband's clothes. That might lead some people to think you knew he wasn't coming back."

"I was hoping he wasn't," Maddie said, and Jane stirred beside her. "I'd found the plane tickets to Rio. I was hoping he was on his way. Henry, none of this makes sense. You're saying I shot my husband who was leaving me anyway? Why? And how? I'd have had to drive Brent up to the Point and put a gun to his head while he just sat there. Henry, we weren't that close."

"Which brings me to means," Henry said. "That's what comes after motive and opportunity. The reason Brent just sat there was that somebody had doped him good with what the coroner called a generic painkiller. Dr. Walton says he prescribed them for you. The pharmacist at Revco says you asked him what effect seven of them would have. The coroner says he'd probably taken the equivalent of seven tablets."

"I asked the pharmacist after he'd swallowed them," Maddie

said. "He took them by accident. I know that sounds dumb, but he did."

"Sheriff," Jane began, and Henry held up his hand.

"You had motive, means, and opportunity, Maddie," Henry said. "No alibi." He sighed, and his voice turned sad and serious. "Maddie, I'll help you get a plea bargain. And if it goes to trial, we'll try the case here in Frog Point. Everybody likes you. Everybody knows how Brent was. The town's on your side."

Jane stood up. "That's enough." She turned to Maddie. "This is the biggest load of crap I've ever heard. He doesn't have means because he doesn't have the gun. He doesn't have motive because none of the things he cited are strong enough to be conclusive. And he doesn't have opportunity because he can't place you at the scene on the night of the crime. In short," she turned to Henry, "he has zilch."

"I didn't do it, Henry," Maddie said.

"Plus she didn't do it," Jane finished. "Nice seeing you, gentlemen."

"Maybe I'll just forget the guy from Columbus," C.L. said as he followed them out into the parking lot. "You're doing pretty good."

"No, I'm not." Jane turned to Maddie. "Get a criminal lawyer fast. He's got some nice circumstantial evidence going there; if he gets anything concrete, you're toast. He's not a dumb man, that sheriff."

Concrete evidence. Maddie thought of the gun in Treva's freezer. "I didn't do it," she said again, but she sounded forlorn, even to her own ears.

The next afternoon, Em felt stiff and tired and dizzy and achy. Her black velvet dress that Grandma Helena had bought her was too hot even if Grandma Helena did say it would be okay because of the air conditioning, and she was crowded around by people, and everything in the funeral room was heavy, the curtains and the carpet and the furniture and the big closed box (*"Coffin,"* Mel had whispered before her mom had jerked her away) that Em didn't want to think about. Everything was too heavy except for the skinny folding chairs that looked like they didn't belong, and everything was sort of muffled, and her eyes hurt, and she stood there like a dummy, just waiting for it all to be over. She felt like somebody had been beating her up. Every part of her body hurt, and she'd cried so much she was dry inside, and the pain still wouldn't go away. She'd go to sleep and when she woke up, the pain was still there. Even when she wasn't quite awake, before she knew what it was, she knew there was something bad waiting for her when she finally woke up all the way, something really bad, sitting like a monster on the edge of the bed, like a shadow, and it never went away. And now she was at the funeral, her daddy's funeral, and he was in that coffin with the lid shut so she couldn't even see him, and she didn't know if that was good or bad, and people kept patting her shoulder and saying, "Poor little thing," and she knew that was bad, and she just wanted to sit down and cry. Except that wouldn't help; she'd been doing that for three days, the kind of crying that tired her out and didn't make anything better at all, but she kept on doing it because there wasn't anything else to do. Nothing made anything better and it was going to be like that forever and she was so tired she couldn't stand it, but she had to because she was at her father's funeral and people were watching her.

Her head wobbled a little, and her grandma Helena came and bent down beside her. "You be brave, Emily," she whispered to her, and her perfume was so strong Em wanted to throw up. "You be a brave little soldier for your daddy."

Em felt like rolling her eyes, but she couldn't. Her other grandma, her grandma Martha, had told her that people would be watching her at the funeral, so she should try to remember to be a lady. A lady wasn't what Em wanted to be, but it beat being a brave little soldier any time. Even when he was alive, her daddy hadn't ever asked her to be a brave little soldier, and she couldn't imagine him ever asking her that, and he was dead now, so he wouldn't care anyway, right? Em clenched her teeth together. What she wanted to be was Emily Faraday, with a father and mother, even if they fought, even if they never talked, but she wasn't.

But she wasn't going to be a brave little soldier either. When her grandmother stood up, Em slipped out from under her grasp and slid behind the row of people before her grandma could grab her again. Any place was better than this.

Down at the end of the hall there was light, which turned out to be a porch. She didn't think funeral parlors had back porches, but probably other people had wanted to get out of funerals before, too. She sat on the steps and missed Phoebe and tried not to think about the funeral. She missed Mel, too, Mel who was back in the awful room, stuck between her mother and father, Mel who still had a father, Mel who looked across the room at her with red eyes that she'd gotten crying for Em, Mel who never cried. It all made Em's head hurt, but most of all it made her head hurt not thinking about her daddy, and not thinking about what was going to happen to her mom and to her.

She was rubbing her eyes when C.L. came out in his suit and sat down beside her without even looking to see if the step was clean.

"You okay?" he asked, and she said, "No. My daddy's dead."

"Right," he said. "Dumb question."

She nodded. It was that kind of day, the kind of day when

people said dumb things because they couldn't think of anything right to say. She sighed and forgave her grandma Helena for the brave-little-soldier bit.

"What I meant was, is there anything I can do?" C.L. said. "I mean, I know I can't bring your dad back, but is there anything I can do that might make you feel better?"

"No," Em said.

C.L. nodded. "Sorry. That was another dumb thing to say. Okay, the thing is, the thing I want you to know is—"

Em lifted her head to look at him when he stopped. He was frowning, but not at her.

"I don't know how to say this right," he said. "I want you to know if you need me, I'll be here. I'm going to be away during the week for the next couple of weeks, but I'll be here on the weekends and then I'm moving here. I'll be here."

Em took a deep breath. *You're not going to be my daddy, nobody's my daddy but my daddy,* she wanted to say, but he was trying to be nice, and that would be mean. And besides, she was too tired to talk.

"Listen, I know I'm not your dad," C.L. said. "I know I never will be. And I know it must be hell knowing he's not coming back. I'm not trying to tell you that I'll take his place, that everything's going to be all right."

Em nodded, feeling tears behind her eyes again.

"But I'll be here." C.L. bent down so he could look into her eyes. "I will be here for you. Always. You can count on it. If you never need me, that's okay, too, but I'll be here."

Em nodded, trying to keep the tears back.

"Okay?" C.L. said, and Em nodded again, her head wobbly, and he said, "So if you want to cry, I mean if you really want to howl on somebody, I'm here and I won't tell, it's okay."

She nodded again, and then she felt herself fall against him, and she sniffed once, she meant it to be just once, just a couple of little tears, but this time the tears came from her stomach, not wimpy little tears but big fat hacking ones, and she pushed her face into his coat and cried out everything: how mad she was, and how afraid she was, and how sorry she was, and how good it felt to just howl, and it all just kept coming and coming while he rocked her back and forth and didn't say anything at all.

Maddie had seen Em leave, her face so tight with pain that she looked old, and she saw C.L. follow and almost followed, too, but she stopped herself in time. That was all this funeral needed, the three of them leaving together. All eyes were on her anyway, and had been from the moment the doors to the viewing room had opened. People dutifully drifted over to Norman and Helena and murmured their regrets while avidly watching Helena glare at Maddie, and Maddie remain as oblivious as she could under the circumstances. Let her glare. Maddie's concern was with her daughter. She'd give C.L. some time to comfort Em, but then she was going out, funeral or no funeral, to make sure Em was all right.

"That woman," Maddie's mother said under her breath ten minutes later. "She's making a spectacle of herself."

"That's just Helena," Maddie said. "She always needs somebody to blame."

Her mother glared at her, and Maddie shut up. She was already in trouble for allowing a small arrangement of yellow irises and daisies into the room. The arrangement was beautiful, but the card had been signed "B," and when her mother had come to her with a question on her face, Maddie had said, "It must be Beth's. Put it over there with the rest."

"Are you out of your mind?" her mother had said, appalled. "It can go in a closet."

"No," Maddie told her. "This isn't about us, it's about Brent. And she probably loved him better than anyone else. Let her have her flowers."

Her mother had complied, but the flowers still rankled, glowing among the mums and lilies, outshone only by Helena Faraday's glare.

Kristie had sent flowers, too, the card signed in a neat little chicken scratch that bore no resemblance to the loopy hand on the pregnancy letter. Whoever was having Brent's baby, it wasn't Kristie. Guilt made Maddie kind when Kristie came into the room, and Kristie burst into tears and said, "I'm *so* sorry," and went to sit in the back, alone.

"I didn't know she was that close to Brent," Maddie's mother said.

"He was close to a lot of people," Maddie said, and when her mother gave her a sharp look, she added, "This is awful, but we just have to make it through this and the funeral and the people at the house, and then we can rest. It'll be over."

"Where's Emily?" her mother asked, distracted by her granddaughter's absence.

"Outside," Maddie said. "C.L. went after her."

"Well, really, Madeline," her mother said, and began to move toward the door.

Maddie caught her arm. "Let them be."

Her mother glared again, but when C.L. and Em came back half an hour later, Em's face was white and tearstained but calm, the tightness all gone, and Maddie sent a silent thank-you to C.L. with her eyes. C.L. smiled back, a slow, reassuring smile that made her want to go to him so much she almost stepped forward. Then her mother nudged her, and Maddie saw Helena's face go into meltdown at the sight of her whore of a daughter-in-law flirting at the funeral.

Go away, C.L., Maddie thought. She felt hemmed in, even

the people who were on her side were making her crazy, and she turned away from him to find Treva for a moment's sanity.

"Nice funeral," Treva said, when Maddie found her in a chair by the door. "The gargoyle in the black silk is a gruesome touch."

"He was her son," Maddie said. "She lost a lot here. Think if it was Three."

"Don't," Treva said. "Don't even say it. I couldn't stand it." She searched the crowd until she found her son and smiled in relief, and as Maddie watched, Three caught the smile and came to them.

"How are you doing, Aunt Maddie?" he said softly, and she looked up at him and frowned.

"Your voice sounds different," she said, and he said, "Well, Mom told me to keep it down, so I've been whispering all day. Makes me feel creepy."

"Don't attract attention to yourself," Treva said tensely. "Here, sit down. You're looming over everybody."

Maddie looked at Three in surprise. He was behaving perfectly well, so why was Treva scolding him? Three shrugged at her and sat, and Treva put her hand on his knee and said, "We'll go soon."

He nodded and leaned forward, his arms on his knees, to watch the people. "Mel's with Em," he whispered, leaning forward even farther to see. "They look all right. Em's not crying anymore."

Maddie glanced over to see and then back to Three, his head bent before her, the cowlick at the crown of his head making him seem so much younger than he was. "Why don't you take them—" she began and then stopped, the cowlick, and his voice, and his height, and the shape of his jaw all coming together for her, familiar and horrible, the reason for Treva's agitation suddenly clear.

"Aunt Maddie?" he said, and the room swung around, and she stopped breathing and looked down at Brent's son and thought, *Treva wrote the pregnancy letter in the box*. Treva. Not Kristie. Treva. Twenty years ago. Her handwriting had changed in twenty years, but her secret hadn't.

"Aunt Maddie?" Three said again, and she said faintly, "Why don't you take the girls outside for a while? It's cooler out there."

Three gave her a strange look and went to get his sister. *Sisters*. Em had a brother.

Treva had lied to her for twenty years. She'd slept with Brent in high school—*my best friend*—and she'd lied to Maddie, to Howie, to Three, to everyone.

Maddie stared out into the crowd, trying to make sense of it. How could she have missed it for twenty years? Three had grown up in front of her. Maybe that was the problem. He'd grown up in front of her, so she'd grown accustomed to his face, that face that was so much Treva, but now so much Brent, too. It was only in the past two or three years that Three had gotten his height. It was only today that she'd seen him in a suit. It was only today that she'd noticed the cowlick in his new short haircut he must have gotten for the funeral. His father's funeral.

It was only today she knew the truth.

For a moment she thought, *I wish I didn't know. I wish Treva had told her lies better so they'd lasted forever.*

"Maddie, are you all right?" Treva said, and Maddie said, "No," without looking at her and went to sit next to her mother, who was talking to Mary Alice Winterborn.

Treva. She'd told Treva everything; for her entire life Treva had been her best friend. And now she was gone, she'd never been there, it had all been a lie.

"Are you all right, Madeline?" Mary Alice said.

"No," Maddie said. "I just lost somebody I loved very much. I may never be all right again." She looked into Mary Alice's eyes and saw all the disbelief drain away into sympathy.

"I'm so sorry, Maddie," Mary Alice said, sincerely.

"So am I," Maddie said, and sat in dull quiet until Mary Alice went on to Helena.

"That's more like it," her mother said. "That's the way to behave at a funeral."

Maddie stared at the flowers. When she was calm, when this was over, she'd go talk to Treva. She had no idea what she'd say, but she'd talk to Treva. But they'd never be the same again. They weren't the same now. Treva had slept with Brent and given birth to his son and in twenty years had never told her. They were best friends, but they weren't. They'd been a lie, the way she and Brent had been a lie, the way the things she told her mother to keep her happy had been a lie, the way C.L.'s reason for coming to her had been a lie, the way the person he thought she should be was a lie. Everything in her life was a lie. She'd been happy while she believed the lies. And now she knew the truths, and nothing mattered anymore. Except for Em.

Maddie clutched the thought of Em to her. Em was truth, and she'd hold on to Em, and go back to teaching, and live the life her mother had, quietly, concentrating on her child. It was awful, but everything else was lies, and if she didn't get arrested for murder, that was going to be the best she could do. She didn't need Treva or C.L. or anybody but Em. At least in that kind of life there wouldn't be betrayals.

And the only lies she heard would be the ones she told herself.

Maddie threw herself into picking up the pieces of her life and mothering Emily for the next two weeks. Em was starting school, Em was training the puppy, Em was still crying herself to sleep, Em was the center of everything, and Maddie even cut short her mother's phone calls, impatient with the gossip because so much of it was lies and none of it mattered and she had to get back to Em. Her mother was cold at first, then apologetic, and then concerned, and Maddie stonewalled her in all three phases, willing to cope only with Em.

Getting the right things for school was important, never more important than now. She remembered the hell she'd gone through when her mother had insisted she wear Mary Janes to school instead of Keds like everybody else. She'd been on one end of the untouchable spectrum with her shiny black strapped shoes, and people like Candace and Stan had been on the other end in cracked leather sandals or ancient Buster Browns, and in the perfect middle had been Treva with an entire wardrobe of Keds she'd decorated with markers and glued-on charms. Treva had danced through the halls while Maddie had plodded behind in her good-girl shoes. Em was not going to plod behind anybody, so Maddie cut her mother short and went back to planning school shopping with Em.

Henry came by the day after the funeral and parked his sheriff car out in front while Leona ogled it from her porch.

"I brought you Brent's effects," he said when Maddie opened the door.

"I don't want them," Maddie said, and he'd sighed and said, "There are some valuables here, Maddie, and a lot of money. And a letter. You should see the letter."

Maddie let him in and watched while he went through the inventory of Brent's things: watch, wedding ring, signet ring, wallet, a ton of stuff. He'd been carrying a lot, but then he'd been leaving town. He'd had some clothes with him in a gray gym bag, Henry said, and there'd been a letter in the bag, too, stamped and addressed to her.

"Looks like he meant to mail it before he left." Henry handed it to her. "We'd like you to take a look at it."

The envelope was already open. "Opening my mail now, huh?" Maddie said, and slid the letter out. It was one piece of notepad paper that said *Basset and Faraday Construction* at the top, and Maddie read it with a growing sense of unreality.

Dear Maddie,

You have to read it all the way through so you know I'm not leaving you. I just have to get out of Frog Point. If I stay, I'll go nuts. So I'm taking Em and we'll be waiting for you when you come down to Brazil. I know you'll come to get Em, and then I'll explain in person. Trust me, I know what I'm doing.

People are going to say I took money, but I didn't, and I'm leaving Howie the company so it's a fair trade. I sold Stan my quarter, so you sign your quarter over to Howie, and we'll be all square. Some other people will say I don't love you, but I do. That thing with Gloria was just once, but she wouldn't let go. Don't listen to her if she tries to say it was more. Once you come down south, we'll be fine again. Em's going to love it, you know how she loves new things, and you will, too. Go ahead and put the house on the market now. It should sell fast and you can pay for your plane ticket out of that and bring the rest down when you come.

All we ever needed was to get out of Frog Point. And now we're going to. It's going to be great.

Love, Brent

"Em hates new things," Maddie said when she'd finished reading. "What was he thinking of?"

"Do you know what he means about Gloria?" Henry asked.

"I think he slept with Gloria," Maddie said, "but I have no proof. This letter makes no sense. What's he mean, he took money from the company?"

Henry looked uncomfortable. "As near as we can tell, he hiked up the price on some houses they built, and then skimmed the increase for himself. C.L.'s trying to sort it out with Howie now. It looks like he hit Dottie Wylie for about forty thousand."

"The money in the golf bag?"

"Hard to tell." Henry stood up. "It does look like he was doing it by himself, though."

"He couldn't be," Maddie said. "He never even balanced our checkbook. I did the taxes. Where would he learn to do this kind of stuff?"

"Greed's a powerful motivator," Henry said, and after he left, Maddie thought, *Not even greed could teach Brent math; he had help.* Then Em came down and asked why Henry had come, and Maddie went back to her full-time preoccupation of keeping Em shielded from everything.

Treva had called, too, the first time to tell Maddie that her mother had faced Helena down in front of the bank, right there in the center of town.

"Helena's been telling everybody you killed Brent," Treva had said in disgust. "She's a real piece of work."

"Nobody takes her seriously," Maddie had said, trying to cut the call short.

"Your mother does," Treva said, the satisfaction thick in her voice. "She backed her up against the bank building and said, 'I heard the most awful thing, Helena. I heard you've been spreading rumors about my Madeline, and I told everyone that couldn't be true because you'd never do anything that un-Christian.'"

"In front of the bank?" Maddie said, distracted. "On Main Street?"

"It was beautiful," Treva said. "Helena backed down, and then, according to my mother-in-law, your mother hinted that if Helena didn't shut up, she'd start telling a few truths about Brent. Irma said it was the closest she's ever seen your mother come to losing it."

"Like I don't have enough troubles," Maddie said. "My mother has to throw a fit on Main Street. Now what will people think?"

"I thought it was great and so did Irma," Treva said. "Are you all right?"

"No," Maddie said, needing to get away. *Your friendship is a lie.* "I have to go to Em. She's still pretty bad."

"Sure," Treva said, sounding unsure. "Listen, I still have plenty of room in my freezer for more stuff if your fridge is full of casseroles. The stuff you sent over didn't even make a dent. You want me to come pick up more?"

"No," Maddie said. Six casseroles and a gun were plenty, and the last thing she wanted was to see Treva. "Thanks for calling." She hung up over Treva's good-bye.

After a few more abortive conversations, Treva gave up and stopped calling which made things easier. Maddie had torn up the pregnancy letter after the funeral, trying to tear up the memory, but the betrayal stayed with her. She was going to talk to Treva again, of course, but not now. Not until she could look at her without wanting to cry and say, "How could you?" and all the other stupid things that wouldn't do any good.

Unlike Treva, C.L. couldn't take a hint.

Chapter Fifteen

C.L. called Maddie for the first time on Saturday after the funeral, stubborn as always. "You're going to have to talk to me sometime," he said when she picked up the phone. "Don't hang up. I'll just call back."

"C.L., I've told you, I can't see you," Maddie said, so tired from holding the fort she was ready to scream. "My mother is having fistfights on Main Street to defend my reputation; the least I can do is give her something to defend."

"I heard about that," C.L. said. "I told her I'd be glad to hold her coat next time."

"What do you mean, you told her?" Maddie said. "What have you been doing?"

"Having lunch with your mother," he said. "Nice woman.

Worried about you, though. Says you're not talking to anybody."

"I have to get ready to go back to school on Monday," Maddie said. "I'm busy."

"So's Treva," C.L. said. "But she's got time to talk, and she says you won't. What's wrong with you?"

"Nothing's wrong with me," Maddie snapped. "Your uncle thinks I killed my husband and is going around town asking questions to make sure everybody else thinks so, too, and my kid walks around like an old lady trying to deal with the fact that her father is dead, and everybody in town wants me to drop what I'm doing and gossip. I can't gossip. I am the gossip. Which is why I'm hanging up now. Good-bye."

"Wait a minute," C.L. said, and she hung up on him anyway, only to pick up the phone when it rang a minute later and find him back on the line.

"Okay, fine," he said when she'd said hello, "you don't want to talk to me. Maybe your kid does. Put her on."

"No," Maddie said, and he said, "I'll just keep calling until she answers instead of you. Put her on."

Em had come to stand by the door, wan and quiet, and Maddie covered the phone and said, "This is C.L. He wants to talk to you, but you don't have to."

Em held out her hand. "I will," she said, and took the phone, stretching the cord so she could go sit on the stairs. "This is me," Maddie heard her say, and then Em's voice went low and she talked and listened for half an hour before she hung up.

After that C.L. called every day. At first Maddie hung up, but he'd call back, and Em started grabbing the phone before Maddie could get to it, so she gave up and let Em and C.L. have their time on the phone. Anything that helped Em was wonderful, even if it was C.L.

On Sunday her mother came over, subdued and cautious, and sat with Em while Maddie went to visit her grandmother.

"I heard," Gran said as she came through the door. "Shut the damn door."

Maddie did and went to sit beside her.

"It's too dark in here," Gran complained, so Maddie got up and opened the drapes halfway. "Now tell me how you did it."

"How I did what?" Maddie collapsed into the chair beside the bed.

"Killed the bastard, of course," Gran said, leaning forward. "I heard you used pills. That's what I used. Did you bring candy?"

Maddie had stopped for a moment in the act of taking the candy out of the bag when she heard *That's what I used*, but now momentum made her continue and she handed the gold box to the old lady. "I didn't kill him."

"This is your gran, Madeline." Gran ripped the red ribbon off and clawed at the box lid. "Don't be stupid. I also heard you shot him. Which was true?" Gran picked up the milk chocolate turtle and bit into it.

"I didn't kill him," Maddie repeated. "How's Mickey?"

"Still flashing." Gran spit out a nut. "Stop stalling. How did you do it?"

"I didn't," Maddie said. "Nobody believes me, but I didn't."

Her grandmother looked at her with palpable contempt. "I did."

"Gran," Maddie said. "I know you like attention, but this is the wrong way to get it—"

"Listen, bubble-brain. Everybody in this place knows I did for Buck. The whole town knew, just the way they know you did it." Gran took another bite, smushed it around in her mouth, and spit out another nut.

Maddie gave up. Unless they drew her jury from the care

home, it didn't matter anyway. "So fine. You killed your first husband. Congratulations."

"Oh, you're so smart." Her grandmother put the half-eaten turtle down and reached for a cream. "But I was the smart one. I didn't even do it on purpose." She stopped and stared into the distance for a moment. "I don't think I did."

"Gran—"

"He hit me all the time, just like yours." Gran frowned and ate the cream while she remembered. "He was ruining my looks. When he broke my nose, the doctor did a real good job of setting it, but when he asked me how I got it, and I told him Buck hit me, he gave me some pills to make me calm."

Maddie blinked at her. "He gave *you* the pills?"

Gran nodded. "Yep. So I wouldn't get on Buck's nerves." She grinned. "But he got on my nerves a lot more, so I started slipping one into his beer when he came home. Two beers, he'd be out like a light. I didn't get punched for a good long time."

Maddie nodded, too fascinated to interrupt her.

"Then one day," Gran went on, pushing chocolates around in the box as she searched for her next, "your grandfather called from the machine shop and told me Buck had been fired for fighting, and he was coming home mad."

"Grandpa called?" Maddie said. "You knew Grandpa then?"

"Don't interrupt." Gran popped another cream in her mouth and talked around it. "So I put two in his beer and he hit me anyway when he got home before I could hand it to him. Then he drank the beer, and I put two in the next one, too, because I didn't want my nose to go again, and he sat down and went to sleep listening to the radio and he just never got up." Her grandmother smiled at the memory. "How was I to know the jackass had a weak heart?"

Terrific. Spousal murder ran in her family. Just what she

needed. "That's some story, Gran," Maddie told her in a futile attempt at damage control.

"It's not a story, it's the truth. It was even in the papers." Gran smiled at the memory. "Everybody knew what happened, but the sheriff told the paper heart attack, and that's what they printed."

"Why?" Maddie frowned at her grandmother. "I don't get it."

"This town takes care of those who help themselves," her grandmother said, in saner tones than Maddie had ever heard before. "When Buck hit me, there wasn't any point in me making a fuss that'd upset everybody. It got too bad, and I took care of it without a fuss, and the town took care of me. It'll take care of you, too. Reuben Henley took care of me back then, and his son will take care of you. He'll protect you."

"I don't want him to protect me," Maddie said. "I want him to find out who really did it. I want people to know the truth."

Her grandmother shook her head. "The truth is in whatever deal you make with the town. And you've always kept your bargains with this town, Maddie, I'll say that for you. You got no imagination and no flair, but you've been a good wife and a good mother and a good daughter and a good teacher to the town's kids. They'll remember that."

Maddie went cold. Her grandmother was right. Frog Point was perfectly capable of protecting her into a guilty verdict with no sentence. "That's not enough," she said. "I can't let Emily think I killed her father. I can't do this to my mother."

Gran sat up in bed and pointed her finger at Maddie's face. "You listen to me. It doesn't matter. Nothing matters except what it takes to survive. You remember this, Madeline: You're born alone and you die alone. In between, you make deals. You stick to your deal with the town, and Emily and your mother will be all right."

Gran picked up her mangled turtle again and sank back

against the pillows, and Maddie couldn't stand it anymore. "I've got to go," she said, standing. "I'm sorry, but I can't stay. I have to get back to Em."

"Sit down," her grandmother said. "I want to hear about this man who spent the night at your place."

"I can't." Maddie shuffled sideways to the door. "I have to go back to Em."

Her grandmother stopped chewing. "You're going to be just like your mother, aren't you? Hide in your little house with your kid even though there's a man around. What a bunch of white-faced wimps I brought into the world." She glared at Maddie. "I was never a coward like you. I took my lovers, and the hell with the rest of them. And now we've come to this. You. Bunch of cowards."

Maddie frowned at her. "What man? There was no man around my mother."

"She had a thing with that bowling-alley person." Gran sniffed. "Nice enough, I suppose, and better than nothing, but not for your mother, oh, no. She'd spent her whole life trying to live me down, she said, and she wasn't going to have you doing the same with her." Gran's face was full of pain for a moment, and then it lapsed back into its normal querulous folds. "Acted like I hadn't done enough for her, like I was something to be ashamed of." She peered at Maddie from under heavy lids. "The only thing to be ashamed of is being afraid to live, and that's your mother all over. Who'd have her life? I ask you."

"It's not a bad life," Maddie said, from the experience of the past week. "It's quiet and nobody lies to you and nobody talks about you."

Gran snorted. "Oh, yeah, that's life. And nobody makes love to you and makes you laugh and makes you glad you're alive either." Her chin came up, and she looked at Maddie proudly.

"I've had eight men in my life, and I'm not sorry about one of them. The town talked, and I didn't give a damn."

"You cheated on Grandpa?" Maddie said, appalled.

"Hell, he slept with me when I was married to Buck," Gran said, unrepentant. "What did he think I was going to do? Turn over a new leaf?" She laughed. "At least I had passion, which is more than my respectable daughter ever did." She glared at Maddie. "I had hopes for you, but you're as limp as she is. What a pair."

"I don't believe it," Maddie said, and her grandmother said, "Scott, that was his name. Sam Scott."

Sam Scott had come out to the bowling alley parking lot the night she'd been looking for Brent. "I recognized your mother's car," he'd said. Had he been watching her mother for thirty years? Is that what her mother had given up? Would C.L. do the same thing? It was awful, an awful thought. She had to get out of here, away from her grandmother who lied. Her mother had said she lied.

Maddie turned to go, ignoring her grandmother's grumbling, and then stopped, remembering the paste necklace she'd brought. "Would you like this necklace?" She took it off while she spoke and held it out to her grandmother.

"Why would I want a piece of cheap junk like that?" Her grandmother shoved the chocolate box away and glared at her. "What do you think I am? Helpless? I don't need your junk. You sit down and tell me about that man you were seeing."

"Gran, I'm sorry." Maddie shoved the necklace in her jeans pocket. "I have to go to Em. She's upset. I have to go."

"Just sit and talk for a while," her grandmother whined. "I'm not going to be with you much longer."

"Good-*bye*, Gran," Maddie said, and escaped out the door, and it sounded as if the whole box of chocolates hit it before she could step away.

She went home and almost asked her mother about Sam Scott, but one look at her mother's face reminded her that "Did you sleep with Sam Scott?" wasn't the kind of question her mother would appreciate. She'd just get another lecture on how her grandmother lied. And Maddie had enough problems, so she sat down to the Sunday dinner her mother had made and was polite until her mother gave up and went home. She spent the rest of the next week at school and at home the same way, polite and withdrawn. It was a cold life, but it wasn't as bad as the one she'd been living before, and she was pretty sure she could make it work. It was the only thing she could bear, anyway. People were just too painful, and she was through with pain for a while.

So she smiled and ached inside anyway because she was so alone.

Chapter Sixteen

C.L.'s two weeks after the funeral weren't much better.

The worst was that Maddie not only wouldn't talk to him, she wouldn't talk to anybody. Maddie's mother seemed concerned but remote, polite while she was having lunch with him but unwilling to discuss her daughter. If it had been his kid who was withdrawing, he'd have talked to anybody and everybody, but Martha Martindale liked quiet.

"I'm grateful you've kept your distance from Madeline," she told him. "There's so much talk after a funeral anyway."

He wanted to point out that the problem was that there *wasn't* talk, at least not from Maddie, but her mother had that stubborn look in her eye, and he'd heard about the showdown with Helena in front of the bank, so he let her be. She was doing her best in her own way.

His way was different.

He went to see Treva and Howie and didn't get much further.

"Hey, C.L.," Howie said when C.L. pulled up next to the Basset garage where Howie was working. "I've been meaning to call you. You still want that house?"

"Of course I still want the house," C.L. said, getting out of the convertible. "The loan should be in place by the end of the month. Candace is pushing it through for me. Why wouldn't I want the house?"

"Well, I thought with you and Maddie not together anymore—"

"We're together," C.L. said. "We've just got some distance in our together right now. How's Treva?"

"Fine," Howie said, but he looked unhappy. "She's in the house."

"Mind if I go in for a while?" C.L. said. "Few things I wanted to ask her."

Howie nodded, and C.L. knocked on the back door and then went in without waiting.

Treva was cooking a vast pot of something, her frizzy blonde hair made frizzier from the steam.

C.L. inhaled and said, "Chicken soup?" and startled her into dropping her spoon.

"Good Lord, C.L.," she said when she'd jerked around. "You scared me to death." She peered into the pot. "And now I have to fish for that damn thing."

"Let me." C.L. picked up a knife next to the cutting board.

"Not that." Treva yanked open a drawer and gave him a long-handled ladle. "Go fish."

"So what's new with you?" he asked her as he stirred, listening with half his attention for the clank on the side of the pot that would tell him he'd connected. "You okay?"

"Fine," Treva said cautiously. "Why?"

C.L. hooked the ladle under Treva's stirring spoon and brought it to the surface. "Wondered if you'd talked to Mad."

"Not much." Treva reached for the spoon as it came clear of the broth. "Ouch. Hot."

"Like that's a surprise." C.L. tasted the broth in the ladle. "Good stuff. I didn't know you cooked."

"Take it to Anna," Treva said, turning off the heat. "We have plenty."

"Taking food to Anna is like taking gossip to Frog Point," C.L. said. "Unnecessary and insulting. Why haven't you talked to Mad?"

Treva put the lid on the pot. "Because she's not talking to me. I figure maybe she just needs some time to recover. So I'm giving it to her." She met his gaze with a stonewall stare that said, "That's my story and I'm sticking to it," but she looked unhappy and angry and guilty. C.L. thought about staying to worm it all out of her, but he had enough problems with Maddie and Em, and besides, Howie might not take kindly to having his wife cross-examined.

"She won't talk to me, either," he said. "I'm just a little concerned."

"She'll be all right," Treva said. "Maddie Martindale is always all right."

On that note, he gave up on Treva and focused his attentions on his uncle.

"You cannot possibly believe she did it, Henry," he said after dinner one night for the thousandth time, and Henry, trying to read his paper, finally snapped.

"You want a list of all the evidence we have against her?"

"No," C.L. said. "But I don't see you arresting her, either, so you must have doubts."

"Yeah, I got some doubts," Henry said. "I'm working on them. But Maddie is still looking pretty good here."

"But you have doubts," C.L. pressed.

"I'd like a murder weapon," Henry said. "And there are a few people around here who might be telling lies." He picked up his paper and went back to reading.

C.L. fought back the urge to rip the paper out of Henry's hands, a stupid move if there ever was one. "So what are you doing about it?"

"Nothing," Henry said from behind the paper.

"Henry," C.L. began, and Henry put the paper down.

"None of these people are going anywhere," Henry said. "I'm watching them. And I'm waiting. And after a while, they're going to get nervous and then one of them will say something. And if it's Maddie, she'll still be all right because any fool knows she was pushed to it, and we'll try it here, and she'll get a real light sentence, and we'll all look after her and the little girl. So don't worry."

He picked up his paper, and C.L. pushed it back down again.

"Henry," he said to his outraged uncle, "putting an innocent woman in jail is not your style."

"C.L.," Henry said. "Get your goddamned hand off my goddamned paper."

C.L. gave up and let go.

He didn't give up on anything else. He called Maddie's house every day, at first to hear her voice, and then after a while to talk to Em, to find out how the first week of school was going ("Okay," Em said, but her tone said, "Awful"), to talk about Phoebe and make her smile and once even laugh a little, and to tell her to take care of her mother. "Are you ever coming over here?" Em asked toward the end of the week, and his throat had gotten tight when he'd said, "Not for a while, honey, but I'll call you every day."

He was being patient, he understood that Maddie needed time to recover, but there was a limit. Sooner or later, she was going to have to see him, even if she was only there to open the door so he could see Em.

Em's two weeks after the funeral were hell. Some days she'd wake up from dreams about her dad, and they were so real that she thought the funeral must have been the dream, but then she'd remember and it would be awful and she'd cry. Some days she woke up knowing, like waking up with a weight on her chest, and that was worse, almost, because there was no time to be happy at all. And sometimes she just woke up and lay there, wondering why she and her mom even bothered to get out of bed. There was nothing to do, not even Mel to talk to because Mel was trying so hard to be nice that it was too awful to talk to her. And it was no use to talk to her mother at all because her mother lied. She told Em they'd go back to school and things would be better, but they were worse. And she looked awful, but when Em asked what was wrong, she said nothing, she was fine, and that was a lie.

School was a lie, too. Everybody pretended everything was fine, and everybody knew it wasn't. All the teachers were really nice and looked at her like they were really sorry, and the kids all looked at her like she was from a zoo, so she ignored them all except for Mel, and she didn't talk to Mel much. Then after Thursday lunch, she didn't talk to Mel at all. They'd been opening their milks, and Mel said, "The kids are saying your daddy was shot, is it true?" Em had heard the whispers, too—the first time she'd heard it, she'd almost thrown up—but she got up now and said, "That's a lie," and moved away. Mel called, "I'm sorry, Em," but Em kept on moving, and on Friday she sat alone at lunch. Anything was better than talking to people. Later that afternoon, Em didn't have her math homework done, and her teacher said, "That's all right, Emily," and she wanted to scream, "I forgot to do it, it's not because my daddy died, everything isn't because my daddy died," but she didn't. They would have thought something was wrong with her if she'd screamed that.

Em was starting to really want to scream.

When she got off the bus after school and walked in the house, it was quiet, no phone ringing, nobody talking, just Phoebe running to her. She took Phoebe out and five minutes later she watched her mom pull into the driveway in the rental car C.L. had gotten them, home from the high school. Her mom got out of the car like she was old. When she saw Em, she waved and smiled, but it was an awful smile. Nobody would believe a smile like that.

Em waited until her mother went in the house, and then she called to Phoebe and went in and sat down at the kitchen table, folding her hands in front of her so they didn't shake. "I need to talk to you," she said, and her mother looked at her as if she weren't sure she knew Em at all.

"What, honey?"

"I need to talk to you." Em made her voice sound strong even though inside she was sick. "Mel said Daddy was shot. She said Daddy died because somebody shot him. With a gun."

Her mother sat down hard in the chair across from her and closed her eyes. "Em, I told you it was an accident. I told you—"

"I want to know the truth." Em gritted her teeth, trying not to scream. "You tell me the truth."

"Somebody shot your daddy by accident," her mom said, but her eyes didn't meet Em's and Em felt sick. *Another lie.* "I told you, it was an accident. He didn't hurt at all, Em. He didn't even feel it. I didn't tell you because I didn't want you to think about it. Just try not to think about it. It was an accident."

Another lie, another lie. Em felt so mad she was sick with it, and that scared her. If she was mad at her mom, if she didn't have her mom, who would take care of her? But her mom was lying and that was wrong and Em wanted to yell, *You tell me the truth*, but she couldn't, so instead she said, "Who did it?"

"We don't know," her mother said, sounding tired, but sounding like she was telling the truth, too. "Sheriff Henry is trying to find out. He's working hard on it." She raised her eyes to Em's and she looked so awful that Em felt ashamed for making her talk. "We don't know who shot him, Em."

"I just want to know the truth," Em said. "I want to know what you know."

Her mother jumped a little at that, and then shook her head. "I don't know anything, baby. I've never been so confused in my life."

"Okay." Em stood up, knowing she should go hug her mother and make her feel better, but somehow, she just couldn't. "Okay," she said again, and walked out of the kitchen feeling really mad and really sad even though Phoebe was trotting behind her.

It wasn't until about four that Maddie realized Em was gone. She called to ask her what she wanted for dinner and got no answer, and when she went to look in the backyard, Em's bike was gone and so was Phoebe.

This is nothing, Maddie told herself, and did a quick search of the house, ridiculous since the bike was gone, and another sweep of the backyard and the garage, and then she stood in the middle of the backyard and told herself not to panic, that everything was fine.

Who to call? Calling the police would be overreacting, except maybe not. Maybe Em had gone to her grandmother's or to Mel's or—

"Maddie, is everything all right?"

Maddie focused on Gloria, myopic over the fence. "Have you seen Em? She was out here just a minute ago."

"No." Gloria moved down the fence to get closer to Maddie. "No, I haven't. Is she lost?"

"Oh." Maddie flapped a hand at Gloria and made her escape up the back steps. "Of course not. She just left without telling me, which will get her grounded for life, that's all."

"Because she might have been kidnapped," Gloria said. "That's on the news all the time now."

"Not in Frog Point, Gloria," Maddie said as she pulled the screen door open, not even pretending to be polite. "She was not kidnapped." She let the door slap shut behind her and then stood in the kitchen for a moment, trying very hard not to be terror-stricken.

She was not kidnapped. She was probably at Mel's.

"Treva?" Maddie said as soon as somebody picked up the phone at the Bassets'.

"What's wrong?" Treva said. "Why are you squeaking? What's wrong?"

"Have you seen Em?"

"Oh, dear God." Treva's voice faded as she turned to yell behind her. "Mel, have you seen Em?"

Maddie strained to hear the faint conversation, but it didn't last long enough for her to hear.

"She hasn't seen her, Mad," Treva said. "She says Em's been real quiet at school all week, so everybody's sort of letting her alone. She said she's tried to talk to her, but Em just looks at her."

"Oh." Maddie tried not to think about Em just looking at a kidnapper or the murderer. "Listen, it's probably okay. She probably went to my mom's. I'll call there. Don't worry."

"If you don't find her, we'll look for her," Treva said. "We've got three cars here, we can cruise the whole town. Call me back and let me know."

"Right." Maddie nodded at the phone and let her head wobble. "Right."

Her mother was even less help.

"Where is she? Oh, my goodness, Maddie, that child could be anywhere. Why would she run away? What did you do?"

"Mother." Maddie took every iota of self control she had and shoved it between herself and the phone. "You are not being helpful. If she's not there, she probably just took Phoebe for a ride. I'm going out to look for her. You stay there in case she shows up."

"Well, I'm calling Henry Henley," her mother said sharply. "Somebody has to find that child."

Maddie banged the receiver down and tried to think. If not Mel's or her grandmother's, where would Em go? Not back to school, she'd been miserable there all week. The Revco downtown maybe. Or the bank to do the stamps again. Or—

The hell with thinking. Maddie grabbed her purse and headed for downtown Frog Point, driving slowly so she could check out the side streets as she went. Em wasn't at Revco, but Sheila was, and when she heard Maddie ask Susan at the checkout counter if Em had been by, she promised to keep an eye out and bring her home. At the bank, Candace did the same.

"This is awful," she said. "She's such a little sweetie. I'll check with the rest of the tellers, but she always came to me."

The counter help at Burger King hadn't seen her and neither had the clerks at the Dairy Queen, nor had Kristie at the company. "I haven't seen her since the funeral," Kristie told her. "I'll watch for her and call you if she comes in."

Maddie went out to the car and put her head down on the steering wheel.

This could not be happening. She had a deal with God, one she hadn't recognized before, but still a definite deal, that she would put up with anything He threw at her as long as Em was safe. Em was off limits. This couldn't be happening.

Maddie drove home by a different route, staring down side streets as if she could make Em appear if she just strained her eyes enough, and she even made a loop around the school, but it was hopeless. When she turned in the driveway, Em's bike still wasn't back. She went inside in time to catch the phone.

"Maddie? This is Henry Henley. Have you found her yet?"

Right. The guy who wanted to convict her of murder for her own good. "No, Henry. I looked downtown and at the company, but no, I didn't find her."

"Well, we got everybody out looking for her, so we'll find her. You stay home now in case she calls, okay?"

"Right." This was good advice, and Maddie felt a stab of guilt that she was being so flat with the man who was trying to find her child. "I appreciate this, Henry, I do. I'm just . . . scared."

"I know, honey," he said. "I'm not happy about it, either, but we'll get her. I have to. Anna'd never let me in the house if I didn't."

"You would anyway, Henry," Maddie said. "That's just you."

"That's my job," Henry said. "Now, you sit tight and wait till she calls, you hear?"

"I hear," Maddie said, and five minutes later when the phone rang again, she prayed it was Em.

Instead it was somebody with laryngitis, whispering over the phone to her in a raspy voice. "Mrs. Faraday? You have a nice little girl."

"What?" Maddie's mouth went dry. "Who is this?"

"Emily is real nice."

"*Who is this?*"

"If you want to see Emily again, you tell Henry about the gun and the money you found. You turn yourself in or you won't see your kid again."

Chapter Seventeen

Where is she? Who are you?" Maddie's voice rose to a shriek. "*Where's my daughter?*"

The voice rasped again. "You know you're guilty. Turn yourself in. Do it. Do it now."

"*Listen to me,*" Maddie said, rage making her voice sharp. "If anything happens to my daughter, I will find you and kill you. If there's a mark on her, I will find you and kill you. If—"

"*You're wasting time.* You only got fifteen minutes to call Henry. Do it or you won't ever see her again. *Ever.*"

"*Wait a minute,*" Maddie screamed into the receiver, but all she got in return was a dial tone.

She hung up the phone and shook for a moment, trying to think. She had to find Henry's number. No, she could do 911. Her fingers fumbled with the phone buttons. Em was somewhere with a maniac. The police switchboard answered and she screamed, *"Get me Sheriff Henley."* Henry's voice came on seconds later and said, "What the hell is this?" and Maddie said, "I did it, Henry, I killed my husband, get over and arrest me and make sure you use the siren, *hurry!*"

Henry said, "Maddie?" and she said, *"Hurry.* And use the siren, promise you'll use the siren, and *hurry."*

He used the siren. By the time he was at her front door, the whole street was on their respective front porches, and Maddie didn't give a damn. All she could think of was Em scared, Em hurt, Em with a kidnapper, and panic made her weak.

"What the hell is going on?" Henry asked when she met him at the door, and Maddie pulled him in and said, *"The kidnapper called."*

"Slow down." Henry took her arm and marched her into the front room. "Go slow and tell me everything."

"He said I'd done it, and he wouldn't give Em back until I confessed," Maddie said, her voice shaking.

"You sure it's a man?"

Maddie nodded. "Pretty sure. He was whispering and his voice was raspy, but it was a man." Some man had Em. "He said I had fifteen minutes to call you and confess."

"Well, if he missed those sirens, he's deaf," Henry said. "You're doing all right. Did you recognize the voice?"

"No, no, *of course not."* Maddie couldn't believe how dumb he was. "If I'd recognized the voice, I'd be after her now. Henry, *somebody's got her.* It might be the murderer. Nobody else would care if I confessed. *Em could be with the murderer."*

"Stop screaming for a minute," Henry said, and went out to his car. The whole street watched while he talked into his handset, and Maddie prayed he was giving good instructions. Em was lost, Em was kidnapped, she couldn't get her mind around it, it was so awful, *Em*, her mind screamed, and her arms ached because they were empty instead of holding Em.

Henry came back inside. "I know you're scared," he said, sitting beside her again. "But I need you to concentrate. Could it have been somebody from the bank?"

"The bank?" The thought was so incongruous that Maddie blinked at him. "You think Harold Whitehead killed Brent?"

"How about Webster?" Henry said. "The one who went down to the safe-deposit box with you. Did you watch him put the box away?"

"No," Maddie said. "As soon as I found the passport, I ran." The impact of that hit her. "Webster? You think Webster took the money? You think Webster has Em?"

"It was his little brother that rear-ended you Thursday," Henry said. "I'm suspicious of coincidences. Could the voice have been Webster's?"

"Henry, the voice could have been yours," Maddie said. "What are we going to do? Em—"

"Em needs you not to panic," Henry said. "Think. Could it have been Stan Sawyer?"

"Oh, God, I don't know." Maddie put her head in her hands. "I swear, it was just a raspy voice. I couldn't tell Stan's voice or Webster's voice if they were talking normally. I just don't know."

"Howie?" Henry said, and Maddie said, "No. *No.* I'd know Howie's voice. It wasn't Howie."

"Tell me exactly what he said," Henry said, but then her phone rang. "Let me listen, too," he said, following her as she ran to answer it, but when she picked it up and held it turned out so they both could hear, it was her mother.

"Maddie, what's going on? I heard sirens and there are flashing lights down the street. Is that your house? Is it Em? What's going on?"

"It's not Em." Maddie fought to keep her voice calm. "We still haven't found her. It's just Henry come to help."

"Well, tell him to turn those lights off. The whole street will be thinking you're in trouble."

"Mother, I can't talk now," Maddie said, and hung up while her mother was still protesting. "The sirens worked," she told Henry. "Do you suppose he knows?"

"The whole town knows," Henry said. "Now, tell me what he said, just the way he said it."

Maddie closed her eyes and tried to remember. "He said, 'Mrs. Faraday' first, and then he said something like 'You have a really nice little girl,' something like that, and then he said if I didn't confess, I wouldn't see her again."

"That's what he said, if you didn't confess?"

Maddie let her head fall back against the wall. "I can't remember. He said I had to tell you. He said to call Henry."

"Henry? Not Sheriff Henley?"

"Henry. I'm pretty sure it was Henry."

"Try to remember his exact words, Maddie," Henry said. "There might be something there."

"He knew about the money," Maddie said. "He said I had to tell you about the money." *And the gun.* Maddie went cold. Whoever it had been knew about the gun in the Civic. It was the murderer.

Oh, God, the murderer had Em.

The phone rang again, next to her ear, and she screamed from surprise and fear, and Henry said, "Take a deep breath before you answer it," and all she could think of was Em.

The bike wobbled as Em pedaled down the gravelly road, so tired she wasn't sure she could keep everything from falling over. The idea of going to the farm had been a good one, she was sure of that. And she knew the way because she'd memorized the road turns with C.L.'s memory trick, telling herself there were Thirty-one people on the Porch eating Hickory nuts. But she'd been on Route 31 now for what seemed like hours, and there hadn't been any Porch Road, or if there had been, she'd missed it, so she was lost. She was lost out in the country and she could get kidnapped or run over or shot—she swallowed hard—and Phoebe wasn't happy about riding in the basket of her bike after the first half hour, and Em wasn't happy about riding her bike after the first hour, so now the idea of going to the farm didn't sound quite so good, although if she could get there, she'd be so happy—

At that point, Phoebe whined again, and Em gave up and steered her bike off the road and under a tree. She managed to park the bike and scoop Phoebe out of the basket just seconds before the puppy jumped and hung herself on her leash. Em collapsed on the ground under the tree and watched Phoebe sniff the ground in a wide half circle, straining at the end of her leash.

She could turn around and go home, but that would put her back where she'd started. And that was the last place she wanted to be. She'd had a week of school, a week of kids talking in low voices when she went by, which was worse. And Mel wanted to ask questions about it, too. It was the first time in her life she'd ever not wanted to be with Mel.

Not that Em didn't understand what Mel was doing. She wanted to ask questions, too, but her mother kept lying, and finally she just had to know. So she'd set out for the farm and C.L. They could fish and talk about Phoebe and maybe things wouldn't be awful for a while. Maybe she'd even get some answers.

If she ever got over being lost. Which she wasn't going to do if she didn't get off the ground and get pedaling again. It was an awful thought, but she couldn't spend the rest of her life under this tree, and sooner or later it was going to get dark and then she would be in trouble.

"Come on, Phoebe," she called, and when the puppy came trotting over, she put her back in the towel-lined basket. Phoebe sighed and tried to get comfortable, and Em said, "I know, I don't want to, either, but we have to," and that's when she heard the car coming and looked up and saw the bright red Mustang.

"Hey," C.L. said when he'd pulled up beside them. "Your mom's having a heart attack."

"I'm sorry," Em said, not meaning it. If her mom hadn't been acting so awful, Em wouldn't have had to ride her dumb bike a thousand miles.

"Yeah, you sound sorry." C.L. got out of the car, trying to look mean and blowing it completely. "I'm against you making your mom unhappy."

"You're not mad," Em said, really tired now. "Don't lie."

"Hey." C.L. frowned. "What's with you?"

"I got lost." Em got off her bike, and C.L. reached out and steadied it with his hand. "I wanted to come talk to you, but I got lost and couldn't find Porch Road. I screwed up."

"You didn't get lost." C.L. lifted Phoebe out of the basket and put her on the ground. "You got tired. Your turn's about a mile up the road. You'd have been fine once you got going again."

Em eyed him narrowly. "Really?"

"Boy, you don't trust anybody." C.L. rolled the bike toward the car. "Get in and I'll show you." He lifted Em's bike into the back and opened the front door so Phoebe could scramble in, and Em felt all her troubles lighten.

They were still there, they were just lighter.

Em walked around the car and got in the passenger side,

glad not to be pedaling her bike anymore and really glad she was with C.L. Phoebe climbed into her lap and leaned over the edge of the door, and Em held on to the puppy's stomach so she wouldn't jump out, hugging the warm little body to her. Really, things were a lot better. She let her shoulders relax a little against the soft seat, tipping her head back to rest her neck. Necks got really tired when you pedaled on gravel for a thousand miles.

C.L. got in and patted her knee, and then he turned the car around and drove for two minutes before he slowed. "See?" he said, pointing to the sign that said Porch Road. "You'd have been fine."

It really was there. She'd almost made it. She hadn't screwed up. C.L. turned down the road, and Em sighed and relaxed completely. "It was too long a way to ride on a bike."

"That's true," C.L. said. "But you didn't know that. It seems shorter in a car. Stop beating up on yourself. The only thing you did wrong was scare your mom. And me."

Em looked at him sideways. "You were scared?"

"Yes." C.L. didn't take his eyes off the road, but he said it strong enough—a real "Yes," not a "Yep" or anything—so that she knew he was telling the truth. "You scared the living hell out of me and Henry and Anna and your mom and about a million other people, so don't do that again."

Em stuck her chin out. "Did you think I might have been shot?"

C.L. slowed the car so he could look at her. "No. That thought never crossed my mind. I was thinking about being kidnapped or hit by a car."

"Oh."

"What's this all about, Em?" C.L.'s voice was easy, but he was serious, and Em sighed again and gave up trying to be cool.

"My mom lies to me." C.L. started to interrupt, but she kept going and he stopped. "She told me my dad died in an accident, and then I found out he was shot, and she said that was an accident, but the kids at school said it wasn't, that he was . . . killed." She sank down in her seat, clutching Phoebe tighter. "Most of the kids at school are geeks, but I bet they're right." She looked over at C.L., daring him to lie to her. "Aren't they?"

He pulled off to the side of the road again and parked. He stared straight ahead for a couple of seconds, and then he turned and looked straight in her eyes and said, "Yes. They're right. He was shot on purpose by somebody who was mad at him."

"Who?" Em said, sick at heart.

"We don't know."

Em snapped her head up, angrier than she'd ever been in her life, but C.L. said louder, *"We don't know who, Em."* She took a deep breath, and he said, "That's the truth. Henry is trying to find out, but we really don't know who."

"Is he going to shoot my mom, too?" Em's voice shook as she finally said the part that had been terrifying her.

"No." C.L.'s voice was strong. "If I thought your mom was in danger, I'd be right there. Whoever shot your dad was mad at your dad, not your whole family."

"Somebody broke into our house," Em said, and C.L. said, "Yes, but whoever it was took what he wanted and hasn't been back. He's not going to hurt your mom."

He seemed a little uncertain at the end, and Em shot him a sharp look. "Don't lie," she said, and he said, "If you don't quit accusing me of lying, you and I are going to have words. I told you, I don't lie."

"That last part about my mom sounded like a lie," Em said. "You didn't sound sure."

"Nobody's trying to shoot your mom," C.L. said. "If I thought they were, she'd never get out of my sight. Cross my heart."

"Don't treat me like a kid," Em said.

"You are a kid," C.L. said. "Stop trying to be an adult and let us take care of you."

"I just need to know what's going on," Em said. "All the whispering, all the kids at school, Mom looking so awful, it's all awful. I hate it."

C.L. started the car again. "Tell you what. I was going to take you back to your mom's after I showed you the road, but I think we should go on out to the farm instead and have your mom come pick you up. And then maybe she'll stay for supper and you can both relax some. Sound good to you?"

Em nodded. "Yeah. But I still want to know what's going on."

"So do I, kid," C.L. told her. "So do I."

Maddie closed her eyes, took a deep breath, picked up the receiver, and said, *"Hello?"*

"It's all right." C.L.'s voice came over the line, warm and sure. "Call off the dogs, babe. I've got your kid, and she's fine."

"What?" Maddie's knees gave way and she sat down on the stool by the phone. *"You've* got her? She's all right?"

Her hand shook so much she couldn't hold the phone, and Henry took it from her. She heard him say, "Who is this? C.L.? What the hell is going on?" and she put her head down on her knees while Henry listened and then said, "Tell it to Maddie." She picked up her head and he handed her the phone. "Em is fine. I've got to make a call or two. You stay here and talk to C.L. and calm down."

Maddie took the phone, trying to swallow back tears of relief. "C.L.?"

"It's okay, honey. She's fine," C.L. said, and there was so much love and concern in his voice that she felt weak and leaned back against the wall, moving the phone away from her mouth so he wouldn't hear her cry.

"She was trying to ride her bike out here to the farm," C.L. went on. "She did pretty good, too, considering. She's really tired but she's fine."

"She's all right?" Maddie started to rock back and forth, holding herself while she cried with relief. "She's all right. Where did you find her? Who took her?"

"Nobody took her," C.L. said. "That was my first thought, too, but she took off on her own. Anna's giving her lemonade right now. She's fine."

Maddie sniffed and told herself to breathe slowly or she'd hyperventilate. Em was all right. She wasn't kidnapped. She was all right. Maddie wiped her tears away with the back of her hand. Some jerk had heard Em was missing and called for a prank, and all along she'd just taken her bike for a ride. "I don't ever want to be that scared again. Tell her she's grounded forever. I can't believe she did this. After everything else—"

"She did this because of everything else," C.L. said. "You have to talk to her, Mad. She's scared and confused and she needs to know what's going on."

Maddie's tension focused on C.L. Some jerk had threatened her daughter and now C.L. thought he was Dr. Spock. "Thank you for the advice. I'll come get her."

"Why don't you let her stay out here for a while? I think she could use a change of scenery."

"C.L., I don't—"

"And Anna's crazy about the idea. I already asked. They're going to bake cookies tomorrow."

Maddie gritted her teeth. "C.L., I *really* don't—"

"Humor me," he said in that tone of voice that meant *Do it.* "Pack some stuff for yourself and come out here where you're safe and you can get some rest. The two of you have had enough Frog Point for a while."

"C.L.—"

"I know you're mad," he said. "I know you were scared and now you're mad and I know you've been through hell and it's not over. Come out here and let us take care of you." He dropped his voice a little, and Maddie knew there was somebody listening on the other end. "Come out here and let me take care of you. You don't get extra points for doing it by yourself, Mad."

You should, Maddie thought. You should get bonus points. But she was so tired of doing it herself, and going out to the farm didn't mean she was giving up. It just meant she was resting a little.

Maddie closed her eyes to keep from crying because it sounded so good. C.L. Anna. The farm and the river and no kidnappers because Henry and C.L. wouldn't let any near. Not that C.L. was a hero just because he'd tripped over her kid and was keeping her safe. Maddie tried to hold on to her anger because it was the only thing keeping her from running out to the farm without the car and throwing herself into his arms and saying, *Somebody's out to get me, stop them.* She could save herself. She was going to save herself. And Em.

"Anna's making fried chicken and gravy," C.L. coaxed. "Em can't wait. And there will be mashed potatoes. The only thing you love more than mashed potatoes is Em. And me."

There was a grin in his voice, and she felt lighter just listening to him. "Cholesterol," Maddie said.

"Em's eight," C.L. said. "She won't need a bypass until high school at least."

She should not go out there. C.L. was out there, and she'd made careful plans to stay away from him, from everybody, until things were calm again, until she could handle people and phone calls again. Until she could handle being with C.L. again.

"C'mon, Mad," he said. "Em's happier out here. And safer. Come on out."

He was right. "All right," Maddie said. "I'll come out."

She hung up the phone and sank down on the stool and tried to find her place in the world again. Em was all right. If Em was all right, there wasn't anything else in the world that could be too wrong.

Except there was. Maddie straightened on the stool. The voice had said, *Tell the police about the gun and the money.* Which meant that the caller wasn't some miscellaneous jerk. It was the murderer and he was out to get her.

The phone rang again, and Maddie stared at it. It could be anything, the murderer, the police, her mother-in-law, Treva, dozens of people she didn't want to talk to, dozens of problems she didn't want to handle. The phone rang again, and she answered it and told her mother that Em was fine and she'd call later and explain everything, and then she called Treva and told her that Em was fine and she'd call later and explain everything, and then she went to get Em's PJs and a change of clothes, telling herself that things were going to be fine.

She couldn't wait to get out to the farm.

Em sat on the porch and waited for her mom, drinking lemonade slowly to make it last. Anna said she could have as much as she wanted, but slowly was better. Especially since she had to get a lot of stuff thought out before her mom got to the farm.

Then her mom came down the road in the rental car and parked at the edge of the lawn and got out and marched across the grass to her, and Em wanted to run to her, but she wasn't going to. Not this time. Em put the lemonade down carefully on the steps and stood up and crossed her arms in front of her.

Her mom stopped before she got to her and looked at her funny, and Em raised her chin a little. Her mom said, "I was worried *sick* about you, don't ever do that again," but Em just stared at her until her mom said, "Em?"

The screen door slammed and Em heard C.L. walk across the porch behind her. "Em is tired of being lied to," he said to her mom. "She wants to know what's going on."

Em saw her mom's jaw get tight. "I can raise my child on my own, thank you," she said to C.L. over Em's shoulder.

"Well, you know, you can't," C.L. said. "That's why she tried to bicycle fifteen miles to find me."

Em's mom took a step closer, still glaring at C.L. *"Listen—"*

"He's right," Em said. "You can yell at him if you want, but he's right."

Em's mom looked shaky. "Em—"

"He doesn't lie to me," Em said. "I know he doesn't tell me everything, I know he knows stuff that I don't know, like why he's worried about you even though he says you're not in trouble. But he doesn't *lie* to me. And you do. You lie and you *lie.*"

Once the words were out, Em started to shake, too. The words were so awful, but she had to say them. "You lie all the time," she said, and then she turned and walked away from the house to the dock, trying not to cry. When she got to the dock, she took off her shoes and sat on the edge of the splintery boards and dangled her feet in the warm water. Phoebe came bounding along and Em grabbed her collar to keep her from falling in and hugged her warm squirmy body close and tried really hard not to think about what she'd just said.

. . .

Maddie wanted to run after Em and hug her and make her be the child she'd been a month ago instead of this rigid bundle of misery walking stiff-legged toward anyplace there weren't any grown-ups. Then Em sat down at the edge of the dock, and Phoebe romped over to sit beside her, and Maddie thought, *I have to fix this and I don't know how.*

"You have to stop lying to her, Maddie," C.L. said, and she turned on him because he was the only person she could yell at.

"You want me to tell her that her father was murdered?" she demanded. "You want me to tell her that he was an embezzler and that he was having an affair, and that he was planning on kidnapping her and taking her to South America without me? You want me to tell her about you and me?"

"Yeah." C.L. looked grim, but he nodded. "Yeah, I do. Because she already knows something's really wrong, and the truth is better than all the things she's afraid of. And you're all she's got, Mad. If she can't trust you, she's all alone, and she's too damn little to be all alone. And I'll tell you something else, now that I'm at it. Em is not that fragile. You treat her like she'll break any minute, and I know she's having a hard time, but she's tough as an old boot as long as you're straight with her. If you're straight with her, she'll be fine."

No. Maddie swallowed and took a step back. Losing a father was enough of a nightmare for Em; losing one to a killer who was still out there would be unbearable. *No.* "I cannot tell her that her father was murdered. I won't."

"You don't have to." C.L. sat down on the porch steps, bending slowly as if he'd aged suddenly. "I already did."

Maddie went cold. "You *what*?"

C.L. looked up at her, and she could tell he was resigned to her anger. "She asked me. The kids at school had told her, so she asked me if it was true. And I'm not going to lie to that kid. Ever. Even if it means you hate me."

"Well, good for you," Maddie said, her head wobbling with anger. "You must be feeling *very* virtuous. *Do you realize—*"

"I realize what it's like to be lied to," C.L. snapped. "I realize what it's like to look at you and love you so much it hurts and know you're lying in your teeth to me because you don't trust me. And I'm not doing that to your kid. Forget it."

He had it all wrong, as usual, but she didn't have time to argue her point. "Listen, you. Em and I are fine. We do not need you or your help, so kindly *butt out.*"

C.L. flinched. "You may not need me, but your kid does. And I need her to need me. If you and I aren't going to make it, well, that's how it goes, I guess. But don't mess with Em and me. Because we are going to make it."

Maddie really looked at him then, grim and determined on the porch steps, telling her he wasn't going to desert her daughter no matter what. He'd be there for Em. He wanted to be there for Em. And Em trusted him, she'd come to him.

And Maddie thought, *I trust him, too, damn it.* He was solid and sure and funny and sweet and exasperating and inescapably desirable, and he wanted to protect Em forever, and all she had to do was go back to being the old Maddie he wanted and she could have him. That was all she had to do.

"I can't do it," she told him. "I cannot be that insipid wimp I was twenty years ago. I can't even be the sarcastic wimp I was a month ago. I'm not the woman you fell in love with in high school. Forget it."

C.L. blinked at the shift in the conversation, and then picked up the thread. "Her? Forget her. I have. She was a terrific memory, but you're not her. You're stubborn and bitchy and you have a hell of a mouth on you, and most of the time

I don't know whether to jump you or scream and get the hell away from you, but I love you and that's the way it is. God knows why, but I do. I love your kid, too. So deal with that, babe." He scowled at her, and she almost laughed except everything was too miserable.

No more lies, he'd said, and she thought about the last two weeks, about not having him with her, and avoiding Treva, and pretending with her mother that everything was fine, and about Em not trusting her anymore, and about how she'd felt an hour ago, her whole world ripped away, and how she never wanted to feel that way again. She'd tried to protect Em by pushing everyone away, but the loneliness of it had been overwhelming, something she'd never felt before because she'd always had Frog Point wrapped around her, keeping her safe. Well, she'd gotten what she wanted, away from Frog Point. Away from everybody.

And she'd been miserable and vulnerable and afraid, and she hadn't protected Em at all.

So maybe it was time to go back.

"Don't move," she said to C.L. "I have to go talk to my kid, but I want you to stay right here until I get back."

"I don't have anyplace else to go," C.L. said. "I'm building a house here."

She turned and headed for the dock, pushing herself toward the worst of several conversations she didn't want to have but was damn well going to have.

Maddie sat down beside Em on the splintery dock and pulled off her own shoes so she could feel the cool green water on her feet. The relief spread up through her ankles and calves and relaxed her body, and she sighed because it all felt so good.

Em splashed her feet a little, and when Phoebe slipped from under her arm to climb into Maddie's lap and lunge to lick her face, Em set her jaw and turned away a little.

Maddie picked the puppy up and put her on the dock behind them and took Em's hand.

Em took it back.

All right. Maddie folded her hands in her lap and started over. "Okay, you're right. I should have told you the truth. I was trying to keep you from being hurt because the truth was so ugly, but I guess there really wasn't any way I could do that." She ducked her head a little to look at Em's face. "Was there?"

"No," Em said. "No. And it's awful not knowing what's going on. I can't stand it."

"What do you want to know?" Maddie said.

Em bit her lip and looked up at her. "C.L. said somebody shot Daddy."

Oh, hell. Maddie nodded. "Yes, but he died right away. He didn't feel anything, Em. That's the truth."

Em pressed her lips together for a minute. "Who did it?"

"I don't know," Maddie said. "Truly, I don't know. Henry is working on it, but we really don't know. I don't even have a guess."

"Tell me what happened," Em said. "I want to know."

"Okay." Maddie swallowed. "We don't know a whole lot. But that Friday night, your dad met somebody in his car. And he was feeling really sleepy because he'd drunk some wine that had some of my pills in it. So the other person drove the car up to the Point and parked it. And we don't know exactly what happened next, but your dad must have fallen asleep from the pills, and then"—Maddie put her arm around her daughter's rigid shoulders—"and then the other person shot him."

Em nodded, not leaning into her mother. "That's what the kids said. Grandma said he got sick and died real fast, but the kids said he got shot." She looked up at Maddie. "But I didn't know about the pills. Does that mean he didn't even know he was getting shot, even for a minute?"

"Probably," Maddie said. "Even if he was still awake, he was probably so groggy that he didn't know what was happening. It didn't hurt him, Em. That's no lie. He didn't hurt at all."

Em sighed and leaned against her mother. "That's better. A little. It's still awful, but I didn't like thinking if he'd been scared or something."

"No." Maddie kissed the top of Em's head. "No. He was probably fast asleep."

"Is the person going to shoot you?" Em asked.

"No." Maddie pulled back a little to look in Em's face. "No, of course not. Don't worry about that at all."

"He shot Daddy," Em said, her voice quivering. "He could shoot you, too."

"I think he was mad at Daddy." Maddie tried to think of a way around all the messy details without lying. "There were some people who were mad at your dad, but they're not mad at me."

"Because a lot of really bad stuff happened to you, too," Em said. "Like the car accident and your face."

"Those were accidents, Em," Maddie said. "The car thing was just an accident." *Webster's little brother rear-ended you*, Henry had said. "I think it was just an accident. People get in car accidents all the time."

"Was your face an accident?" Em asked, and Maddie swallowed again and said, "No."

"What happened?" Em's eyes narrowed as Maddie hesitated. "Don't lie."

"Your dad came home that night really mad," Maddie said.

"And I was mad, too. And we had a fight." She stopped again, and Em sat stone-faced next to her. "And he hit me."

Em blinked, and then she pulled away and said, "*No, he didn't.*"

All right. All right.

"He didn't do that," Em said.

Maddie sat silent, determined to keep her promise and not lie, equally determined not to batter her daughter with the truth.

They sat staring at the water, watching the fish dart just below the surface, and the sun highlight the ripples, and the reflection of the dock wavering on the cool green water. Behind them, Phoebe scratched at fishy smells.

Finally Em said, "Why?"

Maddie took her hand, feeling how fragile Em's little bones were against her fingers. She was so little. Too little for the truth, but that was all that Maddie had anymore. "He was just really mad, Em. He said he was sorry." Maddie remembered Brent on the other side of the door saying, "I'm sorry. I just need to know what you know." Everybody wanted the truth. "He was really, really sorry. He lost his temper. Listen." She bent down closer to her daughter. "He never, ever hit me before or after that. Ever. He wasn't like that."

"I know." Em stared back down at the water and sniffed. "I know. He was a good daddy."

"Yes, he was."

Em nodded. "So nobody is trying to hurt us."

"No," Maddie said, ignoring for the moment the kidnapping call. "Em, I'm sorry about all this. I'm sorry you heard all this."

"It's better," Em said. "It's better than not knowing what's going on. It was scary not knowing."

"I know," Maddie said. "I don't like it much myself. Are you okay?"

"Yeah," Em said. "I'm really, really sad, but I'm okay." She lifted her chin and stared around her, as if she were looking at the farm and the river for the first time. "I'm glad we're out here, though. I like Frog Point, but I'm glad we're out here for right now."

"Me, too, kid," Maddie said. "Frog Point wears on a person."

Em tilted her head to see her mother. "Are you mad at Aunt Treva? Because you haven't been talking to her at all, even when she calls."

Treva. One more lie to confront. One more betrayal. Maddie let go of Em's hand and hoisted herself up off the dock. Phoebe leaped for the sky in ecstasy because they were going someplace and ran back and forth across the end of the dock. "No. I'm not mad." That wasn't a lie. She was disappointed and hurt and betrayed, not mad. "Listen, I've got to go into town and talk to your grandma and tell her you're all right. You and Phoebe will be fine here with C.L. and Anna."

"Do you like C.L.?" Em's eyes were back on the water, carefully not looking at her mother.

"Yes." Maddie looked up at the sky and thought, *I am not discussing my sex life with this child. Forget it.*

"Is that why Daddy was mad?"

"No. Oh, God, Em, *no.*" Maddie dropped down onto the dock, and Phoebe came loping to lunge into their laps. "Listen, your dad and I hadn't seen C.L. for twenty years. He just came back into town for a couple of days. Your dad wasn't jealous. I swear."

Em pulled Phoebe under her arm without looking at her, staring all the time at the water. "Because C.L. likes you a lot."

"Well—" Maddie felt herself nodding like an idiot "—I like him a lot. Too."

Em faced her mother. "Are you going to marry him?"

"No," Maddie said. "I am not going to marry anybody for a long time and maybe not even then. You and I are okay together." Phoebe squirmed under Em's arms, and Maddie reached out and scratched the dog's ears. "You and I and Phoebe."

"And Grandma," Em said. "And Mel."

"Right."

"And Three. And Aunt Treva and Uncle Howie."

Three. Em's half brother. Three, tall and smiling and careful with Mel and Em. He was a good kid. No, a good man. He was twenty years old. He was grown. So many years. Did what happened twenty years ago really make a difference now? Was what had happened worth losing Three?

More than that, was what had happened worth losing Treva? She'd known Treva her whole life. There wasn't a memory she had that didn't have Treva somewhere in it, even if it was just telling Treva about it later. Thirty-eight years of whispering and giggling and *you're going to love this one* and knowing that whatever happened, Treva would be there, with chocolate and wisecracks and unconditional support.

Maddie closed her eyes and thought, *I miss her so much* and then *I've been so dumb.*

"Mom?" Em said.

"Yes," Maddie said with a quaver. "And Three and Treva and Howie. We're not alone. We're going to be okay."

"And Anna," Em said. "And Henry."

"Lots of people," Maddie said.

Em nodded. "And C.L."

"And C.L.," Maddie said. "We have people. We're going to be okay."

"Okay." Em bent to bury her head in Phoebe's soft furry neck. "Okay."

C.L. watched them from the porch, tensing whenever one of them moved. Whatever was going on down there, at least they were talking, and that was good. And they were together at the farm where he could take care of them, and that was good. And then Maddie came walking up the yard to the porch and she looked worn-out but relieved, and that was better than anything.

"How is she?" C.L. called out to her when she was close enough to hear.

"Considering what she's just been through, pretty good." Maddie slowed as she reached the porch. "I have to go to town. Can you keep an eye on her for a couple of hours?"

"I can keep an eye on her for the rest of my life," C.L. said.

Maddie closed her eyes. "Let's start with a couple of hours and see how it goes."

"It'll go fine," C.L. said. "Em and I understand each other. It's you and I who aren't communicating."

"Later," Maddie said. "One trauma at a time. I have some loose ends to tie up. I'll be back later."

He watched her walk to the car and thought for the thousandth time how great it would be if she would just trust him enough to lean on him. Then he went inside the kitchen to get the poles so he and Em could get in a little fishing before dinner.

Maddie drove into town and turned down Linden Street. Her street. Hers and Treva's for almost twenty years. They'd shared the street the way they'd shared everything else all their lives, laughing and crying together and supporting each other without question.

Now it was time to get that back if she could. It had only been three weeks since she'd stood at Treva's back door and said, "Brent's cheating on me and I have to divorce him," and she'd thought that was the end of the world. Amazing the kind of perspective three weeks could give you. Now she didn't care much about the adultery. Murder, she was still upset about, and kidnapping, but adultery? The hell with it.

She parked at Treva's and knocked on the back door.

Treva opened the door and said, "Maddie, my God, it's you." She reached out and grabbed her sleeve. "What's wrong? Is it Em again?"

Maddie looked at her and thought, *I didn't lie to Em. I'm not mad at Treva. I'm not mad at all.* But all she said was, "We have to talk, Treve. It's way past time for us to talk. Come for a walk."

Treva froze for a moment, and then she looked behind her. The light from the kitchen poured out around her into the early September twilight, and Maddie could hear two masculine rumblings counterpointed with one thin little soprano. Family time. "All right," Treva said. "If that's what you need." She slipped back inside, and Maddie listened while she told her family she was going for a walk, "just a little one with Maddie to unwind," and the silence that followed was heavy, but not even Mel was clueless enough to ask questions.

Treva came out with two windbreakers and handed a green one to Maddie before she pulled the door shut behind her. "It's getting colder," she said as she shrugged herself into the red one. "I love September, but it's nothing to fool with at night."

Maddie slipped her arms into the green windbreaker and shoved the sleeves up over her wrists. The jacket was an extra large, the kind Brent used to wear. They walked silently past the neighbors' houses—Mr. Kemp's, Mrs. Whittaker's, and Mrs. Banister's—toward the end of the block and Maddie asked, "Is this Three's?"

"Yep," Treva said. "He's huge."

"Like Brent," Maddie said, and then she stopped walking because Treva had.

Chapter Eighteen

It's okay," Maddie said, turning back to face Treva. "That's what I came to tell you. It's okay. I was upset at first, but I don't care anymore."

Treva blinked hard, as if she were trying not to cry, her mouth pursed so shut it almost disappeared. "Brent told you."

"No." Maddie took a step closer. "No, I realized it at the funeral. Three has Brent's voice. And his build. And his cowlick."

"That's why you stopped talking to me." Treva started to nod and couldn't stop. "That's why. I knew it. I thought you found the letter or Brent told you or—Maddie, I'm so sorry. You don't know how sorry. I'm so, so sorry."

The tears did come then, hard tears, and Treva choked and pushed the drops back from her cheeks with her palms and gulped for air, and said, "I'm sorry" over and over. Maddie put her arms around her and held her tight and then began to cry with her, and it felt good to let the pent-up rage and loneliness out.

"I don't care, Treve," she said, letting her tears drip into Treva's frizzy curls. "I don't care at all. It was just a stupid screwup. It could have happened to me and C.L. It could have happened to anybody. It doesn't matter at all."

"I hated it," Treva sobbed, clinging to her. "I hated it so much, but I couldn't tell you, and I couldn't tell Howie, God, I tricked Howie into marrying me because of it, how could I tell him, I couldn't tell anybody, and I'm so, so, so sorry—"

She bounced her head on Maddie's shoulder with each "so" and Maddie clamped her hand on Treva's head to keep her from beating her brains out. "I know. I couldn't tell you about C.L. because I was so ashamed. I remember how it was. I understand. It doesn't matter anymore." Maddie sniffed one last time and began to pat Treva on the back, now conscious of the cars that were slowing down to look at the two women locked together. "I'm not kidding. I don't care. I thought I did, but I don't."

Treva stepped back to palm away her tears again. "I would. If it were you and Howie, I'd care."

"I know," Maddie said. "I know, but the thing is, I love you so much more than I ever loved Brent. That's such a terrible thing, but it's true. I didn't realize it until I was talking with Em, but I miss you so much more than I miss him. And I love Three, so how could I wish he wasn't born? And I don't think I could get through the day without talking to you, and that's what I've been doing for the past two weeks, and I've really hated it, so all of the other stuff doesn't matter. It really doesn't. It was twenty years ago. It doesn't matter anymore at all."

"Oh, *God*." Treva sat down on the steps to Mrs. Banister's house and cried harder, gasping her words between sobs. "I'm so relieved. I'm so, so sorry, but I'm so relieved." She grabbed Three's windbreaker sleeve and pulled on it until it went past Maddie's wrist. "I didn't do it to hurt you, I swear, I didn't."

Maddie sat down next to her to get her sleeve back. "I know, Treve. It's okay."

"Brent was just—" Treva's sobs slowed down, and she began to search through her jacket pockets for a Kleenex and then gave up and wiped her nose on the sleeve. "Brent was just everything back then, you know? I couldn't believe he was paying attention to me. He was what everybody wanted. He was just it. And I was dumb. I was so dumb—"

"It's okay, Treve, I know. I married him, for heaven's sake." Maddie patted her, but now that she had started, Treva couldn't stop.

"And then I missed my period and wrote that letter—" Treva clutched at Maddie's arm. "*The letter.* Where's—"

"I tore it up." Maddie patted harder. "It's gone. I flushed it down the john. It can't hurt you anymore. I swear it."

"Oh." Treva drew a deep shuddering breath. "Oh. Oh, my God, I can't believe it." She started to cry again. "I can't believe it. Brent was going to tell you. He said he'd tell you and Howie. I screamed at him. I even threatened to kill him, but he said he'd tell if I didn't keep my mouth shut about the money." Treva started to sob again. "I betrayed Howie all over again. I knew he was cheating the company because Dottie Wylie told my mom, and I didn't tell him. I called Brent and yelled and he threatened me and I did it again, I betrayed Howie."

"It's all over," Maddie said. "Nobody will tell Howie." She stopped for a minute, confused. "Wait a minute. What does Dottie Wylie have to do with this?"

Treva gulped back the last of her tears. "Brent charged her too much for her house. She told my mom it wasn't worth what she paid for it, and Mom told me, and I didn't tell Howie, but it turns out she was right. He came in a couple of weeks ago, right before we found out about Brent, and he said he and C.L. had gone over the books, and Brent had skimmed about forty thousand off Dottie's house alone by double-invoicing, but they couldn't find the invoices. He said there were lots more, going back two years, he could tell by looking at what Brent had actually billed them for in the computer, but they needed the invoices, too."

"Yellow carbons," Maddie said. "There were a stack of them in that damn box we found. That's why Brent was so mad about it. His invoices were in there." Pieces began to fall into place for her. "I thought he was mad because I'd found out he was cheating. I told him I'd been with C.L. and he said, 'What did you tell him?' He didn't care I'd been with another man, he cared I'd been with an accountant. This whole thing has been over money. We went through this hell because of *money*. Can you believe it?"

"No," Treva said. "I went through it because I made a terrible mistake twenty years ago and betrayed the two people I loved most."

"Well, that's over," Maddie said. "That's what I wanted to tell you. I know you need to cry, so go ahead, but it's all over. I don't care." She put her arm around Treva and pulled her close, the way she'd held Em only an hour before. "We're going to be okay."

"Are you going to tell Howie?" Treva straightened. "I understand if you do, I deserve it."

"Of course I'm not going to tell Howie," Maddie said. "Haven't you been listening? What do you think I am?"

Treva's head swayed a little. "I think you're wonderful. I'm the one who's awful. I knew Brent was stealing from the company and I let him *blackmail* me—" Treva collapsed on Maddie's shoulder again.

"Are you girls all right?"

Maddie lifted her chin over Treva's head to look behind her. Mrs. Banister stood on her front porch, squinting through the twilight.

"We're fine, Mrs. Banister," she called back. "It's just Maddie Martindale and Treva Hanes. We're talking about old times."

"All right, girls." Mrs. Banister waved as she turned to go back inside. "You need anything, you just come ring the bell."

"Thank you," Maddie called back as Treva burst into tears again.

"Everybody's so nice to me," Treva sobbed. "And I'm the scum of the *earth*."

"Okay, that's it." Maddie stood up and hauled Treva to her feet by the collar of her windbreaker. "Pull yourself together and let's walk some of this off. You are not scum, you're the best person I know, and if I go to jail, I want you to raise my kid, so get over this self-pity thing."

Treva clutched at her again. "You're not going to go to jail. Even if they convict you, they'll give you temporary insanity or something."

"Well, Treve, that's not much help," Maddie started them both walking again. "I don't think it's going to do Em a whole lot of good to live in a town that thinks her wacko mother shot her cheating father." That made Maddie think of her grandmother. "They'll shut me up someplace, and Em will come to visit and bring me Esther Price candy, and I'll spit the walnuts at the walls."

"What are you *talking* about?" Treva said.

"Heredity," Maddie said. "Do you ever look at your mother

or your grandmother and think, 'Dear God, someday that'll be me'?"

"Sometimes I think I'm them now," Treva said. "That's why I've been watching Three like a hawk for twenty years. I've been terrified I'd wake up one day and he'd be Brent."

"It'll never happen."

"Or that Howie would look at him one day and say, 'My God, he looks like Brent.' Because he does, a little."

They passed two more houses before Maddie said, "Look, I know you're relieved, but you do have a good point about Howie. This is something he should know. I'm not going to tell him, ever, but you probably should."

"I can't." Treva grabbed Maddie's windbreaker sleeve. "I absolutely can't. He'll think I just married him because I was pregnant with Brent's baby."

"Howie Basset is a lot of things, but dumb isn't one of them," Maddie said. "He's lived with you for twenty years. He's known you all your life. Give him some credit."

"I can't," Treva said, but her voice sounded less quavery.

"I have just this day become a big proponent of telling the truth," Maddie said. "I highly recommend it. You wouldn't believe what a *relief* it is."

Treve inhaled on a huge quavering sigh. "Well, actually, I would. I'm feeling pretty giddy myself right now just because this is all out for us."

Maddie nodded. "So imagine you and Howie. Do it."

They reached the corner of Linden Street under the street-light, and while Maddie waited for whatever Treva was going to say next, the light came on and flooded Treva's blonde curls, and just for a minute she looked exactly the way she had when they were kids, a little dizzy and absolutely a part of Maddie's world.

They'd been together a long time. And they'd be together

a lot longer now. This was the reason she'd never leave Frog Point, not just Treva or her mother or Em, but all the memory and tradition and sureness that thirty-eight years in the same place gives you. "Streetlight's on," she told Treva. "You know what that means."

Treva grinned at her, a little weak and watery, out still a grin. "Home in ten minutes, or we're grounded."

"Whatever happens," Maddie said, "nothing changes us. You may change, I may change, but nothing changes us. Okay?"

"Okay," Treva whispered. "Okay."

"Okay," Maddie said. "Jesus, what a day."

She went to Helena and Norman's next. She hadn't been there for weeks, since before the funeral, and she knocked on the back door with her heart pounding. Helena's face, when she opened the door and saw Maddie, was not a help.

"What do you want?" Helena said, and Maddie said, "I want you to stop talking about me and upsetting my mother."

Helena glared at her through the screen door. "I told the truth."

"You told part of the truth," Maddie said. "You didn't mention all the times Brent cheated on me, and you didn't mention that he hit me, and you flat out lied when you told people I killed him. My mother hasn't mentioned any of that, either, but she will if you don't stop, and then my child will have to deal with all the talk about what lowlifes her parents are because her grandmothers are too damn dumb to shut the fuck up."

Maddie hadn't meant to end the sentence that way, but she did, and it felt good. It felt like the way the new Maddie would talk, the person she'd been trying to be before she'd gotten blindsided by Brent's death. She'd had a plan. She should have stuck to it.

Helena came out and let the screen door bang behind her, and Maddie almost stepped back but didn't. She wasn't ever going to step back again.

"Come here," Helena said, and Maddie followed her down the walk to the garage.

Helena unlocked the door and turned on the light, and Maddie said, "Oh, no."

The garage was full of posters and placards and bumper stickers, and all of them said "Brent Faraday for Mayor." Maddie felt sick, for Brent, and for his parents, too, for how much they didn't know their son.

"He didn't want this," Maddie said. "I know you meant it for the best, but—"

"He wanted it," Helena said. "It was you who didn't. You were the one who said you didn't want to be a mayor's wife. I heard you at our Christmas party."

"I didn't care," Maddie told her, still overwhelmed by seeing Brent's name plastered everywhere. "Big deal, mayor's wife. I just knew he hated it, and I was trying to take the pressure off. He really didn't want this."

"He would have made a great mayor," Helena said, in the same tone most people would have used for "He would have made a great president."

"Helena—"

"And you wouldn't help him," Helena said. "If he went to other women, it was your fault. You weren't there for him."

"Oh, hell," Maddie said. "I was there for him. I've been there for everybody. He didn't want to be mayor."

"He wanted to be mayor. He'd filled out the forms, he'd done all the work. All we needed was the financial disclosure statement, and we'd have his name on the ballot. It was your fault, and now he's dead, and you're running around—"

"I have been pure as the driven snow for two weeks."

"—and I want the town to know what you did." Helena rolled the last words with vicious satisfaction.

"Well, good for you," Maddie said, her own anger flaring at her mother-in-law's venal stupidity. "But you know my mom, and she wants the town to know some things, too, and I'm not going to let Em get caught in the middle. He was leaving town, Helena. He'd sold his share of the company. He had tickets to Rio. He was leaving and taking Em because he'd been stealing money and you were pushing him to be mayor. Do you really want that to get out? Do you really think it won't if you keep stirring up talk?"

"It shouldn't be about him." Helena quivered with rage. "It should be about you. People think you're so good. They should know."

"They will," Maddie said. "They've got a whole new me coming. But I'm not going to put up with this stuff. Stop slandering me and annoying my mother before she tells the whole world about Brent."

"Nobody will believe her," Helena said, but she sounded a little unsure for the first time in the conversation.

"Just stop," Maddie said. "Just stop it before Em finds out what Brent was."

"Don't be ridiculous," Helena said, but she turned off the light and left without pushing any further, and Maddie was satisfied.

Poor Brent, she thought as she got in the car. Helena for a mother and Norman for a father. He'd have ended up mayor after all. No wonder South America had looked so good.

Especially with a financial disclosure form in the offing. If there was one thing Brent wasn't interested in disclosing, it was his finances, although he must have hidden most of the money he'd skimmed somewhere other than their accounts and his golf bag. She had no idea where, and she wondered how he had known. He really couldn't have been doing it on his own. He had to have had a partner.

Maybe the man who'd made the kidnapping call. Somebody was going to pay for that.

But first she had the last of her unfinished business.

"What happened?" her mother said as soon as Maddie came through the door. "It's past *nine*. I've been worried sick. You've been crying. What with the prowler and the murderer and—"

"Em went out to the farm to see C.L.," Maddie said. "She wanted to know the truth about things, and she thought he was the only one who would tell her."

Maddie's mother sighed and slumped a little. "Well, my word, Maddie—"

"Sit down," Maddie said. "We have to talk."

"You wouldn't believe what a day I've had," her mother said, moving toward her pink flowered couch. "That Helena—"

"Good point," Maddie said. "I've just come from there. The two of you are going to have to stop doing this Godzilla meets the Thing bit or you're going to ruin Em's parents' reputations. Knock it off."

"She started it," her mother said.

"Well, I finished it," Maddie said. "Find something else to talk about, please."

Her mother took her literally. "Gloria took Barry back, can you believe it?"

"Yes," Maddie said. "I can now believe anything of anybody."

"Really? Well, listen to this one." Her mother leaned forward. "Candace from the bank is dating Bailey, that guard out at Brent and Howie's company."

Maddie was momentarily distracted. "That is weird."

"Well, she's a Lowery."

"Right," Maddie said. "Blood tells. Which is why I'm turning into Gran before my own eyes."

"What are you talking about?" her mother asked.

"Em ran away because nobody was telling her the truth." Maddie sat down in the rocking chair across from her mother. "So I've spent the evening being Gran, telling the truth even when nobody wants to listen. It's been pretty interesting so far. I may start spitting walnuts."

"Maddie, what are you talking about?"

Maddie took a deep breath. "We're all so busy protecting each other that we lie right and left. We have to stop doing that or we're never going to be free of the lies. We *all* have to stop doing that."

"Are you referring to me?" Her mother sat stiffly, not amused by the tack the conversation was taking.

"Yes. But you're just one among many."

"Really, Maddie—"

"Em went to C.L. because she couldn't trust us. I don't want that to happen again."

Her mother looked perturbed. "I fail to understand what C. L. Sturgis has to do with any of this. I thought he was out of your life."

"I did, too," Maddie said. "I was wrong. We were lovers and we're going to be again. And I'm not feeling like sneaking around anymore, so you'll probably know when we resume."

"Well, really, Maddie—"

"It's sort of like you and Mr. Scott," Maddie finished.

Her mother seemed silenced for a minute, but then she got her second wind. "I have no idea—"

"Forget it. I told you, I'm not doing lies anymore. I talked to Gran, and she told me everything."

Maddie's mother's face turned grim. "Your grandmother is senile. Pay no atten—"

"Oh, no she's not." Maddie frowned at her mother. "She's a pain in the ass, but she's all there. She told me you gave up your love affair to protect me."

The expression on her mother's face boded ill for her grandmother. "Maddie, I don't see—"

"And I did the same thing for Em." Maddie rocked a little in the chair and felt comforted. She'd rocked Em there as a newborn, so tiny she seemed weightless, and then later as a toddler, reading *Are You My Mother?* reassuring Em on every page everything would be fine. So much for art reflecting life. "I thought as long as I kept all the worry out of her life, she'd be safe. I did what you did. But she wasn't, and C.L. was the one she trusted."

"Maddie, your husband has only been dead two w—"

"I liked Mr. Scott," Maddie said. "I liked it when he came over. He listened to me. I liked him a lot."

Her mother met her eyes for the first time in several minutes. "I did, too," she said finally. "But I just couldn't do it. It would have been so confusing for you. And if we'd kept on seeing each other, well, you know this town."

Maddie wanted to cry, *Mother, you are this town*, but it didn't matter. "I can't do the same thing," she told her mother. "I could wait for a little while if that made it better, I suppose, but I don't want to. I haven't loved Brent for so long, I haven't had that for so long, and now it's right here in front of me." She leaned forward. "I feel wonderful again, Mama. When I'm with him, everything's better. I know it might not last, but it almost doesn't matter because it's so good to be with him right now. Not for the future, not so I'll have a respectable relationship to show people, but for right now, for me. I've made love with C.L., and I've laughed with him, and I've watched him with my daughter, and I'm going back to him tonight and tell him everything because I trust him more than anyone else in the world, and I'm pretty sure that means I love him."

"Think of Emily," her mother said, and Maddie leaned back, defeated.

"I'm not like you, Mom," she said. "I'm selfish. I want it all. I can't give it all up to keep Em in cotton wool. I love her, and I will keep her safe, but I'm not going to live a lie, and I'm not going to walk away from happiness when it's right there in front of me just because it's the town's idea of the right thing to do."

"You sacrifice for your child," her mother said flatly. "That's what a mother does. You put your child first."

"I know." Maddie stood up, seeing no point in arguing with a betrayed brick wall. "I have been putting her first. But I'm putting myself a damn close second, and that means C.L. now, not next year. Em likes him, and he helps her. She's not as sad when she's with him. I'm going back to him. I never should have left."

Her mother leaned forward, tense with sincerity. "Will you please remember how people talk? Brent's been gone less than two weeks. What will the neighbors think?"

"If Em's happy and I'm happy, I don't care about the neighbors." Maddie began to turn away and then stopped, hopeful, ready to give it one more try. "In fact, it's more than I don't care. I'm glad. You have no idea how tired I am of being Maddie the good girl. Now I'm going to be a screwup. And I'm going to enjoy the hell out of it. And I wish you'd call Mr. Scott and join me."

"Maddie, I am sixty-three years old, too old to act like a fool." Her mother set her jaw for a moment and went on. "I gave up a lot to keep you safe," she said, measuring the words out carefully. "I raised you on my own, and I put you first always. And you're going to throw it all away because this Sturgis man—"

"See," Maddie said, "this is another reason I'm not going to mortgage my life to Em, so I can't blackmail her with speeches later on."

"*Maddie.*"

"I love you, Mom." Maddie bent and kissed her mother's cheek. "You'd give me the world, I know you would, but you want my body and soul in exchange. And you can't have them. I'm an ungrateful child, and I know it, and I sure as hell hope Em is, too, someday." She turned and headed for the door. "Don't worry, I'm fine and Em's doing better. I'll call you on Sunday after I've seen Gran."

"That *woman*," Maddie's mother said.

"I like her," Maddie said. "She's selfish as hell. Good role model."

Maddie drove to Dairy Queen and ordered the triple hot fudge sundae. She sat near the front window in the glow of the neon from the street and spooned chocolate like a fiend while she tried to figure out what the hell was happening in her life, who was out to get her, and what she really wanted. People who once would have waved to her bent their heads and whispered to each other, and that would have laid her low once, but now she didn't care. Em was safe. She had Treva back. She'd stopped Helena. Now all she had to do was find out who had killed her husband and get C.L. back in her life.

She had some ideas about the first one, but she knew exactly how to do the second one, so she started with that.

. . .

C.L. was sitting on the porch steps untangling two fishing poles when she drove in at ten.

"You know, if you'd fish from different sides of the dock, that wouldn't happen," Maddie said as she started toward him.

"Phoebe helped." C.L. scooted over to make room for her on the steps.

She sat down closer to him than she needed to. "Give me one of the poles. I'll help untangle."

"You know, there's a metaphor here." C.L. leaned a little toward her so their shoulders touched.

"I know, you want to help untangle my mess." Maddie picked up the bobber. "Wouldn't it be easier to unhook these?"

"I was using them as markers." C.L. took the pole away from her and dropped them both on the grass beside the steps. "It's hopeless. Let's work on something we have a chance of solving."

"All right." Maddie leaned over and kissed him. It was wonderful to taste him again, to have his shoulder to lean on and his mouth hot on hers, and his arm around her, which it was almost immediately, and when she came up for air, she said, "Oh, God, that's good." She put her forehead against his and said, "Remind me not to leave you again. I'm still not getting married, but I want all the other good stuff."

"You're kidding." C.L. looked poleaxed. "No, forget I said that." He kissed her, pulling her close, and she felt his tongue tease her lips and opened for him, sinking against his broad chest while he invaded her mouth. "You're not kidding," he said, a little breathlessly. "Your mother's going to have me killed."

"I already told her," Maddie said. "It's all my fault. I told her I was going to come out here and jump you, so you're the victim here. Kiss me again."

"We've got to get off this porch." C.L. yanked her to her feet.

"Nope." Maddie moved into his arms, loving the way her arms felt around him. "I'm through hiding. I know I'm a widow, but the whole world and his wife knows about Brent, so why should I pretend? Kiss me here."

"Yes, but there's *Em*," he said, and pulled her into the shadows beside the porch. Then he did kiss her, putting his whole body into it now that they were standing in the dark, sliding his hands down her back and pulling her hips to his, and she let herself ease into him and his solid warmth, kissing him just to be kissing him instead of for rebellion or vengeance or independence. "I'm crazy about you," she told him breathlessly, and he said, "Yeah, but what about tomorrow when you're sane again?"

"I'm sane now." She kissed him again and felt her breath come hard, and it took all her concentration to remember when the kiss was done that she had to tell him something before she dragged him to the ground.

She stepped back and felt a little lost until she mentally kicked herself. She was fine. She did not need anyone to lean on. From now on she leaned for love, not need. "We have to talk."

"No." C.L. reached for her. "Let's go back to the insane part before you change your mind."

"I'm not changing my mind. But I have a few things I have to tell you."

"This is going to be bad, isn't it?" C.L. said.

She led him back to the porch steps, and he sat next to her and put his hand on the nape of her neck and rubbed the muscles there. His hand was warm and heavy, and it felt wonderful, not just to have her neck rubbed but also to have him there beside her again. "Okay, shoot," he said.

Maddie sighed. "Well, since you mentioned it, there's the gun."

C.L.'s hand stopped. "Do you know where it is?"

Maddie nodded, as much to feel his hand move against her neck as anything else.

"Would you like to tell me?" C.L. said, sounding faintly exasperated.

"Treva's freezer."

C.L. jerked his hand away. *"Treva?"*

Maddie lifted her head. "She doesn't know. It's in Mrs. Harmon's Spam-and-whole-wheat-noodle casserole."

C.L. looked as if somebody had just smacked him upside the head with a ball bat. "Jesus Christ."

Maddie nodded. "I know. She wants to be New Age, but she doesn't quite get it that Spam is not health food."

"Not Mrs. Harmon," C.L. said. "Although that is disgusting. I'm talking about the gun in Treva's freezer."

"I put it in a plastic bag before I stuck it down in the noodles," Maddie went on, "so I'm sure it's still okay. Freezing doesn't hurt guns, does it?"

"For a minute there I thought you meant Treva had done it," C.L. said. "I know she didn't have motive, but still it was—"

"She had a motive," Maddie said, feeling a little giddy as all the truth came flooding out. "Brent was blackmailing her."

C.L. sat still for a minute and then he said, "Why?" as if they were having a completely normal conversation.

"I can't tell you," Maddie said, "but she didn't do it."

C.L. nodded, processing this new piece of information. "You know, when you start telling the truth, you really let it rip."

"Well, that's the problem," Maddie said, exasperated. "This stuff is not small. It's all very well and good to go around preaching the truth, but people have built their lives on some of these lies, and for good reason. You don't just go blowing up people's lives so you can brag about being honest. You can't just tell people everything and think that's the end of it. You have to pick up the pieces. You wouldn't believe how much damage I did tonight."

"Right," C.L. said. "I think. But I still think we're better off sticking with the truth. Anything else you want to tell me?"

"Yeah," Maddie said. "There's almost a quarter of a million dollars in your wheel well."

"*What?*" C.L. said.

"Two hundred and thirty thousand," Maddie said. "Somebody planted it in the Civic and the gun in the glove compartment and hoped I'd get caught with it."

"I suppose you had to put the money in *my* wheel well."

"It was handy," Maddie said. "You want to tell Henry about this or should I do it alone?"

"Let's do it together." C.L. stood up and took her hand to haul her up the steps beside him. "But first let's go look in my wheel well."

"Get a big bag," Maddie said. "There are a lot of hundred-dollar bills in there. God, I am so relieved to get this off my chest."

"Yeah," C.L. said. "I can see why, now that it's on mine."

Henry was not amused, and Maddie braced herself for the worst.

"'Dyou just find out about this?" he bellowed at C.L. when the three of them were sitting around the kitchen table with the money in front of them.

"Hell, yes, I just found out about it." C.L. scowled back at him. "How damn dumb do you think I am? I've been driving around with a fortune in my trunk for two weeks. She just told me not ten minutes ago, so stop yelling. And don't yell at her because she's family. We're getting married."

"No, we're not," Maddie said, and he looked at her and laughed.

"Yes, we are," he told her. "You just don't know it yet."

Henry spoke to C.L. as if Maddie weren't there. "You know, boy, it's a possibility that this woman shot her husband. She's a nice woman, but he was going to take her little girl, and I think she'd do almost anything to keep that little girl safe. You might want to think this over."

"Well, I'd do just about anything to keep that kid safe, too," C.L. said. "Which is why she's never going to shoot me. Go on inside and call about that gun and we'll wait for you. It's in Treva Basset's freezer in Mrs. Harmon's casserole. Spam and whole wheat noodles."

"Damfool woman," Henry said, not specifying whether he meant Maddie or Mrs. Harmon, and went to call.

When he came back, he was slightly mellower but not much. "I have a couple of questions," he told Maddie, and she swallowed and nodded.

"Why don't I just tell you what I know?" she said. "I've been thinking about this, and I've got some ideas."

Henry exhaled and then nodded. "Go ahead. Just don't keep anything back."

"Well," Maddie said, "I think this all started because Helena Faraday wanted Brent to be mayor, and because Dottie Wylie is good friends with Lora Hanes, and because my husband's mistress wanted him to leave me."

"You're kidding," C.L. said. "What the—"

"Shut up, C.L.," Henry said. "You've forgotten how things work around here." He focused back on Maddie. "Who told who what?"

"About a month ago, Helena told Brent he had to fill out

financial disclosure forms for the mayoral race, and Brent knew that could be bad. And about the same time, Dottie told Lora that her daughter's husband's company had swindled her, and Lora called Treva, and Treva knew that Dottie was as straight as the day is long and that Howie was, too, which left Brent. So she called Brent and asked him what the hell was going on and threatened to raise a stink. And then about a week later, I found those crotchless pants under the seat of my car, and I figure they had to be planted there, so his mistress must have been pushing him about the same time—"

"Crotchless pants?" Henry said.

"What crotchless pants?" C.L. said.

"—because I don't think it was an accident that those pants ended up in the car. I thought of this a while back, but I didn't put it together then, but the thing is, you don't take off crotchless panties to make love." Maddie stopped and looked at C.L. "Do you?"

"Probably not," C.L. said, trying to look virtuous while Henry scowled. "Not that I'd know from experience since I don't do that kind of stuff."

"Anyway, I do not believe a woman wouldn't notice she wasn't wearing underpants. I noticed that night we went to the Point and I didn't have any on."

Henry scowled harder at C.L. and she hurried on. "And they wouldn't make love in the front seat, either, because there's no room, and I saw them get into the back the night I watched them. So she left them on purpose, which means she wanted me to find them and confront him. She was pushing him. Which makes me wonder if that accident I had was an accident."

"Paranoia is not pretty," C.L. said.

"My car was so old that any damage would total it," she told him. "And that would mean I'd have to drive the Caddy, and

I'd clean it out, and I'd find the pants and divorce Brent. Another thing is, I got hit by the brother of the guy that saw me open the safe-deposit box at the bank. And Brent couldn't have been working a swindle alone, he wasn't that good with money, and the bank would be a good place to find a partner who did know money."

"You're right about that," Henry said. "You were having an awful lot of bad luck all at one time, so I did sort of lean on the Webster kid a little. He's not talking, but he's awful nervous. I was just going to wait until he folded, but I could step things up a little, I guess."

"Well, thank you for that," Maddie said. "I thought you suspected me."

"I still do," Henry said, "but that doesn't mean I don't think there aren't other interesting possibilities. Keep talking."

C.L. looked from one to the other. "I don't believe this. Neither one of you told me anything."

"I was trying to handle it myself," Maddie said. "I knew I was innocent, even if Henry did think I was my grandma all over again."

"What grandma?" C.L. said, and watched Henry grimace at a memory. "There's a grandma in this?"

"Shut up, C.L., and let her talk," Henry said.

Maddie was talking again, giving Henry everything she had, and C.L. could see the tension ease as she talked.

"The way I think it was is this. Brent turns everything he can get his hands on into cash and gets ready to leave. But then I find the pants, and C.L. comes to town and chases him, and Treva and I search the office and take the box with the invoices, and he gets so freaked, he hits me. He's still got two days before the plane leaves, and he knows Dottie's yelling is going to cause some trouble with his partner, who probably doesn't know he's leaving, so he calls his partner to control the damage and gives himself away." She stopped and looked at Henry. "Especially if he called that Friday night. He was really drunk and you could see right through him. If you'd arrested him that weekend, he'd have given you everything. I think his partner killed him to protect himself. Except the voice I heard on the phone that night saying 'Fine' was female. There's a teller at the bank named June Webster. Is she any relation to Webster?"

"Sister," Henry said. "I checked. Harold Whitehead's wife was a Webster. The place is full of them."

"I'm starting to not like them," Maddie said.

"Tell me about the money," Henry said. "If you didn't move it, how did it get to the Civic?"

"I don't know," Maddie said. "But I bet whoever did it was the prowler I had Saturday night. That's when my safe-deposit key went missing. I know that isn't enough to get the guy to the safe-deposit box, but it's something. I think the killer took the money and sat back and waited to see if you'd arrest me. When you didn't, he planted the gun and most of the money in the Civic and waited for Leo to find it. Only I found it first. And then he hears Em is missing, which wouldn't be tough since I'd screamed it all over town—" She stopped for a minute and then said, "I went to the bank, Henry. Everybody in the bank knew Em was gone."

"Everybody in town knew Em was gone," Henry said.

C.L. finally spoke up. "This guy must be getting really frustrated. Every move he's made, you've ducked. He must be about ready to come out of the woodwork for you."

"That's only if Maddie's right," Henry said. "There are a lot of loose ends. Like the problem that nobody came off the Point after Brent that night except for her."

"That's according to Bailey," C.L. said. "I want to talk to him tomorrow."

"We need to do a hell of a lot of things tomorrow," Henry said. "Starting with that damn gun."

"That's another thing," Maddie said. "Bailey's dating Candace at the bank, so he's been there. He could be tied in, too."

"He worked security there for a while," Henry said. "He knows everything about the place."

"We're definitely talking to Bailey tomorrow," C.L. said. "Especially now that we know Maddie's innocent." He glared at Henry.

Henry was as impervious as usual. "Maybe. There's still the money and the gun she didn't tell us about. I should run her in for withholding evidence."

"You can't," Maddie said. "I've given you all I've got now, so you'd just look spiteful. And I might marry your nephew, and then where would you be?"

"About where I've always been with C.L.," Henry said, but there was no venom in his voice.

"Em's upstairs asleep in my bed," C.L. said when Henry finally left them to go to bed himself. "She folded pretty soon after dinner. Rough day."

"No kidding." Maddie moved closer to him. "I missed you."

C.L. backed up. "I missed you, too. Go to bed."

Maddie stopped. "What?"

"Your kid's upstairs, and my uncle is waiting to hear you join her. Get moving."

"You've been hanging out with me too long." Maddie moved in fast and wrapped her arms around him. "I *missed* you."

C.L. kissed her once, hard, and she breathed him in and loved him for it, and then he pushed her away. "I missed you, too, which is why I plan on meeting you at your house tomorrow while Anna baby-sits Em and Henry does sheriff stuff, so leave your morning open because you're going to be busy naked. But right now, get upstairs."

She felt empty without her arms around him. She'd just liberated herself from an entire town for him, and she was feeling as if she could and should do anything, and she was empty. "You're kidding."

He took a step back and frowned at her, a lousy attempt at discouragement. "No. Go upstairs."

Maddie put her hands on her hips. "I finally decide to be depraved, and *you* turn over a new leaf?"

"If I'm going to be your husband and Em's stepdaddy, I have to," C.L. said. "I have people to protect. Go upstairs."

He looked determined and stubborn and miserable.

"Oh, hell," Maddie said, and went upstairs, but when she was in bed beside Em, she began to plan.

C.L. evidently still hadn't gotten the idea that the old Maddie was gone since he was trying to turn himself into her twin. And if she had to spend the rest of her life sleeping with her old self, she'd have to kill him. Therefore, she had to do something fast to corrupt him again, corrupt him enough that there was no way he could come back as the old Maddie's double. She wanted him evil and rebellious and full of scandal, and the more she thought of him that way, the more she wanted him. She fell asleep thinking hot thoughts that made her itch under her skin, and they were still with her when she woke up.

Em wasn't cheery at breakfast, but she was relaxed, talking to Anna about cookies and Phoebe without any quaver in her voice at all.

"Can I stay with Anna all day?" she asked. "I don't want to go back there yet."

Maddie said, "All weekend if Anna can stand it."

"I'll take her forever," Anna said. "We'll make cinnamon cookies and then this afternoon we'll crochet. That's a quiet thing to do. Takes a lot of concentration." She smiled at Maddie over Em's head. "Good thing to do when you've got a lot on your mind."

C.L. honked outside, and Maddie pushed her plate away and bent to kiss Em's cheek. "C.L. and I have to go into town, sweetie," she said. "We'll be back this afternoon. Be good for Anna."

Em shot her a scornful look. "I'm always good."

"We're going to work on that, too," Maddie told her. "But I have other fish to fry first."

She went down the steps, and C.L. picked his suit coat up off the passenger seat and said, "Ride in with me."

He probably had an ulterior motive, but so did she, so she got into the convertible, trying to decide how to implement her plan for maximum impact. She couldn't do anything about the Webster mob who were ruining her life—that was up to Henry—but she could do something about taking her life back and making it her own and not her mother's or the town's. She figured she had to do something so bad, she couldn't ever recover her reputation. Even while one part of her knew she was nuts, the other part, the part that had been freed when she'd faced down so many lies the day before, egged her on.

Today was the day she got rid of the old Maddie completely. And C.L. was going to help her. Maddie patted the condom she'd found in C.L.'s drawer and stuck in her shorts. He was going to help her naked.

He threw his coat in the backseat, his muscles flexing under his cotton shirt, and she shivered and smiled at him, the sizzle from last night percolating up again just because he was warm and possible beside her. He tossed her the scarf she'd worn before, and she tied it over her head while she plotted her next move. She had to have him soon.

Amazing how your libido came back when you weren't depressed anymore and your possibly future uncle-in-law was thinking about arresting somebody else.

"I have to go see Henry first," C.L. said, pulling out into the road. "He's talking to Bailey and I want to be there. But then it's you and me, babe, so you stay home." He grinned over at her, and she bit her lip because he looked so good. "I'll leave the car at Henry's so nobody knows."

Maddie laughed, passion making her loud. "C.L., the whole town knows. You'll leave it in my driveway."

"I will not." He glanced at the speedometer and slowed down.

So he was going to be a hard sell. Maddie looked at him sideways from the corner of her eye. No, he wasn't. Whatever else he was trying to be, he was still C.L. underneath.

She pushed a Springsteen cassette in, and turned up the volume, and "Born to Run" boomed out in the sunlight.

C.L. turned the music down. "Farmers are still working the fields along here. No point in calling attention to ourselves."

All right, that was it. She'd fallen in love with a screwup, she was not going to spend the rest of her life with somebody bucking for a good-citizenship medal. She waited until they were on Porch Road, C.L. driving tensely at forty miles an hour, and said, "Go faster."

"There are speed limits," C.L. said, and she rolled her eyes and said, "Yes, and the limit is fifty-five on this road. Go faster."

He sighed and let the needle creep up to fifty, and the song changed to "Thunder Road." It was a great song, and Maddie scooted herself up to sit on the back of the seat in honor of it, holding on to the windshield with one hand. C.L. said, "What the hell are you doing?" but the wind blew against her, pressed against her, and she wanted to yell and strip off her clothes and drag C.L. into the backseat. Instead she took off her scarf and held it above her head and let the wind blow it away.

"Would you get *down* here?" C.L. said, grabbing her calf, and Maddie tipped back her head and felt her heart kick up another notch as the wind blew through her hair and his fingers closed hard on her leg. Every hot memory she'd ever had of C.L. came back, and she let go of the windshield and stretched her arms out to feel her muscles move, and all the while C.L. yelled at her from below.

"Are you nuts? Get down here." C.L. tugged on her leg.

She planted her feet on the seat and sat firm, but she dropped her arms. Her muscles should have been moving naked against him, and instead he was bitching at her. She was going to have to take steps.

"You know, I think this is our song," she yelled down to him. "Definitely our song. Especially the 'town full of losers' part. Pull over and let's make love."

"Maddie," he said, and she stripped her T-shirt over her head and let that go in the wind, too, so that when he glanced up, he swerved. *"Maddie,"* he said, and she laughed at the way the wind blew hard on her skin. The Drake Farm was coming up ahead on the right, and she yelled, "Pull in at that driveway, C.L."

A farmer on a tractor loomed up ahead on the left, and C.L. yanked her feet off the seat so hard she bounced down after all, but it was too late. The farmer's eyes were huge when they passed him.

"That was Todd Overton," C.L. said with false calm. "I'm

going to hear about this from Henry. I suppose you had to do this."

"Turn," Maddie said as the farm entrance grew closer. "*Turn.*"

"Forget it," C.L. said, and Maddie pulled her bra off over her head and threw it in his lap where it immediately blew back over to her side and out of the car.

C.L. looked over and said, "Oh, *hell*," and yanked the steering wheel to get them off the road and into the driveway, just the way she knew he would, the car fishtailing sideways as he stopped.

She had the car door open as soon as the car skidded to a halt, and she was out and into the soft grass along the edge of the driveway before he could catch her.

Chapter
Nineteen

M addie, knock it off," C.L. said from the car. "This isn't
funny. There's a house right there."

"It certainly isn't funny," she said, and shoved off her shorts,
underwear, condom, and all, and tossed them toward him.
"This is the Drake place. It's deserted." She sat cross-legged on
the grass and said, "Make love to me here, right here. In the
sun. In front of God and everybody. I don't want to hide anymore."

C.L. watched her and swallowed. "I'm with you right up to
the God-and-everybody part." He slid out of the car and
came over to her, holding his hand out to her. "We're fifteen
minutes from your house. Why don't we—"

"Here." She yanked him down to the grass beside her. His
shirt was crisp against her skin as she rolled into his arms,

and he was hot under it, solid and hard against her. She kissed him and felt his hands move down her back as the breeze blew across her skin, and she let herself fall against him, pressing him down into the cool earth.

"Not a good idea," he said when he came up for air, but his hands slid over her body as he said it. He rolled her over so that he was on top of her, all heat and weight, and her pulse beat quicker, kicked up by the music that still blared from the radio. "Now," she said, and his hands slid up her sides until she shivered. He kissed her neck, and her ear, and finally her lips again, licking inside her mouth as she moved under him.

"I really want you," he said when he came up for air. "But not here. Not without protection."

"There's a condom in my shorts pocket," she said. "Get it. It's been too long." She pulled his face down to hers to bite his lip. "I want you *now*. Here. While the neighbors watch. So everybody knows." She moved under him and watched his eyes grow dark and felt him hard against her through his jeans.

"Dumb idea," he said, but his voice was husky and faint, and he kissed her again, softly, his tongue a tickle against her lips, then harder as she pulsed against him. His mouth moved to her breast, and her breathing kicked faster as he made her mindless with his tongue.

"Do it," she whispered in his ear as his body moved against her. "I've been thinking about this all night and I'm so hot for you. We're behind the car, people can't see, and I want you so much. Do it hard, I want you now—"

She broke off when he brought his knee between her legs, his hands sure on her, and she moved to help him, the cool air between her thighs reminding her how empty she was and how she ached for him. He rolled to one side to unzip his jeans and she said, "Do it fast, just *take* me right here."

He sat up to get the condom from her shorts and then

smiled as he rolled back to her, a lazy, sexy screwup's smile, and said, "Nah, let's take it slow and make sure everybody sees us." He slid his hand between her thighs as his body touched hers, hot and strong and broad looming over her, and she moved against his hand, closing her eyes against the sun, feeling the cool grass under her and his hot fingers slick inside her, making her breath stutter and her blood pound. "I love you," she said, mindless with wanting him, and he said, "I know," and kissed her, driving her into oblivion with his hands and mouth under the late summer sun while she touched him everywhere, mindlessly claiming everything about him as hers.

Cars drove by, and there were birds chirping, and some kind of farm machinery growled somewhere, but it was all just hum and chatter; the only thing Maddie heard was C.L. whispering in her ear, telling her the impossible erotic mind-bending things he wanted to do to her now, later, forever, while his body pinned her down and his fingers made her breathless with need.

She moaned against him, her hands fumbling at his zipper while her mind went clumsy with wanting him. And when she finally felt him hard against her hand, he said, "I lied, I can't take this slow, we do this *now*."

She lifted her hips to his, and after a moment with the condom, he moved inside her, muffling her cry of relief with his mouth while he rolled so she was on top, pulling her hips hard down onto his. Maddie straddled him, her thighs spread across his broad body, and then shuddered as she felt him high inside her. She exhaled as he moved, watching him close his eyes, his lashes dark against his skin as he sucked in his breath. His face was strong, the most beautiful face she'd ever seen. She drew her breath sharply and pulsed against him, feeling his body tighten under her hands, and he rocked into her and made her dizzy with heat. "You're beautiful," he said, and she realized he was looking at her now, moving deliberately into her to make her shudder while he watched. "You're brand-new," he said, "but you're still mine."

She smiled down at him, biting her lip against the pleasure that lapped inside her. "Maybe," she whispered, and he rolled to pin her beneath him, moving even harder into her. *"Mine,"* he said, and she tried to shake her head, but he moved again, deeper inside her, and she forgot to pretend and just clutched at him. "Harder," she said through clenched teeth, and he took her without stopping again for words or laughter, surging into her in the soft grass beside his bright red car not twenty feet from the road, oblivious to everything but her. They were shameless and mindless for each other, and knowing that pushed her screaming up to meet him, all heat and light and then shudder and twist as she came hard, digging her nails into him as the spasms took her, until he collapsed against her.

And when it was done, all her self-doubts evaporated into the air with her reputation.

They lay gasping in the grass, tangled together in so much mindless pleasure that they both laughed, and she thought, *That's the end of the old Maddie.*

Gran would be so proud.

C.L. gave her his suit coat when they got back in the car. "Personally I prefer you naked," he told her. "But you know the neighbors." Then he kissed her so hard she was breathless again.

When he dropped her off at her house fifteen minutes later, Gloria's head was bobbing down the other side of the fence. Probably edging her grass. "It's hard not to know the neighbors," Maddie said as she got out of the car. "Maybe I'll move. That old farm has nice vibes."

"So do I," C.L. said. "You move, you're moving in with me."

"Maybe," she said, but she went around to his side of the car and bent over to kiss him just because it felt so good.

"Are you nuts? We're in public," he said, and she kissed him again anyway, a good, long, thank-you-for-great-sex-in-the-sunshine kiss with lots of tongue that left him breathless and appreciative. "I'm coming back for my jacket," he said. "As soon as I've seen Henry, I'm ripping that jacket off you."

"This jacket?" Maddie flapped it open. C.L. closed his eyes and she grabbed his keys out of the ignition.

"Hey," he said as she backed away.

"Walk," she said. "I want a scarlet Mustang in my driveway."

"Very funny, Hester," he said. "Give me back my keys."

Maddie walked away into her backyard, paying close attention to the way the silk lining of his jacket moved against her skin. If he followed her, that was fine. Great animal sex was wonderful, but she was due for some leisurely stuff, too, assuming C.L. was up for it. She was pretty sure he would be.

She turned to see if he was following, but he'd evidently read her mind and was slamming the car door.

"Fine," he called to her from the front seat. "I could use the exercise. Stay here so I can get some more when I come back."

She watched him walk away because she liked watching him move, and when he turned the corner she went into the yard and up her back steps.

"Maddie?"

Maddie turned and squinted at Gloria over the fence.

"Maddie, what are you wearing?" Gloria looked equally shocked and delighted. "Is that a man's jacket?"

"It's C.L.'s jacket," Maddie said. "We just made love out at the old Drake farm. I'm naked underneath it. Anything else you want to know?"

"Well, really, Maddie." Gloria's nose went up. "Brent's only been gone two weeks."

"That's a long time to go without sex," Maddie said. "Which reminds me, I understand you slept with my husband, and while I didn't like him much, I'm not real happy with you, either. So you just keep your comments about my sex life and my grass to yourself."

Gloria flushed. "I don't know what you're talking about. I never—"

"He wrote me a letter, Gloria," Maddie said. "Give it up. He ratted on you. I'm guessing you had sex with him in the garage, right in front of the neighbors. Which, come to think of it, was me. Tacky."

Gloria's lips were moving, but no sound was coming out, so Maddie went inside and let the screen door bang.

Maybe when Henry found the killer, he'd let her yell at him, too. It was starting to feel good, being the new Maddie, the one who wasn't nice and got to tell people off.

And the new Maddie had great sex, too. Heartened, Maddie went to put on some good female country music. It was that kind of sunny, kick-ass day.

"I thought you wanted to be here for Bailey," Henry said when C.L. came in rumpled without his suit coat an hour later than he'd promised.

"Had a little trouble on the road," C.L. said, trying to look like he hadn't just had great sex.

"Oh, hell, C.L., in broad daylight?" Henry said. "If you aren't a shit-for-brains moron, I don't know who is."

"Well, there's Bailey." C.L. tried to tuck in his shirttail better. "What did he have to say?"

"He said Maddie shot Brent."

C.L. jerked his head up.

"Slow down," Henry said. "It's possible he's telling the truth. We traced the gun and it's licensed through the construction company. Maddie could have gotten it there."

"Let me see him," C.L. said grimly, heading for the door. "I want to hear this truth."

Maddie put on a new T-shirt and shorts and turned Lorrie Morgan up higher on the stereo in order to annoy Gloria. Then she sat down and went through the mail that had accumulated over the past week. She wrote checks for bills and put them to one side until the weekend when her paycheck would be automatically deposited and she could cover her expenses again.

It really had been particularly cheap of Brent to empty their accounts, especially since he'd had a quarter of a mil for his own expenses. It wasn't like him, really. He'd had his faults, but he'd never been cheap. And he must have known she'd be bouncing checks all over town.

Maddie sorted through the mail again. She should be bouncing checks all over town; she'd never made that deposit Candace had called about. Where were the returned-check notices? Had Candace covered them somehow? And if she had, why hadn't she told Maddie?

Maddie let the mail drop back onto the desk.

Suppose there weren't any bounced checks.

Suppose Brent hadn't emptied the account.

Suppose somebody at the bank had emptied it, so that Candace would have to call her and get her in there to open her safe-deposit box and incriminate herself.

Harold Whitehead couldn't plan a night out, but the Websters probably could. So they'd empty her account, and then get Candace to call so they could stand around as witnesses—

Why would they get Candace to call? Why wouldn't *they* just call?

Candace was the one who'd suggested the safe-deposit box. "Anything in your safe-deposit box?" she'd asked. Hell, yes.

Candace?

Maddie tried to make the pieces fit with Candace in the middle instead of the Websters, but it didn't seem right. True, Candace was blonde, but she was also sane and established and not a little dull. The thought of Candace wearing crotchless underwear under her beige suits was absurd.

Except maybe she didn't wear it. It had been a plant, something so shocking Maddie would have to confront Brent. A smart woman had stuck that underwear under the seat.

Candace was a very smart woman.

Candace had pulled herself up to become loan manager at the bank, but that was all she was ever going to be. Candace would have loved being the mayor's wife. She wouldn't have been a Lowery anymore. All she had to do was get rid of Maddie.

You are paranoid, Maddie told herself, but then where were the overdrawn notices? Her mother said Candace practically ran the bank; she could have gone down alone to get that box with Brent's key.

Once Maddie looked at the possibility, it seemed obvious. Candace was a financial whiz. Candace would know everything Brent needed to skim money from the company. She even handled the deposits and the company accounts. It had to be Candace.

Except the kidnapper's voice had been male.

Candace had been seeing Harold Whitehead, but Maddie couldn't imagine Harold making a kidnapping call, not even if Candace was dancing naked in front of him.

But Candace was dating Bailey, too. He wouldn't kidnap anybody, that would be illegal, like blackmail, but if there wasn't any real kidnapping, he might make the call. The finer points of the law had never been really clear to Bailey. The voice had been raspy like his. It could have been Bailey. But Bailey couldn't kill anybody.

Candace might have.

Maddie frowned at herself. She'd known Candace all her life, all the way back to Mary Janes and cracked sandals. The whole idea was ridiculous.

Except it made sense. In spite of the kidnapper. Because of the cracked sandals. If Brent had been embezzling with Candace, if he'd decided to skip town and leave her holding the bag, if he'd dumped her and she'd realized he was panicking and she was going to go to jail—

Candace could have shot him. She'd worked too hard to be somebody to let Brent make her a nobody again. Or worse, make her the scandal of Frog Point. *Just like a Lowery*, people would say, and for the first time, Maddie wondered what it was like on the other side. She'd hated being born the good girl; how had Candace felt being born a loser?

Maddie had just had naked sex in public to get out of her straitjacket identity.

What would Candace do to keep from going back to hers?

Candace had had a lot at stake. She could have shot Brent.

There was really only one way to find out. Maddie picked up C.L.'s keys and headed for the car. She'd go confront Candace and watch the look on her face.

. . .

"Maddie did it, C.L.," Bailey said, and C.L. looked in his eyes and knew he was telling the truth. Bailey couldn't lie for squat. He really believed Maddie was the shooter.

"Let's take this again," C.L. said, and Bailey sighed loudly.

"She walked up to the Point and she saw Brent sleeping and she shot him," Bailey said, singsong from long practice.

"He slept at the Point a lot, did he?" C.L. asked.

"Sometimes he'd come up there just to get away. I didn't ask. Things weren't good at home." He glanced slyly at C.L. "But I guess you know that."

"That reminds me," C.L. said. "You try to blackmail Maddie again and you'll be picking your teeth up off the street. What the hell was that about?"

"It wasn't blackmail," Bailey said in outraged honesty. "I just thought since she had some money, she could give me some since I was doing her such a good turn."

C.L. looked at him, at first in disgust and then in renewed interest. Bailey was telling the God's honest truth. Or in this case, Bailey's honest truth. C.L. glanced over at Henry and saw him narrow his eyes.

"Tell me again what you saw at the Point," C.L. said, and Bailey shifted a little, but then he answered, honest as a judge.

"Maddie walked up the hill—"

"You see her walk up the hill, Bailey?" Henry's voice was deceptively mild.

"No, I seen her footprints. Then she walked over to the car and shot him." Bailey nodded, virtuous.

"You saw her do it," C.L. said.

"Yep," Bailey said, and his eyes shifted and he moved his feet and C.L. said, "Bailey, you shit-for-brains moron, you are lying in your yellow teeth."

Bailey shifted his eyes to Henry. "He can't talk that way, can he?"

"Normally, no," Henry said. "But it appears he has a point. Let's try this again. Tell us what you saw, Bailey."

"She did it," Bailey said. "I didn't see, but she did it."

"Who told you that?" Henry said.

Bailey shifted in his chair again.

"Bailey," C.L. said, leaning over him. "You are slandering the woman I love. Have you any idea how annoyed that makes me?"

"Police brutality," Bailey said.

"I'm not the police," C.L. said. "It'll be private-citizen brutality, and I'm damn good at it."

"Henry," Bailey said nervously.

"He won't touch you here," Henry said. "You know I don't work like that. Problem is, I can't protect you after you leave here. Now, once he puts you in the hospital, I'll put him in jail. You can count on that."

Bailey looked from Henry to C.L. and back again. "She can't tell you about it herself because there'd be this big scandal. You know how this town is."

C.L. started to cut in, but he caught Henry's glare and shut up. Whoever had done a snow job on Bailey had done a good one. Might as well sit and listen.

"This town's a real bitch," C.L. said instead. "Tell me about it."

Maddie pulled up at the traffic light beside the bank at high noon. Harold Whitehead was getting ready to close the doors, an odd thing for a bank president to be doing, Maddie thought, and then he opened one and let Candace out. She was dressed in her usual smooth beige, a pale leather handbag looped in one hand.

She was carrying a suitcase in the other.

"Hey, Candace," Maddie yelled from the convertible. "Wait a minute."

Candace turned and saw her, waved the hand with the bag, and kept on going. "Candace," Maddie bellowed again, as the light stayed stubbornly red. *"Candace."*

Candace kept on walking, the light smooth step of the professional woman without a care in the world but with a sudden case of deafness.

"The hell with it," Maddie said, and got out of the car, leaving it parked in the middle of the intersection. The light turned green as she reached the sidewalk, and cars began to honk.

The hell with them.

"Candace!" Maddie called again, and ran to catch her.

Candace stopped then; she had to. "I'm in a hurry, Maddie," she called. "Labor Day weekend. Three-day vacation. Plane to catch." She turned to go. "I'll talk to you Tuesday."

"No, that'll be too late." Maddie lunged and caught hold of the handle of her suitcase. "I need to talk to you now."

Several people turned and took an avid interest in Revco's mirrorlike window.

"Really, Maddie." Candace tried to tug her case back.

"We need to talk." Maddie held on for dear life as Candace pulled.

"Maddie, I know you've had a hard time lately," Candace began soothingly, "but I really have to catch that plane."

"With all this money?" Maddie said, and unzipped the bag with one vengeful motion.

Some really beautiful silky underwear slithered from the bag, followed by a lot of very expensive-looking beige and gold clothing that Candace tried and failed to catch before it fell to the pavement.

No money.

Candace dropped the suitcase and looked at Maddie as if she were insane. Several people came to help, one a friend of Maddie's mother's.

"Maddie, dear," she said. "Maybe you need to go home and lie down."

"Oh, hell." Maddie ignored her to concentrate on Candace. "Where did you put it all? In your garter?"

"Maddie, what is wrong with you?" Candace went down on one knee to stuff her clothing back in her bag while people around her made sympathetic sounds and glared at Maddie, and a red-faced man came up and said, "Lady, move your god-damned car."

"I'm a little upset about my checking account," Maddie said to Candace.

"You're joking." Candace zipped her bag shut and stood up. "This is about a checking account? Maddie, you've been under a strain. Go home and we'll figure this out when the bank opens up on Tuesday."

"Lady, *your car*," the man said.

"It's not overdrawn," Maddie said, and Candace's eyes flickered. Just for a moment, but it was there. "You did it, didn't you?" Maddie said.

"*Lady*," the man said.

"I don't know what you're talking about." Candace brushed off her skirt, avoiding Maddie's eyes. "And I don't have time to humor you. Get help. You need it." She picked up her suitcase and bag and turned to go, so sure of herself that Maddie almost let her go.

"No, you don't." Maddie grabbed her arm again. "I don't know where you're going, but I bet it's someplace we can't get you back from, and you are not going to leave me in this mess."

Candace jerked her arm and tried to walk away, but Maddie held on for dear life, and they tugged at each other, Maddie determined, Candace with as much dignity as possible. People had given up the Revco window and were frankly staring now, and even the guy with the car had shut up to watch.

"You're making a scene," Candace whispered to her savagely as she tried to tug away. "You're making a *fool* of yourself. My God, think of your mother."

"The hell with my mother," Maddie whispered back. "And if you think this is a scene, just wait. You come with me to see Henry or I'll stage a complete production."

Candace wrenched her arm out of Maddie's hands and took one long stride before Maddie lunged and caught up with her, knocking her a few steps ahead with her momentum.

"This woman has gone crazy," Candace said to any and all, dragging Maddie with her as she struggled along. "Somebody get her off me."

It wasn't like this in the movies, Maddie reflected as Candace dragged her another couple of feet. Physical stuff was quick in the movies; there weren't these moments of contemplation that made you think you were a moron. No wonder so many fights were over so fast.

"Help me," Candace said, with more irritation than panic, and Harold Whitehead came forward, tentatively.

"Don't do it, Harold," Maddie said, holding on for dear life. "You'll be aiding and abetting a murderer."

"That's ridiculous," Harold said. "Candace is a loan manager."

"She killed my car, shot my husband, and threatened my kid," Maddie said, loudly enough for everybody to hear, and people looked at Candace with new interest. "That's who you hired, Harold."

Candace wrenched free, and Maddie went after her and gave it her last shot. She caught her arm and said, "Of course, that's what you'd expect from a *Lowery*."

Candace swung around with murder in her eye. "You *bitch*," she said. "You complacent, moronic *bitch*."

She tried to tug her arm away, and when that didn't work, she kicked Maddie on the knee. Maddie yelped in pain and said, "*Listen*, you," and that's when Henry pulled up.

"We got a report of a disturbance," Henry called to them, getting out of the car. "I imagine that would be you, Maddie. What'll people think?"

"I've had it with people, Henry," Maddie said savagely around the pain in her knee, but not letting go. "Fuck the neighbors, I don't care anymore. I am not going to jail, because I didn't kill my husband. Now, will you please arrest this woman?"

"She's gone crazy," Candace announced to the general crowd. "She killed her husband and now she's blaming me. She's nuts. Make her let go of me, Henry. She's hurting me."

"Let go, Maddie," Henry said.

"Henry, that's not—"

"*Let go*, Maddie," Henry said, and Maddie understood why C.L. felt the way he did about his uncle. She let go and rubbed her knee instead.

"I think you're right, Candace," Henry said soothingly. "Maddie has some problems—"

"Hey," Maddie said.

"—so why don't we all go down to the station and you can press charges?"

Maddie shut up. Anything that got Candace to the station was a step in the right direction.

"Because I don't have the time." Candace straightened her suit jacket. "I have a plane to catch." She picked up her bag and turned to go, and Maddie grabbed the handle of her bag again, just as Henry stepped forward.

"You are *not* getting out of Frog Point," Maddie said, and Candace turned to her, her face a mix of horror and rage, and swung her free hand with her purse into the side of Maddie's head. The last thing Maddie saw as she folded into darkness was a lot of hundred-dollar bills floating through the air.

"You couldn't wait for Henry," C.L. said when she came to.

She was in a hospital bed, and the first thing she said was, "Where's Candace?"

"In jail," C.L. said. "Henry was coming to take her quietly when you threw your fit. Of course, I can't marry you now. You're such a screwup my family would never live it down."

"What's she in jail for?" Maddie struggled to sit up and he pushed her down again.

"Lie still. The doctor is coming to see if you have a concussion. Then I'm going to make them X-ray you to see if you have any brains. Why the hell did you attack that woman?"

"She was leaving." Maddie gave up fighting because her head hurt and lay back. "She killed Brent. I figured it out, but she was going away. Labor Day vacation, my ass. She was skipping town."

"Right," C.L. said.

Maddie glared up at him. "Do not tell me you already knew."

C.L. shook his head. "We only got it a little while before you did. The safe-deposit box made Henry suspicious from the beginning because if you weren't lying, which he was pretty sure you were, then it had to be somebody at the bank. He'd already tracked the prowler rumor back to Candace, but he couldn't figure out why she'd started it."

"So Brent would bring her a gun," Maddie said, remembering the phone call. "That's premeditated."

"I don't think Candace ever did anything in her life that wasn't," C.L. said. "That's one determined wench. But you were still chief suspect until we broke Bailey, who admitted

Candace had come down the drive that night and said you'd killed Brent, so of course he believed it, especially when she started going to dinner with him." He grinned at her. "Boy, is she pissed at you. Once she started confessing, the thing she wanted to talk about the most was how you'd screwed everything up. She used Brent's house key to leave the safe-deposit key in the desk drawer on Friday after she killed Brent so you'd open the box the next morning and take the money. But you left it there, you dummy, because you're honest, so she had to come back and steal the key again while you were at the farm so *she* could get the money."

"So the Websters were never in it at all?" Maddie felt guilty. "And I've been thinking horrible things about them."

"Well, the youngest one was. Candace mailed him half a hundred-dollar bill anonymously with instructions to total your car if he wanted the other half. She assumed he'd hit it parked somewhere, but the dumb-ass rear-ended it with you in it, instead. He was so terrified he never talked, but Candace had a fit about how damn dumb he was. He's second only to you on her list of people who don't know how to act right." C.L. shook his head. "She said she couldn't understand why you weren't just letting the town take care of you since it always had. She never expected you to fight back."

"I never expected her to confess," Maddie said. "I figured she'd just sit there and blonde it out."

"The lab found her fingerprint on the gun clip. Henry had to get Candace's prints to check, and he was trying to ease her on down to the station when you decided to become the Talk of the Town."

"But I wiped the gun off," Maddie said.

"That was helpful of you," C.L. said. "The clip was inside. She checked the clip and then fired into Brent's head."

"Oh." Maddie swallowed. "Tough woman."

"Not as tough as you. Do you realize you mugged some-body in broad daylight *and* said 'fuck' in front of about forty people including my uncle?"

"I was overwrought," Maddie said. "I couldn't let her leave, but at the same time I couldn't believe she'd done it, so things were tense. I still can't believe it. I know Candace. I went to high school with her. She's lived in this town all her life."

"I think that's why she did it," C.L. said. "She got tired of killing herself with work to get out and decided to kill some-body else instead."

"That can't be it." Maddie shifted carefully on the bed. Her head didn't come off, so she relaxed. "Candace could have left any time she wanted. She had a degree and experience. She must have wanted something else. She left the pants in Brent's car. She must have wanted him."

"She should have asked for him. You'd have handed him over. Hell, I'd have gift-wrapped him for her."

"Wait a minute." Maddie sat up slowly. "Em's safe now. I'm safe now. Right?"

"Well, not exactly," C.L. said. "I'm still here." He gazed deeply into her eyes. "Your pupils look all right. If you don't have a concussion, you want to go back to Drake's farm later? Your reputation is shot to hell anyway."

"Thank God," Maddie said. "My life is going to be so much simpler from now on."

"Don't count on it," C.L. said. "I'm in it now."

Maddie went into Revco the next morning to buy a necklace for her grandmother to con her out of later. Everyone she passed there stared, and some people even craned their heads around displays to get a good look at the new disgrace. They weren't unfriendly, but they weren't slapping her on the back, either. It was as if they didn't know when she'd go rogue on them again, and they certainly wouldn't approve if she did, but they didn't want to miss it if possible. *Get a life*, Maddie wanted to tell them. *I did.*

A gold cat pendant with enormous green glass eyes caught her attention, and she'd just picked it up when somebody poked her in the back.

"I hear they're putting up a plaque here in memory of the battle," Treva said from behind her. "Your name is to be featured prominently." Maddie turned and Treva added, "God, that's an ugly necklace. It's one thing to throw your reputation away, do you have to look like a skag, too?"

"It's for Gran." Maddie sat on the edge of the counter, so glad to have Treva and conversation back that she didn't care that Susan behind the register was giving her dirty looks for leaning on the merchandise. "And you can spare me the hassle about yesterday. My mother has more than discussed my ruin. The Olympics don't get the slow-motion replay that I've had to put up with."

"Well, at least this time they have an expert commentator," Treva said. "I suppose you just endured."

"No, I was great," Maddie said. "I told her that being a scandal was a hell of a lot more fun than talking about one and that she should go out and be one, too."

"So she did," Treva said. "Wow."

"Of course she didn't," Maddie said. "I got another hour on what it means to be a Martindale. I've never heard anything like it. Evidently, for the purposes of Frog Point, we're the Kennedys with morals. And now she and Em are left to tell the tale."

"I think it's just Em," Treva said. "My mother saw your mother last night at the bowling alley having coffee with Sam Scott, and she told Esther. There goes the neighborhood."

"You're kidding." Maddie laughed and leaned toward Treva in shared delight. "Oh, this is so great. I love this. Wait'll I tell Gran. Blood tells after all."

"Oh, I've got better than that," Treva said. "I told Howie about Three."

Maddie's smile faded and she braced herself until she realized that Treva was more relaxed and content than she'd seen her in months. "I gather he took it well?"

"He's known all along." Treva sat down beside Maddie, her smile wide with remembered relief. "Something about blood types in the hospital. I carried that damn secret for twenty years, and he's known all along." Treva rolled her eyes to the ceiling. "He doesn't care. He says he raised Three, and that makes him his kid, and that's all that matters. I couldn't believe he was so calm, but he said he'd been mad and hurt for about a day twenty years ago, and then he held Three and thought, 'The hell with it,' and it didn't bother him again until a couple of weeks ago when he thought I was sleeping with Brent again." Treva shook her head. "Like I'd sink that low twice." She realized what she'd said and jerked her head toward Maddie. "Not that you were low for sleeping with him. He was your husband."

"Dear God," Maddie said, still back on Howie. "All that guilt for nothing."

"I know," Treva said. "I wanted to kill him, but I love him. What can you do?"

"Go scream 'fuck' out in front of the bank," Maddie said. "I'll wait here."

"My mom said some lady at the bank shot your dad," Mel said later that morning when they were out at the farm, trying to fish.

"Yeah. Candace." Em swung her feet against the dock. "I don't want to talk about it."

"Okay," Mel said. "But it's pretty awful."

"Yeah." Em swung her feet harder. "Is Phoebe close to the water?"

Mel craned her head to look. "Nope." She pulled her pole out of the water and got serious. "Are you okay, Em?"

"Yes." Em said the word strong, the way C.L. always did when he was serious. "I talked to my mom and I talked to C.L. and everything's over. I wish my dad wasn't dead—" she stopped and swallowed and gripped her pole tighter "—I really wish that, but everything else is okay. Nobody is trying to hurt us. We're okay."

"All right." Mel dug into her backpack and pulled out a box of cookies, Archway soft chocolate chip this time. "Here. These are the best."

Em took one of the big cookies and stared at the blue September sky while she ate it, trying to think only about being okay. She wished Mel would stop talking about her dad, but that's the way it was. People always wanted to talk about the stuff you didn't want to talk about.

"So is your mom going to marry C.L.?" Mel said. "I mean, you never talk about this stuff and I'm dying to know."

Em sighed. "I think so. Not right away, and Mom says no, and she means it because she promised she'd never lie to me again, but I bet C.L. talks her into it. Probably next summer 'cause that's when the house will be done, and that way we can live out in the country where Phoebe can run around and I can see Anna every day. Mom says no, but C.L. says it's going to happen, and he never lies."

Mel sat up. "Wait a minute, if you live out in the country, I'll never see you again."

"Sure you will." Em bit into her cookie and talked around

the bite. "C.L. will come get you and bring you out or bring me in. I asked him, and he said sure because he'll be working in town. I think he's going to work with your dad out at the company. Everything's okay." *Except my daddy's dead*, she added silently, but the thought didn't hurt the way it once had, it hurt bad but not like it once had. Em closed her eyes and thought of her dad again, baseball cap on and butter pecan ice cream cone in hand, and she remembered him perfectly. "We're going to be okay," she told Mel, and took another bite of cookie.

"Well, that's good," Mel said. "Now, did I tell you what Cindy Snopes told me about Jason Norris?"

"No." Em sat up straighter. "What?"

"Have another cookie," Mel said, passing the box over. "This is going to take a while, but it's good."

"You blew it," her grandmother said when Maddie visited her that afternoon. "You could have had it easy, but you had to push your luck and now there's all this scandal. Adultery. Embezzlement. Murder. Screaming obscenities in public. You couldn't keep quiet."

"Yeah, I decided I wanted to be like you." Maddie handed the extra large five-pound gold box to her grandmother, who was temporarily speechless with delight. "Lots of chocolate," she said finally. "Wonderful." She ripped the plastic off and then the red ribbon and when she opened the lid, the box positively teemed with calories.

Maddie took the milk chocolate turtle before she could get it.

"Hey, that's my favorite," her grandmother said, and Maddie said, "You spit the nuts out. It's disgusting. Besides, there's a dark chocolate one, too."

Her grandmother leaned back against her pillows, pouting. "I don't like dark chocolate. I'm not going to be with—"

"Good," Maddie said. "Then I'll eat that one, too." She picked it out of the box and bit into it. The chocolate was rich and dark and the caramel strung out between her teeth and the nuts were savory and crunchy. "Heaven."

"You're eating all my candy," her grandmother snapped, seriously annoyed. "You're a terrible girl." She ducked her head and went back to her refrain. "I'm not going to be with you for much longer, you know."

"You're going to outlive all of us." Maddie sat down to finish off the dark chocolate turtle. "You're like this town. It'll take a stake through the heart to stop either one of you."

"Damn right," her grandmother said. "But you're still a fool to have let that all come out. All that scandal. And now there's your mother, flaunting herself at the bowling alley with Sam Scott. I'm appalled."

"You'll get over it," Maddie said. "I can't believe you heard about Mom already. I just got it an hour ago."

Her grandmother sniffed. "I talk to people. You're probably spending all your time in bed with that man. Tramp. You'll never live it down."

"I don't want to." Maddie bit into the other turtle. "You know, this is excellent chocolate. I can't think why I haven't been eating it with you for years."

Her grandmother picked a walnut-topped cream out of the box and put the whole thing in her mouth. Maddie waited until she'd spit the walnut across the room and then she said, "That's really gross, Gran."

"That's why I do it," Gran said. "Tell me about this man."

"He's excellent in bed," Maddie said. "Em loves him. He bought her a dog. I'm thinking of marrying him."

"Can't be too soon," Gran said. "Your reputation is shot to hell."

"You must be so proud," Maddie said.

"I am," Gran said. "You wouldn't believe the attention I'm getting. That's a pretty necklace you're wearing."

"A gift," Maddie said. "From my new fella. Couldn't possibly give it up."

"I'm not going to be with you long," Gran said. "My heart."

"A symbol of his love," Maddie said. "I sleep with it on."

Gran hacked and wheezed herself into a coughing fit that didn't end until Maddie had gotten some water down her and the nurse had come in to make sure drastic measures weren't required.

"Don't do that again," Maddie said when the nurse had left. "You're scaring me. I'm just starting to appreciate you, so you can't die on me yet."

"I'd feel so much better with something pretty to keep me company," Gran said. "That cat necklace sure is pretty."

"You win." Maddie handed it over. "Just don't do that coughing thing anymore. Now tell me about Mickey."

Gran moved the candy box out of Maddie's reach and strung the pendant around her neck. "The hell with Mickey. Tell me about this new man of yours. I want to meet him. How good is he?"

"Incredible," Maddie said. "Absolutely the best. I come screaming every time."

"Well, keep it quiet," her grandmother said. "We have to live in this town."

Maddie put Bonnie Raitt on the stereo when she got home, but before she could turn up the volume on "Something to Talk About," the phone rang. Maddie thought about not answering it and then gave up. What if it was something good?

"This is an obscene phone call," C.L. said when she answered, and just the sound of his voice made her warmer. "What are you wearing?"

"A smile and what I wore at the Drake farm. Why aren't you here inside me?" Even as she said it, the thought of the weight of him and of his hands and his mouth and his smile and his love made her breath go and the heat spread, and it evidently had the same effect on C.L. because she heard him exhale over the phone.

"That's it, play hard to get," he said. "Jesus. Where was I? Who cares? Brace yourself, I'm on my way."

"Wait a minute," Maddie said. "What about Em? Is Henry going to call?"

"Anna's planning on watching Em and Mel into the next century, and Henry's got the books and the invoices from that box at the station, and I have nothing to do but make you come your brains out."

Maddie bit her lip and leaned against the wall. Phone fore-play. For the first time in weeks, she thought warmly of AT&T. "Couldn't think of anything else, huh?"

"I thought about rotating my tires, but if you're going to talk dirty, I'll come rotate yours. I have tools, and I know how to use them."

"My grandmother's going to love you," Maddie said.

"So are you, babe," C.L. said, and the determination in his voice made her laugh.

"I already do," Maddie said, giddy with it. "I love you madly, passionately, hopelessly, loudly. Break the speed limit and park in front of my house. We're going to leave the windows open."

C.L. hung up without saying good-bye, and Maddie pictured him leaping over the door of the convertible and fishtailing down the road. He wouldn't, of course, he was a sane and sober citizen now, but she could still see it, and she loved it.

But it would take him at least twenty minutes to get there. She could call her mother and demand details, but she didn't want to do anything that might discourage her from making a fool of herself at sixty-three. She could call Treva, but she'd be spending the rest of her life talking to Treva. She could sit and think obscene thoughts about C.L., but she was already hot and shivering from the phone call. Twenty minutes . . .

There were brownies in the freezer. Cashew brownies. And she had a functional microwave thanks to her functional lover, and she could nuke one into hot heaven in thirty seconds.

Hot heaven made her think of C.L. again. She stripped off her baby blue bikini underpants and left them on the hall floor for him to find, and then reconsidered and went out on the front porch and hung them on the doorknob instead, waving to Mrs. Crosby, who was squinting at her from her own porch. Then she went back inside. She was sure finding the pants would have an electrifying effect on an already electrified C.L., and her afternoon, already a good one, would turn out to be cataclysmic.

And in the meantime, there was chocolate.

Turn the page for a sneak peek at
Jennifer Crusie's new novel

Maybe This Time

Available Fall 2010

The human heart dares not stay away too long from that which hurt it most. There is a return journey to anguish that few of us are released from making.

—*Lillian Smith*

This book takes place in 1992.
Because.

Chapter One

Andie Miller sat in the reception room of the North-Archer Legal Group, holding on to ten years of uncashed alimony checks and the unresolved rage that had swamped her as soon as she'd walked back into the old Victorian where her ex-husband lived and worked. *This is why I never came back here. Nothing wrong with repressed anger as long as it stays repressed.*

"Miss Miller?"

Andie jerked her head up and a lock of her hair fell out of her chignon. She stuffed it back into the clip on the back of her head as North's secretary smiled at her. If that secretary had a chignon, nothing would escape from it. The secretary was discreetly dressed and probably efficient and undoubtedly in control of her emotions. North was probably crazy about her.

"Mr. Archer will see you now," the secretary said.

"Well, good for him." Andie stood up, yanked on the hem of the only suit jacket she owned, and then wondered if she'd sounded too hostile.

"He's really very nice," the secretary said.

"No, he isn't." Andie walked to the door of North's office, opened it before the secretary could get in ahead of her, and then stopped, taken aback in spite of herself.

North sat behind his massive desk, his cropped blond hair almost white in the sunlight from the large, mullioned window behind him. His wire rim glasses had slid too far down his nose again, and his shirt sleeves were rolled up over his forearms—*Still playing racquetball*, Andie thought—and his shoulders were as straight as ever as he studied the papers spread out across his massive desk. He looked exactly the way he had ten years ago when she'd bumped her suitcase on the door frame on her way out of town—

"Miss Miller is here," his secretary said from behind her, and he looked up at her over his glasses, and the years fell away, and she was right back where she'd begun, staring into those blue-gray eyes, her heart pounding.

He stood up. "Andromeda. Thank you for coming."

She crossed the thick rug, smiled tightly at him, decided that shaking his hand would be weird, and sat down. "I called you, remember? Thank you for seeing me."

He sat down and said, "Thank you, Kristin," to his secretary, who left.

"So the reason I called—" Andie began, just as he said, "How is your mother?"

Oh, we're going to be polite. "Still crazy. How's yours?"

"Lydia is fine, thank you." He straightened the papers on his desk into one stack. A lot of really heavy trees had died to make that desk. His mother had probably gnawed them down and used her nails to saw the boards. "I'll tell her you asked after her."

"She'll be thrilled." Andie opened her purse and took out the stack of alimony checks and put them on the desk. "I came to give these back to you."

North looked at the checks for a moment, the sharp planes of his face looking drawn in the dim light.

Say something, she thought, and when he didn't, she said, "They're all there, one hundred and nineteen of them. October nineteen eighty-two to last month."

His face was as expressionless as ever. "Why?"

"Because they're a link between us. We haven't talked in ten years but every month you send me a check even though you know I don't want alimony. Which means every month I get an envelope in the mail that says I used to be married to you. And every month I don't cash them, and it's like we're nodding in the street or something. We're still *communicating*."

"Not very well." North looked at the stack. "Why now?"

"I'm getting married."

She watched him go still, the pause stretching out until she said, "North?"

"Congratulations. Who's the lucky man?"

"Will Spenser," Andie said, pretty sure North wouldn't know him.

"The writer?"

"He's a great guy. He makes me laugh." *And he never forgets I exist.* "I'm ready to settle down, so I'm drawing a line under my old life." She nodded at the checks. "That's why I came to give you those back. Don't send any more. Please."

After a moment, he nodded. "Of course. Congratulations. The family will want to send a gift." He pulled his notepad toward him. "Are you registered?"

"No, I'm not registered," Andie said, exasperated. "Technically, I'm not even engaged yet. He asked me. I haven't told him yes yet. I needed to give you the checks back first." She didn't know why she'd expected him to have a reaction to the news. It wasn't as if he still cared. She wasn't sure he'd cared when she'd left.

"I see. Thank you for returning the checks."

North straightened the papers on his desk again, and then looked down at the top paper for a long moment, as if he were really reading it. He'd probably forgotten she was there again because his work was—

He looked up. "Perhaps, since you haven't said yes yet, you could postpone your new life."

"What?"

"I have a problem that you could help with. It would only take you a year, maybe less—"

"North, did you even hear what I said?"

"—and we'd pay you ten thousand dollars a month, plus expenses, room, and board."

She started to protest and then thought, *Ten thousand dollars a month?*

He straightened the folder on his desk again. "Theodore Archer, a distant cousin, died last year and made me the guardian of his two children. I went down to see them at the family home where their aunt was taking care of them and they seemed fine. Unfortunately, the aunt died in June. Since then I've hired three nannies, but none have stayed."

Ten thousand dollars was ridiculous. He had to be up to something.

But ten thousand dollars would pay off her credit card bills and her car. In one month. Ten thousand dollars would mean she could get married without debt. Not that Will cared, but it would be better to go to him free and clear—

"We wanted to bring the children here in June after their aunt's death, but the little girl had a psychotic break when the nanny tried to take her away from the family home. The boy was sent away to boarding school at the beginning of August, but he's been expelled for setting fires. I need someone to go down there and stabilize the children, bring their education up to standard for their grade level so they can go to public school, and find a way to move them up here with us."

Andie shook her head and another chunk of hair slipped out of her chignon. "North, I teach high school English," she said, as she stuffed it back. "I have no idea how to help these kids. You need—"

"I need somebody who doesn't care about the way things are supposed to be," he said, his eyes sliding to her neck. "I think that's where the nannies are going wrong. These kids are . . . different. I need somebody who will do the unconventional thing without blinking. Somebody who will get things done." He met her eyes. "Even if she doesn't stay for the long haul."

"*Hey*," Andie said.

"I would take it as a personal favor. I've never asked you for anything—"

"You asked for a divorce." As soon as she said it, she knew it was a mistake.

He looked at her over the tops of his glasses, exasperated. "I did not ask you for a divorce."

"Yes, you did," Andie said, in too far to stop now. "You told me that I seemed unhappy, and if that was true, you would understand if I divorced you."

"You were playing 'Any Day Now' every time I came up to the apartment. As hints go, it was pretty broad."

He looked annoyed, so that was something, but it didn't do anything for her anger. "There are people who, if their spouses are unhappy, try to do something about it."

"I did. I gave you a divorce. You had one foot out the door anyway. Do we need to review that again?"

"No. The divorce is a dead subject." *And the ghost of it is sitting right here with us.* Although maybe only with her. North didn't looked haunted at all.

"I realize you're getting ready to start a new life," he went on. "But if you haven't made plans yet, there's no reason you couldn't wait four more weeks. You could use the money for the wedding."

"I don't want a wedding. I want to get married. I can do that at a courthouse." *That's what we did.* "And another thing, why are you offering me ten thousand dollars a month for babysitting? You didn't pay the nannies that. It's ridiculous. For ten thousand a month, you should not only get child care, you should get your house cleaned, your laundry done, your tires rotated, and if I were you, I'd insist on nightly blow jobs. Did you think I wouldn't notice that you're still trying to keep your thumb on me?" She shook her head, and the lock of hair fell out of her chignon again. Well, the hell with that, too.

He sat very still, and then he said, "Why have you got your hair like that?" sounding as annoyed as she was.

"Because it's *professional.*"

"Not if it keeps falling down."

"Thank you," Andie said. "Now butt out. This is a *business meeting.* It's not personal."

He closed his eyes and then said, calmly, "Andromeda, I'm asking for a favor, a big one, and I don't think the money is out of line. We didn't leave our marriage enemies, so I don't see why you're hostile now."

"I'm not hostile," Andie said, and then added fairly, "Well, okay, I am hostile. You didn't do anything to save our marriage ten years ago, but every month you sent a check so I'll think of you again. It's passive aggressive. Or something. You know the strongest memory I have of you? Sitting right there, behind that desk. You'd think I'd remember you naked with all the mattress time we clocked, but no, it's you, staring at me from behind all that walnut as if you weren't quite sure who I was. You have no idea how many times I wanted to take an ax to that damn desk just to see if you'd *notice me*."

North looked down at his desk, perplexed.

"You hide behind it," Andie said, sitting back now that she wasn't repressing anything anymore. "You use it to keep from getting emotionally involved."

"I use it to write on."

"You know what I mean. It gives you distance."

"It gives me storage. Have you lost your mind?"

Andie looked at him for a moment, sitting there rigid and polite and completely inaccessible. "Yes. It was a bad idea coming back here. I should go now." She stood up.

"She said the house is haunted," North said.

"Excuse me?"

"The last nanny. She said there were ghosts in the house. I asked the local police to look into things to see if somebody was playing tricks, but they found nothing. I think it's the kids, but if I send another nanny down like the previous ones, she's going to quit, too. I need somebody different, somebody who's tough, somebody who can handle the unexpected. Somebody like you. And you're the only person like you that I know." He met her eyes, and suddenly he was the old North again, warm and real with that light in his eyes as he looked at her. "They're little kids, Andie. I can't get them out of there, and I can't leave them there, and with Mother in France, I can't leave the practice long enough to find out what's going on, and even if I could, I don't know anything about kids. I need you."

"I don't—"

"Everybody they've ever been close to has died," North said

quietly. "Everybody they've ever loved has left them. They need you. Not somebody, *you*."

Bastard, Andie thought.

"I can't give you a year," she said. "That's ridiculous."

North nodded, looking calm, but she'd been married to him for a year so she knew: he was going in for the kill. "Give them a month then. You can draw your line under us, we don't need to talk, you can send reports to Kristin, hell, take your fiancé down there with you."

"I'm the least maternal person I know," Andie said, thinking *ten thousand dollars*. And more than that, two kids who'd lost everyone they loved.

"I don't think they need maternal," he said. "I think they need you."

He was pushing it too hard now. *Don't fall for this*, Andie told herself. "A psychotic little girl and a boy who's growing up to be a serial killer."

"They're growing up alone," North said, and Andie thought, *Oh, hell*.

The problem was, he sounded sincere. Well, he always did, he was good at that, but now that she really looked at him, he had changed. She could see the stress in his face, the lines that hadn't been there ten years ago, the tightening of the skin over his bones, the age in the hollows under his eyes. His brother Southie probably still looked as smooth as a boiled egg, but North was still trapped behind that damn desk, taking care of everyone in the family. And now there were two more in the family, and he was still handling it alone.

"Please," he said, those gray-blue eyes fixed on her.

"Yes, damn it," Andie said.

North drew a deep breath. "Thank you." Then he put his glasses back on, professional again. "There's a household account you can draw on for any expenses, and a credit card. The housekeeper will clean and cook for you. If you come by tomorrow, Kristin will give you a copy of this folder with everything you need in it and your first check, of course."

"My only check. I'm only staying for a month."

"Of course," North said.

Andie sat there for a moment, a little stunned that she'd said yes. She'd felt the same way after he'd proposed.

"I'd appreciate it if you could go down as soon as possible."

"Right." She shoved her hair back into the clip, picked up her purse, and stood up again. "I'll drive down tomorrow. You have a good winter terrorizing the opposing counsel."

She headed for the door, refusing to look back. This was good. She could spare a month to save two orphans. Will was in New York for the next two weeks anyway, and he'd come home to a fiancée with no debt, and then—

"Andie," North said, and she turned back in the doorway.

"Thank you," he said, standing now behind his desk, tall and lean and beautiful and looking at her the way he used to. *Get out of here.* "You're welcome."

Then she turned and walked out before he could say or do anything else that made her forget she was done with him.

After Andie left, North sat for a moment wondering what the hell he'd just done. He'd had the résumés of several excellent nannies on his desk, and he'd hired his ex-wife instead because she was getting married and he didn't like it. *Fuck*, he thought, and deliberately put her out of his mind which was difficult since she'd mentioned blow jobs. Which were irrelevant because he and Andie were over. She was right: draw a line under it. He went back to work, making notes on his current case file as the shadows grew longer and Kristin left for the night, his black capital letters spaced evenly in straight rows, as firm and as clear as his thinking—

He stopped and frowned at the page. Instead of "Indiana" he'd written "Andiana." He marked an "I" over the "A" but the word sat there on the page, misspelled and blotted, a dark spot on the clear pattern of his day.

There was a knock on the door at the same time it opened.

"North!" his brother Sullivan said as he came in, his tie loosened and his face as genial as ever under his flop of brown hair.

"Sullivan." North nodded. "You're looking well. Paris must have agreed with you."

"Everything agrees with me. You, however, look like hell." Sullivan lounged into the same chair Andie had taken and put his feet on the desk. "You can't work twenty-four-seven. It's not healthy."

"I like my work. How's Mother?"

"Now that's health. That woman was built for distance."

North pictured their elegant, white-haired mother running a marathon in her pearls, kicking any upstarts out of the way with the pointed end of her heels as she crossed the finish line.

"It's you I'm worried about," Sullivan was saying. "You're working too hard, too much on your plate, trying to run the whole practice with Mother gone—"

"My plate is fine. However, I am in the middle of—"

"No, no, it's time I helped out." Sullivan smiled at him. "I've been thinking about what I could do, but I figure you'd fall on your number two pencil before you'd let me help with the practice."

North looked down at the black pen mark that made "Andiana" such a blot. A number two pencil would be a good idea if he was going to start making mistakes.

"So I was thinking of something a little more in my area and out of yours," Sullivan said. "You know. People. You're not a people person, North. I am."

"People." North turned the top sheet on his legal pad over so he didn't have to look at the blot.

"You remember those two kids that second cousin left you awhile back?"

"Yes," North said, fairly sure that had been a rhetorical question, although with Sullivan, you never knew.

"I thought I might drop in, check on things for you, see how they're doing."

North nodded. "You want to 'drop in' to the wilds of southern Ohio to visit two children you've never met."

"Yes."

"Why?"

Sullivan grinned at him. "I want to see the house."

"The house isn't worth anything. It's in the middle of nowhere."

"It's haunted."

"Sullivan, there is no such thing as ghosts," North said, and for a moment he was twelve again and Sullivan was six, staring wide-eyed into the room where their father was laid out in his coffin. "He's not going to sit up, Southie," North had said then. "He's dead. There's no such thing as ghosts."

"I know that," Sullivan said now. "But I want to see a house that everybody thinks is haunted."

"'Everybody' being a nanny who got bored and wanted out."

"Other people have thought so, lots of rumors. So I thought I'd go down there and talk to some of the people. See what's going on."

"And how did you find out about these rumors?"

"I did some research for a friend of mine. She's interested in hauntings, and she looked me up at a party and talked to me about the house and, you know, it *is* interesting."

"She," North said, Sullivan's motives becoming much clearer now. The combination of a shiny new hobby and a shiny new girlfriend must have been irresistible.

"Suzanne Twomey. The ghost thing is fascinating. I've talked to—"

"Suzanne Twomey?" North thought of the tiny, sharp-faced, sharp-tongued newscaster he'd avoided after one viewing. "The little blonde with the teeth on channel twelve?"

"They're very good teeth," Sullivan said, going for indignant and missing.

"They look like they were very expensive," North said and remembered Andie the first time he'd seen her, her big eyes dancing , her curly hair wild, her wide smile flashing her overlapped front teeth. She'd never had her teeth fixed.

"Well, you need good teeth for TV."

"True." That had been the first thing his mother had said about Andie. "For god's sake, North, get her teeth fixed."

"The close-ups are murder," Sullivan said.

And he'd said, "I like her teeth. I like everything about her. And now you do, too, Mother."

Sullivan was looking at him oddly. "Are you okay?"

"I'm fine," North said.

"Okay. Well, then, I'd like to take Suzie down there and look into the ghosts. I can check on the kids for you while I'm there."

"I'd prefer you didn't," North said bluntly. "I don't see Suzie Twomey being a good experience for them."

"No, no, she's not interested in reporting on kids anymore, she's on to ghosts now. She found out that the house was originally a haunted house in England and she's very excited about it. Did you know they brought the house over here in pieces and rebuilt it?" Sullivan shook his head, incredulous. "Suzie could be really grateful if I took her down there. Plus, I'd get to investigate a haunted house. I've been reading a lot about this, North, and I think there might be something in it for me."

"Investigating ghosts?" North said.

"I've talked to two highly regarded ghost experts and there's something behind this stuff. Plus I told them that there's a haunted house in the family and one of them would like to see it. Suzie would like to see it. *I'd* like to see it. We won't talk to the kids."

"The children own the house, so it's not in our immediate family," North said, picking up his pen again. "And you're not going to disrupt their lives because you think you might like to be a Ghostbuster."

"No, no, I told you, we won't bother the kids. My plan is that I take Suzie and Dennis, the expert, down there, we talk to people—not the kids, the adults around there—I see what's going on and report back to you, you get to know the kids are safe, Dennis gets more research, Suzie gets her video whatsis . . ." Sullivan shrugged. "We all win. Plus, I get away from Columbus before Mother gets back from Paris. She doesn't like Suzie. Says she's all teeth and hair."

North looked at his little brother with an exasperation he hadn't felt in years. *Southie's permanently thirteen*, Andie had said. *Thirty-four hobbies and a hard-on.* But she'd been laughing when she'd said it. . . . "Southie, when are you going to stand up to Mother?"

"Southie?"

"What?"

"You called me Southie. You haven't called me that in years."

North sighed. "Well, grow up and I'll never call you that again. You're running down there because you don't want to face Mother with your latest career plan or girlfriend. It's not much of a rebellion if you keep running away."

"I'm not rebelling. I don't have anything to rebel against. I have a great life. And to keep my life great, I'd like to avoid unpleasantness while learning about something that interests me and makes my girlfriend happy. Plus the last nanny quit last week so the kids are there alone. That's not—"

"The children are not alone."

"You hired another nanny?" Sullivan shook his head. "She won't last. Better I should go—"

"This one will last," North said. "I sent Andromeda."

"*Andie*?" Sullivan whistled and then grinned. "Ghosts versus Andie. The supernatural is going to get its ass kicked. I didn't even know she was back in town. When did you talk to her?"

"Today. She's going down there tomorrow."

Sullivan smiled. "Called me Southie, did she?"

"What?"

"That's why you called me Southie. Andie did it first."

"Yes," North said, realizing it was true. Half an hour with Andie and ten years were yesterday.

"She changed much?"

"Her hair's . . . different," North said, remembering her sitting in that chair, bundled up in an awful suit jacket, all those crazy curls yanked back, her face scowling as she argued with him. And then that one lock of hair, sliding down her neck—

"Her *hair's* different?" Southie said. "You see your ex-wife for the first time in ten years and that's all you got?"

"She looked . . ." Serious. Tense. Her old smile gone. ". . . quiet. I think she's had a bad time."

Southie's face clouded over. "Aw, hell. That's a shame." Then he smiled. "She can probably use my help."

North thought of Andie opening the door and finding

Southie and his toothy, microphone-wielding girlfriend on the step with some charlatan ghost expert. "No."

"Maybe she could use your help," Southie said, grinning. "The two of you used to—"

"She's getting married again. Now if we're finished here . . ." North looked back to his notes as a hint, but when Southie didn't say anything, he looked up.

"I'm sorry," Southie said, his face kind. "I really am."

The twinge he'd felt when she'd told him stabbed at North and he put a lid on it again. "Why? We've been divorced for ten years. It's not as if I thought she was coming back."

"Yeah but it was still a shock, wasn't it? At least it is to me. Maybe I thought she was coming back."

"Well, she's not," North said, more sharply than he'd intended.

"So, who's the guy? What do we know about him?" Southie looked serious now which was always a bad sign.

"Will Spenser. The writer."

"The true crime guy?" Southie said, raising his eyebrows.

"I think he writes mystery fiction, too."

"Probably not much difference. What did Gabe find out about him?"

North gathered his patience. "I did not put a private detective on my ex-wife's fiancé."

"Right, she was just here, you haven't had time. Want me to call him?"

"No."

Southie shook his head. "You know, she used to be family. As far as I'm concerned she still is. We need to look out for her. This guy could have anything in his past. He's a writer, for Christ's sake."

"No," North said.

"And I should go down and check on her in that house," Southie went on as if he hadn't spoken. "I can't believe you sent her down there without backup. God knows what's down there."

"Two kids and a housekeeper. You're not going."

Southie sighed. "Suzie's not going to be happy."

"Such is life."

Southie hesitated and the silence stretched out. "All right then," he said, standing up. "You going to see Andie again?"

"No. You have a good evening." North flipped the page back to where it had been as a signal for Southie to leave and saw the "Andiana" in the middle of the page again. "Damn."

"What's wrong?" Southie said.

"I made a mistake." North flipped the pad shut, annoyed with himself.

"Sending Andie down there?"

"What?" he said, looking up.

"You think you made a mistake sending Andie down there?"

"No," North said and then thought about Andie, down in the wilds. It was probably her natural habitat. She'd been wandering around ever since they'd divorced, moving someplace new every year, teaching in some really godforsaken places. Maybe that had been his mistake, keeping her in the city. Trying to keep her at all. He shook his head. "No, it wasn't a mistake. She'll handle things."

"Yeah, she will," Southie said, his voice odd, and when North looked up, he saw Southie regarding him sympathetically. "Maybe you should go down. Get out of the office, check to make sure she's all right. Spend a night in the place so you know what it's like."

"She's fine."

Southie waited a moment and then said quietly, "You could have gone after her, you know."

North looked at him blankly. "Why would I go after her? She'll be fine down there."

"Not now. *Then*. When she left. You could have gone—"

"No."

"You ever think maybe that divorce was a mistake?"

"*No*," North said, putting as much *you-should-leave-now* in his voice as possible.

"Because I always thought it was," Southie said. "If you'd gone after her, you could have gotten her back. That's all she wanted, she was just lonely—"

"Was there anything else?" North said coldly. "Because unlike you, I have work to do."

"Right. Well, you have a good time with your work," Southie said and left, shaking his head.

Damn it. The divorce hadn't been a mistake. She'd been miserable. He'd been miserable because she was miserable. Going after her wouldn't have changed that. They were both happier now. He had work to do.

She'd looked so good, so warm, so everything he'd once wanted, rushing back in one afternoon—

And now she was getting married again. Good for her. Moving on.

He pulled his notebook back in front of him and then thought, *Maybe good for her*. Because Southie was right, he didn't know anything about this yahoo she was getting engaged to. She probably didn't either. She'd married him after twelve hours of sex, she could be lunging into another mistake. And she hadn't smiled, she'd smiled all the time when they were married. In the beginning.

He picked up the phone and called the detective agency that the firm used and ordered a background check on Will Spenser.

Then he flipped open the notebook to go back to work, saw the "Andiana" blot, and thought, *Hell*.

He ripped out the page and copied the whole thing over again. With no mistakes.

By late afternoon the next day, Andie had finished packing and tying off the loose ends of her life. There weren't many loose ends since she'd been moving around the country for ten years, which tended to limit most ends, loose or otherwise, but she did call Will in New York to tell him the good news. "Ten thousand dollars, Will. It'll pay off all my debts with some left over. I'm being practical and mature here."

"I don't care about your debts, I'll pay your debts. What I'd really like to hear is that you're going to marry me."

Of course, Andie thought, and said, "Maybe." She heard a thunking sound on the other end of the phone. "What's that?"

"That's me beating my head against my desk."

Andie grinned. "That's you beating the phone against your mouse pad."

"Same difference. Do you take this long to answer all your marriage proposals?"

It took me five seconds to say yes to North. "Yes. I ponder them, and the guys get bored and wander off. Will, I want to do this, it really is important to me to be free and clear financially before I . . . do anything."

"Okay," he said in that easy-going voice she loved. He was so Not-North. "Call me often. Tell me you love working with kids and want to have twenty."

"Twenty?" Andie said, alarmed. "I don't want any."

"Well, maybe you'll change your mind." Will hesitated and then he said, "You won't be seeing North, will you?"

Andie frowned at the phone. "Are you jealous? Because, trust me, he'd forgotten I'd existed until I showed up in his office. And no, I won't be seeing him."

"Nobody has ever forgotten you," Will said with feeling. "Just remember who you're potentially engaged to."

"How could I forget?" Andie said, and moved on to the I-love-yous before North became a permanent part of their conversation. Then she picked up the last of her suitcases and went out to deal with her mother, who was standing on the sidewalk in front of her little German Village row house in her jeans and faded Iron Maiden T-shirt, looking worried.

"I don't like this," Flo said, for the fortieth time, her long, curly graying hair bobbing as she shook her head. "I dreamed about you last night. You fell into a well."

"Thank you, Flo," Andie said as she opened the back of the car. "That's encouraging."

"It means your subconscious is calling to you. You've been repressing something. That's what the water means anyway. The falling part is probably about being out of control, or since it's you, maybe it's about running away. You know what a bolter you are."

"I am not a bolter," Andie said to her mother, not for the first time. "I go toward things, not away from them."

"I think you got the bolting thing from your father," Flo said. "You're very like him."

"I wouldn't know," Andie said coldly. "Except that I don't desert children, so no, I'm not."

"Don't go," Flo said.

"Because you had a dream? No." Andie put the larger of her suitcases in the trunk of her ancient Camry next to the sewing machine she'd already stashed there.

"There was so much negative energy in your marriage," Flo fretted.

That wasn't negative energy, that was raging lust. "I'm not revisiting my marriage. I'm taking care of two orphaned kids for a month—"

"This is a terrible time astrologically," Flo went on as if she hadn't spoken. "Your Venus is in North's Capricorn—"

Andie slammed the trunk closed. "Mother, my Venus isn't anywhere near North. If his Capricorn was in my Venus, I could see your point, but it's staying here in Columbus while I go south." She went around and opened the back door of the car and shoved the boxes of school supplies that Kristin had given her over to make room for her last suitcase while her mother obsessed about her life.

"North is a very attractive, very passionate, very powerful man, and you're still connected to him." Flo frowned. "Probably sexual memory; those Capricorns are insatiable. Well, you know, Sea Goat. And of course, you're a Fish. You'll probably end up back in bed with him."

Andie shoved the last suitcase into the back seat. "You know what I'd like for Christmas, Flo? Boundaries. You can gift me early if you'd like."

"Andie, if you keep seeing North, he's going to get you again, and you were so miserable with him—"

"I'm not seeing North. I'm with Will. I'm going to have a stable, secure relationship with a good man who loves me and won't desert me for his career. Which reminds me. I left that stupid suit jacket on the bed, so the next time you're at Goodwill, drop it off, will you? I don't know why I kept it. I'm never going to be near anybody who'll want me to wear a suit again."

Flo folded her arms. "Will's a Gemini. Volatile. Well, he's a writer. You're not sexually compatible, you're both so scattered. You must be all over the place in bed."

"*Boundaries*, Flo." Andie closed the car door, thinking, *the sex is just fine*. Not wall-banging, earth-shattering, oh-my-god sex, but fun and energetic and damn satisfying just the same. Wall-banging, earth-shattering, oh-my-god sex was probably for people in their twenties. At least that was the last time she'd had it. "Will and I are good. And I don't believe in astrology. Or dreams." She looked sternly at Flo.

"Of course, you don't, dear. Did you get the birth signs for the children?"

"The boy is a Taurus and the girl is a Scorpio. And yes, even if it turns out that means they're going to kill me in my sleep, I'm still going."

"Well, the boy will be all right. You can always count on a Taurus. Steady as they come. Strong. The Bull." She looked thoughtful. "They like *things*, you know? Good food, comfort, they're very materialistic. If you need to win him over, that could help."

"I'd think good food and comfort would win anybody over," Andie said and Flo looked at her curiously.

"Now why would you think that? The little girl's going to be completely different. Intense. Secretive. You won't buy her with comfort. And you won't be able to bamboozle her, either. Scorpios. They'll kill you as soon as look at you. They like sparkly things, though. You might get her with sequins."

"Flo, she's a little girl."

"Although I've always liked Scorpios. They're *interesting*. And they're survivors. Taurus, too, those are both survivor signs. Tough kids. They'll make it without you." Flo bit her lip. "Andie, don't go."

"I'm going." Andie opened the driver's side door to escape before her mother started on rising signs. "I'll be back in a month, and everything will be fine."

"No, it won't." Flo took a deep breath. "It's not just the dreams and the stars. I read your cards last night. The Emperor was crossing you. That's power and passion, so it has to be North. It was a bad, bad reading. You're going down a path that's all conflict and struggle. There's no peace there.

Will can't help you, he's not strong enough for you. North's too strong."

"*Mother*—"

"Leave both of them," Flo said, serious as death. "Don't go. I'm scared for you, Andie."

"Well, stop it," Andie said and got in the car. Then she got out again and hugged Flo, who hugged her back, hard. "Sorry, Mom. I love you much. Don't worry. In a month, I'll be back and living here in town and you can run the cards for me every day if you like."

"You don't understand," Flo said. "You're not a mother. When you have a child, you can't let her go into danger, you have to be there for her—"

"Flo, I'm thirty-four. The child part is over."

"*It's never over,*" Flo said, and Andie shook her head at her obtuseness and got back in her car.

"I'll call you while I'm there," she said, and put the car in gear, and then waved at her mother in her rearview mirror as she drove away.

Sea goat, she thought, and shook her head.

A little Flo went a long way.

Andie headed south on I-71 and then turned off the interstate onto a succession of increasingly deserted back roads that became more treacherous as she got farther from civilization. The road moved in and out of heavily wooded areas that grew darker and closer together, and she began to see how a nanny could lose her grip just from the landscape. By the time she turned down the long dead-end road that the house was supposed to be on and found the narrow gap of the drive fifteen miles from the turn with its battered sign that said ARCHER

HOUSE, the sun was going down, so she pulled off to the side of the road and got out to investigate in the deepening twilight.

There had been a drive there, but it seemed to have collapsed. What was left was a steep and rocky slope, not anything she'd want to drive down if she had a choice.

She got back in the car and drove slowly over the edge.

The car dipped down sharply, scraping its front fender, and then slid into the pot hole–laced lane that wound through the trees for about a quarter of a mile and came out into a meadow gone to seed with a large greenish pond in the middle of it, and beyond that an ancient three-story dark stone house flaunting two rose windows, a crumbling tower, and a moat, all its windows dark and ominous in the twilight. "Oh, god," she said and followed the drive around to the side, finding a little bridge that crossed the moat onto an untended stretch of pavement that split, the right going to the front of the house and its stone-arched entrance and the left to the back and a large flagstoned yard beside a row of garages.

She pulled the car up in front of the garages and got out, looking around the deserted yard as she slammed the door, which echoed in the gloom.

It wasn't surprising the other nannies had left; it was surprising they'd gotten out of the car when they'd arrived.

She got her suitcases out of the trunk and headed for the house, pushed the back door open, banging the cases on the frame, and then went through a small mudroom, a big, gloomy sitting room filled with uncomfortable-looking Victorian furniture including a massive green-striped couch, and another room with a long, heavy dining table surrounded by ornate chairs. Light seeped around a door in the side wall, and she opened it.

It was a kitchen, large, white, and warm compared to the other rooms she'd dragged her suitcase through, and empty except for a long wood table in the center.

A boy sat at the end, all shoulder blades and elbows in his black T-shirt, hunched over a bowl of something orange, his brown hair falling into his eyes as he looked up at her from under his thick lashes, his mouth set in a tight, hard line. Sitting close to him was a thin little girl cupping her hands around her own bowl of orange, her pale gray-blue eyes narrowed under her long, tangled, lank, white-blond hair, her T-shirt almost covered by all the stuff she had strung around her neck: an old strand of discolored plastic pearls, an ancient locket on a frayed pink ribbon, a string of tiny blue shells, a blue Walkman on a black cord, and a glittery bat on a black chain.

Oh, dear god, Andie thought, and said, "Hi."